from NOTTING HILL *with* LOVE...ACTUALLY

ALI McNAMARA

sourcebooks
landmark

Published by Sourcebooks Landmark, an imprint of Sourcebooks, Inc.
P.O. Box 4410, Naperville, Illinois 60567-4410
(630) 961-3900
Fax: (630) 961-2168
www.sourcebooks.com

Originally published in 2010 in Great Britain by Sphere, an imprint of Little, Brown Book Group.

Library of Congress Cataloging-in-Publication Data

McNamara, Ali.
  From Notting Hill with love-actually / Ali McNamara.
    p. cm.
  (pbk. : alk. paper) 1. Fiancés—Fiction. 2. Weddings—Planning—Fiction. 3. Housesitting—Fiction. 4. Notting Hill (London, England) I. Title.
  PR6113.C5685F76 2012
  823'.92—dc23
                              2012022255

Printed and bound in the United States of America.
VP 10 9 8 7 6 5 4 3 2 1

For those who wished on shooting stars...

One

I didn't feel much like Julia Roberts as I emerged from the hot and crowded London underground. There were no paparazzi ready to photograph my every move—unless you counted the two Japanese tourists snapping away at a black London cab that was just dropping off a fare. And neither did I probably resemble her that much, trundling my old blue wheelie suitcase along the pavement while I looked in awe at the Notting Hill area of London I thought I knew so well.

It was usually another movie star people compared me to, but one from Hollywood yesteryear. With my black hair and green eyes, I suppose I did bear a passing resemblance to *Gone with the Wind*'s Vivien Leigh. And since my parents had kindly christened me Scarlett as a baby, this only added to the illusion.

It certainly doesn't look much like the movie, I thought as I made my way down Portobello Road, which was lined with many antique and craft shops. Where was the vibrant market that Hugh Grant had walked through, with its eccentric market traders selling their wild and wacky wares? So there were a few stallholders, but I really didn't think a fruit and veg stall and a man selling dodgy-looking watches equated to a Hollywood movie.

I've always loved any film Hugh Grant was in. I don't really know why—I don't fancy him exactly, I just love watching him up on the screen. I was certainly at my happiest during the *Four Weddings, Notting Hill, Bridget Jones* era. There's something very comforting about watching a Hugh Grant movie. You know no one's head will be blown off in the first three minutes, no one will be tortured, and the worst thing that might happen is seeing a lanky Welshman eating mayonnaise in his underpants.

*Now I'm sure it said I have to turn off somewhere near a coffee shop...*I glanced at the piece of paper in my hand. *I must concentrate on finding the house first. The movie stuff can all come later...*

I looked around for a street sign.

Oh, but isn't that the house with the blue door where Hugh Grant lives in the movie? No, Scarlett, concentrate for once in your life—stop daydreaming. You're here to prove something. Not to let them be right about you!

I found the exit off Portobello Road and set off on my way again. But I was distracted almost immediately—this time I felt justifiably so. This time it would just have been rude not to stop and take a quick look. Because I'd only gone and stumbled across *the* bookshop.

You know the Travel Bookshop? The one in the *Notting Hill* film where Hugh and Julia meet for the first time? I hesitated in the doorway for a few seconds...I really should go and find the house...but it was *the* bookshop...a few minutes couldn't hurt.

I hurriedly pulled my suitcase inside and tried not to look too overjoyed when I saw just how much the real shop resembled the movie version.

As I moved farther into the shop and stared at the bookshelves, I pretended I was actually interested in buying a book, hopefully not looking too much like a tourist, just lurking there hoping to spot Hugh Grant serving behind the counter.

"Wonderful area, Nepal," a voice said next to me. I hadn't even noticed anyone standing there, so entranced was I to be virtually "inside" one of my favorite movies. "Have you ever been before?"

I looked down at the book on the Himalayan Mountains I was holding.

"Wha…er, no I haven't. Have you?" I asked, turning to see a young man replacing a book on the shelf beside me.

"Yes, quite a few years ago now, though—I highly recommend it if you are thinking of going."

"Thanks—I'll bear that in mind. Erm, do you work here?" I asked hopefully, thinking I'd struck it lucky right away. This was too good to be true, being chatted up in a travel bookshop in Notting Hill. Perhaps you should call me Julia after all.

"No, why on earth would you think that?"

On closer examination I realized the man was wearing a long black raincoat, holding a briefcase and carrying a bag full of groceries.

"Oh sorry, no, of course you don't," I said, chastising myself for getting too carried away in a movie moment as always. "Silly mistake."

"Yes," he said, looking me up and down scornfully. "It was."

Then without saying another word, he turned smartly away and walked out of the shop.

I stared after him for a moment, the sound of the shop's

doorbell still ringing in my ears. "Charming!" I muttered as I grabbed hold of my suitcase again. "I hope everyone's not that friendly here. Now I really *must* concentrate on finding the house. Where on earth did I put that address?"

I stood on the pavement outside and fumbled around in my pockets for a few minutes, and then my bag, and then my pockets again, desperately searching for the piece of paper with the address on it. Beginning to panic now, I quickly turned, meaning to return to the shop to see if I might have dropped it in there.

So caught up was I in my own turmoil I didn't see the man hurrying toward me along the pavement. As I stepped to cross in front of him, a dog being carried in the man's arms yapped, making me jump with fright. Unfortunately as I jumped, I stopped suddenly, and to prevent himself colliding with me, the man had to stop abruptly too. He managed to save himself from falling, and the contents of his shopping-bag-laden arm from spilling. But not the inside—I noted as it ran down the front of my white shirt—of a large cup of freshly squeezed orange juice.

"Oh my dear, I'm so dreadfully sorry," the man said, quickly putting his shih-tzu dog and shopping bags down on the ground.

"No, it was my fault for stepping out in front of you like that," I said, trying to pull my soaking wet shirt away from my skin. "I wasn't thinking."

But the man didn't seem to be listening to me; rather unnervingly he just stared at my chest. "Quick, take off your jacket before the juice seeps on to that too."

I hesitated for a moment, wondering just what sort of guy I'd bumped into. He seemed incredibly fixated by my chest and getting me out of my clothes at this very moment. I glanced at him again. He was wearing black jeans, a black leather jacket, and dark glasses. But he had topped off his look with a pink cravat and a black beret. And the bags that he'd placed carefully down on the pavement next to the dog were all emblazoned with "Harvey Nichols."

I relaxed a little.

He was right, I didn't really want orange juice all over my new suede coat, so I did as he said and carefully removed my jacket to reveal the offending orange stain.

"You simply must get that shirt in to soak immediately," he insisted. "Orange juice is a devil to get out if it's left. Go home immediately and sponge, sponge, sponge, darling. Then I can rest easy that Delilah and I haven't ruined your gorgeous outfit forever!"

I smiled at him, my earlier fears now subsiding. "Don't worry—I'm sure it will be fine."

He rummaged in his bag and produced a business card. "Look, this is my number. If the stain doesn't come out, be sure to call me and I'll reimburse you for a new shirt."

"No really, it's fine," I said, waving the card away.

"My darling, I won't hear of it—here, take the card, I insist."

I took the card from him. It read:

MARY MARY QUITE CONTRARY
Fabulous Fashions and Divergent Designs
Oscar St. James—Proprietor

"I have a shop on the King's Road," Oscar explained. "But

Delilah and I live just around the corner in Elgin Crescent. Are you somewhere nearby too?"

"Er...well I think I am."

"What on earth do you mean, darling?"

"I've just arrived, and I was on my way to where I'm supposed to be staying, but I seem to have lost the address." I shrugged in embarrassment. "I think I'm going to have to phone my friend to get directions again. I'm only here for a month, you see."

"Oh *really*, why? No, ignore my last question," he said with a flourish of his hand. "Far too probing! My mouth gets completely carried away with me sometimes. Well, most of the time actually, isn't that right, Delilah?"

Delilah looked up at him disdainfully while she peed on a nearby lamppost.

"Look, darling, I can't just leave you out on the street like this. Why don't you come back to my house? You can ring your friend and find out where you're supposed to be going, and while you're getting yourself sorted, I can get that juice out for you in a jiffy." He leaned toward me in a conspiratorial fashion. "I have this fabulous little product, given to me by the Red Hot Chili Peppers' ex-stylist. It works in an instant on every type of stain you can think of." He lowered his voice. "And as you can imagine, with them—there were a lot of stains to deal with."

I grinned. "Really, it isn't necessary. I'll be fine." I knew I didn't have anything to worry about with Oscar by now, but I wasn't used to random strangers being this nice to me, especially in London.

"I insist, darling. Besides, I don't get many opportunities to rescue damsels in distress. Old queens," he said, giving me a wink, "now that's a different story. So what do you say?"

"Sure, why not," I finally agreed. "It really is very kind of you, Oscar."

Oscar fed his arm companionably through mine and turned me in the direction of his house. "Not at all, darling. Oh, do come on, Delilah," he said, impatiently tugging on her pale blue leash when she didn't move. "It won't do you any harm to walk, just this once."

When we arrived at his house, Oscar quickly unlocked the door and swiftly turned off his alarm.

"Now then," he said, turning toward me as Delilah trotted off into the kitchen for a drink. "Let the battle of the stains commence!"

We followed Delilah into a kitchen that could have jumped straight off the pages of *Elle Interiors*.

Oscar looked pleased by my obvious amazement. "Welcome to my pride and joy!" he flamboyantly announced. "Designed by none other than Iko Katwatchi himself!"

"It's simply—*fabulous*," I said, thinking this was the type of endorsement Oscar would like.

"Isn't it just? He's *the* most important name in kitchens right now."

"Indeed," I agreed, even though I thought Iko Katwatchi sounded more like one of those newfangled exercise regimes.

"Now first, the offending stain, please?" Oscar said, holding out his hand like a surgeon asking to be passed his scalpel.

I looked hesitantly down at the front of my shirt.

"Oh my dear, how rude of me. Let me give you something of mine to change into while I work."

Oscar went through another door into what appeared to be a laundry area. "Here," he said, reappearing. "Freshly laundered this morning." He smelt the T-shirt. "Ah, lily of the valley, how appropriate for you with your exquisite lily-white skin."

"Thank you," I said, blushing a little as I took the shirt from him. I'd always been self-conscious about my pale skin and often tried to hide it with fake tan and makeup. But here was someone complimenting me on it for a change. I felt myself warming to Oscar.

"I will return in two shakes of Delilah's tail," Oscar said, leaving Delilah and me alone in the kitchen.

Delilah glanced at the door Oscar had just gone through, and I could have sworn she rolled her eyes.

Quickly I changed into the T-shirt before Oscar could return.

"All decent, are we?" he asked, popping his head around the door.

"Yes, fine now, thanks."

He winked. "Not that you've anything to worry about from me, you understand."

I'd kind of gathered that.

"Would you like to ring your friend now?" Oscar asked. "Then I'll make a start on your shirt."

Oscar made us both a cup of herbal tea while I rang my best friend, Maddie. After a few of the pointless questions that people always ask in these situations, like "Where did you lose it?" and "Have you looked in the last place you had it?" Maddie said she didn't have the address on her but promised to get back to me as soon as possible.

I watched while Oscar went to work on my shirt. While he soaked, sprayed, and scrubbed, I learned how he had inherited his house when his aunt died and how he had started his boutique with the rest of the money she'd left him.

"So, darling, are you going to tell me just why you're moving to Notting Hill for only a month?" Oscar asked while he was finishing up my shirt. "Or do I have to guess?"

"No big mystery. I'm house-sitting, that's all."

"Oh, is that it?" Oscar said with disappointment. "I thought it was going to be a much more interesting tale."

"Well," I said, eager not to let him down but also desperate to tell someone what I was up to—I was never great at secrets, "there is a bit more to it, actually. But I warn you it's rather a long story."

"I knew it!" Oscar said, clapping his rubber-gloved hands together ecstatically. "Wait one moment. I'm almost finished here. Let's go through to the lounge and *then* you can tell me all about it."

We settled down comfortably on Oscar's sofa in his equally chic lounge. I wasn't sure why I hadn't just stopped at the "house-sitting for a month" excuse. That's what I'd planned on giving everyone before I arrived in Notting Hill as the reason for my being here. But Oscar seemed to have a way about him that made you want to open up and tell him your whole life story.

"Right then, darling—tell me everything," Oscar instructed as he tucked his legs underneath him on the sofa, while Delilah curled herself up into a furry ball on his lap.

So I did.

I began to explain the strange chain of events that had led to my arrival in Notting Hill earlier that day...

Two

"And the Oscar goes to…"

Johnny paused dramatically, and his chocolate-brown eyes darted up from beneath his long, dark lashes to survey the audience in front of him.

Yes, we were in the palm of his hand, and so probably were the millions of people watching around the globe, as he toyed with us all before he tore into the fateful gold envelope that would mean joy to one and misery to all the others.

Did I imagine it or had he glanced at me just then before he ripped open the envelope? *Does he know something? Does he have some inside information on who the winner is? Or maybe there's another reason he might be looking at me like that?* I'd always suspected Johnny Depp and I would make a fine couple, and now it seemed, on this most significant of nights, I was about to discover the feeling might be mutual.

"Scarlett O'Brien!"

Yes, it was me! Johnny was calling *my* name. I was finally going to claim *my* Oscar from one of my favorite actors, *and*, I hoped, by the look on his face as I glided elegantly toward him in my Stella McCartney gown, soaking up the congratulations of my fellow Oscar nominees as I passed by, a whole lot more. It was what dreams and fantasies were made for.

"Scarlett," he called again, but this time his voice was more of an urgent whisper. "Scarlett, will you get a move on or is your bum permanently glued to that seat? The show is over now!"

I shook my head.

That certainly wasn't Johnny Depp's velvety voice calling me gently from the stage. It sounded much more like—

Oh my God. I turned my head from where I'd been staring into space and realized that I wasn't in Hollywood after all. And yes, I was in a theater, but it wasn't the Kodak theater in Los Angeles; it was the Royal Shakespeare theater in Stratford-upon-Avon. And the person standing there in a suit and tie calling my name wasn't the gorgeous Mr. Johnny Depp but my fiancé, David.

"I...I'm sorry, David," I apologized, hurriedly gathering my belongings up from the floor. "I must have drifted off there for a bit."

"Hmm." David gave me one of his looks. (Which, considering that he had the exact same coloring as Mr. Depp, sadly was nothing like the "look" that Johnny had given me a few minutes previously.) "We'll talk about this later, Scarlett," he said, lowering his voice as he leaned toward me. "But for now we've got other things to deal with. Over there are twelve Japanese businessmen waiting for us to take them out to dinner. So if you're finally back from whatever fantasy world you were away in, I think it's time we did just that, don't you?"

Hesitantly, I turned to my right to see a line of immaculately dressed oriental gentlemen watching our every move, and I closed my eyes for a moment. Damn it, I'd wanted tonight to go so well for David. Why couldn't I for once just have enjoyed what was going on in the real world and not brought one of my cinema fantasies into it?

I mean, I had tried, really I had, but it's what always happens when I'm bored—and tonight had been really, *really* boring.

I'd had to spend the evening sitting in the front row of a theater, with a dozen Japanese businessmen sitting either side of me, and David hidden somewhere among them. Up on the stage, people appeared to be dying left right and center, and for most of the performance I had quite felt like leaping up there and joining them.

As I sat watching the tale of *King Lear* unfold in front of me, my head was filled with questions like, "Could it possibly go on much longer?" and, "Were these Japanese men really understanding all of this, or were they just grinning and nodding out of politeness?" And more importantly, did I have enough movie fantasies to fill an entire Shakespearian tragedy?

I'd hoped my first attempt at a real Shakespeare play would be something like *Shakespeare in Love*. If Joseph Fiennes or Ben Affleck had been up there on the stage it might have been a tad more interesting. Although I'd always had issues with Colin Firth playing the baddie in that film; Colin to me would always be Mr. Nice Guy in whatever movie he was in.

I tried picturing several movie heroes of mine wearing tights, but that didn't take much time: men in tights didn't really do it for me—even superheroes. When I got to Johnny Depp in full Shakespearian costume, he soon began to merge into Captain Jack Sparrow and that passed a good few minutes.

I'd done my imaginary Oscar walk down the center aisle of the theater when we came back from intermission. This was something I usually did at the end of seeing a movie in a cinema: when you walk down the steps toward the screen when the credits are rolling, I like to imagine my name has just been called as the winner of an Oscar. It's usually Best Actress, but sometimes I vary it. Sometimes it will be for Best Screenplay or something like that. The person presenting me with my Oscar is usually Will Smith, but if I'm feeling particularly annoyed with David that day it's either Brad Pitt or Johnny Depp, who then sweep me off my feet and tell me they've not only always admired my work for many years, but fancied the pants off me too.

And that was the fantasy I was in the middle of tonight when unfortunately David caught me.

No one else seems to understand my love of the movies. I don't think *I* even know why I love them so much. It's almost as if it's a genetic thing that's been bred into me. But my father doesn't take any interest in them; in fact, I can't ever remember him watching a film on TV, let alone paying to go to a cinema. And I never really knew my mother.

Still, David's cool with it. He usually puts up with my "nonsense," as he calls it, just as long as he gets to watch his nature programs on TV, or those building ones he seems to have become obsessed with recently. In fact, lately our Sky+ box is constantly full of DIY programs. All since we bought our first house together—a period property in need of some renovation—and David decided that to save us money he would have a go at doing the place up himself.

This would have been absolutely fine had David been the

DIY type, but my David is less Bob the Builder and more SpongeBob SquarePants when it comes to home renovation, and now some six months down the line, I was living in a house that it would have been kinder to put out of its misery had it been an animal in distress.

Tonight's effort to impress the Japanese businessmen had been David's idea—he'd never included me in any of his company's business dealings before. But David said now we were soon to be married things should be different and he would like me to accompany him on business dinners and, in the future, to begin entertaining clients at the house once it was ready.

I wasn't too worried by this talk of entertaining clients; by the speed of the progress David was making with the renovations, I wouldn't have to worry about entertaining anyone in the next few decades. Not unless David thought they'd be impressed by eating off the top of an upturned bucket or a Black & Decker Workmate.

"I once had a boyfriend like that," Oscar mused, reaching for a biscuit. "His house was a complete tip whenever I went round to visit. I couldn't stand it. I spent all my time tidying up when we were there."

"Well I may have exaggerated slightly—it's not *quite* that bad, I suppose." I took a chocolate HobNob from the plate Oscar was offering me. "But I did once write a letter to the BBC asking them if the *DIY SOS* team could come in and help me out."

"And did they?"

"No, apparently they've stopped making the show now. I don't think they do *complete* house makeovers anyway."

Oscar laughed. "That's the benefit of getting someone in to do the work for you." He admired his immaculate home. "Although that Nick Knowles can turn up on my doorstep any day with his power tools, I quite like the rough 'n' ready look."

"I can imagine," I said, grinning.

"Still, not everyone can afford to have designers in to decorate, darling, can they?" Oscar patted my knee reassuringly. "I'm sure your fiancé's doing his best."

"But that's the thing, Oscar, David isn't short of a bob or two; we could easily have afforded to get someone in to do our renovations between us. But no, he thought he'd save us a few pennies by doing it himself. Although by the amount of things that keep going wrong and have to keep being redone, it's going to work out more expensive in the long run than hiring a few Jack-the-lad builders."

"Bit on the cautious side with money, is he?" Oscar asked, politely sipping at his herbal tea.

"No, he's not cautious, or even careful. He's tight. That's what all the DIY is about. Oh, Oscar, it's like living in purgatory with power tools." I picked up my cup from the glass table and took a comforting gulp of the hot filtered coffee.

Oscar laughed. "Oh, Scarlett, I'm sorry. I shouldn't find it funny, because it's your life. But it's the way you tell it."

I had to smile. "It's OK, at least I'm not boring you."

"No, darling, far from it. But I want to get back to the story. Now, where were we? Let's see now, rewind, rewind..." Oscar circled his hands around like film spooling from a reel. "Oh yes, you were at the theater with your fiancé and the hordes of Japanese chappies…"

So, although my first attempt at "business entertaining" hadn't got off to an awfully good start, I was determined to make up for it.

After the slightly embarrassing incident earlier, David and I had managed to gather our oriental guests together outside the theater, and we were now standing on the pavement trying to hail enough taxis to drive us to the restaurant where we were about to have dinner, when the familiar tones of "Let Me Entertain You" began reverberating from my bag.

You'd have thought by the look on David's face that the real Robbie Williams was calling to confirm a date with me next week.

"Sorry," I mumbled, rummaging about in my bag. "I'll just silence it."

"Ah Wobbie Williams—Take That," one of the Japanese men said as he climbed into the taxi. "Vey good singer—I like. You like?" he asked as David went to close the taxi door on him.

"Er yes, Mr. Yashimoto, I like," David lied, nodding enthusiastically at him.

I looked down at the phone as I pulled it out of my bag, meaning to silence it immediately, but I saw the Grand cinema's number flashing on the screen.

Gosh, it must be important if the cinema was calling me.

"I'll just be a minute, David," I called, moving away from the curb. I knew the manager of my local cinema well and he'd once had Kate Winslet in to watch a movie when she'd been appearing as Ophelia with the Royal Shakespeare Company. I'd never forgiven him for not calling me to let me know she was there. Maybe he'd got someone else famous in his cinema today?

But no, my life was never quite exciting enough for me to bump into passing celebrities on a Friday night. As I spoke to George on the other end of the line, I quickly found out it was just work.

"Come on, Scarlett," David called from the open door of a taxi. "We've got to go now, to catch up with the others."

"I'm really sorry, David, but that was George at the Grand," I said, holding up my phone by way of apology. "It's their popcorn machine, it's broken down again and I've got to get over there immediately."

"What, now? You are joking, Scarlett. You can't mean to say that you're going to work tonight?"

I nodded.

David rolled his eyes. "If you were a doctor on call I could understand the emergency, but surely they can manage without you just this one night?"

"You don't understand," I said, approaching the taxi. "George has got a big meeting of his Movie Club on tonight and he has to have popcorn! You can't possibly have one without the other. This is work, David. I thought you of all people would understand."

"But so is this, Scarlett," David said, gesturing at the remaining

Japanese businessmen waiting to depart in the taxi. They were managing to stare at us but still do it politely as always. "This is *my* business."

I could feel the unsaid words, *And it's more important than yours*, hanging in the night air between us.

"Don't force me to choose, David," I said in a low voice.

David stared at me and I saw a challenging look flicker across his eyes. But he obviously decided now was not the best time for a face-off. He slammed the taxi door closed and rolled the window down.

"How long will this machine take you to mend?" he asked, looking straight ahead.

"Not too long, I hope."

"Shall I order for you, then?" he asked as he turned his head slowly toward me.

"Yes, please."

"I'll do my best to try and pad them out a bit with drinks at the bar first, but you'd better be there by the first course, Scarlett," David said, his voice low so our guests couldn't hear him. But his expression remained resolute.

"I'll do my very best, David," I said, grateful he'd calmed down and not just stormed off in a rage. He could be so childlike sometimes.

David looked at his watch. "You've got one hour, Scarlett, so no daydreaming. I know what you're like once you get inside a cinema. You're bad enough out of one."

I smiled at the departing taxi. No daydreaming, indeed. As if I would. Ahem.

"So you mend popcorn machines for a living?" Oscar inquired politely, when I paused to see if I was still keeping his interest.

"My father and I jointly own a small company that supplies popcorn machines to cinemas, but I do all the call outs when there's a problem. David's business is movie-related too—his family owns a large chain of cinemas."

"Oh really?" Oscar said, starting to sound bored. "So come on, you're not going to stop there, are you, darling? What happened next? Did you manage to fix the popcorn machine and still make it to the restaurant on time? Or did you start daydreaming once you got to the cinema?"

Hmm. Oscar had only known me for an hour or so, and already he knew me a bit too *well.*

As I climbed out of the taxi at the front doors of the cinema I rummaged for my purse to pay the fare.

"I sometimes think this thing must have belonged to Mary Poppins once," I joked with the taxi driver as I groped about in the depths of my bag.

"Bit dressed up for the cinema, aren't you?" he quipped, determinedly ignoring my joke. I looked down at what I was wearing. My theater attire, although not quite the Stella McCartney gown I'd fantasized about earlier, was a very nice black and white shift dress from Zara.

"I'm not going to see a film actually," I informed him, as

at last I found my purse and thrust a £10 note through the window of the taxi. "I'm here to fix their popcorn machine." And without waiting for a response, I rushed purposefully into the cinema like a paramedic on her way to tend an emergency.

"Scarlett, thank the Lord you're here," George panted as we rushed across the foyer together. "It just packed up again—there was a sort of sizzling noise and then nothing. The Movie Club's holding their AGM tonight—they simply *must* have popcorn!"

"Don't panic, George," I said calmly. "I'm sure I'll be able to sort it out." I knelt down behind the machine and began to examine the familiar inner workings with the toolkit George had prepared for me.

I loved George. He looked just like Jack Black, only a quieter and much more reserved version of the Hollywood actor. He was a brilliant cinema manager, always keeping me up to date on what new movies were coming out, and he always knew just which ones I'd enjoy watching. He was more like a friend than a business contact, so I hadn't minded at all rushing over to the cinema to help him out that evening.

"Is she going to be all right?" he asked after a couple of minutes, peering worriedly over my shoulder.

"*She*, George?" I asked without turning my attention away from the machine. *If I just tighten up that nut, then we should be in business again.*

"Er, yes. She's been with me for a while, has Poppy."

I bit hard on my lip. "Poppy? You've given the machine a name, George?"

"Scarlett, you know how important this cinema is to me. We're like one big happy family here, including all my machines."

"Yep, one big happy family, that's what we are!"

I looked up and saw Marcus, one of the cinema attendants, dispensing Fanta into a plastic cup next to me. He winked. "Isn't that right, Naomi?"

Naomi passed a packet of Maltesers across the counter to a customer. "Hmm?" she asked distractedly as she opened the till to get change. "What's that, Marcus?"

"George reckons we're just one big ol' happy family here at the cinema."

Naomi rolled her eyes and carried on serving her customers and I felt sorry for George. He obviously loved this cinema in a way that no one else understood. Probably in the way that I loved movies in a way that no one else seemed to understand either.

"There you go, George, all sorted," I said, closing up the back of the machine. I brushed some stray pieces of popcorn off my dress as I stood up behind the counter. "Best keep an eye on it though—it...I mean she could still be a bit temperamental. Erm, George..." I thought I'd better tread carefully, so I lowered my voice. "It's possible we may have to replace Poppy soon. She is getting quite old, you know, and we do have some lovely newer models."

George looked horrified. "Newer models—but what's wrong with Poppy? She's done me well up until now, why would I want to trade her in for a new model?"

"Let's just see how she goes, eh, George?" I said gently. "I've patched her up for now, but how much longer she'll run for..."

"Sure, Scarlett," George said, and he patted Poppy lovingly as white fluffy popcorn began dancing about inside her glass cabinet again. "I understand." He turned to me. "I'll give you a call if there's any change in her condition. I guess I'll be seeing you pretty soon, though—the new Hugh Grant movie's out next week."

I nodded eagerly. "You know me too well, George. I'll be in to see it one evening or even one afternoon if I can get away from work for a couple of hours."

George winked at me. He knew that "occasionally" I would sneak away from work to catch a movie. There had to be some benefits to doing the job I did, and having to visit cinemas to mend their popcorn machines was one of the few times I got to set foot outside the office.

I bade farewell to George and shivered as I stepped out into the cold January evening once more. The warmth and comfort I always felt at being inside a cinema was at once replaced by the cold reality of life. I pulled my long coat around my shoulders and looked quickly at my watch. If I got a move on I might just make it to the restaurant in time for the first course. I was about to hail a taxi when my mobile phone rang again. I grabbed it from my bag, expecting it to be David checking up on me—but it was Maddie.

"No, don't take the call," Oscar squealed. "You'll be late if you do!"

I laughed. "Something tells me you're getting quite into this, Oscar."

"Ooh, I like a good soap, me, and this has all the makings of a classic episode. So did you take the call?"

"Yes, I had to. It was my best friend and I hadn't heard from her in ages."

"Why? Oh sorry, I'm being nosy again."

"Since I'm sitting here telling you virtually everything that's happened in my life over the last week or so, I don't think that's classed as being nosy. Maddie's getting married soon, so she's been really busy lately…"

"Maddie, I haven't heard from you in ages."

"Scarlett, I know—I'm so sorry about that. It's just with my wedding so close now life's just been manic."

"It's fine. I quite understand."

"Do you? I would have thought you having a wedding planner to organize your big day took all the stresses away. That's the whole point, isn't it?"

I thought about the wedding planner that David's parents had insisted we hire to help us plan for our big day. Or Cruella, as I'd renamed her. I could feel stress beginning to seep into my body at the thought.

It wouldn't have been quite so bad if my wedding planner had been at all like Jennifer Lopez from the film of the same name, as I'd envisaged. Or even Martin Short in *Father of the Bride*, just for the comedy value. But no, my wedding planner was more like Meryl Streep in *The Devil Wears Prada* crossed with Glenn Close playing Cruella De Vil in *101 Dalmatians*.

"So," I said, quickly changing the subject away from my own wedding which was never something I chose to dwell on for too long, "when *are* we going to see each other? When have you got a window for me in your busy schedule?"

Maddie laughed. "Don't be daft, Scarlett, you know I always have time for you. How about this weekend?"

"I could do tomorrow," I said, thinking it would get me out of David's planned trip to a DIY warehouse he'd found on the Internet that did discount prices in tiles. What were we supposed to be looking at this time? Was it floor tiles for the kitchen, or wall tiles for the bathroom? I could never remember.

"What would you like to do, Maddie?"

"I don't know, Scarlett, why don't you decide—wait, as long as it doesn't have anything to do with the movies."

"As if!" I said, trying to sound affronted. "I *do* have other interests."

Maddie laughed. "Scarlett O'Brien, I could count on one hand the times we've got together and *you've* chosen what we're doing and it's not been movie-related. If I have to sit through *Thelma & Louise* one more time, I swear I'll scream or, worse, stop fancying Brad Pitt—and *that* would be a real tragedy."

I was smiling at my end of the phone, but I felt I had to defend my girls. "But wouldn't you just like to take off like them sometimes, Maddie? Get away from it all and have an adventure, find out what might *really* be waiting for you out there in the world?"

Maddie sighed; we'd had similar conversations many a time. "No, Scarlett, I wouldn't. Been there, done that, I'm afraid. I'm quite happy with what life's dealt me now, you know that. And can I remind you while we're at it just how that film ends?"

There was no point in arguing with her. Maddie was a super-organized, practical person, who'd made just about everything in her life happen for herself. She didn't believe in fate, destiny, or any of my "airy-fairy" nonsense as she put it, even though she'd met her own fiancé, Felix, in the strangest of places. And you don't get much stranger than on top of one of the parade floats at Disneyland Paris.

"OK, OK, you win. I know there's no point in arguing with you. Plus," I said, looking at my watch again, "if I don't get to a restaurant soon, I might not have a wedding of my own to organize..." My voice trailed off as I wondered for a moment if that might not be such a bad thing.

"What on earth do you mean, Scarlett?" Maddie asked. "Where are you now? Wait, let me guess—at the cinema, right, just for a change?"

"*Yes*, I am standing outside a cinema, but only because I was here fixing a popcorn machine. I got called out on an emergency."

Maddie snorted with laughter. "Only you could call fixing a popcorn machine an emergency!"

"It was for the manager—his cinema is very important to him." I could feel myself starting to get irritated by yet another person's apparent lack of regard for what I, and now also George, it seemed, considered important in life. But I didn't want to start an argument with Maddie—I didn't have time.

"Look, Maddie, I really do have to go. David is waiting for me at a restaurant. What are we going to do this weekend? You pick something if you don't think I can."

There was silence at the end of the line for a moment and I just knew that one of Maddie's more wacky ideas was about to be revealed. Well, it would seem wacky and off-the-wall to me, but completely sane and normal to Maddie.

"How do you fancy an art gallery?" came back her casual reply.

"An art gallery?" I answered cautiously. Our hometown of Stratford-upon-Avon was famous for many things but art wasn't usually one of them.

"Yes, there's a touring exhibition I'd quite like to go and see. It's only here for a week."

"A touring exhibition of…?"

"Russian Jewish painters."

There it was—the sting in the tail. "The Madness of Maddie," as I liked to call it, escaping once more. I'm sure there were plenty of fine works of art by both Jewish and Russian artists, but I couldn't think of any off the top of my head. Why couldn't it have been a Monet exhibition or even the guy that cut off his ear? At least I knew some of his paintings—but I had to admit that was only really because I'd once watched an old movie about him that starred Kirk Douglas.

But it had been so long since I'd seen her properly that I decided even a day looking at obscure paintings would be worth enduring.

"Right then, you're on; the art gallery it is. I'm supposed to be going DIY shopping with David tomorrow but it should be OK—especially since there's no films involved either."

Maddie laughed. "Yes, Scarlett. Even *you* can't find anything to do with movies at an exhibition of Russian Jewish art."

"And did you find anything?" Oscar asked, bringing me back to the present day again. "And what about the meal, Scarlett? You still haven't told me whether you made it on time."

I couldn't believe someone was finding my mundane life so interesting. "All in good time, Oscar," I smiled.. "I'm just coming to that."

Three

I dashed into the restaurant just as the first course was being served.

Hastily I apologized to our Japanese guests and slipped into my seat while David frowned at me from across the table. As I took a good swig of the wine which the waiter had very efficiently poured into my glass the moment I sat down, I noticed that David was doing something strange with his hand. It was almost as if he'd got some sort of nervous affliction. He kept brushing his hand across the side of his head in very small, swift movements—almost as if he didn't want anyone else to see.

I looked at him oddly—*what the hell was he doing?* It was a most effeminate gesture, like he was trying to smooth his hair down. But David's very short hair was, as always, immaculately presented, so I couldn't understand what he was up to at all.

I turned my head to one side as I tried to figure it out. But David just continued to get redder and redder, and his eyes wider and wider as he stared across the table at me. Now he was actually flicking his head to one side—back across his shoulder.

He looked like a very camp advertisement for hair conditioner.

"Escuss, Miss," the Japanese man sitting next to me said as I turned toward him. "I think Mr. David is trying to tell you this." He reached into my hair and pulled out a very large piece of fluffy white popcorn.

"Oh...oh right. Er, thank you," I said, nodding at the Japanese gentleman.

"My pleasure," he said, giving a small bow in return.

I turned to look back at David who'd stopped doing his Black Beauty impression, but now was doing animal impersonations of a different kind as he growled silently across the table.

I sighed and took another large gulp of my wine.

Perhaps tonight just wasn't meant to go well...

After the popcorn incident, the gentlemen from Japan were very pleasant and polite to me in the little bit of conversation we had together through the rest of the evening, but they were there primarily to talk business with David, and talk business is what they did *all* through dinner.

The topic of their conversation was, strangely enough, my favorite subject, but it was the business side of the cinema they were discussing not the fun part, and they weren't really interested in a little company that supplied popcorn makers to local cinemas.

I tried to sit there being the dutiful hostess for David's sake—looking pretty and smiling in all the right places—really I did. But I soon got bored and I began to look around for something to amuse myself as I sat there. None of the waiters looked like movie stars; neither did any of the other diners. I'd tried to accept my Oscar earlier in the evening and that had got me into trouble. Plus, I felt Johnny Depp should probably wait for another night when we were less likely to be disturbed.

And unfortunately for me, there were not even any snails on the menu, so I couldn't have any fun shooting them across the room and calling out "slippery little suckers" as a passing waiter expertly caught them in his outstretched hand à la Julia Roberts in *Pretty Woman*.

Eventually it was all over, and we bade farewell to our guests. As David and I saw them into taxis bound for their hotel, the last of the Japanese men, the one who had pulled the popcorn from my hair, paused next to me.

"I thank you, Miss Scarlett, for vey pleasant evening," he said. "But I think you would be enjoying the *Romeo and Juliet* story more than the *King Lear*—yes?"

I smiled at him. "Yes, Mr. Yashimoto, I think I probably would like that one better."

He nodded. "I thinking this is so. Mr. David is good man, Miss Scarlett, but you are special lady too. I am thinking Mr. Shakespeare vey right when he say, 'The course of true love never did run smooth.' Hmm?"

I stared at him for a moment. "Er, yes, you could be right there, Mr. Yashimoto. I'll bear that in mind, thank you."

"You are vey welcome, Miss Scarlett," he said and bowed.

I watched with David while he was driven away in his taxi, the words ringing in my ears. Whatever did he mean? I may not have remembered any of the Bard's other quotes from tonight, but I certainly remembered that one.

"The Japanese chappie said that to you?" Oscar asked, aghast. "How very odd!"

"I know, isn't it? Have you had enough yet?" I asked apologetically. "I did warn you it was a long story."

"You mean there's more?" His mouth dropped open.

I nodded. "Oh yes, much more."

"Then do you know something, darling?" Oscar said, a solemn expression appearing on his face.

I shook my head. Had he had enough? I'd been babbling on for quite a while now.

"If there's more story to be told, then we're definitely going to need—*more* biscuits!" Oscar cried, as he leaped off the sofa and hurried back to his kitchen for supplies.

The taxi journey back to our house that night was very quiet. David didn't seem to be in the mood for pleasant chitchat.

And when we got home things weren't much better.

"Look, David, I've said I'm sorry about earlier," I said, straightening up a plug socket that was hanging off the wall by its wires before I could plug the kettle in. I thought if I made David his favorite hot drink of baby marshmallows in drinking chocolate before we went to bed, it might make up for tonight's minor disasters on my part. "But I thought it went quite well in the end. The Japanese men all seemed to enjoy themselves."

"No thanks to you," David mumbled as he undid his tie and threw it on his Black & Decker Workmate.

"Hey, I heard that," I said, spinning round.

"You were supposed to."

I looked around the kitchen—if you could call it a kitchen. At the moment it looked more like the middle of an episode of *Changing Rooms*. Did I really want to start an argument with David now? It was late and I was tired…but still…

"So what was I supposed to do then? Just ignore George's call?" David shrugged and began to walk into the hall.

"Don't just walk away from me, David. You started this."

David turned around. "I started this?" he said, his eyes flashing dangerously. "I started this? I started this complete obsession you have with the cinema, so that it interferes with anything and everything we do?"

Oh, so that's his opening gambit tonight? This is a new one.

"I do not have a complete obsession with the cinema; tonight was about my job." I corrected myself. "My *business*, actually."

"I'm not just talking about tonight, about taking the call from George; I'm talking about everything. About the daydreaming for instance, like you were in the theater this evening."

I opened my mouth to protest.

"Don't tell me you weren't, Scarlett, because I know that look on your face. God knows I've seen it often enough."

I folded my arms. But I couldn't deny what he was saying. And OK, yes, I may be a bit of a daydreamer—but I wasn't a liar.

"It's not so bad when you're a bit bored; I suppose we all have our own ways of passing the time when life becomes dull, and trying to live your life like a movie is certainly different. It's when it starts to encroach on our lives together that I have a problem with it."

"I have no idea what you mean, David," I said haughtily. Even though I had a feeling I knew *exactly* what he meant. I turned away from him and began to clatter mugs and spoons about on the kitchen worktop in an effort to deflect the conversation.

But David wasn't going to be so easily distracted by a mug of hot chocolate tonight. "So then," he continued, "how many times do we watch a movie together and you sit there comparing me to the hero, Scarlett, hmm? I can't be Tom Cruise or Daniel Craig or whoever else it is that night. I'm me, David, not some superhero in tights."

It was a good job I wasn't facing him just then because I almost laughed out loud at the image of David prancing about in tights. Luckily I managed to suppress my laughter, and as I turned back to reply to his accusations, another thought occurred to me. If David knew me well at all, he should have known that those were the two least likely Hollywood actors I'd have been comparing him to; they were hardly my favorites.

"David, I can honestly say I've never wanted you to wear tights," I managed to say with a straight face. "And yes, maybe I have compared you to the odd film star on occasion, but that's not a crime, is it? I bet most women do it when they're watching a movie."

"When they're watching the movie, yes, but not later that day when their man is washing up or shaving or...well, do I have to spell it out for you?"

I swallowed hard. He knew about that?

"So," I said, desperately grasping at something to change the subject with and to use as ammunition. This argument was becoming decidedly one-sided. The boiling kettle not only made me jump, but also helped me with my task. "How do you think it is for me living in this...this skip of a house?"

David looked blank.

"Well, I'll tell you. It's like living in a permanent episode of *DIY SOS*, without the hope that a bunch of purple-shirted experts are going to come along and rescue me from this Homebase hell."

David looked completely shocked at my outburst.

"But I thought you liked our house project?" he asked in a small voice, as though I had just come along and knocked down all his sandcastles. "I thought you *liked* us doing up the house together?"

"No, *you* like doing it, David. You're the one who likes the DIY and makeover programs, not me. I'd just have got someone in to do it all up for us if I'd had my way."

"But that would have cost a fortune. We're saving ourselves so much money doing it this way."

"Are we?" I asked, looking round me. "Take that wall for instance. How many times have you re-tiled it now because it keeps going wrong and the tiles aren't on straight or the grouting's not right? We've had to buy at least three new lots of tiles that I know of. We might as well have just paid someone to do it right the first time."

"But I haven't done tiling before," David said, smoothing his hand over the tiles. "It isn't easy to get right the first time."

"All the more reason to get an expert in then."

"But they charge so much, Scarlett. It's just money down the drain."

I rolled my eyes. "Oh, David, for someone who has money, you're so tight with it!"

"I am not tight. I'm just careful. That is one of the first rules of good business, Scarlett. Look after the pennies and the pounds will look after themselves. You should take note of that and then maybe one day your little business might be as big as ours."

Whether he'd meant to or not, with that one comment he'd now got me completely riled.

"No, David, you are not just *careful*. *You* are the Ian Beale of the cinema industry. What about our holiday last year?"

"Yes, and what about it? We had one, didn't we? After I'd been made to sit through yet another of your *girlie* films." David folded his arms and looked at me meaningfully as if he'd scored yet another point.

"David, we'd been watching *Thelma & Louise*, and I seem to remember you promised me a road trip?"

David nodded. "Yes—and?"

"And we ended up taking a dilapidated motor home around the Peak District for a week."

"I got a good deal from this chap I know."

"Exactly. It was hardly a road trip across America in a Ford Thunderbird, was it?"

David shook his head. "Scarlett, if you're not happy with the way things are..."

"You know something, I'm not...but it seems I'm not the only one, am I?"

David looked at me. "Perhaps we both need to have a think about some things then?"

"Perhaps we do!"

"Look, I'll go to the tile warehouse on my own tomorrow if you like. Give you a bit of space here to have a think."

"No need. I'm going out with Maddie tomorrow so I'll be out all day anyway."

"Oh well—that's good."

"Yes it is."

"And should I sleep in the spare room tonight?" David asked, looking at me with big, sorrowful eyes that suggested he hoped I'd say no.

"I'd say yes if it was in a fit state to sleep in," I said matter-of-factly. David's face lifted for a moment. "But since it's not, perhaps you could make up a bed on the sofa."

And then it fell again.

"Oh, all right," he said. "That's probably for the best then."

"Yes, I think it is."

While David made himself a cup of tea, and then a bed on the sofa with a pillow and a sleeping bag, I perched on a stool in the kitchen and silently watched him. I didn't regret my decision for a minute, knowing the last person on earth I wanted sleeping next to me in my bed that night was Ian Beale.

Oscar burst out laughing.

"Oh my dear, I can quite understand why you're here now. I would have wanted to escape from that DIY freak too. But how on earth did you find the house here in Notting Hill?"

"No, Oscar, that's not the only reason I needed to get away—far from it. I'm coming to that. And to how I got the use of the house. If you still want me to tell you, that is?"

Oscar sat back against the sofa, wide-eyed.

"Well of course I do! Forget sleeping with Ian Beale. This is better than a Sunday omnibus of *EastEnders*, *Hollyoaks*, and *Corrie* all rolled into one!"

Four

I stood outside the art gallery the next day waiting for Maddie, still mulling over my argument with David.

I knew things hadn't felt right between us for a while, but I always thought I'd be able to get past his little idiosyncrasies—especially since David never seemed to have had any issues with my love of the cinema before. But now, after last night's outburst, I was starting to wonder whether I could go through with this wedding. If I *could* actually make this arrangement work.

Getting married to David was permanent; there was no going back. I mean, in cinema terms, we were talking *From Here to Eternity, The Full Monty, Diamonds are Forever…*

After a few minutes of me torturing myself with every movie I could recall with a forever theme, Maddie came floating down the street in a suitably artistic outfit. She wore a long, velvet coat with a burgundy and gold Monsoon dress, and she had completed her look with a large gold butterfly in her hair and gold sandals. So pleased was I to see my best friend again that I even restrained myself from making any comment about sandals in late January.

As we began our quest for artistic and intellectual enlightenment among the many paintings and works of art the gallery had to offer, I put all thoughts of David from my head. He could wait for another time.

While Maddie stood and scrutinized every single painting and sculpture she came across, reading the small yet informative card that was placed beside it in full, I wandered quickly from exhibit to exhibit, wondering on more than one occasion just how depressed these people must have been to create some of the stuff. If they'd worked in offices and lived in houses just like mine, then perhaps some of their artistic output could be rightly justified.

I was just about to give up the will to live when my eye was drawn to a cluster of paintings at the end of the room; actually, it was one painting in particular that had caught my attention. Unlike all the other exhibits I had passed, this painting was instantly familiar. It was as if it had once hung on a wall in my own home.

I sat down on the bench in front of the painting, and all at once was lost in my own familiar world as I stared up at it. Now this was a piece of art I understood.

The painting was of a young woman floating against a dark blue sky. She wore a red dress and a long white veil which a man was adjusting on her head to make sure she was perfectly presented for her wedding. In the background was a church, and all around her animals, some playing musical instruments—a violin-playing goat was especially prominent.

I glanced at the card next to the painting:

La Mariée (The Bride) ~ Marc Chagall 1950
Young women or couples can often be seen in Chagall's work. But few of his paintings are as striking as La Mariée, depicting a yearning for something that's lost.

In the 1999 film Notting Hill, *Julia Roberts' character, Anna Scott, sees a print of* La Mariée *in the home of Hugh Grant's character, William Thacker. Anna later gives William a gift of what is supposed to be the original painting.*

A yearning for something that's lost…

The words circled around in my brain for a while before they descended to my heart, where they tried to poke and prod at a part of it where I never allowed anything to go.

I'd always loved the painting that now hung in front of me. I thought it was because of *Notting Hill*; it wouldn't be the first time I'd taken to something because I'd seen it in a movie.

Like when I'd first seen *Sleepless in Seattle* I'd taken to listening to late-night radio call-in shows…just in case. But the callers in this country were rarely in the mold of the gentle Sam character portrayed by Tom Hanks. They were normally far scarier, and much more your usual daytime talk show–style troll.

With *Bridget Jones* I'd kept a daily diary. Internet chat rooms with *You've Got Mail*. I'd even taken dance lessons at our local community center when I'd first seen *Dirty Dancing*. But our dance instructor didn't bear much resemblance to Patrick Swayze or even Patrick Dempsey. No, imagine if you will an effeminate Patrick Stewart of the Starship *Enterprise*, crossed with Patrick Star of SpongeBob SquarePants fame, and you will have the perfect image of my salsa instructor. And when I'd seen *Pretty Woman* for the first time, I'd firmly decided never to try out *any* part of that movie.

"Found something you like at last?" Maddie asked, sitting down next to me. "You've whizzed through the rest of the exhibition pretty quick."

She looked up at the painting with me for a moment then inspected the white information card. "Oh, Scarlett," she sighed, sitting back. "How *do* you do it? I should have known you'd find something film-related—even here."

"It's not my fault. Anyway that's not the only reason I'm looking at this painting."

"It's not?" Maddie looked at me in disbelief. "What other reason is there, then?"

"Because…it's a bride, isn't it…and we're both going to be brides soon. And to tell you the truth, Maddie, it's what it said on the card that's really made me think about this painting."

"Yeah, I know, about *Notting Hill*."

"No, not just that. I mean obviously I recognized the painting from the film, but the part about 'a yearning for something that's lost.'"

Maddie wrinkled her nose. "What *are* you talking about, Scarlett?"

"I don't know." I was beginning to wish I hadn't said anything now. Maddie may well have been my oldest friend, but even she couldn't understand how I felt. I barely understood this feeling I constantly carried inside me myself. "I've just always felt like there was something missing in my life, Maddie. Some tiny piece of something that's not quite there, like the last piece of a jigsaw puzzle."

Maddie stared at me. I wished I'd just hidden behind the movie excuse now—it would have been a lot easier.

"Are you having pre-wedding jitters?" she asked. "Is that what you're trying to tell me?"

I closed my eyes for a moment. That wasn't what I meant

at all, but if I didn't know what I meant, how could I expect anyone else to?

"Yes, maybe that's it," I said, opening my eyes again and looking at her. "I have been wondering lately if marrying David is the right thing to do. I keep having these niggling little doubts."

"What sort of doubts?" Maddie asked with a look that already answered my next question, which was going to be if she ever had the same doubts about marrying Felix.

"Er..." I thought quickly. I couldn't tell Maddie the real reason for my uncertainty. "That I'm everything he wants me to be?"

Maddie shook her head and smiled.

"Oh, Scarlett, don't be daft—of course you are; otherwise, he wouldn't have asked you in the first place, would he?"

When Maddie saw I wasn't smiling too, she became serious again.

"What's made you suddenly start thinking like this? You love David and he loves you. You get married, and live happily ever after; it's as simple as that."

It's as simple as that for you and Felix. There's a bit more involved with David and me...

"It's different with David," I padded, as I desperately tried to explain how I felt. "He...he requires more from a wife."

"Like?" Maddie's face looked blank for a moment, and then her eyes suddenly opened wide. "Oh my, are you saying you've just found out he's into something really kinky in the bedroom? Golly, after all this time too, it's always the quiet ones, isn't it? What is it? Rubber? Chains? You know I once knew this chap that liked this weird thing with a banana and an Angel Delight..."

"No, Maddie," I shushed her. "No, it's nothing like that." I sighed. "I guess I should have realized it before, I mean it's nothing new, well it is to me, so I suppose that's why it seems weird."

"What is it, Scarlett?" Maddie demanded. "Come on, spit it out—I have to know."

"OK, OK," I said, wishing I'd never started this now. "Apparently as David's wife I'll be expected to help him entertain people. You know, future clients and the like."

Maddie nodded. "Yes, and…?"

"*And* that's it."

Maddie stared at me again and I saw the corners of her mouth twitch. "That's it? That's why you're having doubts about marrying him? Because you might have to cook for a few dinner parties?"

I flushed; it did sound a bit lame now I'd come out with it, but the business dinner excuse wasn't completely untrue. It just wasn't the *whole* truth. "*You* know how bad I am at cooking, Maddie. Plus you weren't there last night when we entertained some of David's Japanese business clients. That was bad enough, and we were only eating out in a restaurant."

"Why? What on earth happened?"

"Come on," I said, looking longingly toward the exit of the art gallery. "I'm starving. Let's get out of here and find somewhere to eat and I'll tell you all about it."

We found a pretty little wine bar down the road from the gallery and after we'd ordered some food, I quickly told Maddie the story of my own mini-Shakespearean tragedy.

"…and he said the funniest thing to me. He said *the course of true love never did run smooth*."

"He's quite right," Maddie said, taking a sip of her red wine. "The course of true love never does run entirely smoothly, that's part of what makes it so fun. And what was so bad about the evening? It was hardly a disaster."

"No, but it was hardly a roaring success either. Look, I know there's no such thing as the perfect relationship, Maddie, but I'm just not sure David and I have that special something between us. You know, that special something that you and Felix have...the magic?"

Maddie looked at me, then she raised her eyebrow and cocked her head to one side. "Special something?" she repeated. "Magic? Scarlett, successful relationships require give and take, love and understanding, not special somethings and a magic wand."

I was about to point out to Maddie that the "magic" in question was not the sort that could be conjured up with the wave of a wand when our waitress returned to the table carrying plates of spaghetti carbonara and chicken salad. (Maddie was dieting because of her wedding.)

We'd eaten a few mouthfuls of our food when I decided to ask Maddie a question.

"Maddie, if I ask you something, will you answer it honestly?"

Maddie looked at me. She finished chewing before answering. "Of course I will, you know that."

"Do you think I'm a little bit obsessed with films?"

"Yes," Maddie said without hesitation.

"You didn't even think about it!"

"I didn't need to. You are."

"But...I'm not," I protested. This was not the answer I was hoping Maddie would give. I thought she'd say no, and why did I ask? Then we'd go on to have a good old moaning session about how David had got it all wrong as usual, and weren't men just stupid and only good for one thing.

"Don't be daft, Scarlett, of course you are."

"But what's wrong with visiting the cinema occasionally?"

Maddie put down her fork, folded her arms, tilted her head to one side, and looked at me with a challenging expression.

"What?" I asked.

"Come on. Don't you think it's a little bit more with you than only *occasionally*?"

"But I have my job. It's not my fault that's cinema-related."

"And?"

"And what?" I asked in genuine amazement. I hadn't expected this at all.

"And the rest."

I looked blankly at Maddie.

"OK," she said, "let me help you along. Felix and I were watching *The Holiday* the other night—"

"Oh, I love that movie," I interrupted.

"Yes, I know you do. Anyway, Felix said it's a wonder Scarlett hasn't tried to do that yet. He meant house-swapping."

Actually I had thought of it when I'd seen it for the first time.

"My point being that even Felix is making comments about your movie madness now. And he hasn't known you as long as the rest of us."

"There's nothing wrong in having a hobby, is there?"

"No, nothing at all, as long as that hobby doesn't start affecting how you live your day-to-day life. The thing is, trying to live like you're in a movie all the time, Scarlett, it's just not possible."

I stared at Maddie.

"Not you as well," I said sadly. "I thought it was just David."

"What do you mean? There's more to this, isn't there? That's what you were hinting at earlier in the art gallery."

I nodded and began to tell Maddie about David and the fight we'd had the night before.

"But all couples fight, Scarlett," Maddie said when I'd finished. "Sometimes the making up is the best part."

I'd always hated that saying. In all the fights I'd ever had with David, I'd never found our making up "fun." We'd just start mumbling a couple of words to each other again after a few hours or days of silence depending how bad the argument had been. Then things gradually got back to normal bit by bit.

In fact, now I was remembering just why I hadn't been spending so much time with Maddie lately. It wasn't because she'd been too busy at all; it was because when we spent time together, it reminded me just how bad my and David's relationship seemed in comparison to hers and Felix's.

And it was obvious Maddie in her "loved up" state would not understand my current feelings toward my own fiancé. And why should she? The only reason she had for marrying was love. My own reasons were a little bit more complicated.

"Never mind, Maddie, you wouldn't understand."

"I am trying, Scarlett, honestly. But I *can* see David's point of view to a degree. But then again," she said as I stared hard at her across the table, "I suppose if I had to live with Stratford's answer to Laurence Llewelyn-Bowen, I might be in need of a bit of fantasy therapy too."

I had to laugh. David was about as far removed from the floppy-haired interior designer as you could possibly get.

"That's better," Maddie said. "You don't do enough of that these days." She put her hand on mine and looked serious for a moment. "I'm worried about you, with everything you've told me here and what you said before in the art gallery. Maybe you need a break for a while?"

I smiled at her. "What, in another motor home? I don't think so—the last one was bad enough."

"No, I don't mean with David. On your own. Get away from everything for a while—do some thinking."

"And just where am I going to do that?"

I was playing along with Maddie. There was no way I'd be able to get away from work at the moment; a shipment of new machines was due to arrive with us any day. And the chances of David thinking it a good idea for me to go away on my own… well, they were non-existent.

"David would never allow me to spend money on going away on holiday on my own. You know what he's like."

Maddie pulled a face.

"Hmm, there is that. Let me think for a moment…"

I took a sip of my wine while Maddie thought, glad my interrogation was over for now. I couldn't believe Maddie thought I was obsessed too. What was wrong with these people? Movies were just a harmless bit of fun. Why couldn't they see that?

"I've got it!" Maddie said suddenly, when I was just thinking my food was going to get cold if I didn't start eating again soon. "I've had a brilliant—no, make that a fabulous idea! Look I've nearly finished my salad, what little there was of it. Do you mind if I make a couple of calls while you finish your pasta? You'll love me for it when I'm finished, Scarlett, I promise."

I shrugged and picked up my fork while Maddie dived into her bag for her mobile phone. Then she began to make the first of several phone calls, all of which involved much laughter and phrases like, "We must meet up soon, darling." This made me smile because Maddie was so not the "darling" type at all.

"Well," she said when she'd finally finished. "I don't know if I've done the right thing here—because in a way I think it might just be encouraging you more. But you know how you were saying before how you loved the movie *The Holiday*?"

"Yes?" I asked suspiciously. I hoped "The Madness of Maddie" wasn't going to erupt into some tin pot scheme as it had a habit of doing occasionally when left unchecked for too long.

"Well, how would you like to relive some of that movie? Actually, come to think of it, I'm giving you two movies for the price of one here."

"Just what are you talking about, Maddie?"

"Scarlett, I have managed to obtain for you a little luxury pad just off the Portobello Road to house-sit for a month!"

"How on earth have you done that?" I asked, completely amazed at my friend's ingenuity.

"Ah, you just have to know the right people," she said, tapping the side of her nose. "No seriously, it belongs to a friend of my sister," she explained. "I remember Jojo saying a while back that Belinda and Harry needed someone to house-sit for a month while they're in Dubai visiting Harry's parents, and they were having such trouble finding someone reliable. They leave in less than a week, so you, my dear Scarlett, could be the answer to their prayers!"

I thought about this for a few seconds, about trying to live out *The Holiday* for myself. I'd always fancied being Cameron Diaz—or would I be Kate Winslet? Then something occurred to me. "You said two movies, Maddie?"

"Yes." Maddie grinned. "The Portobello Road, Scarlett... it's where?"

"Oh my God!" I said as the penny dropped. "But that's only one of my absolute all-time favorites."

"Yep, I know," she said, her eyes shining. "*Notting Hill!*"

I looked at Oscar.

He'd been sitting listening to me for over an hour now, completely enraptured by my tale. Obviously I'd only told him a condensed version and not the parts that were too personal, but he got the gist.

"So it's your fiancé and your best friend that have driven you here to seek refuge?" Oscar asked.

"There's my father as well. But he pretty much seems to have the same opinion as the other two." If not more so... "I just want to prove them wrong, Oscar. Prove to them there's nothing wrong with me loving the cinema so much, and that life isn't so far removed from the movies as they all seem to think it is."

"Well I think you're already living your dream without even

coming here, my darling. It all seems very Hollywood to me!" Oscar said, his eyes wide with amazement. "I can see it all now," he said, waving his hand in the air with a flourish. "Beautiful young girl sets out into the world to seek revenge for an injustice she feels has been cast upon her by her cruel family. I can hear Red Pepper doing the voiceover as I speak."

I had to laugh; Red Pepper was the chap with the really deep gravelly voice who did all the dramatic movie trailer voice-overs. "It's not quite *that* bad, Oscar. And actually it isn't very Hollywood at all. It's been a bit of a disaster since I arrived." I meant losing the address, but the guy in the travel bookshop's attitude from earlier was still bugging me.

"But you've only just got here, darling. You've yonks of time if you're here for a month." Oscar thought for a moment and then he smiled. "Actually you've had a pretty good start today, haven't you, if you're looking for proof that movies happen in real life?"

"Have I—how?"

"Oh my dear, what sort of use are you going to be if you can't recognize an opportunity when one arises? For one thing, someone knocked into you today and spilled orange juice all down you…"

He left a long pause while he waited for the penny to drop. When he saw recognition strike, he continued, "That same person invited you back to his home to change…" Again the pause.

"And OK, I may not be Hugh Grant—although in a certain light…" Oscar stood up and admired himself in the mirror above the mantelpiece.

I laughed.

"*And*," he continued, "to top it all, that same person is going to invite you to a dinner party tonight!"

"You're having a dinner party?"

"Well, I wasn't. But what the hey, I shall have to now, won't I? Just to give you another movie scene to help you on your way!"

"Really—you'd do that for me, a total stranger you've just met on the street?"

"My darling Scarlett," Oscar said with his hands on his hips. "You can't be a *total* stranger now, can you? No total stranger would be sitting in my lounge, eating my biscuits, and wearing my T-shirt, now, would they?"

I left Oscar's house with a spring in my step, and a Fortnum & Mason shopping bag swinging from my arm, complete with my clean white shirt inside. Along with some very precise instructions from Oscar on how I should continue to dry it out when I got to the new house.

As I whizzed along the streets and finally found my way to my new home, I felt confident that at last things were looking up. I'd actually met someone nice here, someone who wanted to help me, plus I was going out to dinner tonight!

Maddie had phoned with new instructions on how to get to the house, but now as I looked at the scribbled notes on the crumpled piece of paper in my hand I wondered if I'd misheard her.

"This can't be right," I said, looking around me. "I must

have got the wrong area." I was sure Maddie had said a *little* house off the Portobello Road; these all looked like mansions. But the street sign at the top of the road had the correct name, so I slowed down and continued trundling my case along the pavement, carefully inspecting the numbers on the houses as I passed.

At last I came to a house that matched the number on my note and stared up at a large cream-fronted residence, much like all the others on the street. I reached for the black iron gate and cautiously pushed it open. I was sure my new neighbors would be twitching their net curtains (if they had anything so common) at the sight that was creeping up Belinda and Harry's steps right now.

I stood on the doorstep and rummaged in my handbag. Belinda had had some keys couriered over to me by motorbike the day before, saying she couldn't possibly trust anyone else to let me in when I arrived.

There was obviously a good neighborly spirit in the area, then.

I really must get a new bag, I thought, as my hand groped around for the keys.

"Good evening," I heard a voice call from the next house.

I looked across at the voice, and standing in the same place I was, on the steps next door reaching for his own keys, was the young man from the travel bookshop earlier. He wasn't wearing his coat now or carrying a shopping bag, but was dressed casually in a brown leather jacket, white T-shirt, and jeans.

"What are you doing here?" I blurted out.

He looked surprised. "I could ask you the same thing. Where are Belinda and Harry?"

"They've gone away on holiday for a few weeks. I...I'm house-sitting for them."

I'm not surprised they didn't want their neighbors letting me into the house if you're anything to go by, I thought as at last I found the keys.

"That sounds a plausible excuse, I suppose."

How very neighborly of you, I thought sourly, as I put the key in the lock. "If there's nothing else?" I inquired, turning to face him and raising my eyebrows in what I hoped was a haughty, "I really don't have time for your silly questions" kind of way.

"Actually yes, there is. Why did you think I worked in the bookshop earlier? Do I look like a shop assistant?"

He looked anything but as I stood face to face with him now. His attitude was definitely much more "Don't mess with me" than "Can I help you?" My new neighbor was tall, with tousled, sandy hair, and as he stood looking accusingly at me, with one of his eyebrows raised in a quizzical manner above his pale blue eyes, there was almost a look of *The Holiday*-ing Jude Law about him. I quickly shook this vision from my head. No, that was taking this movie thing a bit *too* far.

"No, I mean yes, you did back then obviously, or I wouldn't have said it. Look, my head's been all over the place today; it's my first day here and everything is new to me."

I hoped he'd feel sorry for me and embarrassed that he'd been so mean. But instead he just continued his interrogation.

"This head of yours," he asked, slowly looking me up and down. "Is it often all over the place? Do you often have problems putting your thoughts in a sensible order?"

OK, I'd thought Oscar had been a bit off the wall to begin

with, but he now seemed positively sane in comparison to this dude.

"Not usually, no, why do you say that?"

"No reason," he said, turning away. He unlocked his own door and pushed it slightly ajar. "It's just your T-shirt suggested to me otherwise." He gave me a smug smile as he stepped into his house and swiftly closed the door behind him.

I looked down between the lapels of my jacket. I'd been so engrossed in everything that Oscar and I had been talking about earlier that I hadn't paid any attention to what was on his T-shirt.

It was navy, and emblazoned across it in big bold white letters was the phrase: I CAN'T EVEN THINK STRAIGHT.

Five

After I'd successfully unlocked the door a piercing, high-pitched wail bombarded my eardrums. The alarm—Belinda had warned me about that.

I ran over to the small black box that sat on the wall opposite the doorway, realizing that I'd had the alarm code earlier on my original piece of paper, but Maddie had only given me the address over the phone.

Think, Scarlett, think.

I knew the six-digit code was something personal to me—I'd thought that when Belinda had told me it the first time, now what was it again?

The wailing seemed to be getting louder. How long did I have before the police would come out? I couldn't remember what Belinda had said now. If only that damn wailing would shut up for a minute so I could think. Oh, that was the point.

I thought hard.

Now…the first two numbers were my birthday—that was easy, I could remember those. The next was…oh, my bra size minus the cup, yep, got it. And the last two…come on, Scarlett…think…oh, of course, how many times I'd seen the movie *Notting Hill*!

Hastily I reset the security code, all the time praying I'd remembered it in the correct order. Within seconds of pressing the buttons, the wailing ceased.

I breathed a sigh of relief, pulled my suitcase in off the step, and shut the door behind me. It was only then that I noticed the elegant surroundings I found myself in.

"Wow," I exclaimed as my eyes ran over the coffee and cream decor of the hall. "Triple wow!"

I quickly explored the house, opening doors and expelling further sounds of pleasure as I became more and more excited.

Belinda and Harry certainly had plenty of money, that was for sure—but I thanked the Lord they had taste too. Plain walls were simply adorned with bold works of art, and every room was light and airy but managed to remain warm and cozy too. Everywhere was decorated in a chic, minimalist style, and I loved it.

I selected one of their five bedrooms to sleep in. It had a lavish purple and lilac theme. There was a beautiful silk duvet cover and scatter cushions on the bed, with full-length raw silk curtains at the window. *This will do nicely*, I thought, as I launched myself face down on to the bed, arms and legs outstretched just like Kate Winslet had done in Cameron Diaz's mansion in *The Holiday*. Then I flipped over and lay back on the bed for a moment, admiring my new surroundings. "Ha ha, you lot," I said to the empty room. "Strike one! There's my first completely spontaneous and totally harmless movie moment and I've only been here five minutes!"

My intention was to go back home at the end of my month away with a list of evidence of things that had happened to me that were the same as things that happened to people in the movies, therefore proving my point to those that doubted me. I was determined to show that what they considered my strange little obsession was not as eccentric and bizarre as they thought it was.

Movies weren't that different from real life a lot of the time—I just had to find a way of proving that.

I mean, obviously there wasn't any chance of me sailing on a 46,000-ton passenger liner when it hit an iceberg, but what was to stop me from going to as many weddings as I could find, in the hope that the best man would forget the rings or the bride would be jilted in sign language by the brother of the groom?

OK, those might not be the best two examples, but it couldn't be that hard to find movie scenes in everyday life. And after all I *was* in Notting Hill, which had already given me a good start in meeting Oscar.

I know the others just thought I needed some time away- to get my head together, to think about my life and what I really wanted from it. Dad had seemed especially keen that I do just that.

I thought about my father.

I'd only mentioned him casually to Oscar, saying he felt the same as Maddie and David. But the truth was Dad had just as much to do, if not more so, with me being here as they did.

The day after I'd gone to the art gallery with Maddie, David and I had spent a very awkward day in the house together, desperately trying to spend as little time as possible in each other's company, therefore ruling out any possibility of needing to discuss the argument of Friday evening.

So for once, when Monday morning came and I found myself climbing the concrete stairs in the plain gray building that housed our tiny two-room offices, I actually felt quite relieved to be coming into work.

The building I seemed to spend most of my life in these days had once been home to a psychiatric hospital, or mental asylum as they were called back then, until a forward-thinking architect in the 1970s had converted the then derelict building into offices. As I passed through the corridors on a daily basis, I could sympathize wholeheartedly with how the past inmates must have felt at being incarcerated here all those years ago. At least I got to leave this drab institution for a few hours at the end of every day. They would have been stuck here permanently, with no light at the end of their tunnel.

Mrs. Jameson was our part-time secretary, or Miss Moneypenny, as I secretly called her when I was trying to inject some interest into my long, boring days, and I would pretend these rather boring, tiny offices were the hub of MI6. She was already hard at work when I arrived. She smiled at me over her gold-rimmed spectacles as I opened the door.

"Morning, dear, how are we today?" she asked, looking up from her typing. "There's an awful wind out there this morning; fair blew me away when I got off the bus."

"Yes," I agreed, as I hurriedly unbuttoned my coat. "It is a bit brisk. Is Dad in yet?"

"Yes, dear, he's in already. I believe he's on the phone just now."

"Oh, right. Thanks, Mrs. J," I said as I hung my coat up on the old wooden coat stand in the corner of the room. I'd hoped to get in early today and make a good impression on Dad. It might have helped soften the blow a little when I mentioned the possibility of taking up Maddie's offer.

The office door burst open—my father had obviously finished his phone call.

"Morning, Scarlett, glad to see you made it in at last," he said, brushing past me. He placed some papers on Mrs. Jameson's desk. "This is the account I was telling you about, Dorothy. Can you check the invoices back from August, please?"

"I'm not late," I said, looking at my watch. "Actually I think you'll find I'm early, Dad."

"That makes a change," he mumbled as he searched through a filing cabinet.

Mrs. J rolled her eyes at me and mouthed the words "bad mood" while my father had his back to her. So I carried on through to the tiny room Dad and I shared as an office. I heard the door close behind me.

"Good weekend?" my father inquired, as he thumbed through the files he was carrying.

"Er, not too bad," I answered cautiously. I figured this was probably not the best of times to mention Maddie's idea. In fact, now I was back here again, I realized it was likely there never *was* going to be a good time. So I decided that the best plan for now was just getting on with some work. I would bide my time and wait and see if a better moment arose later.

For the rest of our Monday morning, I chased up a few unpaid invoices while Dad spoke to potential clients about the benefits of installing a popcorn machine in their refreshment areas. Then, while Dad phoned the bank to talk to them about extending our business loan, I surfed the net while pretending to type a letter. It was virtually the same as any other mind-numbing day at the office.

I'd soon exhausted all the movie websites I had bookmarked and was just about to log on to robbiewilliams.com when I noticed Dad was watching me from his desk.

Quickly I closed the Internet down.

"Scarlett?" he said slowly.

"Yep," I said, opening the letter I was supposed to be typing again.

"Is everything all right with you lately?"

"Yeah," I said, concentrating hard on the screen.

"Are you sure?"

I looked up from the monitor. What was going on? Dad never usually inquired about my state of mind during work hours.

"Yes."

My father sighed. "Scarlett, I do have eyes, you know; you've not been your usual self lately. What's wrong?"

I shrugged. "Nothing."

My father raised his eyebrows.

"It's nothing, really, Dad."

"Is it David?"

"Maybe."

"Scarlett, come on; you've got to give me more than that. I'm a man; I'm not good at this relationship stuff."

I half smiled. "You always coped all right before when I had problems."

"I had to, didn't I?" Dad said in a gruff voice. "There was no one else to. Have you two had a fight?"

"No, it's nothing like that," I lied.

"Really?" Dad said, his brown eyes watching me closely over the top of his reading glasses.

"Yes…" I began. Then I stopped. Wait, something wasn't adding up here…

"He's been to see you, hasn't he?" I said suddenly, as the missing link clicked into place.

My father shuffled some papers about on his desk like a newsreader at the end of a bulletin, and then he placed them back down in exactly the same spot they'd started out in. "David did come to see me on Saturday. He seemed awfully worried about things."

"What sort of *things*?" I asked in a tight voice.

"Now, Scarlett, don't get wound up just because David is showing some concern for your relationship."

"I'm not getting wound up," I said, while under my desk my hands began to form tight fists in my lap. "I just don't see why David came to see you, that's all. What goes on between us is our business."

"Because he's worried about you, that's why." Dad removed his glasses and walked the short distance across the office toward me. He perched awkwardly on the corner of my desk. "He says you don't seem yourself these days. And like I said earlier, I've noticed the same."

I was surprised to hear this. I thought I'd done quite a good job of hiding everything. And in the space of a weekend I'd got David giving me grief about a bit of daydreaming, Maddie about my love of films, and now Dad about…well, what had Dad noticed exactly?

"You do still love David, don't you?" Dad continued after a few moments' thought. "I mean, things aren't that bad, are they?"

As he looked down at me, awaiting my answer, his face was filled with concern.

"Yes, Dad," I replied automatically without thinking, more to put him out of his misery than anything else. "I do still love David...at least, I think I do."

Dad looked relieved for a split second before anxiety filled his face once again. "What do you mean *think*? Oh, Scarlett, why on earth have you agreed to marry the poor chap if you're not sure you still love him?"

"I've nothing better to do this spring?" I shrugged, not wanting to tell him the real reason. And David was hardly a *poor* chap.

"Scarlett!" Dad said, running his hands in exasperation through his graying hair.

"Well, it's true. A wedding is the most excitement I'm going to have for a while."

My father shook his head and got up from my desk. "But I thought you loved David," he said, pacing across the office floor. "I mean you've got the house together and everything now."

Yeah, like a bit of DIY was going to make a difference. The way I felt about David right now it would take all the superglue in the world to bond us together. But Dad looked so upset at the thought of all this that I felt I needed to go easy on him.

"I didn't say I didn't love him—just that I wasn't sure anymore." I paused for a moment. "I mean how do you know when you *really* love someone? What happens to let you know you're doing the right thing when you commit to spending the rest of your life with them?"

My father considered this. "You never know for definite, Scarlett. It's just a feeling you have that this is the right person for you."

"Did *you* have that feeling with Mum?" I said without thinking. I rose from my chair and approached my father carefully. "Did it feel like…" I hesitated. "…magic when the two of you first met?"

I saw my father's body stiffen, and the gentleness and understanding of the last few minutes visibly drained from him. I could have let loose a torrent of obscene swear words and I'd have offended him less. I'd broken the cardinal O'Brien rule.

I'd mentioned my mother.

"I would prefer to keep your mother out of this discussion," he said, retreating across the office floor to the shelter of his own desk.

"I know you would; you always do." I could feel hot blood beginning to pump into my cheeks and my hands were curling up into fists again. "But *I* might want to talk about her once in a while. She was *my* mother as well as *your* wife!"

"I am quite aware of that fact, thank you, Scarlett," my father said coolly, not rising to my anger. "But your mother chose to remove herself from our lives twenty-three and a half years ago. So I see no reason why she should have any part to play in them now."

"I don't want her to play a part—I just want to talk about her occasionally—maybe learn something about her. I don't even know what she looked like, for heaven's sake!" I stared accusingly at my father. "You must have destroyed all evidence of her existence when she left because I was never able to find any in the house. While most kids were searching for where their Christmas or birthday presents were hidden, I was searching for photos of my mother!" I flounced back into my own chair, and for a moment we surveyed each other over our desks like warring armies waiting to see what the other's next move might be.

My father gave first. "Scarlett, I'm sorry." I felt his genuine distress as he spoke. "I didn't realize it bothered you that much."

"It didn't when I was little," I said, my voice softening too. Dad and I could never stay mad at each other for long. "Only having a father at home seemed normal to me then. But as I got older, I wanted to know who I was, and where I came from. I mean, I know she must have loved the movies like I do, or I'm pretty sure I wouldn't have been christened Scarlett. You're not likely to have chosen my name, are you—you seem to hate films." I looked at my father, but as usual he gave nothing away. "But am I like her apart from that?"

"Oh, if only you knew just how much you are."

"You mean the way I look?" I asked hopefully. This was more than I'd ever got before.

"Partly," my father said, coming over to my desk again. This time he knelt down next to my chair so I looked down at him. "Your green eyes..." he said, gently cupping my face in his hand. "Yes, they're definitely hers. I remember the day you were born, your mother's complete joy that you had the same coloring as Vivien Leigh. Everyone else was shocked at the mop of black hair you were born with, but not your mother; she said you were her perfect Scarlett. *Gone with the Wind* was her favorite film."

I watched my father closely: there was a fondness in his eyes and in his voice while he talked. He had never spoken like this to me about my mother—there had always been coldness in his eyes and hate in his voice when her name was mentioned.

But again he snapped out of this reverie just as quickly as he'd slipped into it. "But no, it's not your looks so much as your attitude." He sprang to his feet again. "Your mother was always watching nonsense at the cinema just as you seem to do all the time. The films filled her head with unrealistic hopes and dreams of how life should be so she wasn't satisfied with what we'd got. And *she* always had her head in the clouds just like you do! When David came to me on Saturday, I could quite understand how he felt. It took me back to the situation I found myself in over twenty years ago."

"That's not fair," I said, determined to defend myself but at the same time trying to digest all this new information Dad was feeding me. I'd found out more in the last two minutes about my mother than I'd ever known before. But it was all clashing with this stupid nonsense David was dreaming up. "I do not go around with my head in the clouds. Sometimes my life can be a bit boring, that's all, and I find ways of passing the time— and yes, sometimes those ways do involve the movies, and that does make me start to wonder if there might be more to life out there for me than here in Stratford. Is that such a crime?"

My father rolled his eyes. "Do you mean is there a life out there for you that's more like one of these soppy films you're always watching? With a handsome prince waiting at the top of a tall tower to give you a happy ending? And I'm pretty sure it'll be that type of movie you go to see. I bet there's not any blood, guts, or gore in anything you watch."

"No, but why would I want to see that? I go to the cinema to be entertained, not to be scared and repulsed by what I see."

"But that's real life, Scarlett. Life is not a heart-shaped box of chocolates."

"You never know what you're gonna get?" I suggested helpfully.

"What?" my father asked.

I guess *Forrest Gump* must have passed him by. "Never mind, it doesn't matter, Dad. It's from a movie."

"You see, you're even talking like them now. Scarlett, life is not a movie, and you can't go around trying to live your life as if you're in one—especially not the sort that seem to be filling your head with silly ideas." My father ran his hand through his hair in exasperation and turned his back to me.

"Ah!" I said, banging my hand on the desk. "Why does everyone keep saying that to me all the time? How do you all know that, eh?" I demanded. "How do you all *really* know? Take you, for instance, Dad, you've never been anywhere or done anything with your life. There could be a mountain of exciting things just waiting to happen to you out there—just the same as the sort of things that happen in the movies."

My father spun round. "You seem to forget that the main reason I've never been anywhere or done anything is because I was bringing you up—alone. I was a single parent trying to build a business that I hoped would provide us with a decent living. *And* was doing all this before it ever became trendy—as it seems to be these days—to be a single dad with a young child. I worked hard for you to give you a decent future, not so I could go swanning off around the world having adventures, as you think I should have."

The silence that filled the room was only broken by the gentle *tap tap tap* of Mrs. J's fingers running over her old keyboard in the next-door office.

My father looked hurt, angry, and confused as he stood there, and there was sadness in his eyes that I just couldn't bear to see.

"I'm really sorry, Dad," I said in a small voice as I looked up at him from my desk. "I do appreciate everything you did for me when I was young—you know I do."

My father looked at me, and his face softened. "And I'm sorry too, Scarlett—for shouting at you." He held out his arms. "Are you too big now to give your old dad a hug?"

I got up and moved over to him, burying myself in his warm embrace. "Never."

"You know I was only trying to help?"

I nodded, my head still buried in the comfort of his familiar scent.

"It's just that I've seen you grow up watching movies, reading about movies, pretending to be in the movies. There's nothing wrong with the cinema—for heaven's sake, without it we wouldn't have a business—but I want to make sure you understand that you have to live in the real world, with real people and real situations. I don't want you to end up like..."

My father didn't finish his sentence.

"Like who, Dad?"

"Er...just one of these people that dream their life away and never really do anything with it." Dad held me back and looked at me. "Scarlett, you can't continue to pretend your life is a movie script. And after what David said to me last night, if you continue like this, you're going to risk losing him—along with your mind."

I was about to say that might not be such a bad thing when I remembered one of the reasons I'd agreed to marry David and I stopped myself just in time.

My father let go of me and walked to the window. After a moment's consideration he turned to face me again. "Scarlett, I'm going to tell you what I told David yesterday. I think you need some time away, to get your head together and to think about things. What do you say?"

I tried not to look too overjoyed. Hadn't that been just what I'd wanted when I'd walked into the office this morning? But I hadn't expected my father to hand it to me served up on a silver salver like this, all wrapped up with a big red bow.

"Er...yes that sounds like a good idea," I said cautiously, in case Dad's idea of time away wasn't the same as mine.

"How about a couple of weeks off work?" Dad suggested.

"How about we make it a month? Then I'll have plenty of time to do *lots* of thinking about my life. I'm bound to come to the *right* decisions then, aren't I?"

My father considered this for a moment. "Well, if you think you need that long?"

I nodded.

"All right then, I'm sure Dorothy and I will be able to manage on our own for a while. Any idea of where you might like to go?"

"Er…no. But probably not too far away."

"Well, make sure it's far enough. Because I want you to come back in a month, Scarlett, able to prove you've made some sensible decisions about how you want your life to be in the future. That's the only way David will agree to you going: if he thinks it will make your relationship stronger."

"Yes, I know," I said, thinking about David for a moment. "And don't worry, Dad," I promised. "I'll return in a month with loads of proof that I've done plenty of thinking about my life."

And more importantly, I'm going to come back with lots of proof for you and David, and Maddie for that matter, that I'm not just spending my life daydreaming. Life can be just like a movie, and it doesn't just happen occasionally by accident; it happens every day, over and over again.

I didn't know what my father had said to David that weekend about me going away on my own for a while (maybe he'd agreed to help him with his wallpapering or something?) but David didn't lodge a single complaint. It was most unlike him. I suppose the fact that I was going to house-sit for a month, and wasn't going to spend any money on a fancy hotel or a cottage in the country, softened the blow quite a bit.

Six

As I set out that night for Oscar's dinner party, it was on my third attempt to leave the house that I was finally able to step outside into the cold night air.

I'd had a few "minor" altercations with the house's alarm system before we'd reached a compromise: the alarm would behave, accept the code I was pushing into it, and obediently set itself, ready to bravely protect the contents of Belinda and Harry's home from intruders. And in exchange, I wouldn't rip it down from the wall and stomp on it until all its insides would be good for were the inner workings of a toaster.

Eventually, happy that we were each sticking to our side of the agreement, I pulled the door firmly shut behind me and set off down the steps to the pavement below. As I did so, I heard the front door next to me open and close.

Oh no, I thought, trying not to look up. This was all I needed.

"Evening," he called.

"Hello again," I called back, forced to turn around. "I'm just off out."

"I can see that," he said, nonchalantly descending his own steps.

Clever sod.

"Which way are you headed?" he asked as he reached my side.

Please don't let it be your way. "Er, this way," I said, pointing in the direction of Oscar's house.

"Me too—should we walk together?"

Do we have to? "Sure," I said, forcing a smile to appear on my face.

As we set off side by side along Lansdowne Road, I was glad Oscar's house was just around the corner; at least I knew I wouldn't have to be in this idiot's company for too long. I felt quite self-conscious walking alongside him. While he was still dressed in his casual attire from earlier of a light jacket and T-shirt, I was wrapped up against the cold February evening like something from an upmarket ski-wear catalogue, in my warm winter coat, hat, and scarf.

"I guess if we're going to be neighbors, we should introduce ourselves properly," he said after a few paces. "I'm Sean." He held out his hand.

"Scarlett," I said, briefly shaking it with my gloved hand as we walked.

"That's an unusual name."

"Yes," I said through gritted teeth. *Wait for it, here comes the next question…* The next question usually depended on the person's age. Looking at Sean I guessed he'd go for the obvious—and he did.

"Is it from *Gone with the Wind*?"

Bingo! If only I had a pound for every time someone had asked me that.

"Yes, it was my mother's favorite film." At least I was able to answer that truthfully now.

If Sean had been a few years younger or trying to chat me

up he'd have probably gone for "Oh, like Scarlett Johansson—the actress?"

Sean smiled knowingly.

"What?" I asked.

"Ah, nothing. It's a cool name, that's all."

"Thanks."

We walked along together a bit further. "I have to turn here," I said, stopping to cross the road.

"That's fine," Sean said, standing on the edge of the pavement next to me, "so do I."

We stood silently like two schoolchildren carefully crossing the street together. Look left, look right, and look left again. Then we looked at each other for mutual agreement, before stepping out into the road.

"So where are you off to this evening?" Sean asked. "Anywhere exciting?"

"A dinner party, actually."

"Really? How odd. Me too."

No, it couldn't be, could it? I thought as we reached Oscar's house.

"It wouldn't be here by any chance?" I asked, positive I already knew the answer to my own question.

"Well, actually…"

"Scarlett, you made it!" Oscar called, holding Delilah in his arms as he flung open the front door. "And I see you've already met Sean."

I looked across at my fellow dinner guest.

He grinned. "Looks like I could be learning just a little bit more about you tonight than only your name, Scarlett."

We both made a move to go up the narrow path at the same time. Sean stood back to let me pass. "Ladies first."

"Thank you."

I walked toward Oscar, who was looking quite resplendent in a deep-purple shirt and matching shade of tartan trousers. But I was still having problems with who he reminded me of. Most people I could usually match up with a movie actor or character, or at the worst a mix of two. Currently I was getting vibes of both John Hannah in *Four Weddings* and Tom, one of Bridget Jones's gang of oddball friends, for Oscar.

"I brought you this," I said, holding up a bottle of wine. "*And*"—emphasizing my gesture to Sean, as I held up a shopping bag in my other hand—"I'm returning *your* T-shirt you *lent* me earlier today."

"Darling, you shouldn't have—really, there was no need for either. But do come in, won't you, I can't wait for you to meet everybody. Do come along, Sean," Oscar called down the path. "The gang's all here!"

Once inside, Oscar took our jackets and we followed him through to the lounge. There were five people already sitting on two settees and a chaise longue, drinking wine and chatting.

"Now then, everyone, I'd like to introduce Scarlett," Oscar announced, clapping his hands to gain their attention. "Oh, you all know Sean, of course," he added, almost as an afterthought.

"Wish we didn't sometimes." A woman with extremely short black hair, and an alarming amount of colored beads strung around her neck, spoke. I was relieved to see she was only joking when everyone laughed.

"We'll start with you then, Vanessa. Scarlett, this is Vanessa, she owns the shop next door to mine."

"Hi," I said. "What does your shop sell—clothes, like Oscar's?"

"Erotic lesbian fiction mostly," she replied, looking me up and down. "You should come in and take a look some time."

I cleared my throat and smiled politely. "Maybe I'll do that one day."

"Vanessa, do stop teasing," Oscar insisted. "Now then, next to Vanessa we have Lucian and Patrick; they own one of the antique shops just off the market."

"Hi," they said in unison. Then they giggled at each other like little children.

"Over on the chaise longue we have Brooke. Brooke's a model."

Brooke looked like she was a model for appetite suppressants. If she eats anything tonight it will only be the garnish, I thought sourly.

Brooke waved casually.

"And finally next to her we have Ursula—my best and dearest friend."

Ursula smiled warmly at Oscar, then equally warmly at me. She had sandy-colored shoulder-length hair, pale blue eyes that were just as warm as her smile, and she was wearing a dress covered in daisies that looked like it was from the 1950s. But what really made me take an instant shine to her was the fact that Ursula looked like a delightful combination of a young Emma Thompson and, my all-time favorite, Kate Winslet.

"Hi, how are you?" she asked. "I'm also an interior

designer—since everyone else got their full title. Not just a professional friend to Oscar."

There were a few chuckles around the room, so gratefully I returned her smile while trying not to stare at her too much.

"Well, that's everyone," Oscar sang.

"Ahem." Sean cleared his throat behind us.

"Scarlett's met *you* already, hasn't she? Oh, very well," Oscar sighed, when Sean silently raised his eyebrows at him. "Scarlett, this is Sean. Sean is only here because he's Ursula's brother, and I needed someone at short notice to make up the numbers."

Sean grinned. "Thank you for that kind introduction, Oscar; the feeling is mutual, as you know."

Oscar tossed his head and made a "hmph" sort of noise.

I found myself smiling at Sean.

He grinned back as Oscar flounced off into the kitchen calling something about more wine being needed.

I had wondered, after I'd been introduced to everyone at the start of the evening, just what I'd let myself in for, having dinner with this eclectic bunch of people. But I needn't have worried because the evening turned out to be full of thought-provoking conversation, lots of laughter, and extremely good food. (Which Oscar later admitted he'd had catered in, because of the short notice.)

The chocolate brownies were particularly mouth-watering.

"Oh no!" Oscar cried when he noticed they'd all been eaten. "There's none left; we can't do it now!"

"Do what, Oscar?" Brooke asked. I'd been quite wrong about Brooke—she ate just like everyone else did, even tucking into the brownies with lashings of vanilla ice cream on top.

Oscar looked at me. "Can I tell them, Scarlett?"

"About the brownies?" I asked, bemused.

"No, about why you're *really* here?"

I looked at the others listening expectantly around the table. All except Sean, who lolled back in his chair drinking red wine.

"I don't see why not."

My plan to let people think I was house-sitting for a month just didn't seem to be working out. But after meeting Oscar, and hearing everybody else's life stories tonight, my little "obsession," as everyone at home seemed to think it was, seemed quite normal.

"Oh, are you some sort of secret agent?" Ursula asked excitedly.

I laughed. "No."

"Ooh, ooh, I like guessing games," Brooke said. "An undercover police officer?"

"No." I shook my head.

"On the run from gangsters then?" Patrick called from across the table.

"They're not drugs barons, are they?" Lucian added eagerly.

"Er no, look, I really don't think you—"

"You're a Martian from outer space?" Vanessa mocked.

"Look, it's really not that exciting," I said, feeling a little embarrassed now.

"Oh it is—it is!" Oscar enthused. "Well, I think it is anyway. It's a shame more people don't stand up for what they believe in. Do let me tell, Scarlett?"

"Sure, go ahead," I said, more out of relief than anything else now Oscar had made me sound like some sort of saint.

"Well," Oscar began, his eyes glinting in the candlelight. "Scarlett is really here under false pretenses…"

I glanced around the table while Oscar eagerly explained everything. Everyone listened intently to what he was saying—he was a born storyteller and made it sound much more interesting than I would have done. Even Sean seemed to be taking it all in. He glanced across at me while I was watching him, and I quickly averted my gaze.

"…so that is why Scarlett has moved in across the road—why I'm holding this dinner party—*and* why I wanted the last brownie!" Oscar finished triumphantly.

"Oh, like in *Notting Hill*?' Ursula said. "I love that movie."

"Me too," Patrick agreed. "Hugh Grant is divine in it."

A conversation then followed about the joys of *Notting Hill*, and this quickly moved on to a rather heated debate about the rest of Hugh Grant's films. Sean was strangely silent throughout all of this.

"What's up, Sean—nothing to contribute to our conversation?" Oscar teased. "That makes a change."

"I can't talk about something I know nothing about," Sean responded coolly.

"You've never seen *Notting Hill*?" Brooke asked in astonishment.

"Nope, nor any other of this Grant fella's films."

"You must have seen *Four Weddings*?" Vanessa asked. "Everyone's seen that one."

"Nope."

"But why not?"

"Sean hates the cinema," Ursula answered for him. "Don't you, Sean?"

"I don't hate it—just can't see the point. I'd rather read a good book or go to the theater."

"But a good movie is just another extension to the art of storytelling," I suggested, joining in. "If you like both of the mediums you mentioned, why not the cinema too?"

Sean shrugged.

"It's Dad," Ursula said, nodding matter-of-factly. "He's put him off it."

"But why?" I was enjoying the apparently self-assured and confident Sean becoming decidedly uncomfortable for once.

Sean shrugged again.

Ursula tutted. "Oh, he can be so rude sometimes, Scarlett. Dad's crazy about James Bond, always has been since before we were born. Drove our mother mad—that's one of the reasons they got divorced in the end. But our stepmother, Diana, she's different, absolutely adores movies like Dad. We sometimes laugh that the only reason Dad married her was because of her name."

We all looked blankly at Ursula.

"Oh sorry, when you've lived with James Bond as long as we have, you assume everyone knows the history. Diana Rigg played the only Bond girl 007 ever married."

"Oh I remember that one," Lucian piped up. "*On Her Majesty's Secret Service*, right?"

Ursula nodded. "So that is why Sean hates movies, because we've had to live with them as part of the family since we were small. Well, he says he does. Knowing all about 007 didn't do him any harm when he was younger though, eh, Sean? Go on, tell them your chat-up line."

"This," said Sean, rolling his eyes, "is just why you don't go out for dinner with your sister in tow."

"Oh, do tell us, Ursula," Oscar insisted. He was obviously enjoying Sean's embarrassment as much as me.

Sean fired an *I'll get you for this later* look at Ursula, but she happily ignored him.

"When Sean was just beginning to find out about the joys of the opposite sex," Ursula said, looking gleefully around the table, "he used to try chatting up girls by using this line." Ursula put on her best Sean Connery voice: "'My name is Bond…' and then the girl was supposed to say, 'What, James Bond?' and Sean would say, 'No, I'm Sean, but you can be my Bond girl any time.'"

Everyone laughed. Sean drained the last of his glass of wine and lifted the bottle to pour himself some more.

"May I just point out that I was at school then," he protested. "I was hardly going to use a Shakespeare sonnet!"

"Perhaps 'You've left me feeling shaken and stirred' would have gone down better with the girls?" I suggested, lifting my own glass and trying not to grin as I held it out for him to refill.

Sean glanced at me and narrowed his eyes. But then the corners of his supposedly angry mouth twitched in amusement as he finished pouring the wine, and I was relieved.

"So you are actually a Bond then?" I asked him.

Sean nodded. "Yeah, it's Dad's real surname. Lucky for him, eh? Not so lucky for us, though. I was named after Sean Connery, Dad's favorite 007, and Ursula—"

"After Ursula Andress?" I guessed.

"Yep, you got it—Dad's favorite Bond girl. Mum once told me Dad had really wanted to call me James. Thank the Lord she talked him out of that one!"

I smiled, and his eyes held mine for a moment.

"I think that's quite enough of the Bond family history for now," Ursula said, glancing between the two of us. "I bet we all wish we'd stood up for something we believe in at some point in our lives. Let's have a think for you, Scarlett; we must be able to come up with something to help. You've already done a couple of bits from *Notting Hill* thanks to Oscar...so how about *Four Weddings and a Funeral*, you must be able to find a few weddings to go to?"

"My best friend is getting married this month, but that's the only one. I can't just gatecrash three other weddings."

"You could become a priest," Lucian suggested helpfully. "But I guess you don't have time for that," he added, when everyone looked at him incredulously.

"Join the Women's Institute," Brooke suggested, waving her cigarette casually in the air.

"What?" Oscar asked impatiently. "And just how is that supposed to help?"

"My mum is in the WI, and they are always doing the flowers in our local church. At least it would get you inside."

"Thanks, Brooke." I smiled gratefully at her. "But I don't think I'm the WI type really."

Sean sniggered.

I glared at him across the table.

"Oh my God, I've got it!" Ursula exclaimed. "Sean, cousin Rachel's wedding this weekend!"

"What?" Sean asked, looking confused.

"Rachel, Aunt Hilary and Uncle Jonathan's daughter, she's getting married this weekend, up near Dad."

"Is she?"

"You had an invite, Sean. We both did. I can't go because I'm exhibiting at an interior design fair and you said you just didn't want to go so I sent a *With Regret* card from both of us."

"Ah right—that was good of you."

"Yes—wasn't it?" Ursula shot Sean a look, which he again ignored. "Anyway, why don't you take Scarlett this weekend instead—it could be one of her weddings!"

Sean and I nearly spat our wine at each other in our haste to reject Ursula's idea. We both gabbled various polite excuses, all with the true meaning of, "Not bloody likely."

But Ursula carried on unperturbed. "Oh, go on, it'll be fine. You've not been up to see Dad in ages, Sean. And you, Scarlett, you've got to have a bit more pioneering spirit or you'll never prove your family wrong, will you?"

"But we've said we can't go now," Sean protested. "We'll mess their numbers up."

Phew, nice one, Sean, I thought, relieved.

"That won't matter," Ursula said cheerily. "It's going to be a buffet reception, I remember from the invite. They're quite free spirits, Rachel and Julian," Ursula explained, turning to me. "I think they even said we didn't need to reply to the invite, just see how we felt on the day. If we wanted to come, we should; if not, no bother. But I always like to do things properly, so I sent them a card."

I nodded. "Well, it is good manners."

"Exactly. So what do the pair of you say? Come on, Sean, you can introduce Scarlett to Dad. I'm sure with their love of films they'd have loads in common; he might even be able to suggest some things for Scarlett to do."

Sean looked over at me. His look suggested he'd given it his best shot with the numbers objection and now it was my turn.

"But...I don't have anything to wear to a wedding," I said, thinking hurriedly. "I only brought casual things with me."

Sean nodded approvingly.

"That's not a problem," Oscar said, joining in. "I'm certain I can find you something from my boutique."

"There you go. Now no more excuses, the pair of you. I'll call Dad to tell him you're both coming." Ursula rubbed her hands together in glee. "Oh, I love it when a plan comes together!"

Sean and I left Oscar's house together that night, feeling like children whose parents were forcing them to do something they didn't want to, with the excuse, "It will do you good!"

"I'm sorry about Ursula," Sean said when the door was safely closed behind us and our lives could be organized no more. "She gets a bit carried away sometimes."

"That's OK," I said, smiling up at him while we walked. "Her heart is in the right place."

"Shame her head isn't!"

I laughed. But inside I felt deeply grateful to Ursula, Oscar, and the others. I'd opened up more today to Oscar, and tonight to a bunch of strangers I'd only just met, than I ever did at home to my so-called family.

I'd even ended up telling them about Dad bringing me up alone, and what I'd only learned recently myself, about Mum sharing my love of the cinema when my father didn't.

"You don't mind too much, then, about the wedding?" Sean asked, breaking into my thoughts. "I mean you don't really have to come with me if you don't want to. I'll still have to go now Ursula's phoned Dad, but I quite understand if you want to back out."

I stopped walking as we passed one of the communal gardens that sat in the middle of this part of Notting Hill.

I peeped between the black railings that surrounded the garden. Then I turned back to Sean.

"So it's your call, really," he continued.

"Give me a leg up," I said.

"What?"

"A leg up—put your hand out and help me up, so I can get inside."

"No."

"Why not? You're not scared, are you?"

"No, of course I'm not," Sean said defensively. "Why would I be?"

"No reason." I turned back toward the railings. "Fine, I'll do it myself then."

It wasn't easy, but I managed to get a part hold on the railings and a part hold on a tree that overhung the top of them, and unceremoniously I hauled myself up. I wobbled a bit at the top, but I then managed to jump—well, I guess it was more of a fall—down the other side and into the little garden.

"See, I didn't need you after all." I peered back at Sean through the railings. "Bet you feel a bit silly standing there on your own now!"

"Not as silly as you're going to feel when I do this." Sean pulled some keys from his pocket and held them under the streetlight to select one. Then he walked along the railings to the gate, calmly placed the key in the lock, and turned it so the gate swung open. Closing it securely behind him, he walked over to where I stood.

"Why didn't you tell me you had a key to get in here?" I demanded.

"You never asked."

In frustration, I turned and marched away from him, but I stopped abruptly when I saw a bench. It was only visible in the darkened park because the moon that sat high in the clear night sky cast a luminescent glow over it.

Sean caught up with me. "What is it?" he asked. "What have you seen?"

I walked silently over to the bench. I ran my hand gently along its back before slowly and purposefully sitting down on it.

Sean followed me.

"What on earth are you doing? First you break into private property and now, on a cold February evening, you're going to sit outside on a park bench?"

"You wouldn't understand," I replied, dreamily thinking of Hugh and Julia sitting on this bench together. It could have been the same one for all I knew.

"Try me," Sean challenged, sitting down beside me.

I wondered whether I should try to explain it all to him. He would probably just mock me again.

The answer you give now, Sean, will decide whether I go with you to the wedding on Saturday.

"It's from the movie *Notting Hill*."

"I should have known." But Sean must have seen irritation flicker across my face because he added, "OK…which part?"

"One of the most romantic parts," I said warily. "This is one of the most memorable scenes from the film, when Hugh Grant and Julia Roberts sit on a bench together in a park just like this one. The song that is sung at that point is beautiful too—it's one of my favorites."

"It all sounds…lovely."

I looked skeptically at Sean, but he wasn't being sarcastic for once. He was genuinely trying to say something that wouldn't offend me.

"It is actually—it's very romantic. But I don't suppose Ronan Keating is your cup of tea really, is he?"

Sean wrinkled his nose. "Not really, no. But I've heard him singing that song before, if that helps?"

"Well, that's a start."

"Yes, I suppose it is."

Our eyes met in the same way they had over the dining table earlier.

"About the wedding, Sean…"

"Don't worry," he said, holding his hand up. "I told you, you don't have to come."

"No, I do," I insisted. "Your sister would be so disappointed if I didn't go. She's going to so much trouble to help me—I can't let her down now."

"Yes, of course, you're absolutely right," Sean said keenly, resting his hand on the back of the bench. "We really should go through with this weekend for Ursula, shouldn't we?"

"Yes," I agreed, smiling at him now. "Let's put our own feelings aside. We'll go to this wedding together, simply to keep your sister happy. What other reason would there be for us to go all the way to Glasgow together?"

For a moment Sean was silent. "No other reason, Scarlett," he said eventually, shaking his head. "No other reason whatsoever."

Seven

We decided to travel up to Glasgow by train. We could have flown; Sean seemed quite happy to pay for tickets with whatever airline had the best last-minute flights available. Unlike David, who never booked anything last minute, because in his opinion there was always money to be saved "with a little forward thinking."

But when Ursula was sorting everything out for us and gave me the choice, I opted to travel by rail. I did think about it for a while—flying would have been so much quicker, and really the less time I had to spend with Sean the better. But I could see another movie opportunity in traveling this way, and I didn't want to miss out on any chances to add to my dossier of proof.

We arrived early at King's Cross station on Friday lunchtime, and so had plenty of time to kill before our train arrived.

"Shall we get a coffee?" Sean asked.

"Yes, let's," I said eagerly, pleased he was making this so easy for me.

We walked through the station toward the concourse area of shops and cafes, me dragging my case and Sean carrying a small holdall in his hand and a folded garment bag over his shoulder.

"Aren't you going to try and go through there?" Sean asked, grinning, as he nodded toward a wall. Two children were having their photo taken underneath a sign that said *Platform 9¾*. "Then you'd be able to catch the train to Hogwarts, and you'd have another movie to cross off your list."

"Ha ha, very funny," I said, pulling a face. "Anyway, how'd you know that's in *Harry Potter* if you never watch films?"

"I think you'll find it was in the book," Sean said, raising his eyebrows.

"Oh right, yes, of course it was." I was embarrassed. I didn't want Sean to think I was one of those people who only know the movie version of a story. But then again, why should I care what Sean thought?

We came to a stand selling hot drinks. It was hardly the refreshment room at Ketchworth station, but it would have to do.

"A coffee, please—black no sugar," Sean said to the vendor.

The young man who grunted a reply—which I think was inquiring whether Sean wanted a lid—was hardly Myrtle Bagot, or even Beryl. I sighed wistfully as I remembered *Brief Encounter*.

"What would you like, Scarlett?" Sean asked. "Hey, Scarlett?" he asked again when I didn't respond. "Are you with us? Would you like a drink or not?"

"What? Oh sorry. Er, I'll have a tea, please, milk no sugar." I began to blink hard.

Sean looked at me and narrowed his eyes suspiciously. "What's wrong?" he asked as he paid for the drinks. "Have you got a nervous twitch or something?"

"No, I think I've got something in my eye." I blinked even

harder and it occurred to me I could get two movie scenes for the price of one here if Sean responded accordingly. *The Holiday* contained a similar scene between Kate Winslet and Jack Black.

"Cheers," Sean said to the vendor as he lifted the hot cups from the counter. "What do you want to do, Scarlett—go to the ladies' and take a look at it? I think it's just over there, but you'll need 30 pence to get in. Have you got change?"

"No." I blinked. "I don't think so."

"Let me see if I have, then. Just hold these," he said, passing me the drinks.

"Can't *you* take a look?" I asked in frustration. I was standing in the middle of King's Cross station, holding two steaming polystyrene cups and winking madly at everyone that passed by. One man even winked back. "I think it might be a piece of grit."

"I could, but I don't have my glasses on just now," Sean said, still rooting about in his pockets for change.

"What glasses? I've never seen you wearing glasses before."

"I only need them for close stuff. I can look into your eye if you want me to, but I can't guarantee I'll see anything as small as a piece of grit." He began to rummage in his jacket pocket.

"Oh, just forget it," I said huffily. I handed him back his coffee. "The moment's passed now anyway. I…I mean the grit seems to have gone."

I opened my tea and took a large gulp. It was hot and burned the back of my throat, but I wasn't going to let on. "Looks like our train is here at last," I said, glancing up at the ever-changing information board. "We'd better go."

Sean followed me with a puzzled expression on his face, as

I stomped off in the direction of the platform. We loaded our luggage and ourselves onto the right train, and then looked for our seats. They were facing each other over a table—and after a quick discussion about who would travel forward and who would travel back, we sat down.

I looked out of the window at the people hurrying along the platform toward their carriages and wondered what their reason was for catching the same train as us.

I bet none of them are in the same situation as I am right now, I thought as I silently watched them.

I glanced at Sean, but he wasn't looking out of the window; he was looking at me.

"What is it?" I asked when he didn't immediately avert his gaze.

"I was just wondering what all that was about back there on the platform—with your eye?"

"It was nothing, I told you it's gone now."

"Was it ever there in the first place?"

I sighed. Oh, what was the point in lying to him?

"No," I said quietly.

"Then why would you say...wait a minute, was that charade something from a movie by any chance?"

"Maybe."

"I should have known—which one?"

"*Brief Encounter*, if you must know."

"Isn't that the one about aliens?"

I laughed. "No! That's *Close Encounters*. *Brief Encounter* is a wonderful love story, set mainly in a railway station. It stars Celia Johnson and Trevor Howard."

"Oh, I see." Sean thought for a moment. "And let me guess—this Celia gets something stuck in her eye, and good old Trevor gets it out, right? And then they fall madly in love?"

I tried hard to suppress a smile. "There's a bit more to it than that, but yeah, that's the general gist."

"Sounds riveting."

"It is, actually. It's a wonderful piece of black and white film-making—it's based on a play by Noel Coward."

"Quite the little film buff, aren't we?" Sean said, grinning at me. "It doesn't surprise me though—about Noel Coward, I mean. Most *good* films were originally books or plays. Either that or they're based on true stories or real events."

I thought about this for a moment. "Some are, I suppose—but not all."

"Go on then, name some well-known, *quality* films—you know, the type that have won Oscars—that haven't been based on one of those things."

I thought again. But annoyingly he was right—every film that immediately sprang to mind fell into one of those categories.

"There are *some* exceptions, obviously," Sean continued. "But the ones you always think of first are all just copies. Although I'm sure they would rather be known as a homage to someone else's work."

I smiled wryly.

"I'm right, aren't I?" he asked, grinning.

"Well, I can't think of any right now—so for the minute, yes, I guess you are."

We sat in silence for a moment as the train began to pull out of the station. As it started to pick up speed and the tower blocks of London turned into the hedges and fields of the country, Sean spoke again.

"If we're going to be spending over six hours on a train together, Scarlett, we may as well get to know each other a bit better. So you first, why don't you start by telling me the story of your life?"

I turned my gaze back from the window, thrown off course by his innocent question. Without realizing it, Sean had given me another movie moment for my list. In *When Harry Met Sally*, Harry asks Sally virtually the same thing when they're traveling to New York together at the beginning of the film.

"Er...there's not that much to tell really. I'm almost twenty-four years old. I live in Stratford-upon-Avon, and I work in the family business."

"Which is?"

Here we go, I thought—more fodder for ridicule.

"We manufacture and sell popcorn machines."

Sean laughed.

"What's so funny about that?" I demanded.

"First," Sean said, trying to straighten his face, "what finer career for *you*, a lover of the cinema, than providing the staple diet of any moviegoer. And second, you live in Stratford-upon-Avon—the home of the Bard, recognized as one of the greatest playwrights ever. And you choose to worship *movies*?"

"That's right," I said defiantly, folding my arms. "And what's wrong with that?"

Sean shook his head. "Nothing—nothing at all. Look, I don't want to argue with you, Scarlett, I'll behave." He sat back in his seat, a childlike, innocent expression imposed on his face—which any moment looked like it might break out into a mischievous grin.

"What about you then?" I asked, fighting hard my inclination to grin back at him. "Let's hear all about *your* wonderful life."

"Well, I'm no James Stewart." He grinned, trying to make a joke. "Get it—*Wonderful Life?*'

I chose not to laugh at his poor attempt at a joke. "So you do know *some* films then?"

"Maybe just a few." Sean arranged himself in his seat so that his ankle rested up on his knee. "OK, let's see, I'm twenty-six years old, I have a sister called Ursula, as you know. A father called Alfie—who to my absolute joy is the owner of a James Bond-themed pub in Glasgow, which he runs with my step-mother, Diana. Oh, and I quite boringly work for an investment company."

"And what do you invest in, property?"

"No, companies."

"How?" I asked to be polite, even though I wasn't really interested in what Sean did for a living.

"Well, we help out companies that are having a few problems. We either invest heavily in them until they're rebuilt and back on their feet again, or we just buy them out there and then."

"How do you make money out of that? Oh wait, I know. You buy them at a ridiculously low price because they're struggling, then build them up and sell them on when they're successful again."

"Something like that, yes. That's very astute of you, Scarlett. I'm impressed."

"Richard Gere," I said knowingly.

"What?"

"If you *owned* this investment company, you would be like Richard Gere in *Pretty Woman*."

Sean looked blank.

"In *Pretty Woman*," I explained, "Richard Gere plays this bastard businessman, who swoops in and buys businesses when they're at rock bottom and just about to go bust. Then he sells them on at a later date when they're successfully making money again, for a huge profit."

"Sensible man." Sean nodded approvingly.

"So, if you were the *owner* of this company, then you'd be just like him."

"A bastard, you mean?"

"That's right."

"I am."

I looked at Sean to see if he was winding me up again, but his face was completely serious. "What do you mean—you own this company, or you're actually just a bastard?"

"What do *you* think, Scarlett?" Sean placed his elbows on the table, rested his head on his interlinked hands, and looked at me with a challenging expression.

As I sat back in my seat and tried to consider this, I was much too aware of Sean's pale blue eyes scrutinizing my every move. "Well," I said eventually, meeting his gaze, "you do live in a very affluent part of Notting Hill, so I guess you might be telling me the truth."

Sean grinned and leaned back. "I'll take that as a compliment—I think."

"So why didn't you tell me that to begin with?" I demanded. "Why the pretense?"

"I didn't say I wasn't the boss, just that I worked for the company. And I do work for them. I work damned hard in fact."

"So how come you're sitting here with me then and not out somewhere arranging mega-bucks deals?"

Sean shrugged. "Perks of being the boss, I guess."

"Lucky you."

A porter came through the carriage trundling a food trolley, so we bought some lunch for the journey and settled back to eat it.

"So, your family isn't too keen on this movie obsession?" Sean asked, tucking into his sandwich.

"OK, stop right there," I said, putting down my baguette before I'd even had the chance to open it. "Unless you want me to get off at the next station, you can stop calling it *that* right now."

"Easy," Sean said, raising his eyebrows. "Bit touchy, aren't we?"

He did that a lot, I noticed—raised his eyebrows. In fact his whole face was very expressive. The eyebrows in question were the exact same shade of sandy blond as his permanently tousled hair. He didn't look much like the owner of a large successful business as he sat there tucking into an egg sandwich in his blue jeans and gray T-shirt—he'd also lost his look of Jude Law now too. No, the person sitting opposite me definitely bore more than a passing resemblance to Ewan McGregor.

"All right, how about we use some business terminology?" Sean thought for a moment. "You're having a difference of opinion and are unable to reach a satisfactory conclusion where all parties are in agreement that the subject is in fact in breach of her contract to remain a rational and normal human being? There, is that better?"

I couldn't help grinning.

"Yes, that sounds much more like it, thank you."

"So, Scarlett," Sean asked, brushing some stray crumbs from his shirt, "how on earth did you manage to get your family to let you come away for a month? I mean I know about Maddie and the house, but your father and your fiancé too?"

"You're not the only one that can swing a deal when you want," I said, trying to shake Ewan McGregor from my brain at the same time as I shook open my baguette. I carefully picked out the pieces of cucumber they always insisted on putting in with tuna. "I have my ways when I want to."

"Oh, I bet you do, Scarlett," Sean said, one eyebrow raised again as he watched me. "I bet you do."

Eight

We arrived in Glasgow Central station at about teatime, where we duly queued for a taxi and made our way to the hotel Ursula had booked for us.

Basically Ursula had organized the whole trip. She'd rung her father the night of the dinner party and told him what was happening. The next morning, while I'd gone along to Oscar's boutique on the King's Road to choose an outfit for the wedding, she had booked us two return train tickets for later that same morning and hotel rooms for the next two nights.

Without Ursula we definitely wouldn't have got to Glasgow. She was one of life's organizers (and also a hopeless romantic, she'd admitted to me) and reveled in providing us with everything we needed for the weekend ahead. Although Sean had insisted he should choose and pay for our hotel—in fact he had offered to pay for our whole trip—I, of course, declined his kind, yet surprising, offer, and insisted I at least paid for my own train ticket.

The Radisson in central Glasgow was a beautiful, modern hotel. I was impressed—I hadn't really thought about where we'd stay. I'd assumed maybe a Travelodge, or a similar sort of hotel—that's where David and I usually ended up. But Sean didn't seem the type to stay in hotels where the adjacent restaurant had laminated menus or an all-day breakfast.

"Shall I meet you back down here in, say, an hour?" Sean asked after we'd checked in. "Is that long enough for you to unpack and do whatever you need to?"

"Yes, that's plenty of time," I said, a little bit distracted by the hotel manager, who was currently dealing with a problem behind the check-in desk. He looked exactly like Barney, the hotel manager from the Regent Beverly Wilshire in *Pretty Woman*. Immaculately dressed, gray hair, pointy little gray beard...

"I know an excellent restaurant just down the road from here," Sean continued. "Would you like to go there for dinner this evening?"

"Yes." I pulled my attention away from "Barney" and suddenly felt shy. Sean made it sound like we were going on a date. "I'm sure that would be lovely."

"Good. I'll catch up with you later then." He smiled at me, and for the first time since we'd met, it was not a smile of mockery or laughter. It was a genuine smile that reached all the way up to his eyes.

"Yes," I said, coyly smiling back. "I'll look forward to it."

The restaurant Sean had spoken of was a lovely little Italian—it had oak beamed ceilings, checked cloths covering the tables, and waiters scurrying about brandishing huge pepper grinders.

After we had ordered, Sean took a sip of his wine and then leaned casually back in his chair and watched me.

"What?" I asked. "What is it this time? You keep doing that—you were doing it on the train too."

"You remind me of someone," he said. "Trouble is I can't think who."

"Oh." I hadn't been expecting that sort of answer. I thought it was going to be one of Sean's usual smart remarks.

"I hope that's a good thing," I said, thinking he might say I reminded him of a film star—then we'd actually have something in common. I was hoping for Anne Hathaway or Julia Roberts, and not the obvious Vivien Leigh. Even Angelina Jolie would have done, though I'd never quite forgiven her for stealing Brad's heart. Talking of Brad, was Sean starting to resemble him too? No, he could never be a Brad—a Matthew McConaughey maybe at a push, but never a Brad Pitt.

"Who knows?" Sean continued, still thinking, but his eyes twinkled mischievously. "It could be someone I hate."

"Thanks a lot." I took a sip of my own wine. "Talking of people you hate—I've been meaning to ask why you and Oscar seem to dislike each other so much."

"Hmm…Oscar…now there's a tricky one."

"Why? He seems OK to me."

"He is, I guess. He's been a friend of Ursula's for years, but we've never really seen eye to eye."

"Why not?"

Sean twiddled the stem of his wine glass around in his fingers. "Like I said—it's tricky."

"Come on, Sean, we've got all night. And judging by our past conversations, I really don't think we're going to have that many subjects in common to last the whole evening."

Sean grinned. "Now that is very true. OK, I used to go out with Oscar's sister."

"Oh, I get it."

"No, you don't. You don't know what I'm going to say."

"I can guess. You broke her heart, right, and now Oscar can't forgive you for doing it?"

"No, the other way around actually, she broke mine."

"Oh." I felt guilty for judging him. "Oh right. I'm sorry."

"No need, it's not your fault she fell for some Yankee bastard."

I didn't know what to say, so I sat quietly in the hope Sean would continue.

He didn't. Instead, he picked up his wine again, and this time drank the glass dry. "More?" he offered, as he held up the bottle from the table and hovered its neck above my glass.

"Just a little," I said, not wanting him to suffer further rejection.

For the next few minutes we sat in silence. I politely sipped at my wine while glancing surreptitiously at the other diners. Sean's interest was held solely by the contents of his glass.

"Look, just tell me to bugger off if you want, Sean—and I know you would," I said, hoping to lighten the moment. I smiled across the table at him, hoping he would see the funny side and smile back. But he didn't; he just stared down at the tablecloth. So I carried on anyway. It couldn't get any worse. "But why would Oscar hate you because of that? It wasn't your fault."

Sean sighed and placed his glass purposefully back down on the table in front of him.

He was quiet again for what seemed like ages while I watched his face gradually darken until it was so black that I half expected he was going to throw his wine over me and storm out of the restaurant.

"I introduced them," he said finally, looking up at me, his eyes full of anger. "I bloody well introduced *her* to *him!*"

I didn't dare say anything, so Sean continued. "Rob was a work colleague of mine. They both did the dirty on me for a couple of months before deciding the only decent thing to do was to continue doing the dirty—but to do it as far away as they possibly could and move to the States. He already had a job to return to, and she had some family over there, so they just upped and left one day. So that's why Oscar and I don't see eye to eye. His sister screwed me over, and as far as Oscar's concerned, I was the cause of her going to live as far away from him as she possibly could." He paused to reflect on this. "So, Scarlett," he said, leaning forward and looking me right in the eyes, "now do you see why we're not best buddies?"

I nodded, this time choosing to return his intense glare.

The waiter appeared at the table and began to serve our meals. While he was doing this, Sean silently downed yet another glass of wine.

"Look, Sean," I said bravely, when the waiter had gone. "This is none of my business, I know. But I believe everything happens for a reason in life, and it may not seem like it now, but there *will* be a reason you introduced them to each other. You may not know why just at this moment in time, but I promise you, you will in the end."

Sean stared at me again. "Did you just say everything happens for a reason?"

I nodded. "Yes, it's a great motto to live your life by. I've always thought—"

Sean interrupted, "That's exactly what my stepmother said to me when it happened too."

"What, everything happens for a reason?"

"Yes...and I've just realized, she's who you remind me of."

"I guess that must be a good thing..." I started to say, pleased he seemed to have calmed down a bit now. But then something occurred to me. "Didn't you mention when we were at Oscar's how your stepmother was mad about the movies?"

"Yes, I said that's why she puts up with Dad so easily."

"My mother loved the movies too, and you just said I reminded you of Diana."

"Yes, you do remind me of Diana in that way. And so? Wait, you're not saying what I think you are? Are you?"

"It could be, Sean—although I know it seems like a huge coincidence."

"No, you're just getting carried away, Scarlett. My stepmother and your mother are *not* one and the same person." Sean picked up his knife and fork.

It was my turn to glare across the table now.

"Look, your mother's name," Sean said, pausing before he cut into his steak. "Was it Diana?"

"No, it was Rosemary, but—"

"So, you're suggesting that my stepmother changed her name by deed poll before she met my father, and she never chose to tell him?"

"Well, she might have told *him*, but why would she need to tell you or Ursula?"

Sean shook his head. "I'm beginning to see where your family was coming from when they said you needed some time away. You've got one hell of an imagination, Scarlett. That script sounds like something a Hollywood film studio would churn out!"

He grinned now. But instead of smiling back, I sat back in my chair and folded my arms.

"It's all right for you, Sean. You've been lucky enough to have two mothers in your life. I've never even had one—not that I can remember anyway."

Sean put down his cutlery again and this time had the good grace to look sympathetic. "I'm sorry, Scarlett—about your mother. I don't want to sound harsh, but I don't think pinning your hopes on some crazy idea that my stepmother is also your mother is going to do you any good at all."

"You're probably right," I said, pouring my Bolognese sauce—which I'd asked to be served separately—over my pasta. I picked up my fork and began twisting it around in my spaghetti. "Just forget I ever said anything."

Sean nodded as the atmosphere between us calmed once again, and he happily began to tuck into his steak.

Well *you* can forget about it, I thought, as I lifted a forkful of spaghetti up from my plate. But *I* certainly won't…

That night, before I went to bed, I opened up my purse and pulled out a tatty, folded photo that I'd always kept with me for the past fifteen years. I'd found it at the back of a wardrobe Dad and I had been sorting out for a Brownie jumble sale one day and, on realizing what it was, I'd quickly shoved it in my pocket so he didn't see.

Now, I carefully unfolded it again as I had so many times before over the years, and looked at the creased up photograph that was lying in my hand.

It was a picture of a couple holding a newborn baby. My father was definitely the man in the photo, I could see that easily. I was the baby, and the woman holding me was my mother.

And the reason I knew that it was definitely my mother and me was handwritten in black ink on the back of the photo.

Tom,
  Us & our darling Scarlett—March 1986
  Now at last we are a family.
  All my love for ever,
  Rosie x

Nine

The next morning we were up bright and early.

The wedding was at eleven o'clock, so we didn't have long to get ready before we had to leave for the church on the other side of town. I scrutinized my appearance in the full-length mirror that hung in my hotel room while I waited for Sean to arrive.

I hadn't really known what to expect when I turned up at Oscar's shop early yesterday morning, but I had been pleasantly surprised.

Oscar's tiny boutique was a cornucopia of fashion. He had everything in there from sixties chic and seventies retro, to up-to-the-minute designer wear. Everything was unique—and very "Oscar." The only thing the clothes had in common was that they were all jostling for prime position on the bulging rails and in the shiny display cases.

I had no idea where to begin looking, but Oscar produced three perfectly matched outfits immediately upon my arrival. I tried each one on in turn and was surprised to find I looked quite good in all of them.

In the end we settled on a dress—a simple design, in red

cashmere. It had a high roll neck, short sleeves, and fit me like a glove.

"It could have been made for you, darling!" Oscar cried when he saw me in it. "Now we just need some accessories."

The accessories—a thick black belt, a pair of stiletto-heeled, black suede boots which we purchased from a shop three doors down from Oscar's, and a long, black wool coat—finished off the outfit perfectly.

"Darling, you will look divine!" Oscar approved when he saw the whole ensemble. "What a shame you're only going with Sean to the wedding; it'll be wasted on him."

As I turned back and forth in front of my hotel mirror I knew Oscar was right: it was lovely. Even my self-critical eyes were enjoying what they saw for once. It wasn't that I didn't care about my appearance usually, far from it. I liked a good shopping spree as much as the next Gok Wan or Stacy London—I just didn't do dresses that often. In fact when we'd been to see *King Lear* David commented that the next time he was likely to see me in a dress would be on our wedding day. Which at the time I felt was a little unfair, but in retrospect was probably quite justified.

As if he knew, my mobile phone rang on the dressing table beside me and David's name flashed on the screen. I debated whether to answer it. But David had been so good about not calling me too often since I left that I thought perhaps I should speak to him this time.

"David, how are you?" I asked brightly.

"I'm well, Scarlett, how are you? How's London?" David's voice sounded a bit forced.

"Er...I'm not actually in London right now."

"Where are you then?"

"Glasgow."

"Glasgow! What the hell are you doing in Glasgow?"

"I'm going to a wedding," I replied calmly.

"Whose wedding?"

"Er…" Oh God, what was the name of the bride again? Or the groom, for that matter? "It's a friend's cousin's wedding. I just met up with them the other day in London, and they mentioned the wedding and asked if I'd like to go with them."

"What, just like that?"

"Yes."

I desperately tried to think of a way I could change the subject quickly. "It's a lovely hotel we're staying in, David—the Radisson."

"The Radisson! Blimey, you're not paying, are you, Scarlett?"

Yep, it worked. "No, my friend is, David, don't worry."

There was a knock at my door.

"Oh, that'll be them now; we're just about to leave for the church. I'll have to catch up with you another time. Bye-bye now!"

Quickly I hung up the phone.

It was Sean.

"Come in," I said, throwing the door open. "I'll just get my things."

I gathered my bag and coat up from the bed and turned to face him. "Hey, you've got a suit on—it kind of suits you."

Sean was wearing a deep-purple shirt, unbuttoned at the neck, and what I imagined must be a very expensive, charcoal-colored suit. The fabric had a slight sheen to it, and it hung beautifully on him.

David got his suits in Tesco's. They'd just started doing them in their value range. The day David found out you could get a full suit for only £25 you'd have thought he'd won the lottery.

I bet Sean's suit wasn't even "off the rack," let alone from a supermarket trolley.

"Sorry, bad pun," I said when Sean didn't respond to my comment.

"Oh sorry, yes," Sean said hurriedly. "Your outfit is lovely too. You look so...so..."

"So...what?" I asked, grinning at him.

"Different."

"Gee, thanks."

"No, I mean that in a good way. Oh, I'm rubbish at giving compliments, always have been. What I meant to say was—you look beautiful, Scarlett."

"Oh, oh, right. Well, thank you," I said, as my face flushed a similar shade to my dress.

We stood awkwardly in the doorway.

"We'd better get going," I said. "Did you book a taxi?"

"Yes." Sean looked at his watch. "It should be here by now, shall we wait downstairs?"

We both tried to exit through the door at once, barging shoulders as we did so.

"Sorry, ladies first," Sean said, gallantly holding out his hand.

"Why, thank you, kind sir," I replied, bobbing a little curt-sey, for once trying to act and sound like my namesake.

Sean pulled a face. "You're not really the Scarlett O'Hara type, are you?"

I stopped still in the doorway. "What do you mean?"

"I mean the name—Scarlett. It's a cool name, but it's not really you, is it?"

I stared at Sean. What on earth was he talking about?

"What do you suggest I should be called?" I asked him, stepping back into the room. "If you've got any better ideas perhaps you should let me know now while I've still got the chance to spend the rest of my life getting used to being called something different."

"Easy." Sean laughed. "Maybe I was wrong. Maybe you have got the O'Hara temper on you. You definitely see red whenever someone criticizes you. Perhaps that's why the dress suits you so well today."

I should have known his pleasant manner wouldn't last long.

"In fact that's it. That's probably what you should be called."

I opened my eyes wide to suggest I had no idea what he was talking about.

"Red." Sean grinned. "That's what I shall call you from now on whenever you're getting het up about something."

"Red," I repeated. "You're going to call me Red?"

Sean nodded.

"Fine," I said, turning away from him and heading out of the door again. "Just don't ask me to repeat what I'm calling you inside my head every time you do."

As we traveled down silently in the lift together, for the first time ever it was bugging me that the person I was with reminded me of an actor in a movie. This was one of my favorite games usually. But today, because he was dressed the way he was, Sean was looking much too like Brad Pitt in *Ocean's Eleven* for me to deny any resemblance. I didn't like it one little bit.

Luckily my mind soon had more important things to worry about than my Brad/Sean dilemma, when after twenty minutes our taxi had still failed to appear.

After Sean had to complain twice at reception—and once to "Barney"—the cab driver, full of apologies, finally screeched to a halt outside the front entrance of the Radisson.

"Apologies for the hold-up, folks," she called from the driver's seat as we piled into the back of her cab. "There's a protest march in the city center, so the roads are a pure nightmare. I dinnee know what clown was given the job of arranging the diversions—but he disnee know Glasgow one wee bit!

"Don't yez worry though," she assured us, as we plugged our seat belts in and finally pulled away from the Radisson. "I know a wee short cut—I'll have yez both there in no time at all."

We headed off at such speed that for the first few minutes of the journey we could do nothing but sit bolt upright like statues on the backseat as we both silently prayed for our lives. Then we relaxed a little as our "torturer" had no choice but to slow down, while she twisted and turned in and out of the side streets and back alleys of Glasgow city center.

When she finally had to slow right down because of traffic lights up ahead and I could finally catch my breath enough to speak, I leaned forward in my seat a little so not to disturb her concentration (or her foot on the accelerator pedal) too much.

"I don't suppose you've ever seen a movie called *Taxi*, have you?" I asked. "It stars Queen Latifah?"

"Queen who, hen?"

"Queen Latifah. She plays this feisty, wise-crackin', speed-demon taxi driver in New York, who gets caught up helping this police detective out with a gang of bank robbers."

"No, hen, never seen it. I like a nice wee horror film meself, something that scares the shit out of me."

Like you do to your passengers? I wondered. "You should try and rent it sometime. I think you'd like it."

I glanced at my watch as we sat bumper to bumper in the traffic that crawled along the road. It appeared to stretch way out in front of us too. "At this rate we're never going to make it on time. Is it much further, do you know, Sean?"

"I don't think so." Sean now leaned forward to speak to our own speed queen. "How much longer to the church?"

"At this speed, hen, 'bout another twenty minutes."

"Sean, the wedding is in ten!"

Sean pulled a wad of notes from his wallet.

"Look, this should cover the fare so far—we'll walk from here." He turned to me. "Is that OK with you?"

I looked down at my high heels and sighed. "I don't think we've much choice."

We climbed out of the taxi and began to walk along the pavement on the side of the road.

"Do you think we're going to make it at this speed?" I asked, trying hard to keep up with Sean's great lolloping strides and finding I was having to break into a jog to do so.

"Can't you go any faster?" Sean asked. Then he glanced

down at my heels. "No, I don't suppose you can." He looked quickly around him, then suddenly darted out into the traffic.

"Sean!" I cried. "What the hell are you doing?"

Sean dodged in and out of the vehicles that still crawled along the road. Horns beeped, and obscenities were shouted from car windows, but he kept going until he reached the other side. Two delivery boys standing outside a pizza restaurant having a cigarette idly watched him.

Sean approached them and words were quickly exchanged, and then some money. The boys put on their helmets and climbed aboard their mopeds. Sean climbed onto one of the bikes too, perching on the back where the pizzas usually sat.

Oh no, you can't be serious, I thought, as they wove their way back across the traffic toward me.

"Climb aboard," Sean shouted above the noise of the engines. "They'll get us there on time!"

"But I can't—I'm wearing a skirt!"

My delivery boy smirked at my tight dress. "You could always hitch it up," he leered.

"Come on, Red!" Sean called. "Don't be a spoilsport—it's the only way we're going to make it there on time!"

I glared at Sean, then, swallowing my pride, hoisted up my dress and perched myself gingerly on top of the pizza rack.

My escort turned round and grinned. "I'm Brian," he said, holding out his hand.

"Scarlett," I said, shaking it.

"Nice name. Look, Scarlett, you're going to have to put your arms around me," he instructed. "Or you'll fall off."

"Right," I said, closing my eyes and wrapping my arms

around Brian's skinny torso. *Jeez, this had better be in a movie somewhere*, I thought, as I held on for dear life while Brian expertly wove his moped in and out of the congested Glasgow traffic. *He's not exactly James Dean or Marlon Brando.* But I don't suppose, as I balanced precariously on the back of a pizza delivery bike, I looked much like a starlet of Hollywood yesteryear either.

We arrived at the wedding with minutes to spare. I clambered off the moped as gracefully as I could and hurriedly smoothed down my dress, grateful there had not been any undelivered pizzas on the bike during our ride or my current odor might now have been less Chanel No. 5, and more Order No. 5 with extra pepperoni and cheese. I was grateful we'd been wearing helmets too, for as much as my hair had been flattened from being squashed under the helmet, if it had been loose I'd have had another movie moment to add to my list, and it would have been a most unwanted one—that of Bridget Jones's frizzy hair after she'd been in Daniel Cleaver's open-topped sports car.

"OK?" Sean asked, holding up his hand to the pizza delivery boys as they sped off together, zigzagging back through the traffic.

I nodded. "Yeah, I think so. Well, at least we got here before the bride."

"Only just," Sean said, nodding in the direction of a big black car pulling up outside the church.

I watched as the car door was opened and a young girl wearing white alighted from the vehicle. "Is that Rachel?"

"Yes," Sean said, taking a quick glance. "Now come on, let's get inside before she does."

"It's an unusual outfit she's wearing," I said as we quietly crept into the church.

"Mmm, is it?" Sean said, finding us an empty pew at the back. "I didn't really notice."

It was then I realized something wasn't quite right.

As I looked around me, I saw the congregation weren't dressed in the usual wedding attire of morning suits, dresses, and oversized hats, but were wearing what looked like fancy dress outfits.

"Sean, what's everyone wearing?" I whispered.

"What do you mean?" Sean looked up from his Order of Service.

"Look at everyone, they're all dressed funny."

As we both looked closely at our fellow guests, the realization dawned on us that the wedding obviously had a theme. Nearly everyone had on some sort of costume, the only exception seemed to be a couple of elderly grannies, or maybe they were aunts, who wore the more traditional wedding attire of pastel twinset with matching shade of large feathery hat.

"Didn't you know it was fancy dress costumes?" I hissed in Sean's ear. "I feel a right fool dressed like this now."

"It's worse than just fancy dress," Sean whispered back, a smile beginning to spread across his face.

"What do you mean worse? How could this get any worse than us being at a fancy dress wedding in normal clothes?"

Just then the huge wooden doors at the back of the church

burst open, and everyone stood up as the first bars of the bridal march began.

That sounds familiar, I thought as the notes began to register in my ears.

Then it hit me what the music was, and why Sean was now standing next to me grinning like a fool—as the John Williams theme from *Star Wars* echoed around the church, and Rachel, dressed as Princess Leia—bagel hair and all—shimmered toward us in a long white dress.

I looked at Sean. His eyes shone in amusement.

"It can't be, can it?" I asked, wanting to giggle. "It's not a *Star Wars*–themed wedding?"

"Look at Uncle Jonathan," Sean hissed, barely able to speak for laughing now.

The man walking Rachel down the aisle was dressed in what looked like a monk's habit—a long brown hooded tunic, knotted at the waist with rope.

"I think he's Obi-Wan Kenobi!" Sean squeaked, his hand covering his mouth to try and conceal his mirth from the approaching Jedi Knight.

Following Princess Leia and Obi-Wan were the bridesmaids, two of them dressed as Ewoks, and the other, an older girl, as Queen Padmé from the later *Star Wars* films.

We watched in amazement as the bridal procession passed us. Sean craned his head around the end of the pew to get a better view down the aisle.

"Who is the groom dressed as?" I asked, unable to see clearly through the people in front of me, one of whom had come as Jar-Jar Binks and was wearing extremely tall headgear.

"I think he's Han Solo," Sean said, whispering. "Oh my God, guess who the best man is?"

I tried to look through the sea of costumes and caught a glimpse of something gold shimmering up ahead. "Not C-3PO, surely?"

"It surely is." Sean leaned his head back toward mine. "Shouldn't it really be Chewbacca, though, wasn't he Han's best mate?"

I smiled at Sean. "I thought you didn't know anything about movies?"

"Maybe some I do. Anyway, everyone knows *Star Wars*."

"I guess."

"I suppose we can let them off the Chewbacca thing. After all, who's going to be daft enough to dress up as him? The suit would be stifling inside."

I nodded in agreement. "I can't believe this, Sean. I've been to loads of weddings, but never anything like this before. I mean, what's next—the vicar dressed as Darth Vader?"

Sean took another look. "How did you guess?"

"What? You're kidding, let me see." I leaned across Sean to take a peek. And indeed, up ahead conducting the ceremony was Darth Vader himself, in a long black cloak and full head mask.

I grinned, then realized I was still lying over Sean's lap, so I hurriedly pulled myself up again.

"Sorry," I whispered in embarrassment.

"No worries," Sean said, and our eyes held each other's again for the briefest of moments. Then we noticed that the rest of the congregation was standing, and it was time for the first hymn. Well it wasn't actually a hymn, we all sang "Super Trouper" by

Abba. (Except it was written "Super 'Storm' Trooper" on the Order of Service.)

The *Star Wars* theme continued throughout the ceremony. The rings were brought out on a silver cushion carried by a full-size remote controlled R2-D2. Then it was Yoda's turn to give us a reading, based on his own philosophies and teachings. The part of Yoda was played by one of Sean's cousins—he crouched down behind the pulpit with his hand stuffed inside a children's puppet of the wise Jedi.

The *piece de resistance* of the whole ceremony, though, came during the signing of the registers, when we were treated to a reenactment of a classic fight scene from one of the films. Obviously Darth Vader was a little too busy just now signing paperwork to be fighting Luke Skywalker, so Darth Maul took his place in the battle of the light sabers—in full red and black makeup.

When the battle of good against evil had been won and the registers had been signed, the happy couple walked back down the aisle through an archway of millennium stormtroopers, each holding a light sabre above their head.

"Well, that was certainly different," I commented, as we emerged into the cold February air once more.

"Different is certainly *one* of the words I'd use to describe it, yes," Sean said, squinting into the bright winter sun. He pulled a pair of silver sunglasses from his pocket and the Brad Pitt *Ocean's Eleven* look was now complete. I swallowed hard.

I looked around at the guests emerging from the church behind us to try and take my mind off it. "Oh my God, Sean," I said, spying a rather large woman standing not far away. "Look at all the trouble that woman has gone to—she's well padded up under that dress. What a sense of humor, eh? Jabba the Hutt does M&S! Brilliant!"

"That's Great-aunt Evie," Sean said, looking to where I was pointing. "And I'm afraid to say she's not actually in fancy dress."

"Oops. Sorry." My face flushed the color of my dress once more. I turned in the other direction. "Oh look, Sean, there *is* a Chewbacca here—and he's waving at you."

Sean turned around as Chewbacca and his escort—a female Jedi knight—began to walk toward us.

"That looks like Diana under that hood..." Sean said, peering at them. "Oh no, that means Chewbacca must be..."

"Sean, how are you?" Diana asked as they reached us.

"Good, thanks, Diana." Sean kissed her on the cheek. "And yourself?"

"Wonderful, darling."

"Hello, Dad," Sean said, looking up at Chewbacca.

Chewbacca removed his head. "How'd you know it was me?"

"I should have known, this is right up your street, isn't it, all this movie stuff?"

"Fantastic idea! It's certainly livened up the occasion." Sean's father turned to me. "You must be the Scarlett Ursula was telling me all about?"

"Sorry," Sean apologized. "Dad, this is indeed Scarlett. Scarlett, this is my father, Alfie, and my stepmother, Diana."

"Fantastic to meet you." Sean's father reached out his large paw and shook my hand vigorously.

I turned toward Diana. Underneath the hood was a tall, elegant woman, with long, silver hair tied up loosely on top of her head. She had electric-blue eyes, with which she studied me intently.

"Lovely to meet you, Scarlett," she said, holding out her hand.

"And you, Diana," I said, shaking it.

I knew at that moment she wasn't my mother: Sean had been right once again. I don't know how I knew; it was just a feeling—well, a lack of feeling really. I was certain if Diana had been my mother I'd definitely have felt something...anything, when our hands touched.

Ten

We spent the rest of the wedding celebrations with Alfie and Diana.

They were a lovely couple. Alfie was a large, jolly man, full of mischief and laughter—he reminded me very much of Gareth from *Four Weddings and a Funeral*. Diana was his calming influence—she was elegant and serene, but very approachable and friendly. Honor Blackman with a touch of Helen Mirren were my favored choices for Sean's stepmother.

"You must take after your mother," I said to Sean, as we sat watching Alfie spin Diana around the dance floor at great speed. It seemed it was not only in looks that Alfie resembled Simon Callow's *Four Weddings* character. He'd been dancing with great exuberance for most of the evening; no female was safe once he selected his next dance partner—even me. I had been chosen by Alfie to strut my stuff with him to Robbie Williams's "Let Me Entertain You." Which, considering it was one of my favorite songs, I didn't mind too much. But Alfie's rendition of the song was something I didn't think I'd ever forget.

"Why do you say that?" Sean asked, turning to me.

"Your dad—he's just so spontaneous and full of life."

"And I'm boring, is that what you're saying?"

"No," I said, quickly trying to backtrack. "You're just… more laid back—there's nothing wrong with that. Ursula must take after your dad, and you, your mum."

"Yes, I suppose you're right. Mum and I always understood each other better."

"Do you see each other much?"

"Mum died two years ago."

"Oh, Sean." I was shocked by his revelation. "I'm so sorry, I had no idea—I just assumed your parents had divorced."

"They did, and then Mum went to live in Wales with another man. Her illness came on quite suddenly—but she died without too much pain, so we were grateful for that."

Sean looked so sad as he reflected on his mother's death that I desperately wanted to put my hand over his to comfort him. But I didn't feel it was my place to.

"She was happy, though," Sean continued. "Before she died. She remarried, and her second husband, David, was nothing like Dad. He was a very quiet chap, calm and conventional, good at his job. Ursula thought he was boring, but Mum was happy with him, so we were happy for her."

"Davids often are," I said, not meaning to think aloud.

"What do you mean?"

"Oh sorry, nothing really. Please, continue about your mother."

"No, go on," Sean insisted. "I don't want to dampen the mood of this happy occasion. What did you mean, about Davids?"

I stalled for time by finishing off the last of my drink. Then I swirled the remaining ice around in the bottom of the glass. Did I really want to start a conversation about David and myself with Sean? But after what he'd told me about his mother I didn't want to seem insensitive. "David is my fiancé's name," I said eventually, putting my empty glass down on the table. "And it's just...he's quite conventional too."

"You mean boring?" Sean grinned.

"No, not boring. He knows what he likes, that's all."

"What does he do for a living?"

I looked at Sean—I knew what was coming before I even spoke.

"His family owns a chain of cinemas."

Sean threw back his head and laughed. "Scarlett, you really are something else. Is that why you're marrying him, so you can get free cinema admission for the rest of your life?"

"No." And there was me trying not to be insensitive.

"I'm sorry," Sean said, trying to straighten his face. "I shouldn't have laughed. But you've got to see the funny side."

"I suppose it may be mildly amusing. But that's not why I'm with him."

"Why are you then? Wait," Sean said, raising his eyebrows suggestively. "Is he Brad Pitt's long-lost twin by any chance?"

"What my David is or does is none of your business." I was getting cross with Sean now, mother or no mother. Why did he always have to find something about me to ridicule?

"Right, so he's not great looking. He's boring...and you're *not* marrying him to get free movies forever, so that only leaves...his money."

I glared at Sean.

"Oh, Red, you're not, are you? I never thought you would be so mercenary."

Sean was joking, but he was getting a bit too close to the truth for comfort, and I didn't like it.

"Don't be silly—of course I wouldn't marry someone for their money. I love him. There, isn't that enough?"

Sean looked as if he didn't believe me. "Methinks the lady doth protest too much. However, I'll trust you—you don't look the gold-digger type."

"Thanks," I said sarcastically.

Alfie and Diana returned to the table.

"So," Alfie asked, panting heavily after a vigorous rendition of Ricky Martin's "Livin' la Vida Loca." "How are you two getting on?" He looked between the two of us. "More drinks?"

"Yes please, Alfie," I said, holding up my empty glass. "That would be great."

"My round," Sean said, standing up. "I think Scarlett has had enough of my witty repartee for now. Haven't you, Red?"

I chose not to respond and looked out at the dance floor.

Sean just grinned. "Right then, same again for everyone, is it? Good, then I shall return forthwith!"

Sean strode over to the bar, leaving me sitting with Alfie and Diana.

"Oh dear," Diana said with concern. "He hasn't been teasing you, has he? He's a devil for winding people up."

"No, it's fine." I smiled at Diana. "Nothing I can't handle anyway." Perhaps Sean wasn't as different from Alfie as I'd automatically assumed earlier on. His sense of humor was just a little more subtle.

"So, Scarlett," Alfie said. "Ursula has told us all about how you love the movies."

"Yes, that's right," I said, turning to him.

"But your family don't understand you? She said your father isn't keen on the cinema, but that your mother loved it just like you."

I froze on hearing my mother mentioned. I'd spent so many years not talking about her that it now seemed very odd for a relative stranger to want to start discussing her with me.

"Alfie," Diana said softly. "Maybe Scarlett doesn't want to talk about her."

"No, it's fine," I said. "I don't mind. Really."

I told them what I knew of my mother and her love of the movies. While I was doing this Sean returned with the drinks. Then for some unknown reason—as I never usually talked about it to anyone—I told them about her leaving when I was only a baby.

"Oh my dear, how awful for you," Diana said sympathetically. "But your father sounds a fine chap from what you've told us."

"Yeah, Dad is great. I never missed out on anything when I was growing up. Well, I didn't feel like I did anyway."

"What was your mother's name?" Alfie asked.

"Rosemary. But I think she called herself Rosie a lot of the time."

Alfie screwed his forehead up. "Diana, do you remember that barmaid who used to work for us? She was mad about the cinema too. You used to go out together and see films occasionally when I was working in the bar and couldn't go with you. Wasn't *her* name Rosie?"

Diana thought for a moment. "Yes, I think you're right, it was. But, Alfie, you're talking ten, maybe twelve years ago now."

"What did she look like?" I asked eagerly. It couldn't be her, surely—there must be thousands of Rosies who liked the cinema.

Diana thought again. "Er, she had lightish-colored hair, I seem to remember, although I think she may have dyed it. But it definitely wasn't black like yours, Scarlett. And if I remember rightly, light eyes too—blue, maybe green?"

"I may get my hair from my father. But his eyes are brown, so..."

We began to discuss excitedly the possibility that this woman could be my mother.

Sean, who had been sitting quietly at the table until this point, interrupted us. "I hate to be the voice of doom among all this hope. But don't you think you might be getting a little carried away here?"

We all stopped talking and stared at him.

He glanced between the three of us, and his gaze rested on Diana. "You said you hadn't seen this woman for some time. Perhaps your memory might be a little clouded."

Diana considered Sean for a moment, her blue eyes blinking slowly. "Are you saying as I approach old age, Sean, that my mind is starting to go?" she inquired politely.

"No, not at all, Diana," Sean said hurriedly, his cheeks flushing a little. "I'm just saying the chances of it actually being her are millions to one." Sean took a quick gulp of his drink, and his voice slowed to its usual calm collected pace again. "Quite simply you are all possibly letting your shared tendencies to romanticize things, as if they were on celluloid, shroud your better judgment."

"Ah, my son—the voice of reason," Alfie said, leaning back in his chair and surveying Sean. "*That* is your mother talking."

"It's nothing to do with Mum. I'm just being sensible. These are the facts: this all happened a decade ago; you've not seen the woman since and you have no idea where she is now. How is this helping Scarlett, by getting her hopes up that you may have met her mother many years ago? It's not as if you know where she is now, is it?"

I was in two minds as to how I felt about Sean at that very moment. I was mad at him for quashing our ideas with his common sense. But I was touched that he was worried about me getting hurt by all this talk of my mother.

"London," Diana said. "The last I knew of her, she went down to London to work. She met a chap up here who offered her a job in one of the upmarket boutiques on Bond Street. Rosie was always well dressed—she took care of herself, and people noticed."

"You don't remember which one, do you?" I asked hopefully.

Diana thought hard. "No, I'm so sorry, Scarlett, I don't. But this is years ago, it doesn't mean she'd still be there now."

"And even if she was," Sean said, "it doesn't mean this woman is actually Scarlett's mother. We have no proof."

I opened up my bag, and pulled out the battered photo. "I know this is old," I said, unfolding it carefully. "But did the Rosie you know look anything like the woman in this photo?"

Diana took the photo gently from me, and she and Alfie both reached for their spectacle cases.

It was Alfie who took his eyes from the photo first. He removed his glasses and shook his head.

"I'm sorry, Scarlett, it's difficult to tell—I can't say I remember her all that well. Women change their appearance so much from week to week, let alone over several years. I really couldn't say for sure."

"It's OK, Alfie. It was worth a try." I tried not to look too disappointed.

Diana passed me back the photo and removed her glasses slowly. Then she placed her hand gently over mine before she spoke.

"It's her, Scarlett. It's Rosie."

It was as if Diana was handing me a piece of the jigsaw I'd never been able to complete.

I'd told Sean I believed everything happened for a reason. What if my reason for coming to Notting Hill was more than just to prove my family wrong about the movies? What if the reason I'd come here was to get the chance to find the final piece of my jigsaw, the something that was missing from my life—the chance to find my mother again?

Eleven

Our journey home by train the next day was much quieter than our journey up had been. I sat deep in thought most of the time, and Sean was polite enough not to disturb me as we traveled back to London.

When we finally reached Notting Hill and our taxi dropped us off outside our houses, Sean asked if there was anything more he could do to help.

"Thanks, but I think I can take it from here," I replied, carrying my suitcase up the steps.

"No, I mean with the search for your mother," Sean said, climbing his own steps so he was level with me again. "You haven't said as much, but I assume you're going to continue looking for her now you've got a lead?"

"Oh, I see. Yes, you're right, I am. But I think I know what I'm going to do." I smiled at him. "Thanks for asking, though."

"Any time. If you change your mind, you know where I am."

I nodded.

Sean smiled, unlocked his door, and disappeared inside.

I stood for a moment on the steps, gazing at the spot where he'd just been. It seemed odd to be on my own again now.

But as I turned the key in my lock, I wasn't alone for long: my homecoming was greeted by the now familiar wailing of Buster—as I'd christened him—the burglar alarm.

Early the next morning I set off to the heart of London's shopping district. As I emerged from Bond Street tube station I suddenly realized the enormity of what I was about to try and do.

Surrounding me were more designer clothing, perfume, art, and antiques shops—and more Royal Warrant holders—than anywhere else in the city.

Where on earth do I start? I wondered, as I looked along the rows of elegant and expensive shops. Well, as a famous nun once sang in a movie, "Let's start at the very beginning, a very good place to start…"

So that's just what I did. That Monday morning I walked the entire length of Old and New Bond Street, asking in shops, and—if I was lucky to get even the merest flicker of interest from one of the bored assistants—showing my photograph too.

At lunchtime I took a break in a little cafe. I took a seat by the window, and while I was waiting for my panini to be brought to the table, I unfolded my photograph once more, this time for my own benefit.

"*A yearning for something that's lost.*" The words from that painting made sense to me at last. Now I was actually doing something positive about trying to find my mother, it was all clicking into place.

Carefully I folded the photograph and placed it safely in my inside coat pocket. Then I took a sip of my orange juice and stared at the shoppers passing by on the pavement.

Two women across the road bumped into each other as they tried to enter and exit Jigsaw at the same time. I smiled as I saw the two of them apologize to each other, and then bang their heads together as they both bent down to pick up the vast quantity of expensive-looking shopping bags that they'd dropped on the pavement. It was something that you did all the time when you were out shopping, especially in a place as busy as London. But what you didn't usually do, and what the lucky lady had done who had been about to enter Jigsaw today, was bump into Keira Knightley in the process.

I sat watching open-mouthed as I saw recognition strike on the other lady's face. She flushed a shade of bright red after either losing the power of speech or, by the look on Keira's face, more than likely saying something really stupid. Keira just smiled politely at her and began to back away. At first slowly, and then at a much speedier pace. Very quickly she became invisible among the throng of afternoon shoppers once more.

What a waste, I thought, as the waitress brought my lunch to the table. If that had been me I would have been able to engage her in some polite chitchat about her latest movie for a couple of minutes. Not babble some incoherent nonsense that scared her away down the street. Why did I never get those sorts of chances? It was really unfair.

In the afternoon I repeated my morning performance, this time along the opposite side of Bond Street. I knew it was a long shot. I mean, it was over ten years since my mother was supposed to have worked here. But it was all I'd got—I had to keep giving it a try.

My mobile rang just as I was about to enter the Fenwick department store.

"Dad!" This was the first time Dad had contacted me since I'd been away. "How are you?"

"I'm fine, Scarlett. How's it going? Are you having a good time away from us all?"

How could I answer that?

"I'm missing everyone, obviously. But it's been…helpful to get away for a while, yes."

"Good, I'm pleased to hear it. So, what are you up to at the moment?"

"I'm just doing a bit of shopping, actually."

"Ah, I should have known—spending all David's money, are you?"

Chance would be a fine thing.

"I do have money of my own, Dad," I reminded him. "That's why I come to work with *you* every day!"

"Not *quite* every day," Dad said, laughing. "I'm glad you're having a good time, though. You needed a break."

"Yes…" I said, feeling guilty as I thought about what I was doing just then. "Look, Dad, I'd better get going. I'm having a bit of a hectic day." That was putting it mildly.

"You're not the only one. I'm running this office virtually single-handed. Or had that little detail slipped your mind?"

I could hear by the tone of Dad's voice he was just joking with me. "Then you'll appreciate me all the more when I return!" I smiled. "I really have to go now. I'll call you soon."

"OK then, darling. Speak to you later. Love you."

"Love you too, Dad."

I ended the call and looked down at my phone. Perhaps I should have told him. But this search for my mother could all come to nothing so it would be pointless upsetting him. It wasn't as if I was getting anywhere with it. But I had to keep trying.

I put my phone back in my bag and pushed my way purposefully through the revolving doors of Fenwick's.

Right then—where to start?

I walked through all the departments, asking the same questions to any of the more mature assistants I could find. It was pointless asking the younger ones; they wouldn't have been around when my mother worked here—if she had worked here, of course. Diana's information may indeed have been accurate: my mother could well have worked in one of these shops many years ago. But the chances of finding her—or even anyone who had worked with her—were becoming more unlikely by the second.

I returned to the ground floor and began to make my way toward the exit. But I paused as I walked through the handbag department—not to gasp at the extortionate price of the designer bags, but to stare at one of the assistants. She was an older lady, but I hadn't seen her earlier when I'd passed through. The reason I was now staring at her was because pinned tightly to the top of her head was a bun of jet-black hair. And as she looked over her spectacles at a stock sheet, I saw that the eyes that darted to and fro were the exact shade of bright green as my own.

She glanced up and met my stare. "Can I help you?" she asked.

"No. Well, actually, yes, you might be able to." I didn't know what to say—I was in shock. I'd been trailing up and down Bond Street all day, I was tired and exhausted, and now this person standing right in front of me could really be my mother. "Have you worked here long?" I asked stupidly.

"About ten years. Why?"

"Oh, good, erm, well, the thing is…" How the hell did you ask someone if they were the mother that ran out on you when you were a six-month-old baby?

"Miss Sheila!" I heard a voice call. "Could you help me with this customer?"

Miss Sheila looked toward the other side of the counter where an elderly gentleman who was obviously having trouble deciding on a handbag—I presumed for his wife—stood there looking perplexed.

"Excuse me one moment, dear. I'll be right back." Sheila glided effortlessly over and spoke briefly to the gentleman. Expertly she demonstrated two bags by opening and closing them, holding them under her arm, at arm's length, and then slung over her shoulder. Finally, the gentleman pointed at his choice: a tan leather clutch bag with optional chain strap.

"Michelle—gift-wrapping, please!" Sheila called.

"Michelle's on her break now, miss."

"Then you can do it, Leila, please."

"I can't, miss, I haven't been shown that yet—with me being a trainee 'n' all."

Sheila raised her eyes to heaven as if asking for spiritual guidance to give her the patience to deal with these underlings. "It's about time you learned then, my girl. Watch and learn."

I watched too, as Sheila swiftly and expertly dealt with the gift-wrapping. The finished product was an elegant, light blue parcel with coordinating ribbon. It was placed in a clear cellophane bag, which was tied up at the top with a white ribbon, after dried rose petals had been carefully poured into the bag to surround it.

Rowan Atkinson eat your heart out, I thought, storing yet another film scene in my head to add to my ever-growing list.

Sheila returned to my side of the counter.

"So sorry about that," she said. "Now, you were saying?"

"Er yes, that's right—is Sheila your real name?" I blurted out.

Sheila looked as if she was wondering whether she might need to call security in a minute. "Yes, it is—why do you ask?"

"Oh...no reason," I said dejectedly.

"There must be a reason, dear, otherwise you wouldn't have asked in the first place."

I stopped myself from saying. "Because I thought you might be my mother" just in time. Instead, I told her about my search for a Rosemary O'Brien, who might have worked here in the past. Then I quickly showed her my photo.

"Sorry, dear. Neither the name nor the photo ring any bells, I'm afraid."

"Never mind," I said, putting the photo back in my bag. "It doesn't surprise me—I've been getting the same answer all day. Thanks anyway." I began to move away from the counter.

"Wait—you could ask Bill."

"Bill?"

"He's our odd-job man—he's been here for donkey's years. Bill knows everyone, and everyone knows Bill."

"Can I speak to him?" I asked excitedly.

"Wait, I'll just see if he's around." Sheila picked up the internal phone. "Hi, Janice, Sheila here—ladies' bags…yes, yes, I'm fine. Do you know if Bill is about somewhere in the store?"

I waited with bated breath. I'd never had to bate my breath before, and now seemed as good a time as any to give it a try.

"Oh, is he? Oh, that can be nasty…Yes, let's hope so, eh? Well thank you, Janice…yep, we should do that soon. Bye-bye for now." Sheila put the phone down.

"I'm sorry, it seems Bill is off sick at the moment. Touch of the flu, Janice says."

I unbated my breath as my heart sank. "Do you know when he might be back?"

"No, I'm afraid not. Bill must be well into his sixties—these things take their toll when you're that age, don't they? Perhaps you could pop back later in the week?"

I nodded. "Yes, I'll try and do that. Thanks for your help, Sheila."

"My pleasure, dear. Good luck with your search."

It was the last straw at the end of a very disappointing day. I couldn't face any more shops after Sheila's news, so I decided to head home.

A long soak in a hot bath was what was needed tonight, and maybe a bit of cinema therapy, courtesy of the extensive library of DVDs that Belinda and Harry kept in their study. I'd had enough real life for one day.

Twelve

I passed the next couple of days with more visits to Bond Street. I completed the second side of the street fairly quickly on Tuesday morning, but although I felt more positive as I entered the stores and asked my questions, the answers I received were still the same.

Spending the day in and out of all these designer stores should have been fun. It should have been like something from the *Sex and the City* movie. But I didn't feel much like Carrie, Samantha, Charlotte, or Miranda as I trailed in and out of the shops. They'd have been parading up and down here in designer outfits and high heels. I had chosen comfort and was sporting TopShop jeans, a Gap hoodie, Next down vest, and Nike trainers.

After I'd had lunch, I popped into Fenwick's just in case Bill had made a miraculous recovery, and was wandering about the shop with a screwdriver in his hand once more. But the answer from Sheila was still negative, so I left, promising to return again tomorrow, and headed back home.

The same happened on Wednesday morning. Still no Bill. I asked Sheila if it might be possible for Personnel to give me his telephone number so I could ring him. But after a very brief phone call up to Janice again, the answer was a very definite no, they could not possibly give out personal details on a member of staff.

"I'm sorry, dear," Sheila apologized. "They say he probably won't be back until next week now either. Perhaps you could try again then."

I returned to the house once more, dejected and completely fed up with life. Not only was finding out any further information on my mother proving to be virtually impossible, but nothing new was happening to me on the movie front either. This was probably because I'd spent most of the last three days trailing up and down Bond Street. But after the first week's successes I'd been lulled into the false belief that proving you could live your life like a movie would be easy. Now, I wasn't so sure.

That afternoon I flicked through all 400 channels on the TV. When I didn't find anything to watch, I looked once more through Belinda and Harry's collection of DVDs to find someone to spend my evening with—and then I ran yet another bath, hoping that would pass half an hour until dinner.

I was just about to climb into the hot soapy water when the doorbell rang. I tried to ignore it and hoped they'd go away. All I needed was Oscar or Ursula checking up on me again. They'd both popped round several times since we'd arrived back from Glasgow on Sunday night, and even though I was grateful for their interest and concern, I really didn't feel like relaying yet another day's disappointment to them. But instead of my intruder taking the hint that no one was going to answer, the doorbell rang again, this time for longer.

I rolled my eyes, pulled on a white toweling robe that hung on the back of the bathroom door, and hurried downstairs.

"Yes?" I snapped, as I flung open the door. I guess I should have used the peephole first, but I hadn't got used to all this security stuff just yet.

"Oh sorry, am I disturbing you?" It was Sean. He stared down at the bathrobe.

"I was just about to take a bath actually," I said, pulling the toweling collar around me protectively.

"Oh, I see." His eyes rose up level with mine again. "I just wondered how you've been getting on. I imagine you've been up and down Bond Street for the last few days. I've been away on business or I'd have called round sooner."

So that's why I hadn't seen him about.

"Yes, I have."

"And? Any luck?"

"Actually, it's been a complete disaster..." I told him everything that had happened. "Most of the assistants were so snooty—they weren't interested in helping me at all. Just because I wasn't wearing Jimmy Choo shoes or carrying a Gucci handbag..." I paused mid-sentence and stared at Sean, and then smiled as a thought dawned on me.

"What's up?" he asked, looking puzzled.

"*Pretty Woman*," I said, grinning. "That's what! Oh, Sean, it may have been information I was after and not clothes, but they still made me feel the same as her."

"What on earth are you talking about now?"

"*Pretty Woman*—it's another movie. The one I was telling you about on the train. The one where you were a bastard?" I helpfully reminded him.

"Oh, that one."

"In the film Julia Roberts is a hooker, and Richard Gere gives her some money to go out and buy clothes on Rodeo Drive—but the assistants won't help her because she doesn't look the part."

"OK…"

"That's been me over the last few days, but I wasn't in Beverly Hills, I was in London's equivalent—Bond Street."

"If you say so," Sean said with a quizzical expression.

"Yes, I do—I've got to take something positive out of all my efforts. And another movie scene to add to my list will do nicely!" I folded my arms over my dressing gown.

"But what of this woman in Fenwick's—Sheila?"

"I won't be able to do anything about that until Bill comes back to work. So until then I'd better try and forget about my mother and get on with my movie business, and if you don't mind, just now, my bath."

"Sorry, yes, of course. Oh, wait, I almost forgot, the other reason I came round. Are you doing anything tonight?"

"Apart from my bath, and a date with Brad Pitt—nothing, really."

"Brad?"

I grinned at him. "It's a joke. I was going to watch *Mr. & Mrs. Smith* on DVD tonight."

"Oh right, I see." Sean nodded but I still wasn't sure he understood what I was talking about. "It's just some friends of mine have given me tickets to the opera this evening, and I wondered if you'd like to go."

"Thanks, Sean, but I don't really know anyone who likes the opera that I could take."

"No—I meant would you like to accompany me?"

I blushed. Of course he did.

"Oh, yes, I guess I could. Would I have to dress up? Only you know I don't have that kind of garb with me."

"No, it's not an opening night—there's no dress code. What about the outfit you wore to the wedding on Saturday? You looked good in that."

I thought for a moment and was about to say, "But you called me Red in that outfit," when something occurred to me. This got better and better. I might not be having any luck finding my mother, but I could sense another *Pretty Woman* opportunity on the horizon. Two in one week!

"Well, in that case, I should be delighted to accompany you to the opera tonight, Sean."

Or should I call you Richard...

Thirteen

We arrived at the theater in plenty of time and decided to have a drink in the bar before the show.

While I was waiting for Sean to come back with our drinks I wandered over to a display cabinet of posters and programs advertising the show we were about to see: *Così fan tutte*. I was using any diversionary tactic I could to put all thoughts of Sean as Brad Pitt out of my mind—and actually it was proving much easier than it should have been considering he'd turned up this evening wearing another *Ocean's*-inspired suit. As I stared at the glass, I was trying to picture him as Richard Gere and me as Julia Roberts to go with the theme of the evening. But this was proving far from the easy task it usually was. I seemed to be struggling with all my fantasies, both wanted and unwanted, and I couldn't figure out why.

"So," Sean asked when he'd finally fought his way back from the bar with a glass of white wine for me and a beer for himself, "is this your first opera?"

I wanted to reply, "Why, of course not. Opera, ballet, and the theater are the staple diet of my life when I'm back in Stratford." But Sean knew me better than that. "Yes, it is, actually."

"Opera is a bit like Marmite," he said knowingly. "You either love it or hate it."

That was hardly what Richard had said to Julia.

"Right, and I'm assuming you...love it?"

Sean nodded. "Should I tell you a little of what this opera is about?"

"Go on, then."

"Roughly translated, *Cosi fan tutte* means 'they're all like that.' It tells the story of two men who think their fiancées will always remain loyal. But this chap wagers them that the women won't and says he can prove to them he's right. As part of the bet, the two men pretend to be sent off to battle, but instead disguise themselves and return to try and woo each other's girlfriend."

"Sounds different."

"It's good, a bit like one of your romantic comedies, I suppose. Except it's happening live in front of you, not up on some huge flat screen."

"I'll reserve my judgment until I've seen it for myself," I said with indifference. "But I'll give anything a go once, and I like Mozart, so it can't be that bad."

"*You*—like Mozart?" Sean asked, looking surprised.

"Yeah, why shouldn't I?"

"No reason. Yet again you surprise me, Scarlett. The libretto—that's the text of the piece, rather than the music— was originally written for Mozart's colleague, but he didn't complete it, so Mozart took over."

"Salieri," I said knowingly.

"That's right—how'd you know that?" Sean studied me for a moment, his blue eyes darting to and fro across my face as though he was reading my mind. "Oh I know—you've seen *Amadeus*, right?"

"I may have done. It's a good film."

"It stretches the truth a bit, though."

"Most films do."

"And there's another instance of a film being based on one of those criteria we talked about on the train. *Amadeus* is not only based on the life of Mozart, but was a play and an opera before it was a movie."

"How do you know all this stuff?" I asked, looking skeptically at Sean. "You seem like this normal guy but inside you're just a walking, talking encyclopedia."

Sean laughed. "Years of very careful practice!"

The bell rang to summon us to our seats. "The time has come to see what you make of all this, Scarlett." Sean held out his arm to me. "Shall we go?"

I slipped my arm through his, and we walked to the auditorium together to find our seats.

I was slightly disappointed we weren't in a box like Julia and Richard. But once the opera began I soon forgot about re-enacting *Pretty Woman*, as I became more and more absorbed by what I was watching and hearing on the stage in front of me.

"So?" Sean asked when the curtain fell at the end of Act I. "What do you think so far?"

"It's just wonderful," I said, still staring at the closed curtain.

Sean smiled. "I thought you might enjoy it—that's why I got the tickets."

I turned to face him. "But you said some friends had given them to you!"

"Ah, I may have told just a little white lie there."

"But why?"

"I didn't think you'd come if I just asked you straight out. I thought if you figured you were doing me a favor then you'd feel more obliged to accept my offer. I knew you'd love the opera—it's so dramatic, and as I said before, this one is just like one of those romantic comedies you're always telling me about."

Yet again Sean was causing me to feel mixed emotions. I was cross that he'd duped me into coming with him tonight, yet pleased that he'd wanted to bring me.

"The *only* reason I came with you tonight was so I could re-enact a scene from *Pretty Woman*," I said haughtily. "The fact that I'm enjoying it is just an added bonus as far as I'm concerned."

Immediately I regretted what I'd just said, as Sean's face fell and quickly became void of emotion.

"It looks like I've done you a favor on both counts then," he said in a strange, clipped voice.

We silently got up from our seats, following the crowds through to the bar to collect our interval drinks. Then we stood in painful silence sipping at them while we tried to look at anyone rather than each other.

To escape this torture, I downed my drink rather too quickly and then managed to pad out another ten minutes by visiting the ladies' toilets. I was overjoyed when I heard the sound of the bell signaling the end of the interval.

Sean was already back in his seat reading his program when I returned. He threw a cursory glance in my direction as I sat down.

I took a deep breath. "About what I said before, Sean—it was uncalled for, and I'm sorry."

"No need to be—you simply told the truth," Sean said, still staring at the program.

"It was very kind of you to get these tickets for me," I persisted. "I should have been grateful to you, not rude."

Sean lifted his head and turned to me. "You're honest, Scarlett, and I have to say I do admire that about you. But I guess it can sometimes get you into trouble, am I right?" He smiled, and my stomach did something funny, like it was trying to perform a back flip or some other gymnastic move inside me.

"So remind me, what film am I in now?" Sean asked, grinning. "Whatever it is, I hope I'm playing the part well."

I smiled now too. "I'm afraid it's that businessman again," I said as the lights began to dim in the auditorium.

"Not the bastard one."

"Yep, that's him."

"Then I'm not doing too bad so far," he whispered as it went dark. "Since I've managed to annoy you all night."

I was about to protest, but the orchestra struck up its first few notes and we were immediately drawn into the lives of Ferrando, Guglielmo, Dorabella, and Fiordiligi once more.

"Thank you," I said to Sean as we traveled back to Notting Hill in a black cab. "The opera was fantastic."

"My pleasure. I'm glad you enjoyed it. At least it's taken your mind off your various quests for a while."

I thought for a moment. "Yes, I suppose that's what they are, aren't they? Two very different personal quests."

"So what will you do about Bill?" Sean asked. "You can't just sit and wait until he comes back to work. If it's flu and he's elderly, it could be weeks."

"What else can I do? I can't just go in there and demand his telephone number. And they wouldn't give it to me if I did. They don't give out that kind of personal information about staff."

"There must be other things you can try."

"Like? I've visited every other shop in Bond Street now. Fenwick's and Bill are my last hope."

"Hmm, let me have a think." Sean looked out of the window at the passing London streets.

"*You* could always take me back to the shop," I joked. "Tell them that we would spend an extortionate amount of money in there if they pandered to my every need, spoiled me rotten, *and* gave us Bill's telephone number!"

"We could try that, I suppose," Sean said, mulling it over. "I'm not sure it would work, though."

I laughed. Now that I'd met Sean, my father's lack of movie experience suddenly didn't seem quite so odd. "Oh, Sean, you really *do* have to start going to the cinema sometime soon; you're starting to remind me of my father."

"Why? Oh right, was that another movie scene?"

"*Pretty Woman* again."

"Do you particularly like that one? You seem to mention it a lot."

"Yes, it's quite good. I've seen it several times."

I hoped Sean didn't want me to pinpoint a number. Double figures for any film would seem obsessive to him. And I had a feeling that *Pretty Woman*, like *Notting Hill*, might soon be approaching the triple-figure mark.

"So what's your favorite one?" Sean asked to my relief. "Romantic film, I mean?"

"Ooh, that's a good question," I said, thinking. "There's so many of them I like. I mean I love *Notting Hill*—that was one of the reasons I wanted to come here. But I don't really have just one favorite." I thought some more. "There is a scene from a movie I really love, though...it's a bit odd because it's not the sort most people would usually choose as their favorite."

"Why, what happens?" Sean asked, sounding interested in my movie talk for once.

I hesitated. "It's from *Love Actually*—but it's kind of difficult to explain. It involves this chap telling a girl he loves her, without actually speaking once."

Sean looked puzzled. "How does he do that?"

"With signs."

"Signs?" Sean said, the corners of his mouth beginning to twitch.

"You'd have to watch the film to understand properly," I said, wishing I'd never mentioned it.

"Sounds like it," Sean said, raising an eyebrow.

I sighed and turned away from him to look out of the window, but the taxi was just drawing up in Lansdowne Road.

"Would you like to come into mine for a while?" Sean asked after he had paid the driver.

I hesitated again.

"I still haven't come up with a plan for you yet, so a coffee is the least I can offer you until I do."

I got the feeling he was trying to apologize for earlier. "Well—all right then."

I followed him up the steps and into his house. I watched while Sean dealt swiftly with his alarm.

"I wish I was as quick with mine," I said, looking around me. "Damn thing's got a mind of its own."

Sean's house—much to my surprise—was decorated in warm and lively colors and had quite an exotic feel about it. Some of the influences seemed to be African, some Indian, depending on which room you were in. Big comfy-looking settees were adorned with cushions and throws, and everything was set against terracotta and sand-colored walls.

"I like your decor," I said admiringly. "It makes Belinda and Harry's look stark in comparison."

"I think your home is as much an expression of who you are as your clothes," Sean replied. "Maybe that means Belinda and Harry are stark and uninteresting people."

"Well, they're your neighbors."

"Doesn't mean I know them. This is Notting Hill, Scarlett—not Albert Square."

I laughed. "So if everyone who lives here is stark and uninteresting, why are you here?"

"So I'm *not* stark and uninteresting, then?" Sean said, raising his eyebrows. "I thought I was a geek earlier?"

"I didn't say that. I said you were a walking encyclopedia—and I can see why now." I stared at Sean's book-lined walls.

"Nothing wrong in improving your mind with a bit of light reading. Take a look while I get us something to drink. I'll be right back."

While Sean was in the kitchen I cast my eyes over his book-shelves. Light reading? It was like entering a library. There were books on everything—from the history of art to travel guides, to cookery; from crime novels to the classics—Shakespeare, Dickens, Austen, and Bronte...wait...Jane Austen? Charlotte Bronte? Did Sean actually read these? And then I saw it sitting there like a beacon shining out at me from the shelf: *Love Letters of Great Men*—the very same book that Carrie Bradshaw reads in the *Sex and the City* movie. There was no way Sean would read this—was there?

"Wine OK?" Sean asked, returning. "Ah, I see you've been inspecting my library."

I jumped and turned away from the bookshelves. He held two empty wine glasses in one hand and a bottle of red wine in the other.

"Yes, lovely thanks," I said, quickly sitting down on one of the sofas, while Sean poured the wine. "So have you actually read all these books?"

"Yep, every last one. Why?"

"No reason, I just wondered."

"Wondered if they were just here for decoration, I bet. That would be like you having DVDs in your house that you haven't watched, and you just keep them out on show to impress people."

Sean sat down next to me. "Anyway, before we get into another argument, let's concentrate on your problem."

Which one? I thought. *The fact that I'm deceiving my family by not telling them the true reason I've come to London for a month? The fact that the only person that can help me find my mother could be dead from flu by the end of the week? Or the fact that when you sit this close to me my stomach starts doing its Olympic gymnastics routine?*

"Hmm…" Sean looked deep in thought.

I tried hard to think about Fenwick's and Bill. But my mind kept overriding these thoughts, and chose instead to think about Sean and what it might be like to kiss him…His kisses would be firm and powerful—the sort that took your breath away. Not weak and wet, and leaving you wanting to rinse your mouth out with antiseptic.

Oh my God, get a grip, Scarlett—what the hell are you thinking that for? You're engaged to David, for heaven's sake. Plus you barely even like Sean—why on earth would you want to kiss him? You must have thought about him as Brad Pitt once too often. Yes, that must be it.

I took a large gulp from my wine glass.

"So, what do you think?" Sean asked.

"Hmm?" My mind floated back into the room again as I realized Sean was talking to me.

"My idea—what do you think?"

"Run it by me again?"

Sean sighed. "We go into the store with stockings over our heads and hold up the manager at gunpoint until he gives us Bill's address."

"You're joking, right?"

Sean raised one eyebrow at me.

Oh God, my stomach must have won a medal—it's doing a lap of honor now.

"Yes, of course I'm joking. Are you OK? You haven't been listening to me, have you?"

No, I'm not OK. I'm engaged. I shouldn't be thinking about you in this way. He's not Brad Pitt, Scarlett. Or Ewan McGregor or Jude Law or any of those movie stars he might have a passing resemblance to—he's Sean, your temporary next-door neighbor.

"Yes, I'm fine," I said, trying to pull myself together. I took another large gulp of wine. "I was just, er, deep in thought and didn't hear what you said, that's all."

"I said, we'll both go over to Fenwick's tomorrow, and I'll see if I can use my natural charm to persuade them to tell me more about Bill."

"Sounds like a good plan."

"OK—now I *know* something is wrong. I fed you a great line there, Red, and you chose *not* to make a sarcastic comment about me?"

"Oh yes, sorry. Do you know something, Sean? I'm not feeling that great—I think I'd better go home." I stood up and made a bolt for the door. "It's a great idea though," I said, peeping out from behind the doorframe. "What time do you want to meet up tomorrow?"

"Ten?" Sean suggested. "Look, do you want me to help you back to your place—tuck you up in bed, that kind of thing?"

"No!" I insisted a bit too loudly. "No, thank you, I'll be just fine. You stay right here...with your wine...alone. And I'll be next door...in my bed...alone."

"Right..." Sean said, sounding mystified. "I'll see you tomorrow then, at ten."

"Yes—ten," I said, disappearing backward out of the door. I ran down Sean's steps, back up my own, and in through my front door again. And Buster the burglar alarm must have sensed this was not the time to play me up, because for once he behaved impeccably.

It was just as well one of us did. Because I feared if I'd stayed any longer at Sean's tonight my own behavior might have been far from impeccable.

Fourteen

Sean knocked on my door at 10 a.m. as arranged, and after he inquired if I was feeling any better this morning, we set off to Bond Street—a tube journey I knew all too well by now.

At Fenwick's we walked through the store together to the handbag department, where I spotted Sheila behind a desk. She was checking off stock against a delivery sheet.

"Right, you stay here," Sean said, parking me behind a pillar. "Sheila mustn't know we're together."

"OK," I said, wishing he hadn't had to touch me to do so. My stomach was off again—I think it may have been training for the parallel bars event now.

"I'll be back in a few minutes," Sean said, facing me. He still held on to my shoulders and looked deep into my eyes while he spoke. "Wish me luck."

"Good luck," I squeaked, barely able to find my voice with his face this close to mine.

Sean released his hold on me then strode purposefully across the shop floor in the direction of Sheila.

I breathed a sigh of relief. I had to stop this—now.

When I'd got back home last night, I'd given myself a stern talking to in the bathroom mirror. Telling myself that I was getting married in just over seven weeks—and under no circumstances was my stomach, or brain, allowed ever again to repeat anything that had gone on in Sean's house that night. Sean was just a friend—well, hardly that, really, more an acquaintance—who was simply helping me out. He wasn't a movie star or whoever else my brain had subconsciously duped me into believing he was to make me feel this way about him.

Sensibly, after my stern talking to, I'd phoned David. And after a long conversation with him I'd slept extremely soundly, which I put down to a guilt-free conscience, but in reality was probably more to do with David's long and extremely detailed description of how well the grouting had gone on his newly hung kitchen tiles.

But why was Sean still helping me? He didn't need to, he could just as easily have dumped me after Glasgow. He had no reason to continue helping me search for my mother, and yet he did. Why?

Over in ladies' bags Sean was now deep in conversation with Sheila. She was shaking her head, and Sean, still talking, was tapping his index finger forcefully on the glass counter.

Sheila then picked up the same phone she had called Personnel with on Monday. She had a brief conversation, presumably with Janice again, before the phone was quickly replaced.

More shaking of the head, then I saw Sheila lift her hand and point in my direction. Quickly I pulled my head back behind the pillar.

"It's no good you hiding!" Sheila called. "I know you're

there. I've just told your boyfriend here the same as I've told you for the past three days—we *can't* and we *won't* tell you any more about Bill. You'll simply have to wait until he comes back to work!"

I slithered out from my hiding place and joined Sean at the desk.

"Then I shall have to take my business elsewhere!" Sean said in a very loud voice. "I imagine you work on commission, Sheila, right?"

Sheila nodded furiously as she furtively glanced around to see how many customers might be watching.

"Big mistake then, *big* mistake! Because my girlfriend loves handbags—especially expensive designer ones, and I was just in the mood today to treat her to more bags than she could hold in both her hands. But no, sadly, because of you, we'll just have to go somewhere else now. Good day to you, Sheila!"

I was beginning to doubt Sean was telling me the truth about not watching movies. That speech was almost word for word the same one that Julia Roberts had made to the snooty shop assistants in *Pretty Woman*. I was about to question him about it, but he was grabbing my hand and pulling me toward the exit.

"Don't look back," Sean insisted as we hurried toward the doors.

"But—"

"Trust me!"

We reached the exit and were about to go through the revolving door when we heard someone hissing, "Oi, you—mister."

We turned and saw a young lad wearing a navy blue coverall and carrying a bucket and mop.

"Yes?" Sean inquired.

"I might know where Bill lives."

Sean smiled knowingly at him. "That sort of information could be very useful in the right hands."

The young lad—who according to his name badge was called Joe—leaned toward us. "I can't say noffin 'ere, someone will see. Meet me outside in a few minutes—in front of the ladies' knicker window."

"We'll be there," Sean said with a conspiratorial nod of his head.

Still holding my hand he quickly pulled me through the revolving doors. We walked along the front of the shop until we came to a window full of ladies' lingerie being promoted as *The Ideal Gift for your loved one this Valentine's Day*.

It was the type of underwear that was the ideal gift for a *man* on Valentine's Day, but in my experience was far from ideal for any woman I'd ever met.

Sean gazed up at the window.

"Put your tongue away," I said, turning my back to the glass.

"Why, isn't that *your* ideal gift?"

"Hardly."

"Poor David."

"I'd have thought *you'd* have had more taste than that sort of thing," I said, gesturing with my head back toward the window.

"Maybe I do." Sean grinned. "But it doesn't do any harm to look."

Joe appeared again. "I can't be long," he said, looking around furtively. "Or they'll miss me. I heard yous in the shop earlier asking after Bill, and I've seen 'er"—he nodded at me—"come in asking after him too. Is he in some sorta trouble?"

"No, not at all..." I began to explain. "You see—"

"Look, let's cut to the chase," Sean interrupted.

I frowned at him and huffily folded my arms.

"Bill's not in trouble," he continued, speaking directly to Joe. "We simply want to ask him a couple of questions. Maybe this will help." Sean pulled two £20 notes from his wallet.

"Nah, see, me memory ain't that good these days," Joe said, looking up at the sky.

Sean took two more twenties out.

Oh my God, that makes it eighty quid. If David ever carried that amount of cash on him he'd have had his wallet chained to his wrist.

Joe nodded. "That'll help." He reached out for the money, but Sean snatched his hand away.

"Information first."

I was impressed. Now *this* was more like being in a movie.

"Well, I don't know the exact number or anyfin—but he definitely lives down West Ham way. There every other Saturday, he is—in the stands."

"West Ham is a big place, Joe." Sean took another twenty from his wallet.

"I fink he said Chesterton sumfin..."

Sean counted the notes in his hands.

"Chesterton Terrace—that was it. Yeah, 'cause it made me fink of him in the stands watchin' the 'ammers."

"House number?" Sean inquired.

"Nah, I definitely don't know that. Can I 'ave me money now?"

Sean narrowed his eyes and looked at Joe. "Yeah all right, go on with ya then."

Joe snatched the money from Sean's hand and ran back inside the store.

Sean turned and looked at me. "Well?"

I was still staring after Joe, amazed at how easily Sean had just relieved himself of £100.

"Oh, sorry, yes, I'll pay you back of course."

"No, not the money, silly—don't worry about that. Joe's information?"

"Oh...oh right. I guess it's something to go on. But unless this street is a very close community, it's going to be like looking for a needle in a haystack." I sighed. "Oh, why does this have to be so difficult all the time?"

"Come on," Sean said, grabbing my hand again. "Never say never—it'll be a challenge!"

Fifteen

A challenge? Resisting the sweet trolley when hot chocolate fudge cake is calling out to me in a restaurant: that's the scale of my usual challenges.

Trying to find one old man in a street of houses that seemed to run on for miles—that was something else. It was akin to painting the Forth Road Bridge with your toothbrush, but as embarrassing as finding out you had to do it in your underwear.

"Where on earth do we start?" I asked Sean as we stood gazing at the endless row of houses.

"By knocking on the first door?" he suggested helpfully. "Should you do one side and I do the other?"

I didn't fancy knocking on anyone's door, let alone doing it on my own without Sean for backup. "No, let's do it together."

"Right then, no time like the present."

How could he be so cheerful about this? We'd have chafed knuckles and a repetitive strain injury by the time we'd knocked on all these doors.

But luckily for us, many of the houses had knockers—and some, even doorbells—so my hands were spared. Even if my patience wasn't.

After the twentieth time, the routine was becoming all too familiar.

I would knock or ring at the house, and then if the door *was* answered, Sean would ask the question, "Excuse me, does Bill live here by any chance?" And when the answer came in the negative form—as it always did—and the person answering the door didn't immediately slam it in our faces, Sean would follow up with, "You wouldn't happen to know of any Bills that live down this street?"

It didn't take me long to realize the reason this routine was becoming so familiar. It was not the constant repetition of knocking, ringing, and questions, but the fact that I'd seen it all done before in a movie. I couldn't believe I hadn't thought of it sooner.

"D'oh!" I said, sounding like Homer Simpson as I clutched my hands to my head.

"What's up?" Sean asked, opening a small gate leading up to the next front door. "We can't give up yet, we're not even halfway."

The tiny patch of land in front of this house had some plants in it this time and not the usual fridge, mattress, or empty beer crate that the last few houses we'd tried had lying around in them.

"It's another film!" I cried.

"What is? This garden?"

"No, what we're doing: banging on people's doors asking if someone lives here. Except it was Hugh Grant asking if his tea lady—Martine McCutcheon—lived there, not Bill the Fenwick's handyman."

Sean shook his head. "I don't know how you do it. I mean there's no way you could have orchestrated this movie scene."

"I don't *orchestrate* any of my movie scenes, Sean. That's the whole point of what I'm trying to prove, that movies aren't that different from real life. Well, I may have tried a couple of times in the beginning," I said, thinking of King's Cross. "But when I did they only went wrong. And can I remind you that walking down this street banging on doors asking if Bill lives here was all *your* idea.'"

"Well, I'm sorry for trying to help you, but—"

"Yes, Bill lives here," a voice said.

We'd been so busy arguing that we hadn't noticed that the door had been quietly opened, and an elderly woman now stood on the step in front of us. She was wearing a brightly colored pinny and wiping her flour-covered hands on a tea towel.

"He does?" we both asked in surprise.

"Yes, what did you want him for? Only he's not been too well of late. Oh, you're not from the pools, are you? Have we won and that silly fool hasn't checked the draws off correctly? He did that once before, we'd only won £50 that time, but it was still enough to buy us a little something, and when you're pensioners, every little helps. I mean, my Bill still has his part-time job at Fenwick's, but how much longer he'll be there after this flu's knocked him out is anyone's guess. Dr. Hardman says it could be a while before he's allowed back. 'Betty,' he said, 'you can't be letting Bill go back to work until he's fully recovered,' and with the weather being what it is just now, you never know when he might take a turn for the worse again. He's a good doctor is Dr. Hardman—been our family doctor for donkey's years, he has. I remember when—"

"We're not from the pools," Sean interrupted. Trying to stop

Betty when she was in full flow was like trying to stop a verbal tidal wave crashing toward you.

"You're not? Then what are you here for? Oh wait, you're not from *Deal or No Deal*, are you? We applied to be on that *ages* ago now, I just love that little Noel Edmonds, he's such a—"

"No," Sean said firmly. "We're not. We wondered if we might be able to have a word with Bill. Scarlett here is looking for her mother, and it seems Bill might have known her many years ago."

Betty puffed out her chest under the pinny like a mother hen protecting her young. "I'll have you know I'm Bill's childhood sweetheart—we've been together since school, so we have—there's been no *other* women in his life."

"No. Please, it's not like that," I said, holding up my hands in a submissive gesture, hoping to calm Betty down—she'd turned a funny shade of purple and didn't look too good. "We think he may have worked with my mother at Fenwick's many years ago. I'm trying to find her, and we wondered if Bill might know where she went after she left the store."

"Oh, I see." Betty's chest subsided along with her color. "Well, why didn't you say so before, dear? Come in."

Betty opened the door, and we walked into a small hallway. "Bill's right through here," she said, leading us into the front room.

Bill sat in an armchair by the fire with a rug over his legs. He was doing a book of crossword puzzles.

"Bill, these people are here to ask you about—"

"I know what they're here for, woman. I'd have to be deaf to not hear you prattling on, wouldn't I?"

I smiled at Bill. "I'm sorry to bother you when you're not well," I said, approaching him, and for some reason I felt I needed to kneel down beside his armchair. I'd been trying so hard to stop comparing people to movie stars since the Sean incident, but I just couldn't help it with Bill, because there was just no mistaking it. He was so obviously a dead ringer for the late James Stewart, only a bit heavier around the middle—probably much to do with Betty's home cooking, I suspected. "Only I'm looking for my mother, and we think she used to work at Fenwick's between ten and twelve years ago. I can't be more specific than that, I'm afraid. But I do have a very old photo of her." I reached into my bag, but Bill stopped me by placing his hand over mine.

"No need," he said. "It's Rosie you're looking for, am I right?"

"Yes, yes we are. How did you know?"

"Because she's sitting in front of me right now." He smiled. "Well, someone who looks very much like her is anyway. You, my dear, are the spit of your mother. The hair, no, but your eyes and your coloring—they're an exact match."

"So you knew her well?" I couldn't believe it! Someone sitting here in the same room as me that had actually known my mother.

"Everyone knew Rosie. She was the life of that place while she was there—always up for a good time, she was."

I smiled as I tried to imagine. "When did she leave, Bill?"

"Oh let me see, nine, maybe ten years ago now. It's difficult to say, time goes by so fast these days." Bill looked wistfully into the distance as he considered this thought. Then he smiled down at me before continuing with his story. "She got a job offer out in America, from one of them designers whose frocks we used to sell. Rosie was always wanting more for herself. I didn't get the feeling she was one to settle for long. So she took him up on his offer, and was gone within a week. It was all very sudden."

"Do you happen to know which part of America?" Sean asked, while I was still thinking about my mother.

Bill looked up at Sean. "New York, I seem to recall. Yes, it was definitely New York, because we joked about her finding herself in the middle of a movie set one day. Rosie loved the movies."

"And the designer?" I asked, coming back to the real world again. "Do you remember the designer's name?"

"Oh now, you're talking, dear. I don't think I do."

"Please...please try and think."

"Hmm, now let me see." Bill's brow furrowed. "It was definitely a man's name. Because I remember the person that came and offered her the job didn't look like his name at all."

I didn't have the heart to tell Bill that it would definitely have been an assistant to the designer that offered my mother a job, not the designer himself. But we'd narrowed it down to a male name, so that was something.

"You're sure it was a man's name?" I asked, trying to think of some male fashion designers. "It wasn't a one-word name like... Chanel, or...or Gucci, for instance?"

"No, it was definitely a man's name."

I looked at Sean for help.

"Er..." he struggled. "Jean Paul Gaultier?"

Bill shook his head.

"You'll get nowhere with this," Betty said. "He has enough trouble remembering our grandchildren's names, let alone a fashion designer's."

"I'll have you know, woman," Bill defended himself, "my brain is as sharp today as it was…" But his voice faded rapidly, as a nasty coughing fit took over.

Betty rushed to his side to comfort him as he tried to regain his breath.

"Perhaps we'd better go," I said, worrying we'd pushed Bill too far with all our questions.

Bill held up his hand. "Just…wait…a moment…will you?"

Betty rubbed Bill on the back. "He gets like this occasionally," she said. "Takes him a few minutes to recover."

Sean and I stood awkwardly in the room waiting, as Bill's breathing slowly returned to normal.

"I'm sorry about that," he said at last. "This damn flu's taken me real bad, it has. And I'm sorry I can't remember this fella's name that your mother went to work for either, but it was definitely her, I'm certain of it. You really are the spit of her, dear. Be in no doubt of that."

I smiled at him. "Thank you anyway, Bill—and you, Betty, you've been a great help, really you have."

"Any time, dear," Betty said. "You'll let us know if you find her, won't you? I'll be wondering about it now—how you've got on and all."

"Of course I will," I said, smiling at them both. "Now we should really go. No, please, don't get up, Betty—really, we'll see ourselves out. Thank you both again."

We left Bill and Betty sitting together in their front room,

Bill still in his armchair and Betty perched on the arm, lovingly tucking his blanket back around him.

"Well, that's that then," I said as we let ourselves out into the cold afternoon air. I pulled my coat tightly around me as we began to walk back to the tube station.

"What do you mean?" Sean asked in astonishment, pausing from tapping the buttons on his BlackBerry. "I'm just working out when we'll be able to get a flight to New York."

I stopped abruptly and stared at him. "I can't just drop everything and fly to New York!"

"Why not?" Sean asked, turning back to me.

"Because...I can't afford it, for one thing."

"I'll pay."

"No, I can't let you do that. It wouldn't be right."

Sean raised his eyebrows. "Don't be silly, Scarlett—I want to help."

"Why?" I demanded.

"Why do I want to help you?"

"Yeah, what's in all this for you?"

I knew I was being overly cynical and incredibly ungrateful. But Sean's constant generosity of spirit and of wallet bothered me. Or had I just spent far too long living with David's double-knotted purse strings?

Sean shrugged, tucking his phone away in the back pocket of his jeans. "Why does there have to be something in it for me? Can't I just help out a friend?"

I folded my arms and looked quizzically at him. "So we're friends now, are we? When did that happen?"

Sean grinned. "Maybe we did find each other a tad irritating at first—neither of us can deny that." He paused, and his expression changed. "But now…"

"Now?" I repeated. I half expected one of Sean's wisecracks but instead he just looked at me. He wasn't grinning anymore.

"Now, Scarlett, I—"

My mobile phone rang now. "Sorry," I said, hurriedly reaching into my bag. I looked at the name flashing on the screen. "I'd better take this. I'll just be a minute, I promise."

As I flipped open my phone cover, Sean closed his eyes and sighed.

"Maddie, hi."

While I spoke briefly to Maddie about how everything was going in London (well, it was a brief phone call for us—only five minutes long), I watched Sean. He had wandered a little way away from me while I spoke—well, Maddie spoke mainly—and now seemed deep in thought.

"Sorry about that," I said when I finally got Maddie off the phone. "That was my best friend. Anyway, before—you were saying?"

"It wasn't important," Sean said, smiling at me. "I was just going to say that your idiosyncrasies—shall we call them—don't annoy me quite as much now as when I first met you."

"Thanks," I said, pulling a wry face. "I'll take that as a compliment—I think." But I desperately wanted to know what he was really going to say before Maddie phoned. I'd never seen Sean look at me quite like that before—and I think I liked it.

"Now, about New York—" Sean began.

"I've told you—I can't just drop everything and fly over to the States."

"And I've told *you*, I'll pay."

"I know and that's incredibly generous of you, Sean, but it's not just that. That phone call is one of the reasons—actually, Maddie is. She's getting married on Saturday, and tomorrow night is her hen night."

"Oh, I see. Wait, isn't Maddie your friend from Stratford who got you the house-sitting gig?"

I nodded. "Yes, she's the one."

"But I thought the idea was to get away from all your family and friends for a month?"

"It is, but the wedding is different. It's been planned for ages. I can't miss it. Anyway, I'm chief bridesmaid."

"Oh right," Sean said, trying to take all this in. "So this Maddie is having her hen party the night before the wedding?" he asked, looking surprised. "She's asking for trouble, isn't she?"

"Ah, you see there's a bit more to it than that." *When wasn't there with Maddie?* "They're getting married at Disneyland Paris. Both the hen and stag nights are being held on Friday night, and then the wedding is in Sleeping Beauty's castle the next day."

"I'm sorry," Sean said, holding his hands up in front of him in a "time out" gesture. "Just hold on one moment. They're getting married in *Disneyland*? And I thought my family's *Star Wars* wedding was bad enough! I didn't even know you could get married there."

"You can't normally. But they both worked there a number of years ago; they met during one of the parades, when Felix was playing Aladdin, and Maddie, Princess Jasmine. They were on top of the magic carpet together and they've been inseparable ever since. The funny thing is, Maddie would never have got the job if her father hadn't performed surgery on one of the major Disney shareholders—apparently he saved his life on the operating table—and he's felt indebted to Maddie's dad ever since. The job, and now the wedding, is his way of repaying him."

Sean stood open-mouthed. Then he shook his head. "Just when I think you can't tell me anything else that will surprise me, Scarlett, you manage to. That story is madness."

"I know—but it's true. Anyway, we're all meeting in Paris tomorrow night for a joint stag and hen do—well, I think the first part is joint. From what I know they're opening up all the rides for us when the park closes to the public—it closes earlier in the winter, apparently—and then later on we're splitting up into two parties at two different venues."

"It all sounds excellent fun. It's certainly unusual."

"It always is with Maddie—she's like that." I paused as a thought began to form in my head. Then, without thinking it through, I allowed the thought to spill right out into speech. "Hey, why don't you come?" I blurted out. "I'm sure one more won't make a difference. I can clear it with Maddie first if you like, but she's usually pretty laid back about these things."

Sean looked thrilled at my suggestion. "I'd love to—it will make up for me dragging you to my family wedding. Wait, we don't have to dress as Disney characters, do we?"

"No, thank God. It's just the usual wedding attire. Although being chief bridesmaid I do have a pretty amazing dress to wear."

"I'm sure you'd look amazing whatever you wore." Sean smiled at me. "I'd love to be your escort for the day."

My stomach began the usual gymnastics routine it always

started when Sean smiled at me now. But instead of completing the parallel bars with a perfect score like it usually did, it flopped and fell like a lead balloon when he mentioned the word "escort."

"Oh," I said flatly.

"What's wrong?"

"I forgot one thing—David."

Sean's face fell, almost as far as my stomach. "Ah...yes, that could be tricky. I guess *he's* probably expecting to be your escort to the wedding—and rightly so, of course. No worries, Scarlett, I'll just see you after the weekend. It will give me time to sort those flights out, get some paperwork done, that kind of thing."

I could have kicked myself. How could I forget about David?

The annoying thing was I just knew Sean would enjoy Disneyland so much more than David. David would moan about the rides setting off his motion sickness and the weather being too cold and how expensive everything was. And if he came straight from work on Friday night like he was planning to, he'd probably turn up to ride the rollercoasters in a suit and tie.

"Come anyway," I said on impulse. "I don't think David is coming until Saturday anyway—scary rides aren't really his thing—and...I believe he has an important meeting Friday and can't get away in time to get a flight."

"You're sure?" Sean asked, his elated expression returning. "I mean I wouldn't be imposing?"

"No—of course not." I put my arm companionably through his. "It would be great to have you there, Sean."

And for the first time, I genuinely meant it.

Sixteen

Luckily for me, as it turned out, David really couldn't make it to Paris until Saturday, and oddly enough for the exact same reason as I'd told Sean.

"I'm so sorry," David said when I spoke to him on the phone later that day. "This is a really important meeting. Are you sure you'll be all right on your own?"

"I won't be on my own," I said, thanking my lucky stars I didn't have to use any of the weird and wonderful excuses I'd come up with to prevent him arriving for the partying on Friday night. "I know loads of the people who'll be in Paris."

"Yes, I know that. But I meant I haven't seen you for over two weeks, and I'm looking forward to us spending some time together again and hearing all about what you've been getting up to while you've been away."

"It's fine, David, really. I'm sure I'll be able to find some way of keeping myself amused until you get there."

We all gathered at the end of Main Street USA, waiting for the kickoff. We'd been arriving at Disneyland Paris in dribs and drabs all day. Some guests like Sean and me had flown in, but the majority of revelers had arrived by Eurostar about two hours ago. Now, after most of us had already spent the last hour in the bar of the Disneyland hotel, we were getting instructions on where we could go and what we were allowed to do for the next two hours.

"...and at 9 p.m. we will meet back here. Then we can separate into hens and stags and all go off to our own individual parties," Maddie finished reading from her sheet of paper. "And can I remind everyone that tonight's festivities are a huge favor to Felix and myself. So please enjoy yourselves, but don't do anything silly or reckless, will you? If you must tie Felix up and strip him down to his undies—at least wait until you're out of Mickey and Minnie's sight!"

There were a few polite chuckles from the assembled guests.

"So, what are we all waiting for?" Maddie announced, holding up her arms in dramatic fashion. "Let's go party!"

Everyone quickly dispersed into the park, eagerly heading toward the ride they wanted to attempt first.

"So, what do you fancy?" Sean asked me. "Space Mountain, the Indiana Jones ride?"

"Erm..." I wasn't really that keen on rollercoasters. Being spun through 360 degrees while traveling at breakneck speed until you felt sick wasn't *my* idea of fun. "I don't know. Shall we see what we come to first?"

"Righty-ho then," Sean said, in his usual relaxed way.

We wandered into Frontierland. This area, full of timber buildings and Indian tepees, was designed to look like the Wild West.

"Oh, this is the bit that has Big Thunder Mountain," Sean cried enthusiastically. "Come on!"

I had to smile. While we wandered around looking for the Big Thunder Mountain railroad, Sean was just like a big kid—his eyes darting excitedly to and fro, taking in everything and everyone. When we eventually found the ride, Sean almost ran through the turnstiles.

I hung back.

"Come on, Red," he called, turning around when he found I wasn't beside him. "What's up? You're not *scared*, are you?"

"No!"

"Well, come on then."

I cautiously followed him through the entrance. We walked past a sign that stated a one-hour waiting time from this point; a bit further on there was a 45-minute one, and then a 30-minute one followed.

Do people seriously queue this long for this sort of torture? I wondered, as I followed Sean along the path.

"Isn't it great we don't have to queue for any of these rides?" Sean said happily when I caught him up. "We can ride them as many times as we like!"

I'm pretty sure once will be enough for me, I thought as I watched the last train rattle and roll its way around the mountain like a high-speed wooden corkscrew.

At last we found our way to the top, where we stood and waited with a couple of Felix's friends for the "runaway" train to arrive.

"I'm sensing you're not too keen on this kind of thing," Sean said as we stood in silence.

"It's not my favorite way of spending a Friday night, no."

"You'll be fine. This isn't one of those really scary rollercoasters anyway—it's just a baby one."

When the train drew up and we were seated, huge metal harnesses descended into our laps—presumably in case we should come to our senses and want to get off again. This always worried me about these types of ride: if they had to strap you in, it meant you were going to travel fast enough to fall out.

But I didn't have time to worry about that. The train suddenly whizzed off up the track toward a tunnel. The next four minutes were sheer hell, as we hurtled up, down, and around a rickety mountain railroad track. The only thing that made it half bearable was Sean's hand reaching out and holding mine when we had just got to the peak of a long mountain climb and were about to plunge to our doom down the other side.

When at last we screeched to a halt in the station, Sean released my hand while we quickly climbed out of the train, allowing the next group of fools waiting to ride to take our places.

"So, how bad was that?" Sean asked, grinning at me.

"Bad enough."

"Hey, you're shaking," he said. "Goodness, you *really* don't like rides, do you?"

It was true, I was shaking, but that may have been more to do with Sean's hand-holding than the actual ride itself.

"Here," he said, reaching into his back pocket. "Try some of this." He pulled out a hip flask and poured a tot of something into the lid. "It's whiskey. Go on, get it down you."

"How have you got this? I thought Maddie said we weren't allowed alcohol in here."

"All the stags have them. Felix's best man passed them out earlier."

"You mean Will?"

"Yes, that's the chap."

I opened my bag and pulled out a mini bottle of champagne. "And all us hens have got these!" I laughed. "Want to swap?"

"Nah, but you can still have the whiskey. I already had a fair bit to drink in the bar earlier."

I'd noticed. But I swigged the whiskey back anyway and gasped as it caught the back of my throat.

"Where to now?" Sean asked.

"What about that house thing over there?"

"You mean Phantom Manor? You sure you won't be scaaarrred?" he tried to say in a spooky voice.

"As long as it doesn't loop the loop at a hundred miles an hour, I'll be just fine, thank you."

There were a number of us "visiting" the manor, and the hospitality was very good as even more secret bottles were passed around in the waiting room before the main journey began around the supposedly haunted mansion. The purpose of this ride, I quickly discovered, was to unravel the mystery of a ghost bride who waited for her groom in vain. The spooky walls and pictures were supposed to recount their grisly tale, as you rode along in carriages called "Doombuggies."

Can I count this as my third wedding? I wondered, watching the story of a marriage ceremony that never took place slowly unfold.

Sean and I had somehow got split up in the haunted house at the start of the ride, so I ended up sitting next to one of the girls Maddie worked with. But as we spun around the manor in our two-person Doombuggy, in between the ghosts and ghouls that popped up in our faces, I managed to catch sight of him a few times, and on one occasion he saw me watching him and winked.

"Oh, I'm sorry," the girl sitting next to me said. "I didn't realize that was your boyfriend or I'd have let the two of you sit together."

"No, not at all, please don't worry," I said a bit too hastily. "He's not my boyfriend."

"Is he anyone's boyfriend, do you know?" she asked, as the ride came to an end and we prepared to hop off. "He's quite good looking."

I pretended I hadn't heard her and hurried over to join Sean again as soon as I'd freed myself from the ride. "Let's go this way," I said, swiftly steering him in the opposite direction to my traveling companion.

We found ourselves walking toward Fantasyland. "This is the kiddies' bit," Sean said, and I noticed he was having trouble walking in a straight line. "Although after seeing you on Big Thunder Mountain back there, this might be more up your street."

"Stop with the teasing, you," I said, pleased we seemed to have lost Sean's admirer. "This is what Disney is all about."

"You are *not* getting me on one of those elephants," Sean exclaimed as we approached the flying Dumbo ride. "No way!"

"I wouldn't want to—strange as it may seem, flying elephants aren't really my scene either."

"Ah, I know what you'd like," he said, a grin spreading across his face. "Come with me."

Sean, for the second time tonight, grabbed hold of my hand, and I willingly let him lead me toward a sign that declared *It's a Small World*.

"Now this ride isn't scary at all," Sean said as we walked together along a pastel-colored path toward the entrance. "Unless you've seen the *Child's Play* movies—which I very much doubt you have—because then the dolls can take on a whole different light."

"We can't go on this," I protested. "We're too old."

Sean paused by the entrance, his eyes wide in mock horror as he turned to look at me. "No one's too old for Disney, Red—as you so rightly pointed out back there. Come on, it'll be fun," he said, holding out his hand to me again. "There's no one riding it just now."

"No, because they're all over ten years old, that's why."

But I took Sean's hand and we climbed onto one of the small boats that was trundling along in the water and allowed ourselves to be transported into the magical miniature world.

Inside the ride was split into countries, and in each country there were displays of animatronic dolls. The dolls were dressed in their national costumes performing activities fitting to their native country, and they were singing the intensely catchy theme tune of "It's a Small World After All."

"How much did you say you'd had to drink?" I asked Sean, as he began to hum the tune quietly to himself as we rode along. This was shortly after he'd downed the remains of his hip flask.

"Not that much, why?"

"Nothing." I smirked.

"Look here," Sean said, putting on an intensely serious face. "Just because this isn't one of your big budget Hollywood movies entertaining you doesn't mean you can be snooty." He waved his hand in the direction of the passing display. "Those poor dolls are singing their hearts out up there."

I bit my lip and tried not to laugh. Sean was quite funny when he was drunk.

"Right, if they aren't enough entertainment for you, let's create our own movie moment, right here and right now." Sean tried to stand up in the boat.

"Sean, sit down—you might fall."

"No—I'm fine," he said, steadying himself. "Hey, Red, come to the front with me, and we'll act out that scene from *Titanic*—you know the one, where Leo holds on to Kate."

Tempting as it was to see myself as Kate Winslet and add to my tally of films, my better sense kicked in. "We'll do nothing of the sort. Sit down, Sean, or you'll fall and hurt yourself."

Sean clambered right up on the front of the boat, then, wobbling with his arms outstretched, he shouted, "I'm king of the world! Look, Red, I've done a movie for your collection."

"Yes, you certainly have. But I'm afraid it's much more Hugh Grant in *Bridget Jones* than Leonardo DiCaprio in *Titanic*. Now get down from there before you—"

Too late. As we passed under a low bridge, Sean's head collided with it and he was knocked sideways into the water.

The line of boats continued on their merry way.

"Sean!" I shouted when he didn't immediately reappear. "Oh my God, where are you?"

I clambered back along all the boats until I came to the last one in the line. As we passed under the bridge where Sean had fallen, I looked helplessly down into the water.

"Sean!" I called again.

Just then a head bobbed up, and Sean emerged blowing a fountain of water from his mouth.

"Oh my God, Sean, I thought you'd passed out under the water. Quick," I said, holding out my hand. "Climb back on."

Sean shook his head, pushed his hair back off his face, and waded along through the water until he'd caught the boat up again. Then somehow while the boat was still moving, I managed to help him climb back aboard.

"What happened to you?" I asked, moving one seat ahead of him as he dripped water everywhere.

"I got caught in between the rails. I had to stay under the water while the boats went over the top of me." He looked embarrassed.

"Jesus, Sean, that could have been dangerous. What the hell were you thinking?"

"I didn't plan to fall in." He rubbed the back of his head and winced.

"Does it hurt?" I asked.

"What do you reckon?"

"All right, it wasn't me that was stupid enough to injure myself at Disneyland Paris on 'It's a Small World.'" My mouth twitched with amusement. "And when you think of all the ways you could get hurt on the more dangerous rides too. Your heroic story will now always be—'I nearly drowned in a three-foot-deep dolls' lake.'"

Sean pulled a wry face as I held my hand over my mouth in a vain attempt not to laugh.

"Do we have to tell anyone about this?" he asked. "I mean, no one need know."

"I think people might notice when you turn up soaking wet for the party later."

"I'll just go back and change at the hotel."

"You've got to get there first without anyone seeing you."

The ride came to an end and I began to climb out.

"Scarlett," Sean pleaded, still sitting in the boat with water pouring off him. "Help me, please!"

"Oh, so I'm not Red now then?" I asked, standing on the side looking down at him with my arms folded.

Sean just looked up at me with big puppy-dog eyes. "Please, Scarlett," he said again. "I need you."

Seventeen

"Nearly there," I whispered to Sean, as I guided him out of the lift and along the corridor. "Where's your key?" I asked as we reached his room.

"In my jeans pocket," came back his muffled reply.

I felt inside his wet denims that I'd been carrying in my arms across the park, pulled out the key card, and let us both into his room.

"Phew," I said, dropping his damp clothes on the floor. "I didn't think we'd make it."

"Do you think anyone noticed?" Sean asked, pulling off Goofy's head.

I laughed. "Of course they noticed—you're just lucky no one stopped and asked you for a photo."

"I mean they didn't know it was me?"

"I doubt it. But you have to get this costume back to that guy first thing tomorrow or he'll lose his job."

"But gain €300!"

"You're getting €100 of that back on safe return of his costume, that was the deal."

"Hmm, about that, couldn't you have found something

a bit cooler for me to disguise myself in than a seven-foot Goofy costume?"

"Are you kidding?" I said, flopping on the bed. "It was Goofy or nothing. You're just lucky he was still on site; all the other characters have gone home."

"Yeah I know. Thanks for helping me."

"It's OK. It was worth it just to see you dressed like that." I grinned. "Who would have thought it, Mr. Sean 'I hate movies' Bond dressed as Goofy! What would your dad say if he knew? After all the stick you gave him at the wedding for dressing as Chewbacca too!"

Sean struggled with the suit. "Are you just going to lie there mocking me all night, or are you going to help unzip me from this thing?"

I tilted my head to one side as if I was considering it. "All right, all right, I'm coming," I said when Goofy's paws rested on his hips. I stood up again and undid the hidden zip at the back of the costume. "There you go, free again."

Sean stepped out of Goofy's body wearing just his underpants—I'd forgotten he wasn't wearing anything else. Maurice—who had originally been wearing Goofy when we found him—had been wearing leggings and a T-shirt when he'd stepped out of the suit. I'd been keeping watch outside the men's toilets while Maurice helped Sean zip himself back inside Goofy before we made our escape across the park.

I looked away—but not before I noticed what an extremely fine body Sean had. I'd realized he wasn't exactly overweight when I'd seen him wearing T-shirts and jeans. But in the flesh—boy, did he scrub up well. He wasn't overly muscular, but he was toned, and there were reasonably-sized bulges in all the places there should be.

"So what sort of view do you get from your window?" I hastily asked, going over to it and looking outside.

"Er, probably one much like yours," Sean said as he went into the bathroom. "I'll just take a shower to warm me up a bit—that water was bloody freezing."

"It's a good job you fell in near Australia, then," I called, "and not the North Pole!"

"Yes, yes, very funny!"

I turned away from the window now that it was safe to look back in the room again and sat down on the bed. I thought about what had happened tonight. Sean had been lucky; the accident could have been much more serious. He should probably put something cold on his head, or he'd have a huge bump in the morning.

I picked up the phone and called down to reception, asking if we could have either an ice pack or a bowl of ice. The receptionist said she'd see what she could do.

"Calling us some room service?" Sean asked, emerging from the bathroom. This time he had only a white towel wrapped around his middle and his damp skin glistened with tiny droplets of water.

I swallowed hard.

Sean opened up his wardrobe and pulled out a white shirt and blue jeans.

"Well?" he asked, turning to face me.

"Oh…er, no…I was just asking if they had an ice pack we could use. You should put something cold on your head—where you banged it."

"Are you worried about me, then?" he asked, grinning.

My stomach had long ago given up its gymnastic routine. It had now moved up a gear—to another Olympic sport—and was currently involved in a thrill-providing, super-fast bobsled race.

"You did bang your head pretty hard."

Sean gently touched the back of his head. "Ouch." He winced. "Yep, it's still there."

"Let me take a look. You didn't cut it open, did you? I haven't seen any blood. But you never know."

I wished I'd waited until after he got dressed to ask him that, as Sean sat down beside me on the bed, still wearing only the towel.

I stood up and very gently moved his damp hair about on the back of his head. A small moan escaped from Sean's mouth.

"I'm sorry, did I hurt you?"

"No...no, not at all." Sean tilted his head back to look up at me. He had that look in his eyes again—the same one he had on the first day we met and sat on the park bench in Notting Hill. The same one he had when he came to ask me to go to the opera with him and found me in my bathrobe. And the same one he had outside Bill's house, just before he was going to tell me something.

My hand still rested on the top of his head. But it was now stroking, rather than just moving Sean's hair around.

Sean took hold of my hand—he looked at it for a moment before he gently began to trace the lines along my palm with his finger.

"Scarlett," he whispered, his voice husky and low. "Oh,

Scarlett," he sighed. Then he looked up at me again, his eyes telling me everything his voice could not.

There was a knock at the door and we both jumped. "That will be your ice!" I said in an overly bright voice, quickly pulling my hand away.

I don't think the night porter had ever seen anyone quite so pleased to hear him knocking at their door, as I grinned inanely at him like a bizarre mix of Jack Nicholson in *Batman* and the Cheshire Cat on speed.

"Your ice pack, madam," he said.

"Thank you…" I looked at Sean; he was already up and producing a note from his wallet.

"Much obliged, Joseph," he said, handing the porter the money.

"If there's anything else, sir…madam, don't hesitate to call, will you?" He glanced briefly at the bed, and I realized Goofy's head was still lying there. Quickly I moved in front of it.

"We will," Sean said. "Thank you again, Joseph. Good night."

"Good evening, Sir."

Sean closed the door and turned to look at me. "I guess I'd better use this," he said, holding up the ice pack. "It's suddenly got extremely hot in here—I could do with cooling off a bit."

You're not the only one, Sean, I thought as I tried to steady my breathing again. *Believe me, you're not the only one.*

Eighteen

By the time Sean had held the ice pack on his head for a while and had finally put on some clothes, it was 9 p.m. and time to meet up with the others again. There had been no mention of what had nearly happened on the bed earlier, and I was relieved.

We split up into two parties and departed to our allotted venues to spend the rest of the night participating in activities deemed suitable only for persons of our own gender.

I was happily sitting at a table alone downing the last of a bottle of champagne while the other girls were doing some sort of boat dance on the floor, when Maddie swayed over in my direction. She was wearing Minnie Mouse ears, a veil, and L-plates pinned to her front and back.

"Why are you sitting on your own up here?" she asked, slurring her words slightly.

"Because I've seen enough boats for one night."

Maddie furrowed her brow. "What do you mean? I didn't go on any boats. Oh, the paddle steamer wasn't running, was it? Did they start it up and I missed it?"

"No, not the paddle steamer, don't worry about it, Mad—it's nothing."

Maddie draped her arm around me. "I can't be having my chief bridesmaid sitting up here all alone moping, can I? Now tell me how you're getting on house-sitting for Belinda—I've barely heard from you since you left for London."

I told Maddie as much as I thought her sozzled brain could take on board about what I'd been up to since I arrived in Notting Hill. I was deliberately selective in what I chose to tell her—mainly about the new friends I'd met, and how "coincidentally" and "maybe it was something to do with living in Notting Hill," things that happened in movies just seemed to keep happening to me. I left out the part about my mother—that was too complicated to explain to someone who'd had as much to drink as Maddie had tonight. I was glad the wedding wasn't until Saturday evening—at least she would have enough time to sleep off her hangover tomorrow.

When I'd finished, Maddie was strangely quiet while she took another long drink from her glass of...just what *was* in that purple concoction she was drinking?

I watched the girls on the dance floor who were now trying to do the Macarena while Maddie apparently gathered her thoughts.

"Sean seems nice," she suddenly said after a few minutes, as she casually stirred the umbrella around in her cocktail.

I looked hard at Maddie. What did she mean by that comment? Nice in regard to what? Or was it just a throwaway observation? The state Maddie was in it could mean anything. It was hard to tell.

I decided to play it cool. "Yeah, he's OK."

"Remind me again—just why *is* he here with you this weekend?"

"I told you, he's Belinda and Harry's neighbor in Notting Hill, he's been helping me get to know the area—and stuff."

"I wouldn't mind him helping me out with my *stuff* any day!" Maddie cackled, then she winked at me, "There's a definite look of Brad Pitt about him."

"Maddie! You're getting married tomorrow!"

"And you are getting married in April, Scarlett, but you've still brought another man to my wedding!"

I looked at Maddie again. Was she as drunk as she was making out? She was making some very telling observations for one so under the influence of alcohol.

"No, I haven't," I said defensively. "David arrives tomorrow morning, as you well know."

"Yes, that's right, so he does." Maddie thought for a moment. "That's good because tomorrow at the wedding, I'm going to try and set Danielle up with Sean. You met her earlier—she said she was sitting next to you on the Phantom Manor ride. Anyway, Sean is single, isn't he? Because Danielle was asking about him. Danielle has been single far too long, and I reckon Sean looks the type who wouldn't mind a quick shag after the ceremony tomorrow."

"Maddie, no! Don't you dare!"

Maddie looked at me innocently with wide eyes. "Why not? After all if he's *only* your temporary neighbor, what's it to you?"

"OK, what's in that drink?" I demanded.

"What—this?" Maddie held up her glass.

"Yes, that. It's not alcoholic, is it?"

Maddie leaned in toward me. "Do you think I'm stupid enough to get hammered the night before my own wedding?

It's the biggest day of my life—and I'm damned if I'm walking down the aisle looking like death warmed up."

"Have you had *any* alcohol tonight?"

"A couple of glasses of champagne at the start of the evening, that's all. This is just blackcurrant and lemonade. The others think it's vodka Zulu, but I've had an arrangement with the barman all night—under no circumstances is he to put any alcohol in my drinks. Everyone thinks I'm pissed—but sadly, on this occasion, no."

I grinned at Maddie. "You are one crafty cookie, madam."

"And you are one very mixed-up chief bridesmaid." Maddie put down her drink and looked at me seriously. "I did *see* you and Sean together earlier, Scarlett."

"So?"

"So, I saw you laugh more times with Sean tonight than I think I've ever seen you laugh in all your time with David."

"But I love David."

"I know you do. So be careful, Scarlett. Don't let this time-out, house-sitting thing—if that's what you're really doing in London—completely screw your life up."

"What do you mean?"

"I mean, you love David and you want to marry David—but you've been having a few doubts, you told me as much. Then just when you're in the middle of this carefree, living-in-a-movie-type lifestyle that you've always wanted, Sean comes along. He's like this big, handsome movie hero you've always dreamed about meeting, but while you're away living your perfect fantasy life, you're forgetting about the people left behind."

"No, I'm not." I didn't know how Maddie could even think

that. "I just want to be happy, that's all, and to prove Dad, David, and you, for that matter, wrong about the movies." I clapped my hand over my mouth. *Damn it.*

"Oh, so that's what you're really up to, is it?" Maddie said, raising an eyebrow. "I knew there was something else going on."

"Maddie, that's not important now," I said, quickly trying to gloss over my blunder. Plus I had to clear up this other misunderstanding first. "I don't see Sean as a movie star—that's just silly." Maybe I had in the past, but I wasn't lying to Maddie now; it was ages since I'd imagined Sean as anything but himself. I found it virtually impossible to do that now. "He's just a bit different to David, that's all. Sean's....." A smile crept across my face as I thought about him. "He's fun and spontaneous and generous, and, well—he's everything David isn't."

"Including *yours*," Maddie finished for me. "Scarlett, you don't want to be in love—not in the conventional sense anyway. You want to be in love in the movies."

"And what's wrong with that?" I started to say, and then I stopped. "Wait a minute, that's familiar."

"What is?"

"What you just said. Say it again."

"Which bit—you don't want to be in love, you want to be in love in the movies?"

"Yeah, that bit." I rested my head in my hands. "Oh, it's on the tip of my tongue..."

"What on earth are you doing?" Maddie asked, watching me.

"*Sleepless in Seattle*!" I exclaimed, hitting the palm of my hand on the table. "It's from *Sleepless in Seattle*. Meg Ryan's best friend says it to her when they're watching *An Affair to Remember* on TV."

"Wait, is that the one with Cary Grant and…" Maddie paused. "Oh, who's the woman?"

"Deborah Kerr."

"That's it, and he asks her to meet him on top of the Empire State Building on Valentine's Day, and she can't get there because she's ill or something?"

"Disabled," I said, thinking about the movie. "*Sleepless in Seattle* is a similar story. I love both of them."

Maddie shook her head. "You've got *me* at it now! What was I saying before you went off into one of your movie rants?"

"That I only want to be in love in a movie?"

"Yes, yes, that's right. But what I'm really saying, Scarlett, is don't ruin what you've got back home in the real world with some pipe dream that you *really* can live your life like it's a movie—because you can't. This house-sitting in Notting Hill was just a bit of fun, really—I suggested it because I thought it might do you good to get away for a while, to clear your head, that kind of thing. But now I'm beginning to wonder if I did the right thing…" She paused as she took my hand in hers. "Scarlett, please be careful. People get hurt in *real* life; in a movie they just exit stage left."

"Thanks for your concern, Maddie," I said, part of me knowing she was right. I did need to be more careful about Sean. "I appreciate it, really I do. But I'm not intending to let anyone exit from my life—stage left or any other way." I drew my hand away from hers. "But as for me not living my life in a movie, I beg to differ with you—and Dad and David too—because since I've been away, I'm already proving that I can, quite easily, and no one is getting hurt."

Nineteen

I stood in the foyer of the hotel with the other bridesmaids, awaiting Maddie's arrival. We were wearing long, purple satin evening gowns, with matching purple stoles to keep us warm in the cold night air. We didn't really look like bridesmaids. The dresses were so elegant we could have been off to some glitzy party, had we not all been wearing exactly the same design.

I stifled a yawn—it had been a long day already, in more ways than one.

The day had started early when the local experts Maddie had hired arrived to do our hair, then our nails, and finally our makeup.

Then we'd hung about eating snacks and drinking a few glasses of champagne (purely medicinal, Maddie had insisted) until the time had finally arrived—about an hour ago—for us to put on our dresses. Since then, we'd been standing around, first in Maddie's room and then in the foyer of the hotel, trying not to get them creased. Now we were awaiting the horse-drawn carriages that were to take us to the ceremony being held in Sleeping Beauty's castle.

But there was a second reason it had seemed a long day.

David had arrived at about one o'clock, and so I'd had to spend any free time I did have in between hair and beauty appointments with him.

He'd been very attentive to me as always, and when he wasn't on his mobile phone making business calls, he spent the time filling me in on everything he'd got completed on the house while I'd been away.

But David was also keen to hear exactly what I'd been doing too. So just like I had with Maddie last night, I managed to spin him a fairly sporadic yet truthful tale of my time in Notting Hill.

I hadn't spoken to Sean all day.

I had seen him a few times, but only through a window pacing around the courtyard outside, and each time, like David, he'd been talking or texting on his BlackBerry.

At last Maddie appeared down in the foyer wearing a shimmering ivory silk gown. It was long and fitted with an embroidered bodice, organza sleeves, and a skirt that had the tiniest of trains that just kicked out at the bottom, making it look like a baby mermaid's tail. The majority of her strawberry-blonde hair hung loose around her shoulders, but one side of it was pinned up away from her face with a mother-of-pearl hair comb, adding to the mermaid effect. A round of applause broke out from some of the other guests that were staying in the hotel as she walked toward us, radiating joy and elegance. "You look beautiful," I said, going over to her. "Felix will be so proud when you appear, he'll burst!"

"I hope not," Maddie said, smiling. "I don't think we're insured for that!"

I laughed, that was more like the Maddie I knew.

"You scrub up pretty well yourself in that dress, Miss Scarlett. Your two beaus will be dueling at dawn when they see you."

"Stop it—don't be daft, I only have one beau here, and that's David."

"We'll see," Maddie said knowingly.

"Scarlett, our carriage is here," one of my fellow bridesmaids called from the doorway.

"Coming," I replied. "Good luck," I said to Maddie, giving her a hug while at the same time trying not to crease her. "And above all, enjoy it, won't you?"

"I will," she said. "Or is that I do?"

It was 7 p.m. as we left the hotel and there were still a few people in the park, either enjoying the rides before they closed up for the night or buying their last few souvenirs of the day. As we rode through Main Street USA in our horse-drawn carriages I think some of them thought there might be another parade beginning as they stood back to view our procession.

I felt a bit like royalty as I waved from my ornate gold and red carriage at the passing crowds. I glanced back at Maddie; she also looked as if she was thoroughly enjoying herself, as she and her father rode along in the carriage behind us toward Sleeping Beauty's castle.

The castle was illuminated against the night sky in delicate shades of pink and purple. This iconic symbol of Disney almost didn't seem real as it lit up everything that surrounded it. It looked just like a giant birthday cake—the roofs of its pink iced turrets could have been glistening and sparkling with frosting instead of hundreds of tiny twinkling lights.

We pulled up in front of the castle—which had been closed especially for the ceremony—and alighted from our carriages as elegantly as we could. A few photos were taken of us outside, and then finally it was time to go in.

We walked through a guard of honor made up of Disney characters on our way up to the entrance. There was Mickey, Minnie, Donald, and Daisy; in fact, all the characters seemed to be lining Maddie's route into the castle—all except Goofy. There was a gap where he should have stood. I made a mental note to check with Sean later that he'd remembered to return the costume to Maurice.

Surprisingly, the decor inside the castle actually made it look like a tiny, round church. There were huge, bright, stained-glass windows depicting various scenes from "Sleeping Beauty," and an upper gallery all the way around the inside perimeter of the wall. This created a viewing area for the guests, from which they could watch the ceremony take place below. The priest, Felix, and Will stood waiting for the bridal procession to arrive. Felix looked extremely handsome in his black tuxedo, white shirt, and black bow tie. I was surprised it suited him so well, because Felix wasn't the sort of man to dress formally, let alone in a full dinner suit. It was a shame the same couldn't be said for his best man. Will looked like a lanky Charlie Chaplin in his baggy suit and lopsided bow tie. All he needed was a bowler hat and his outfit would have been complete.

Once Maddie had made her grand entrance and we were all

inside, the castle seemed even smaller with everyone huddled so closely together, but that made the unique setting all the more intimate and romantic.

The ceremony was traditional, with a few personal twists from the bride and groom. When it came to exchanging rings, as a joke after their real rings had been exchanged, Felix gave Maddie a huge plastic ring with Tinkerbell on it, and Maddie gave Felix a similar ring, but with Sulley from *Monsters, Inc.* grinning up at him instead. They had written their own vows, and it moved me to tears when Maddie recited hers to Felix. She used their magic carpet connection as an analogy through-out, talking about ups and downs, the need to hold each other tight, and how they were just starting out on another new jour-ney into the unknown together.

During one of the hymns—which I was glad to hear were the traditional arrangements and not cheery Disney versions—I glanced up at the viewing gallery and spotted Sean. He winked at me, and I smiled back.

I looked a bit further around the circle and saw David too—but he wasn't looking down at me, he was peering with a puz-zled expression across the gallery, at Sean.

The whole ceremony managed to go without a hitch. Both parties said "I do" in all the right places, and not too many people laughed when Felix revealed that his middle name was Archibald. When we left the intimate setting of the castle and returned to the Disneyland hotel for the reception, everyone was in high spirits.

It then became time for that dreadful wedding tradition—when as a guest you have to congratulate all the immediate family of the bride and groom and say things like, "You must be very proud" or "You look lovely in that dress." (I've always found that particular one is best saved for female members of the wedding party—unless of course you go to much more forward-thinking weddings than I do.)

But today in my role as chief bridesmaid I found myself in the unusual position of being on the receiving end of the comments. Unfortunately, by the time most of the guests got to me they'd run out of things to say—so I got thirty-five "You look lovely," eleven "Purple really suits you," eight "You did a fine job," two "Are you Maddie's sister?" and one "Do you know where the toilet is, dear?"

As the line got ever shorter, I noticed Sean slowly moving along it in my direction.

"Having fun?" He grinned when he arrived opposite me.

"I will be just as soon as this damn line-up is over with," I said, still managing to talk through the fixed smile that constantly remained glued to my face.

Sean leaned toward me. "You look stunning, Scarlett," he whispered in my ear. "I'll try and catch up with you later on—I might have some news for you by then." Quickly he kissed my cheek and moved along to a waitress holding a tray of champagne.

"Sean, wait…" I called after him, but he'd already sauntered off into the ever-growing throng of guests.

What sort of news?

I thanked the next two people who said I'd done a good job and then I realized it was David standing in front of me.

"Great job, darling," he said. "You looked lovely—purple really suits you."

"Thanks," I said drily.

"Scarlett, you don't happen to know where the toilet is, do you, by any chance?"

After more official photos, it was at last time for some food. As it was a buffet, everyone was allowed to sit where they wanted—everyone except the main wedding party, which of course included me. I had to sit on the top table, next to the best man.

Will was OK in small doses; I'd met him before, and he was harmless enough. But by the time dinner and the speeches were over, I could have happily strangled either him or myself, depending on which I thought might bring a faster end to his never-ending drone about the joys of CB radio.

"I thought all that died out when the Internet came along," I said in a vain attempt to shut him up, or get him on to another topic of conversation.

Will looked stunned that I could even compare the two.

"There will always be a place in our hearts for CB radio, good buddy," he said, placing his hand on his heart in a dramatic gesture of allegiance.

"But don't people just use mobile phones now?"

Will sucked in his breath. "Cell phones! They are a blight on humanity! My good buddy, Transit Trev, was just telling me the other day how his..."

I was just about to bang my head on the white tablecloth in front of me when I heard my name spoken. I don't think I'd ever been so pleased to see David in my whole life.

"David!"

"I thought I'd come over and see how you were doing. Am I interrupting?" he asked, looking at Will.

"No! No, not at all," I answered before Will could say otherwise.

"Good, good. It seems the formalities are over now, so you can come and join us at our table if you'd like to?" He held his hand out toward a table in the corner of the room.

I sighed with relief. "Yes, I copy you—that's a big 10-4," I said as I stood up.

"What?"

"Sorry, I mean yes, I'd love to join you over there, David."

I turned back to Will and smiled. "Well, good buddy, you got your ears on? It's time to pull the big switch on you, I'm afraid, because this beaver is over and out!" I grabbed David before Will recovered from his shock and took up the airwaves once more, and we made our way over to the table he had been sitting at with a few of Felix's work colleagues.

"Oh my God, was I glad to see you just then," I said as David found me a chair and I sat down. I'd once sat through a marathon of trucker movies on one of the lesser-known Sky channels when I'd been off work ill one day. Who would have thought old Burt Reynolds and Clint Eastwood and his orangutan would have come in so handy one day?

"Was Will entertaining you by any chance, with tales of his CB radio?" a young chap—who I think was called Graham—asked me. "Will's always good for those."

"Was he half!" I said, as Graham poured the last remnants of a bottle of wine into a glass for me. "I think sitting next to Hannibal Lecter at dinner would have caused me less pain."

The other people around the table laughed.

"Would you like a proper drink?" David asked. "I'm just going up to the bar."

"Yes, that would be great. I'll have a large Jack Daniels, please."

I chatted with the people around the table while David was gone and then glanced around the room. The hotel staff were beginning to clear the tables, so they could arrange the room into one suitable for dancing to the band that had just arrived and were currently unpacking their instruments up on the stage.

I saw Sean standing talking to a girl who had her back to me. She laughed and when she tossed her hair over her shoulder I caught a glimpse of her face. It was Danielle.

Sean then gestured, would she like a drink? Danielle nodded, Sean took her glass from her and began to make his way toward the bar. He had to pass our table as he did so.

I tried to look like I was deeply engrossed in what the women next to me were saying. They were actually discussing the pros and cons of grocery shopping on the Internet, but I tried hard to look interested in their conversation.

"How's it going?" Sean asked, as he passed our table.

"Oh, it's you," I said, pretending to jump as I turned around.

"Having fun? I saw you got stuck next to ol' Rubber Duck over there at dinner. I met him at the stag do, interesting guy…"

"About as interesting as watching the National Lottery show without a ticket, yeah. Actually I take that back, even watching it with a ticket is bad enough!"

Sean laughed. "But at least you've escaped now. I saw David come over and rescue you. I would have done so myself but…" He looked back at Danielle.

"Yeah, I can see you've been busy."

"Here we go—one large Jack Daniels," David said, returning with our drinks. He looked with interest at Sean.

"Sean, this is David, my fiancé. David, this is Sean...er... he's my next-door neighbor in Notting Hill," I said, not being able to think of a better way of introducing him.

David put the drinks down on the table, and held out his hand to Sean. "Pleased to meet you, Sean."

"And you too, Dave," Sean said, shaking David's hand.

"Id, it's Dav-*id*."

"Of course, my mistake, sorry."

There was an awkward silence.

"Well, I'd better go and get some drinks," Sean said, holding up the empty glasses in his hands. "I'll see you later perhaps, Scarlett."

I watched him walk over to the bar before I turned back to David.

"Your neighbor?" he asked, sitting down next to me. "How does your neighbor in Notting Hill know Maddie and Felix?"

"Er...he doesn't. *I* invited him to the wedding."

"You did? Why?"

When I'd told David the little bit about what I'd been up to since I'd been in London, I'd skirted around the Sean issue by saying that the "friend" I'd met up with I'd also been "out and about" with occasionally too.

I took a deep breath and then a large gulp of my drink.

"He's the friend I was telling you about that I met in London."

"What friend?" David asked, looking puzzled for a moment. "Wait, you mean the one who you accompanied to a wedding and a dinner party *and* the opera?"

I nodded.

"But he's a man?"

"Yeah, and what of it? Are you saying that men and women can't be friends?"

Ooh, ooh, *When Harry Met Sally*, I thought excitedly—storing that one up to add to my ever-growing list of proof. But I kept the thought to myself—I didn't think now was really the time to be sharing my latest finding with David.

"No, but I mean…I just thought he was a girl, that's all."

"Nope, Sean's definitely not a girl," I said, as a vision of him emerging from the shower last night floated into my head.

"Don't be facetious with me, Scarlett, I can see that." David looked over to where Sean stood at the bar. "I saw him wink at you in the castle earlier."

"I know," I said, trying hard to focus on David again.

"And?"

"And what, David? Are you telling me that because a man winks at me it means I'm having an affair with him?"

"No, but…"

Sean walked back across the floor with two drinks in his hand. He winked at me as he passed.

I half smiled back, but then I noticed David frowning at me.

"Look, David, Sean is just a friend, I promise you, nothing more. Anyway, if I was having an affair with him do you think he'd be over there chatting up Danielle?"

David looked to where Danielle and Sean were now sitting next to each other, their heads close together as they laughed at a private joke.

I felt a twinge in my stomach. This time one of the Olympic

athletes—who had been performing their workouts with my stomach—felt like they had torn a muscle, ripped a tendon, or sustained some other career-threatening injury.

I looked away. "Well, do you?" I asked him again.

"I'm sorry," David said, taking my hands in his. "You know how jealous I get when I see you with other men."

"It's fine," I said, deliberately not looking Sean's way again. "At least I know you care."

And at this precise moment, David, for once I understand *exactly* how you're feeling...

Twenty

I tried not to watch Sean too much during the rest of the evening—but I couldn't help myself, because every time I glanced in his direction, I'd see Danielle somewhere near.

"Hey, how's it going? Are you enjoying yourself?" Maddie asked, arriving at our table just as I was staring forlornly in Sean's direction once again. "Where's David?"

I jumped. "Oh, hi, Maddie…er…he's at the bar just now. But yes, we're both having a lovely time. How about you? Is it everything you hoped it would be?"

"Yes it is, and so much more," she said joyfully. "I'm so glad all my friends are here to share this with me. I've never been happier."

I stood up and gave her a hug. "I'm so pleased for you, really I am. When you first told me you were going to get married in Disneyland, I thought you were mad. But it's been fantastic, honestly it has."

Maddie glanced over to the dance floor. The band had now been replaced by a DJ, and some of the guests, including Sean and Danielle, were dancing to a medley of Take That songs.

"I just wanted you to know I didn't encourage her," Maddie

said, staring in their direction. "After what I said last night, I thought you might think...I mean I would never have...after what you said and everything. Oh, am I making sense? I really have had a few drinks tonight."

"Yes, you are. And I know you didn't. Anyway," I said, turning away from the dance floor and looking at Maddie, "it doesn't matter to me what Sean does. Why should it? I've got David."

"Yeah, I had the third degree off him earlier, asking me who Sean was, how long you'd known him, where you met, et cetera."

"Did you? When?"

"Er...a little while ago, when I found him and Felix talking outside by the big fountain. Did you know David's thinking of erecting a water feature in your garden?

Oh no, not gardening as well.

"So what did you tell David when he asked? About Sean, I mean."

"Just what *you* told me—that he's just a friend you've met since you've been in London."

I nodded and glanced over at the dance floor. They were holding hands now. OK, they *were* at arm's length, as Danielle spun around and Sean kept her upright. But they were still touching each other.

Ouch, the athlete in my stomach just tweaked another muscle.

"That *is* all you are—isn't it, Scarlett?" Maddie asked, watching me. "Just friends?"

"Yes...yes, of course it is. Don't be daft." But my eyes were still trained on the dance floor.

"But I thought men and women couldn't just be friends?"

Maddie said knowingly. "That's what they say in the movies, isn't it—sex always gets in the way eventually?"

This time it was Maddie who was the one referring to *When Harry Met Sally*, a movie she'd watched with me many a time.

I lifted my chin, turned toward her, and smiled. "Oh look, your new husband is after you." I beckoned across the room to Felix, who was watching us. He immediately came over.

"Sorry, I didn't want to interrupt you," he said. "You both looked like you were putting the world to rights."

Maddie kissed him on the cheek. "No, not the whole world—only Scarlett's world."

Felix smiled at me. "I've only come over to say your mother is looking for you, Maddie. She's saying something about you having enough time to get changed before we leave."

Maddie rolled her eyes. "Tonight has been wonderful, but it's just flown by. I'd better go and find her. I'll see you later, Scarlett, before I go—yes?"

I nodded.

"Come on then, hubby, let's go find your new mother-in-law!"

I watched them walk away together hand in hand. Then I heard the DJ announce that he was slowing it down for a while and I heard the first few notes of "Angels" by Robbie Williams float across the room.

Oh no, this was one of my favorite songs. I couldn't bear to watch Danielle and Sean smooching the night away to it. Wait a moment—why should I care what they did to Robbie when David was here with me? Then another thought occurred. What if David asked me to dance, and we had to go over there right next to them? But he wouldn't...he hated dancing. But he knew I loved this song and he would enjoy scoring points off Sean. I knew that about him…

"I'm just going to get some air," I called to David, just to make sure, as I hurried past him at the bar. "I'll be back in a while."

"Should I come too, Scarlett?" I heard him call after me.

I shook my head. "No, David, I'll be fine. I'll only be gone for…" I thought quickly. "About four and a half minutes—I promise."

I left David puzzling over my precise timing and walked out of the hotel into the cold night air. Outside was a court-yard, and a little way across from that a large garden with a white picket fence. Inside the garden was a Mickey Mouse face planted entirely in flowers, a large fountain, and some benches high up on a small hill. I climbed the hill, sat down on one of the benches, and pulled my stole tightly around my shoulders. Then I watched the clear flowing water cascade into the large pool below while I tried to collect my thoughts.

What was happening to me? Why did I feel this way about Sean? To begin with, I'd pretended it was because he resembled so many of my favorite movie stars—but now I knew that wasn't the truth. We didn't have that much in common—everything I liked Sean seemed to detest and vice versa. So why should I be jealous he was dancing with Danielle? I mean it wasn't like *I* was alone, was it? I had David, my fiancé, here with me, and yes, David and I had our problems, but he was still the one I'd chosen to be with, the one I was supposed to love. I should have been happy to have been here today with David. I should have been content. So why wasn't I? Sean annoyed me, Sean irritated me, and Sean made me feel…just how *did* he make me feel?

I paused to reflect on what should have been a difficult question for me to answer. But I found I could answer it almost immediately.

Sean made me feel alive; he made my life exciting, and he made me happy. But more than all of that, he made me feel wanted—for all our differences.

I let my head drop into my hands. What was I going to do?

"Hey, what's up, doc?"

I looked up in despair to find Sean standing next to me. He was grinning as usual.

"Sorry, that's not Disney, is it—it's Looney Tunes."

"What are you doing out here, Sean?"

"Mobile rang." Sean held up his phone. "Had to answer it, could have been important."

"Which business are you shafting at the moment, then?" I asked, and instantly regretted it.

"The call was about *you*, actually."

"Me?"

Sean sat down on the bench beside me. "Yup, I said I might have some news for you later, and that was it."

I'd almost forgotten about that, what with the Danielle drama and everything else going on. "What sort of news?"

"Well, my dear Scarlett. It seems if your mother is going to be anywhere, it's not New York after all—it's Paris."

"Paris? But how?"

"Well, I've done some digging with the help of a friend of mine, and she says someone with the same name as your mother moved on to work in Paris after taking her job in New York—with the same company, apparently, just in a different country. It was Louis Vuitton Bill was thinking of; that's where she went to work after Fenwick's."

"Oh, of course, the man's name," I said, thinking fondly of Bill and Betty again. "But how has your friend found all this out?" I asked, looking at Sean in amazement. "I mean, we didn't even know who she was employed with!"

"Jennifer works for one of New York's top fashion magazines—she has contacts with all the major designers. So I told her what we knew, roughly when your mother went over to New York to work, and she rang a few people, got them to check their records, and bingo, came up with your mum's name. But then she found out she'd been transferred to Paris about a year after she went over to New York."

"And is she still here?"

"That, I'm afraid, is where the trail ends. Jen's contacts are all based in New York. Once she tried to continue digging in French soil, the ground—so to speak—became awfully hard."

I thought about this for a few seconds.

"So she *could* actually still be in Paris?"

Sean nodded. "Yes, possibly. So what do you reckon, Scarlett? Shall we take a shopping trip into Paris tomorrow?"

I looked at Sean in astonishment. "I can't believe you've done all this for me. I saw you on your BlackBerry today—several times—and I just thought you were wheeling and dealing."

"Nope, I've been speaking to Jen on and off for most of the day. I didn't know if she'd be able to help at all because our information was so vague, but she's been extremely helpful."

"Thank you," I said, looking up at him. "Thank you so much."

"We don't know for sure she still works at one of the stores yet."

"No, I don't mean for that—well, yes I do—but as well as that, just thank you for...for caring enough to help me."

Sean smiled. "Don't be daft, we're friends, aren't we? Well, I hope we are after everything you've put me through over the last couple of weeks." Then he grinned, and one of the athletes—the gymnast, now recovered from her earlier injury—did a backflip in my stomach.

I reached over to hug Sean, and as I put my arms around him, in reply I felt his own strong arms slowly wrap themselves around me. He felt warm and solid—just what I needed right now. I closed my eyes and rested my head on his shoulder. We held on to each other for longer than we should have, both of us easing each other's body just that little bit closer every second...

"Oi!"

My eyes snapped open, and I saw David hurrying across the courtyard toward us. Instantly we pulled away from each other as he approached, and Sean stood up.

"What the hell do you think you're doing with your hands all over my fiancée?"

"David, calm down, it's not like that," I protested.

"What *is* it like then, Scarlett?" David panted as he reached our side. "He's been winking at you on and off all day, and you've been unable to take your eyes off each other all night."

How could David even think that, when Sean had been all over Danielle? I might have been glancing in *his* direction occasionally, but Sean hadn't been watching *me*—had he?

"Dave, old chap, calm down." Sean put his hand on David's shoulder. "It's not what you think."

"I *think* you'd better take your hands off me," David said in a voice that was just a bit too calm. "And it's Dav-*id*."

"OK, OK," Sean said, holding up his hands in surrender. "Whatever you say, mate."

This appeared to anger David even more. "And I am certainly *not your* mate! Scarlett, come with me, we're going in." He grabbed my arm. "We'll talk about this inside," he hissed in my ear as he began to march me away from Sean.

"David, stop it. You're behaving ridiculously." I wriggled under his tight grip.

"I think you'd better do what Scarlett asks," Sean said, following us.

David stopped abruptly and turned to face Sean. "Or what?"

It was Sean's turn to look angry now. "Just do as she asks, all right?"

David released his grip on my arm. "And I'll ask you again: or what?"

Sean turned away from him and spoke to me. "Are you OK?" he asked gently.

I nodded.

"Don't ignore me, both of you. Especially *you*!" David said, pushing Sean's shoulder.

Sean turned. "Don't do that," he said, his eyes flashing dangerously.

David pushed Sean's other shoulder. "Or what? I know your sort, full of clever words and empty threats."

"And unfortunately, Dav*id*, I've also come across your sort too many times before. Come on, Scarlett," Sean said, putting his arm around my shoulders, "*I'll* take you back inside if you like."

"You're not taking her anywhere. Not now, not ever."

"And just how do you propose to try and stop me?" Sean said, throwing David a pitying look.

David lunged at Sean, who swiftly sidestepped him so that David went crashing to the ground.

"Is that all you've got?" Sean looked down at David sprawled on the tarmac. "Come on, Scarlett."

I hesitated, torn by my desire to go with Sean and my loyalty to David.

"See, she doesn't want to go with you," David said, picking himself up off the floor. "She's mine."

"Excuse me, I'm not any—" I began to say. But my words were lost, as David lunged with all his force into Sean again. This time Sean wasn't ready and they both fell to the ground. They tumbled down a slope covered in bright winter flowers. Over and over they rolled until finally they splashed into the fountain below.

They pulled themselves up in about a foot of water and began to throw punches at each other, most of which missed their target as they kept slipping on the muddy base of the pond.

"Stop it!" I called, running down the hill. I paused halfway down as I heard a commotion—other than the idiots that were splashing about in the water below. At the entrance of the hotel, I saw a horse-drawn carriage pulling up outside.

Oh no, Maddie and Felix were about to leave.

I hurried down the rest of the hill, just as all the guests

began to spill out into the courtyard to see the happy couple on their way.

"Stop it!" I shrieked at Sean and David. "Maddie is about to leave, and I won't have any part of her day ruined by you two play-fighting in a paddling pool!"

To my surprise, they ceased their fighting and looked at me.

"I mean it!" I said, as they stood up in the water like a pair of naughty schoolchildren in front of their headmistress. "Just try and look normal!"

I climbed over the picket fence and stood by the edge of the fountain, hoping to hide the two wet and bedraggled men standing behind me. At least we were over here, a little bit out of the way—perhaps no one would notice us.

Maddie and Felix appeared in their going-away outfits, my wedding gift to them. They'd been outfitted in clothes of their choice (Maddie's choice mostly) from Selfridges, when we'd had a fun day out, just the three of us in London, in the January sales. And as they climbed up into their carriage, Maddie wearing an elegant winter white trouser suit and Felix looking much more casual now in a petrol-blue cashmere sweater and navy blue cords, Maddie was still carrying her bouquet.

"Ladies," she called. "The time has come for us to see who will be the next lucky female to walk down the aisle! Are you ready?"

There was a surge toward the carriage as half the guests piled forward. I held my ground by the fountain—there was no way I was going to leave these two delinquents alone for a second.

Maddie stood up and looked around her, then she peered out into the sea of guests.

Oh no, she wasn't looking for me, was she? *Just throw it, Maddie*, I willed her. *Don't worry where I am!* I prayed she wouldn't see me, or that, if she did, there was no way she'd get the bouquet this far.

But she spied me standing by the water and grinned. Then she closed her eyes, reached way back behind her, and threw the bouquet as far into the distance as she could. I'd forgotten that Maddie used to play in a women's American football team when she was at university and could easily throw a ball twenty meters down a field. As if in slow motion, the bouquet sailed over the heads of the desperate females—who jumped and leaped in the air to try and intercept it—and landed firmly in my hands, ready for a touchdown.

Everyone turned to look at me.

I held the bouquet aloft and quickly moved forward to try and distract attention from Sean and David, still standing in the water behind me.

Maddie waved, then winked at me knowingly, as she saw the two bedraggled men. Then she and Felix sat down, and everyone waved good-bye as they rode off together, out of the park gates and along to a taxi I knew was waiting around the corner ready to take them to their hotel in the center of Paris.

Slowly, the crowd began to disperse as everyone moved back into the hotel.

I turned around to look at the two disheveled specimens behind me.

"I guess I should be saying thank you for providing me with yet another movie scene to add to my collection," I told them sternly. "You two did a fine job of recreating the fight between

Mark and Daniel in the second Bridget Jones film. But I won't, because you're just ridiculous. Two grown men fighting about... well, what *are* you fighting about?"

Sean and David looked at each other and I thought for one awful moment they were going to start again.

"David, just wait there," I said, holding up my left hand like I was directing traffic. "I just want to talk to Sean for a moment. Sean," I said, beckoning him with my right hand, which was still holding Maddie's bouquet, "you come this way."

We left David standing in the fountain, as Sean waded through the water toward me. The wet white shirt that clung tightly to his torso had become almost transparent as he climbed out of the water.

"I'm sorry..." he began as he pushed his hair back off his face.

"Over here," I said, pulling him away from the water and out of David's earshot.

"Hey, did I give you another movie moment there?" Sean asked. "I must have looked a lot like Mr. Darcy coming out of the water just then."

He had, actually, but I'd tried hard not to think about it.

"Don't flatter yourself," I said. "And anyway, you're thinking of the TV adaptation of *Pride and Prejudice*, there was no lake scene in the film."

Sean shrugged. "You're the expert."

"Look, Sean, you'd better go and get some dry clothes on," I said, aware that David was still close by. "And then maybe you should go and find Danielle. She must be wondering where you are—that's if she didn't notice you in the water."

"I doubt it," Sean said. "I think she got the message when I wouldn't dance with her to Robbie Williams. I hate that song."

I smiled. Of course he'd hate it; I should have known.

"What's funny about that? I do. Anyway, I was looking for an excuse to get away from her—she was really starting to get on my nerves."

"But I thought you were enjoying her company?"

Sean frowned. "No. I was just putting up with her for something to do."

"But I thought..."

"You thought what, Scarlett? That I fancied her?" Sean raised his eyebrows. "I don't know anyone at this wedding; she was the only person that wanted to talk to me for more than a couple of minutes."

"You knew me."

"Yeah, but you were with David, and I could hardly play gooseberry all evening, could I?"

"Oh, Sean, I'm sorry. I didn't realize. You looked like you were enjoying yourself."

"I'd rather have been with you."

We looked into each other's eyes and at that moment all I wanted to do was put my arms around him again. I almost forgot David was still waiting in the water.

"Ahem," David said. He had pulled himself out of the fountain and was standing just a few feet away from us.

"Sean's just going inside," I insisted. "Aren't you, Sean?"

Sean nodded. "I think I'd best call it a night," he said, backing away. "I'll see you in the morning, Scarlett. Shall I book us a taxi to go into Paris?"

"Sure, that'll be fine. See you tomorrow."

I watched Sean walk away, and then I turned to David.

"What does he mean, book you a taxi to go into Paris? You're not spending tomorrow with him, Scarlett. Have you forgotten what day it will be?"

"Er…"

"February the 14th. Valentine's Day."

Oh God, I had forgotten.

"The thing is, David—it's complicated."

"You're telling me, Scarlett." David ran his hands through his own wet hair, but he didn't look anywhere near as sexy doing it as Sean had done a few minutes earlier. "I thought we agreed we were going to spend the day together before we flew home tomorrow night? And now you want to spend it with *him*. Who, ten minutes ago, do I need to remind you, was found by me with his hands all over you?"

"No, Sean isn't the complication." Well, he was part of it, but I wasn't going to tell David that. "There's something else."

"You mean to tell me there's more going on than you running off to London for a month's holiday away from me? A month that I now fear I was very much mistaken in allowing you to have? More than you spending all your time with another man—who you've not only tried to make out is nothing more than 'just a friend,' but who you now announce you would rather spend Valentine's Day with than me? There's *more* to it than that, Scarlett?"

"Yes, David, there is."

"Well let's hear it then, because I'm sure this will be very illuminating."

"Why don't we go back to our room? You can get dried off, and then we can talk as much as you like."

David looked down at the puddle around his feet.

He doesn't look anywhere near as good wet as Sean did...

I shook my head—I had to stop these comparisons, they were almost as bad as my movie ones.

"No, Scarlett," David said, staring angrily at me. "I think I want to hear everything right now, before you have time to think up *more* excuses for your behavior. You at least owe me that."

"Yes, you're right," I said, and I told David as quickly as I could about what had been going on with my mother, how Sean and I had been chasing leads all over the place, and why I now really needed to go with him into Paris tomorrow. By the time I had finished, he was starting to look very cold.

"David, let's go inside and finish talking about this. You'll catch pneumonia if you continue to stand out here soaking wet."

"Just answer me three questions," David said, appearing not to hear me. "Do you love me, Scarlett?"

"Yes, of course I do. What sort—"

David cut me short. "Do you love *him*?"

"Who? You mean Sean?"

David nodded.

My mouth went dry and I swallowed hard. "No."

"Do you love your father?"

"What the hell sort of question is that? Of course I do!"

"Then leave it, Scarlett. Leave this whole notion of finding your mother alone. You'll only end up getting hurt. And you're going to end up hurting others too."

I thought about what he'd just said. "What do you mean,

people are going to get hurt? Are you talking about Dad and me if I find my mother? Or me and you if I go with Sean to find her?"

"Everyone, Scarlett—this whole process is going to end in heartbreak somewhere along the line. This started out as a simple—but now I see stupid—idea for you to have some time away, to 'get your head together,' I think was the exact phrase put to me. And it's now escalated into this quite mad notion you're going to find your mother. And what if you do, Scarlett? What if you find her and she doesn't want anything to do with you? She didn't all those years ago. Have you thought about that? How you're going to feel if she rejects you all over again?"

I hadn't even considered that possibility in all my euphoria.

"How will your father feel if by some chance she wants to be a part of your life once more? Have you thought about what that would do to him?"

I shook my head.

"No, I thought not. And have you thought about how I'm feeling in all this, when you, the woman I'm going to marry in a few weeks, is running around the country with another man? Have you ever stopped to think for one moment how that might make *me* feel? Have you?"

I hung my head and looked at the ground.

"When are you going to start realizing, Scarlett, this isn't a movie you're in now—this is real life, real people, and there might *not* be a happy ending if you continue messing with our lives like this."

I looked up at David. He'd given it to me straight, and he

was right. Everything he'd said had been true, and I hadn't ever stopped to consider it.

"But what if I don't see this through, David? I might never find out if I *can* have that happy ending with my mum. And that's all I really want, to be happy, and to know that I did everything I could to give myself the chance to be."

David shook his head despairingly. "If I hadn't given my word to your father..." he muttered.

"What do you mean? What did you say to him?"

"It's not what I said to *him*, Scarlett—it's what he said to me."

"I don't understand. Explain yourself, David."

"I can't. I gave him my word when I went to see him that I wouldn't get involved in this. And against my better judgment, that's just what I'm *not* going to do." He straightened himself up. "Scarlett, you win—I trust you. Go to Paris with Sean tomorrow—go to the moon with him for all I care. Just promise me you'll be at that church, by my side, in April. You do still want that, don't you, for us to be married?"

"I do, David," I said, solemnly looking into his eyes. "Really, I do. I just need to do this one thing first."

"Then that's all I want, Scarlett. For you to be there that day, saying those same words to me."

"David, I promise you that on our wedding day I'll be in London, in my wedding dress, saying the words I do."

Twenty-One

Sean and I stood on the pavement in the shadow of the Arc de Triomphe. We'd been in Paris for most of the day, visiting the many Louis Vuitton stores that were scattered across the city. Now we had just emerged from the Metro yet again and we found ourselves this time on the bustling and ultra-chic Champs-Elysées.

"Right, I think it's this way," Sean said, looking up from his map. "We're looking for 101." Eagerly he set off along the pavement.

With slightly less enthusiasm, I followed.

It had not been a very successful morning so far. To begin with, there had been a decidedly chilly air in the hotel room as I'd packed my things into my suitcase and prepared to meet Sean downstairs after breakfast.

David hadn't said too much after the events of the night before. He'd been polite and courteous, as he always was, but he'd been distant too.

I couldn't say I blamed him. After what he'd told me last night, I realized he was right—I hadn't given any thought to how all this must seem to him. If the shoe had been on the other foot, and it was David racing about with another woman in tow, would I have been as gracious to David as he had been to me, and let him continue? I think, not.

I vowed once this was all over I would somehow make it up to him.

Not that I wanted it all to be over: that was something else I hadn't given much thought to—returning home again. Once my time was up, that was it—I would return to Stratford, to Maddie, my father, and to David, and I would probably never see Ursula, Oscar, or, more importantly, Sean ever again.

I sighed heavily.

"Hey, buck up," Sean said. "She has to be at one of them—it's just a matter of time."

"It's not that. I was just thinking about something David said last night."

It was Sean's turn to sigh now. I knew he hadn't been very impressed by David's actions.

"What has he said this time?"

"He asked me what would happen if we do find my mother and she doesn't want anything to do with me. After all, if she didn't want me when I was a baby, why should she want me now?"

Sean stopped walking, placed his hands firmly on my shoulders, and turned me around to face him.

"Stop this," he ordered, looking directly into my eyes. "You were so enthusiastic about all this before last night—there were no doubts in your mind at all about what you were doing. All you wanted was to find your mother. You weren't worrying about who she was, or what she'd think of you—just that you'd finally get to meet her."

"I know but…"

"But nothing, Scarlett—it's David who has put all these doubts in your mind. I don't know what he said to you after I left last night, but it hasn't done you any good."

"David was very understanding about everything, actually."

Sean let go of my shoulders and spun away from me, rolling his eyes. "Understanding—yeah right, that's what it was. Controlling, more like."

"Sean, please," I said, putting my hand on his arm. "Let's not argue about David. My mind is in enough turmoil thinking my mother could be just around the corner every time we get off the Metro. I can't deal with this right now."

"I'm sorry," Sean said, giving me an apologetic smile. "I won't mention his name again." He put his arm through mine and saluted with his other hand. "Right then, Red, it's full speed ahead. The next handbag shop awaits us!"

We walked a bit further along the Champs-Elysées and there, as promised, was another Louis Vuitton shop, selling its distinctive luxury leather luggage and bags. Sean pushed open the door and we went inside.

"*Bonjour,*" he said to the exquisitely made-up assistant behind the desk. "*Parlez-vous anglais?*"

"*Oui, monsieur,* I most certainly do," she replied in extremely good English. "How can I help?"

It was always a relief when the assistant spoke English. It was hard enough explaining to someone in our own language who we were looking for and why. But in the little bit of French Sean and I could cobble together between us, it was virtually impossible. I watched her while Sean spoke; with her short cropped hair and elfin features, she had an aura of *Amélie* about her, which I felt only boded well.

"Ah good," Sean said. "We are looking for a lady called Rosemary. Do you have anyone who works here called that?"

"Or it could be Rosie?" I added helpfully.

"*Non*, we have no one here of that name, I am sorry."

"Have you worked here long...Chantal?" Sean asked, looking at the assistant's name badge. "I mean, is there a member of staff that's been here a longer time than you?"

Chantal looked puzzled.

"Someone older?" I tried.

"Ah yes, older, now I understand. There is Marie, she has been 'ere for er...long time."

"Could we speak to her?" I asked.

"*Oui*, she is out in the back just now. One moment, I shall return."

While we waited, I glanced at some of the bags beautifully displayed on the glass podiums and shelves. I didn't bother glancing at the price tags, though. No point.

Presently, Chantal returned with an elderly woman dressed entirely in black. She was holding on tightly to Chantal's arm for support; and was almost bent double as she hobbled across the shop.

"This is Marie," Chantal said. "She is the grandmother of our manageress. She likes to come and sit in the shop with us for company since her husband died, but they do not let her sit out front." Chantal put her hand to the side of her mouth and whispered to us. "They say it will...'ow you say...er...put the customers off?" She found Marie a seat and helped her into it. "She does not speak any English, but I shall try and ask her what you ask me."

I nodded and smiled at Marie. She stared hard at me over her tiny pince-nez glasses.

Chantal then presumably asked Marie the same questions we had asked her. But it was hard to tell—I could only really pick out the word Rosemary.

Marie shook her head vehemently.

"She says no," Chantal translated unnecessarily.

"Or Rosie?" I asked, looking at Marie.

Again she shook her head.

I turned to Sean. "We may as well just go; this is getting us nowhere."

"English," Marie said.

We all turned to look at her.

"English," she said, pointing her bony finger at me.

"Yes, that's right, I am."

"Vivien," she said, nodding.

"No, my name is Scarlett."

She nodded again. "Oui…Scarlett…Vivien. Da, daa, da, daa. Da, daa, da, daaa," she hummed.

"Come on," Sean said. "Let's go, we've still got one more shop to try yet. Plus," he whispered, "I don't think this old bird is all there."

"No, wait," I said, listening to Marie hum. "Can't you hear what she's singing? I think it's the theme tune to *Gone with the Wind*."

We all stood and listened to Marie humming. She stopped and smiled a toothy grin at us.

"Vivien," she said again, pointing at me. Then she spoke to Chantal in French.

"What's she saying?" I asked.

"She says you look like Vivien."

"Who, Vivien Leigh?"

Chantal asked Marie.

"No," Chantal explained. "A woman that used to work here. Marie says she very much loved the cinema, and her favorite film, she remembers, was *Gone with the Wind*. So the staff, they called her Vivien, as it sounded more French."

"More French than...?" I asked hopefully. "What was her real name?"

Again Chantal spoke quickly to Marie.

"She does not remember her true name, I'm afraid."

I was just about to give up when I remembered the photo. "Is this her?" I asked, producing the photo from my bag. I pointed to my mother in the picture. "Vivien?" I asked Marie, kneeling down beside her.

Marie peered closely at the photo and then she looked at me.

"*Oui.*" She nodded, looking down at the photo again. "Vivien." Then she smiled at me. "Vivien," she repeated as she took my hand in hers.

"Bingo," Sean said, grinning.

With Chantal translating in between customers, I asked Marie as much as she could remember about my mother.

She described her to Chantal as being full of spirit and life, and with a passion for the cinema, which Marie also shared. She had not worked in the shop for long before she had once again moved on. But this time Marie seemed sure she had not stayed within Louis Vuitton but had gone to work elsewhere. "Mysterious circumstances," Chantal translated it as.

The shop was starting to get busy now, so we decided we should leave. It was obvious to me Marie had indeed known, and liked, my mother very much, but yet again we had reached a dead end. We thanked Chantal and Marie profusely for all their help, then bade them farewell.

"So there you go," I said to Sean as we stood outside on the pavement again. "That's that."

Sean fixed me with one of his disapproving looks. "Scarlett, you have to stop saying that every time we come up against a small hurdle. You can't just give up so easily all the time."

"What else are we supposed to do? We have no other leads. My mother worked here for a while, and that's all we know. Marie has no idea where she went after she left. She could be anywhere, Sean."

"But we were so close," Sean said in frustration.

"I know, but at least I can take something away from all this— I've found out the kind of person my mother was. Everyone we've met has had good memories of her. She left her mark on people's lives, Sean, and she's obviously lived her life to the full."

Just as I'm going to from now on, I vowed to myself.

"But we're giving up, admitting defeat, Scarlett. You can't want that."

"No, Sean, *you* don't want that. I've found out so much more in the last week than I ever dreamed I'd find out about my mother, and I'm happy with that. Meeting her again just obviously wasn't meant to be."

Sean looked like he didn't agree.

"Look, I know this isn't how you would usually go about things, Sean—you're the type of person that never gives up until he's won—but on this occasion we can't win, we can't be the best, and we have to admit defeat."

Sean still didn't look convinced. "Are you sure that's what you want, Scarlett? I mean it isn't just because of what David said, is it?"

"No—no, it's not."

Sean raised an eyebrow.

"Honestly," I insisted. "This is what I want. Besides," I said, trying to sound cheerful as I changed the subject, "this means we now have the rest of our time free to see Paris properly. That's if you'd like to spend the day with me, of course?"

Sean smiled. "You know I would."

"Right then, let's go somewhere now. And, if you promise to be good, I'll try really hard not to find any movie moments while we're here—how about that? Come on, Sean," I urged, taking hold of his hand. "It'll be fun."

Sean's face fell. "Oh, Scarlett, I'd love to—really I would. But I'm afraid I've got some business to attend to this afternoon."

"Oh...oh right." I tried not to sound too disappointed as I felt his hand fall away from mine. "Well, no matter. I'm sure I'll be fine on my own. I bet you've seen most of it before anyway. You'd probably have been bored."

"No, of course I wouldn't. I would have loved showing you around Paris." He glanced at his watch apprehensively. "What about if you wait for me back at the hotel? I could call you after my meeting and we can go somewhere then. It shouldn't take too long."

"Don't be silly. I'll be fine on my own. I'm a big girl. I can cope." I was joking to try and lighten the moment, but Sean didn't smile. "I'll just meet you for dinner tonight back at the hotel, shall I? Then neither of us will feel the need to rush around this afternoon."

"You're sure?"

"Yes, perfectly."

"Well, all right," Sean said, still looking uncertain. "You'd better take this, though." He held out the map. "You won't get lost, will you?"

"Sean, I said I'll be fine. Now just go, please," I said, taking the map from him.

"Right, I guess I'll see you later."

I nodded and watched him while he walked back toward the Metro. It seemed odd to be on my own again. Sean and I had spent so much time together recently that not having him by my side now suddenly felt very strange indeed.

Before I descended to the Metro myself, I couldn't help but pause outside one of the inviting chocolate shops that lined the Champs-Elysées.

They were like nothing I'd ever seen before. The window displays showed chocolate in every flavor and form you could think of, from truffles to marzipan flowers, pralines to ganaches and chocolate sculptures. It was a chocoholic's paradise.

I allowed my gaze to wander from the window display to the inside of the shop, and it was there that my eyes stopped dead in their tracks and remained on something more gorgeous and more delicious than any Parisian chocolate shop could ever hope to contain: a certain Mr. Johnny Depp buying an expensive-looking box of chocolates.

As I stood staring at him through the window I knew I was probably drooling, but I couldn't help it—it was Johnny Depp in there, just a few meters away from me, and if that wasn't enough, he was buying chocolate! I watched while he paid for his purchase and then to my horror I realized he was now walking in my direction as he made his way toward the exit of the shop.

"Ahoy there!" I called as he stepped out onto the pavement. *Oh my God, what the hell was I saying?*

He turned around.

He was just as gorgeous in real life as on the screen. I could feel my knees begin to buckle as his dark-chocolate eyes looked around him.

"Just kids having a joke, I think." I looked over my shoulder, pretending to spot someone who might be responsible for that ridiculous outburst. I smiled and to my surprise he gave me a half-smile back.

"Wouldn't be the first time," he said, his voice sounding as sweet to my ears as all the chocolate in the shop would have been to my tongue. "But it's usually in French over here."

"So...you're buying chocolate," I said as he turned away from me, apparently about to continue down the road.

He paused and turned back. "Er, yes. I do that sometimes. You should go in—he's one of the best chocolatiers in Paris." I think he thought perhaps he'd get rid of me that way, but still I didn't take the hint.

"It's just it seems funny seeing you buying chocolate in a chocolate shop, with you being in that film—you know the one...*Chocolat*?"

Quizzically, Johnny raised one eyebrow at me, and I nearly passed out right there on the Champs-Elysées. "Er, yes, I do remember it."

"And...and then of course you were also Willy Wonka so there's a chocolate link there too."

Oh my God, shut up, Scarlett. What on earth are you saying now?

Johnny smiled at me again.

Well, it was more like a grin this time.

OK, he was laughing at me.

"Yes, indeed there is," he said, his face becoming serious now. "I'd never really thought about it like that. But the thing is I've also played the creator of Peter Pan and I can't *really* fly. An astronaut but I've never been into space. A man with scissors for hands and a murdering barber, yet I can't cut hair and I've never killed anyone. Oh, and as you so kindly pointed out a few minutes ago, a pirate, but do you know something?"

He walked back along the pavement, then, standing right next to me, he leaned in, his face close to mine.

"You've never been to sea?" I whispered, almost unable to speak. He was so close I could smell the aftershave delicately wafting from his oh-so-perfect skin. *David is so getting some of that for Valentine's Day*, I thought, wondering if it would be rude of me to ask what brand it was.

"You got it. However," he said, now whispering into my ear, "when I played Don Juan, the greatest lover in the world..."

He stood up in front of me now and winked. And while he'd managed to render me speechless for a few seconds, he took his chance and bounded off down the Champs-Elysées as fast as his seafaring legs would carry him.

When I finally got over first the shock and then the embarrassment of my encounter with Johnny Depp—I mean, what were the chances of that happening? I knew he had a home in Paris and a French girlfriend, but still—I spent the rest of the afternoon trying to calm myself down by doing the tourist thing of seeing as much of a city as I could in one day. I hadn't been to Paris since I was fifteen on a school trip. Back then I was wandering around with about twenty other teenagers. But this time I was on my own.

I visited the Musée d'Orsay art gallery, staring up in amazement at the huge Monet canvases that adorned the walls of what was once a central Paris railway station. I went to Notre Dame and again gazed in wonderment at the inside of the vast Gothic cathedral, understanding now how it had been the inspiration for Victor Hugo's novel and so many of the film adaptations that featured its infamous inhabitant the hunchback. In Montmartre, I wandered among the artists painting portraits of the tourists that flocked around them. Briefly I thought about Sean and wondered if he had any artistic leanings. Maybe he'd like to sketch me like Leo had Kate in *Titanic*—which would give me another movie to add to my ever-lengthening dossier of proof. Then I remembered what had happened after they had done that in the movie, and I thought better of it. I was already in enough trouble with David as it was. But maybe Sean and I could visit the Moulin Rouge while we were here to catch a show. I'm sure we wouldn't have to sing or swing from a trapeze or anything to find something from the movie there...

Finally, I ended up visiting that tourist haven—the Eiffel Tower.

As I stood underneath the enormous iron structure and looked around me, I saw that even though it was now a very late afternoon in February, there were still people everywhere, mainly tourist groups and families...and couples, lots and lots of couples.

Ah, of course, it's Valentine's Day. Well, I suppose you can't get much more romantic than Paris on Valentine's Day.

I tried hard to think about David. He would probably have arrived back home by now and would be happily pottering away with his latest DIY project. But my thoughts kept disobeying me and returning to Sean.

Even though I'd enjoyed myself this afternoon, I knew I'd have enjoyed it even more if Sean had been with me. I'd had that familiar feeling that something was missing, but this time that something was him.

I watched the people rising to the top of the tower in the lifts, and climbing the long staircases together. I couldn't go all the way up there on my own; what would be the point of getting to the top and then not having anyone to share the wonderful views with?

So I turned away and began to make my way back to the

Metro. Then I stopped and smiled, as an idea began to blossom in my mind.

An idea that could help me make a decision, one way or another...

Twenty-Two

At the hotel, I asked the receptionist for some writing paper before heading upstairs. I knocked on Sean's door as I passed to see if he was back yet. There was no answer.

Once inside my room, I found a pen and sat down and thought for a moment, trying to compose a note.

I screwed up three pieces of paper before I got the wording just right.

> Meet me at the top of the Eiffel Tower tonight—
> Valentine's Day.
> Scarlett x

I thought I'd better put my name—after all, this wasn't a real movie, and with my luck someone else would pick up the note and I'd be stuck up the Eiffel Tower all evening with a night porter called Pierre.

I quickly freshened up and changed my clothes to something warmer, but also more romantic-looking—which is a difficult combination to get right.

I tried to remember the type of clothes Meg Ryan had worn

in *Sleepless in Seattle* but I could only remember the teddy bear bit at the end, and anyway that was on top of the Empire State Building. And in *An Affair to Remember* Deborah Kerr had never even made it as far as that. So in the end I chose smart black trousers, a pale pink sweater, and my long black coat. I finished off the look by tying my hair back in a loose ponytail and arranging a brightly colored scarf that I'd bought from one of the market stalls in Montmartre casually around my neck. I say casually: it took me at least eight attempts to get it just right.

When I was finally ready, I crept out of my room—in case Sean had returned in the meantime—and as quietly as I could slipped the note under his door. Then I walked quickly to the nearest Metro station and made my way back to the Eiffel Tower.

By the time I arrived it was fully dark, and I stood in awe looking at just how beautiful the tower was, lit up against the night sky.

There were still queues to ride up in the lifts—even at this time of night. So I joined one, hoping it would be a while before Sean found my note.

When I reached the front of the queue, I paid for my ticket and rode up in the lift with the other tourists to the first, then the second, and finally to the very top floor—where we all climbed out. I wandered over to one of the barriers that surrounded the upper viewing deck to look out at the city and to wait for Sean. I glanced at my watch—it said 6:45 p.m.

By 7:50 p.m. I'd walked the perimeter of the platform five times. The views of Paris at night were indeed breathtaking, I couldn't deny that—they almost surpassed the beauty of the illuminated tower—but it was starting to become embarrassing being up there all on my own.

Earlier today, the crowds riding up in the lifts and climbing the stairs had been a mix of families and large tourist groups. Now the majority of visitors were couples—they were holding hands and giving each other tender looks and loving kisses. I couldn't blame them; after all, it was Valentine's Day. But I felt like a big French gooseberry waiting up there all on my own.

Hurry up, Sean, I willed, looking through the wire barriers yet again. I shivered—this wasn't fun anymore. I reached into my bag for my phone; maybe he'd tried to call and I hadn't heard it? Or maybe the signal wasn't that good up here?

It took a few moments of grappling about in my bag before I remembered I'd put my phone on to charge in the hotel room. I'd been so busy choosing what I was going to wear and deciding what I was going to write that I hadn't remembered to pick it up again—damn!

By nine o'clock I was starting to get very cold, as well as extremely fed up. I sheltered as best I could toward the center of the tower, on one of the benches tucked away beneath the iron girders.

"If he doesn't come in the next half an hour, I'll go and get a coffee," I promised myself, thinking of the cafeteria on the second floor. I daren't leave just yet—I had to know if he would come.

Two cups of coffee later and seven "Would you mind taking a photo of us?" requests from fellow visitors, Sean still wasn't there.

I looked at my watch again. It was now 10:20. The last lift came up at 10:30 in the winter—he was running out of time.

I went to look out at the view once more—the Trocadero Gardens and the bridges across the River Seine were becoming quite familiar by now—and if I squinted hard enough I could even see across to Montmartre and the illuminated Sacré-Coeur. I'd stood outside this huge Roman Catholic church—or basilica, as my guidebook had informed me it was correctly known as, this afternoon: the Sacré-Coeur was the Basilica of the Sacred Heart. All this waiting around wasn't doing my heart or my nerves any good, that was for sure.

My gaze wandered back to the inside of the tower again. A couple standing a little way along from me were giggling and whispering to each other when suddenly the man dropped to one knee.

Oh no, this was all I needed right now.

The girl apparently answered his proposal in the affirmative because they were suddenly superglued together at the mouth.

Deciding to leave them to it, I dismally began to walk away.

"Excuse me?" I heard them call.

I turned around.

"Do you speak English?" the man asked.

"Yes." I nodded.

"Would you mind awfully taking a photo of us? Only Helen and I, well...we've just got engaged!" They gazed happily into each other's eyes again.

"Sure, why not?" I agreed.

"Just push this button," the man said, holding out his camera. "It's quite easy."

I knew it was, because I'd already taken three photos of couples tonight on cameras identical to this one.

"Smile," I said, trying to sound cheerful.

They didn't need much encouragement.

I took the photo and passed the camera back to the man.

"Thank you so much," Helen said, smiling at me. "It's wonderful, Alexander and I will have this moment recorded for ever now."

"Would *you* like a photo taken?" Alexander asked, looking around.

He was obviously sussing out whether I was with anyone.

"No, no, thank you," I said. But not wanting to look too sad, I added, "I'm waiting for someone."

"At this time of night?" He looked at his watch. "Bit late, aren't they?"

"Alex, stop it," Helen said. "I think it's romantic; it's just like in that film, isn't it…the Meg Ryan one? What was it called now…"

"Oh, do you mean *When Harry Met Sally*?" Alex suggested helpfully.

"No, not that one, er…it had Tom Hanks in it…"

"Hmm…" Alex thought again. "Oh, I know—*You've Got Mail*, they were both in that!"

"No…oh, it's on the tip of my tongue."

"*Sleepless in Seattle*," I answered quickly, before they carried on all night.

"Yes, of course," Helen said with relief. "That's it. But she was on top of the Empire State Building, wasn't she—waiting, I mean?"

"Actually, the son was. But it's a similar situation, yes."

"Oh, how wonderful. Is it your husband you're waiting for?"

"No."

"Fiancé?"

"No."

"Boyfriend?" she asked hopefully.

"Yes," I lied. "My boyfriend." I tutted. "I'll kill him if he doesn't get here soon."

"Quite right too—it is Valentine's Day, after all." She looked up adoringly at Alex again. "And you need to be with the one you love on Valentine's Day."

As if I needed reminding.

"Well, I hope for your sake he gets here soon. I think it's so romantic arranging to meet someone here tonight. Isn't it, Alex?"

Alex nodded lovingly at Helen. "Indeed it is, darling." Then he looked across at me again. "You must love him very much to wait this long. I hope he deserves you." He put his arm around his future bride. "We'd better get going, Helen." He smiled at me. "Thanks for the photo, hope everything works out for you."

"Yes, never give up on someone you love," Helen said dreamily. "Good-bye now."

I watched them walk off, their arms tightly around each other, and suddenly I felt very alone.

How I could I have been so stupid? I could have spent Valentine's Day in Paris with a man that truly loved me, that wanted to marry me and spend the rest of his life with me. And instead I'd spent it running around overpriced luggage shops, sightseeing on my own, and freezing my arse off on top of a pointy French tourist trap. Although…there had been the Johnny Depp incident…I shook my head. No, even that had hardly been a great success.

And if my life really *was* like a movie, I'd turn around right now, just as the last lift of the night was arriving, the doors would open, and Sean would be standing there with a look of desperation about him and have a wonderful story of how he'd been delayed by something dramatic, like a bank heist or a bomb scare.

I turned around, and sure enough the last lift of the night *was* just arriving. I watched hopefully as the doors opened… and inside there was a man standing there…but unfortunately it was just the lift attendant, who did indeed have a look of desperation about him—but desperation of a different sort.

I took one last poignant look out over the Paris skyline before climbing into the lift beside him. While we waited for the last few remaining visitors to be rounded up, I glanced at the uniformed man standing opposite me. He was middle-aged and balding, with a lazy eye and a pot belly that hung over the top of his leather belt. He smelt of tobacco and something else— which I think was his aftershave but smelt more like furniture polish. He grinned at me and I caught sight of his nicotine-stained teeth. Politely, I smiled back then looked away, but not before I'd noticed the badge pinned to the front of his overall, which confirmed my fears from earlier, that if this idea of mine went wrong, like it had so spectacularly, I would indeed end the evening with a Frenchman called Pierre. The lift deposited me safely at the base of the tower again, and as I sat on an almost deserted Metro train, I could think of nothing other than what a complete disaster tonight had been. I was so sure that Sean would meet me at the top of the Eiffel Tower that I hadn't given any thought to what would happen if he didn't.

Had he not seen my note lying at the base of his door? And if not, why not? Why hadn't he come back to the hotel tonight? What if something had happened to him today...an accident...or worse?

Actually the "worse" could be that he *had* come back to the hotel, *had* read my note, and I'd scared him off. Maybe I'd taken it a step too far by suggesting something so romantic as meeting me up there. Maybe Sean did only want to be friends. *Just* friends.

My head was spinning with so many thoughts and scenarios when I finally reached the hotel that I had to stand outside for a few seconds, calming myself with deep breaths before going in.

It was a busy street we were staying in, full of lively bars and pretty restaurants. As I stood outside, the clink of wine glasses and the sound of happy, excited voices wafted down the road toward me. I glanced at the bistro opposite—it looked a charming place. The tables were adorned with red and white checked cotton cloths, and in the center of each one a wine bottle covered in wax held a lit candle. It reminded me of...where? Ah yes, the little Italian restaurant Sean and I had dined in together the night we arrived in Glasgow.

But that wasn't the only thing that reminded me of that night. For sitting at one of the window tables was a couple.

They were chatting and laughing—much as Sean and I had done that night. In fact, when I looked at them more carefully I noticed the man actually resembled Sean quite a bit—he had the same build, hair color…eyes. But as the waiter moved away from their table and the couple stood up to leave, that's where the similarity with my night in Glasgow ended—because the man then kissed the woman on the cheek, and they hugged.

Sean certainly hadn't done that to *me* in Glasgow…but he was definitely doing it tonight, right in front of my eyes—to the woman he was having dinner with in the restaurant across the road.

Twenty-Three

I stared in disbelief at them for a few more seconds before I turned and ran into the hotel. I didn't wait for the lift—I took the stairs instead. Four flights later and a sprint down the corridor I opened my hotel room door, slammed it shut behind me, and flung myself onto the bed, breathing heavily.

As I lay and stared hard at the ceiling, I wondered how I could have been so stupid.

How could I have even thought that Sean would want to meet me tonight? He obviously had other plans. Maybe those other plans had been made even before he'd found out about my mother? And the whole "business" thing had just been to spare my feelings today.

The conclusions I'd reached less than an hour ago at the top of the Eiffel Tower had been right. I should have spent today with David—I'd been selfish and stupid. He was the one who loved me and wanted to be with me—not Sean. I reached over and unplugged my phone, still charging at the side of the bed. I'd call David now and tell him how much I loved him.

I glanced at the screen. There were several missed calls, and two unopened texts waiting for me.

The first text was from David thanking me for one I'd sent him earlier. I hadn't spent the whole day being a complete idiot—I had actually remembered to wish my fiancé a happy Valentine's Day.

The second was from Sean. I hesitated before opening it—did I really want to read more lies and excuses?

But, I had to know—so I pressed OPEN on the menu.

Where r u? Hav been trying 2 call. Won't b back @ hotel till late 2night, something's cropped up. Hope u had fun afternoon, Sean.

PS Call me when u get this, worried about u.

Yeah, I bet you are, I thought, thinking about the restaurant. Then I remembered my note. Damn, he'd see it when he got back tonight. If only I could get into his room and find it before he did. At least then I wouldn't look so stupid. Sean would rib me about this forever when he found out I'd been sitting at the top of the Eiffel Tower alone all night.

I sat up and looked around the room.

Hmm…now what did I have that was flat enough to slip underneath his door…Where was a ruler when you needed one?

I looked through my suitcase for something suitable. Shoes—too wide; comb—too short. Wait, I know…I felt at the bottom of the case underneath my bridesmaid dress carefully packed away in its protective cover and found what I was looking for.

I'd bought the L-plates to pin on Maddie on her hen night, but one of the other girls had got to her first with her own. I'd felt a bit peeved at the time—after all, *I* was the one who was chief bridesmaid. But now that the plates were needed for more important matters I was grateful she'd beaten me to it.

I crept out of my room and knocked gently on Sean's door, just in case I hadn't heard him come back. Then I ran back into my own room and pressed my ear to the inside of the door. The last thing I wanted was to come face to face with Sean tonight unless it was absolutely necessary.

After a minute or so, happy there was no sound from the next room, I crept out into the hall again. I checked up and down the corridor, making sure no one was about. When I was sure the coast was clear, I knelt down on the floor and tried to look into the tiny gap at the bottom of Sean's door.

I couldn't see a thing, let alone whether there was a note still lying there. So I tried to insert one of the L-plates into the gap, and to my surprise it fitted. Slowly I moved the plastic from side to side under the door, and then I felt it catch something—at last, my note! I tried to get my L-plate on top of the paper to pull it toward me but it was having none of it and doggedly remained on the other side.

"Can *we* help at all?" I heard a voice above me say.

I froze, then very slowly turned my face up toward it. An elderly couple were standing over me looking perplexed. They were wearing smart evening dress and were obviously on their way back from a night out.

"Have you locked yourself out of your room, dear?" the woman asked, peering at me over the top of her glasses. Her snow-white hair, which was tied up tightly on top of her head in a bun, glowed like a halo around her head with the fluorescent light of the hallway behind it.

"Er...no..." I looked down at the L-plate still clutched in my hand. "Er...they've just got married and...we thought it would be funny if they found some L-plates in their room in the morning. Yes, that's it...you know, Just Married...'learners' on their wedding night?" I scrambled to my feet.

"Oh..." The man, who was almost bald, cleared his throat. "Oh right, of course, we understand, don't we, Marion?"

Marion looked at me suspiciously and then leaned in toward my ear. "Thing is, dear," she whispered. "I don't think many of them are these days."

"Are?"

"Learners, dear. I know I wasn't on my wedding night." She winked at me. "Never mind though—it's the thought that counts." She put her arm through her husband's. "Come along, Gilbert, should we pretend it's our wedding night again? It'll be better than the usual routine, and at least we won't need any talcum powder for the rubber suits!"

Gilbert's face suggested he thought that was a very good idea indeed.

Marion turned to me again. "Rubber can be so chafing in the most awkward of places, don't you know?"

I hurriedly nodded.

"Well, good night, dear. Enjoy the rest of your evening." She winked again. "I know I will!"

I watched open-mouthed while the couple walked away arm in arm, steadying each other as they went. Shaking my head, I tried to clear my mind of the unwanted images of Marion and Gilbert that were beginning to fill it.

The L-plates weren't getting me anywhere, so I decided to return to my own room.

How much longer do I have? I thought as I paced about the

floor. Sean and his companion had appeared to be leaving the restaurant when I saw them. Maybe they'd gone on somewhere else or were having a drink in the hotel bar? Otherwise they'd have been back by now.

I walked to the window to see if I could make out anything down below. There was a small balcony outside, so I opened the French windows and stepped out on to it. I looked toward the bistro but couldn't see anything, only another couple wandering along the street on their way home.

When I turned to go back inside I noticed that the net curtain in Sean's room was billowing out of his window. If the curtain was able to get out, that meant...

I looked at the distance between the two balconies. It wasn't too bad; I could probably stretch my legs between the two—I shouldn't fall.

Listen to yourself, Scarlett. You shouldn't fall? You shouldn't be going across there in the first place!

But I couldn't bear the thought of Sean seeing that note. It would have been bad enough normally, but now I knew he'd spent the evening with another woman it would make my embarrassment even more painful. I had to get it back.

I took a deep breath before turning to face the wall, then, holding on to a drainpipe with one hand, tentatively dangled my leg over the edge of my own balcony and toward Sean's. "Thank you, God," I whispered, as my foot felt something solid underneath and I was able to place it down on a firm surface once again. So now I was straddled between the two rooms— one leg on each balcony—I had to take the next brave step and bring my right leg over to meet my left.

I took another deep breath, closed my eyes, and, before I could change my mind, quickly swung my other leg over the gap and on to Sean's balcony.

"Phew," I said, opening my eyes again. "That was easier than I thought it would be."

Gently I pried open the French windows and slipped quietly inside. The room was in darkness.

Please don't let him have come back without me knowing, I thought, hurriedly trying to remember where the light switch was in my own room.

I stumbled, literally, into a floor lamp, and after groping about for the switch for a few moments, managed to turn it on. At once the room was flooded with light.

I breathed another sigh of relief when I saw the bed was empty. I looked toward the door and saw my note lying innocently at the base of it. Quickly I ran toward it and was just about to reach down to pick it up, my *Mission Impossible* complete, when I heard a key card being slotted into the other side of the door.

Shit! I thought, looking around me. I grabbed for the handle of a door that in my room would have led to the bathroom. But I hadn't realized the rooms were set out as a mirror image of each other, and I found myself opening the door to a built-in wardrobe. I had no time to go elsewhere, so I quickly climbed inside and pulled the door to as best I could without a handle to help me.

I heard Sean's voice first and then a woman's.

"Sean, I'm impressed," the woman said. "You've certainly come up in the world since I knew you. Better class hotels *and* better class rooms."

"Indeed." Sean spoke now. "There's been a lot of water under the bridge since then, though."

"So it would seem."

There was a slight pause before Sean spoke hurriedly. "Look, let me find you those brochures I was telling you about. I think they're in my suitcase."

Oh God no, his suitcase was wedged in between my legs at this precise moment.

"Forget that for now, Sean," the woman said. "You know what they say about all work."

To my relief the wardrobe door didn't open. But when the room went silent I realized that Sean finding me inside his wardrobe was going to be nothing compared to the embarrassment I might have to endure if what I thought was going on on the other side of the doors right now developed any further.

Now is really not the time to be living in a movie scene, I thought, recalling *Four Weddings and a Funeral*, and in particular the scene where Hugh Grant is stuck in the closet while the bride and groom bonk on the bed outside.

No films, I silently prayed. *Not now of all times—please, not now!*

I think someone must have been listening. Because then I heard Sean's voice—

"No, I'm sorry, I really can't do this."

"Sean, darling...come on, just for old times' sake."

I heard a sort of scuffling noise.

"No, Jen! Really, I can't. There's someone else now."

"Who? You never mentioned anyone else at dinner."

Yes, who, Sean? You've never mentioned anyone else to me either.

But if it means getting rid of this Jen…wait, wasn't Jen the name of Sean's contact in New York?

"Well, there is," Sean said so quietly I could hardly hear him. "And she's very important to me."

"So what was tonight all about, then?" Jen demanded. "Just dinner?"

"Yes," Sean said, sounding apologetic. "That's exactly what it was—just a thank-you for helping me out."

"I see."

"I'm sorry if you thought it was more than that, Jen. I can assure you my intention was not to lead you on."

There was a brief silence and then Jen spoke again.

"I haven't heard from you in years, Sean, and then out of the blue I get a phone call from you asking for help. What am I supposed to think?"

I'm guessing Sean shrugged then because there was silence once more. Oh, it was so annoying being in this cupboard—I wanted to see what was happening. Then I remembered why I was there, and I calmed down again.

"Well, you never contacted me either, did you? You ran off with the Yank, and that was the last I knew. I mean Oscar isn't likely to tell me what you're up to, is he?"

Oh my God, Jen is Oscar's sister…the one who broke Sean's heart!

"He was called Rob, as you well know, Sean. After all, he was your best friend."

Oh my God, his best friend? Sean said he was just a work colleague.

"Exactly, Jen, my best friend, and you ran off with him."

"That's ancient history as far as I'm concerned. And anyway, if you were still so sore about it, why did you call me up wanting my help? You knew I'd be here in Paris right now for fashion week. Admit it, Sean, you wanted to see me again."

Don't, Sean—don't admit anything! I willed from my cupboard.

"I had no idea you'd be here," Sean said coolly. "I assumed you were safely back in New York when I called."

"So why call?"

"Because, for the hundredth time, I needed some information, and, unfortunately for me, you were the only person I knew who might be able to help."

"So why ask me out to dinner then?"

"I didn't; you invited yourself. And because you'd been so unusually helpful, I was too polite to say no."

"You used me," Jen said accusingly.

"I did not."

"So where is she then? This girl you've been helping? I'm assuming she's the someone else you mentioned."

Silence.

"I thought as much," Jen continued. "If that's the case, I may as well just go. You've humiliated me, Sean, letting me follow you to your hotel room like this. I hope you're happy."

"I promise you it was not my intention, Jen. However, if that's how you feel, then..."

There was silence again. Oh how I wished I could see what was happening.

"Then what, Sean?"

"Then I'll look on it as an added bonus. Because now, Jen, you've experienced just a tiny percentage of how you made me feel when you ran off with the Yank!"

Go, Sean! I wanted to yell.

A door slammed shut and the room fell silent. I felt secretly pleased for Sean—he had definitely won that battle.

But my euphoria was somewhat short-lived—for it dawned on me I was still stuck in the wardrobe. It was getting hot and stuffy in here now, and my legs were starting to cramp from straddling Sean's suitcase. How on earth was I going to escape?

Hmm…I thought hard for a moment. Let's assume Sean will probably just go straight to bed now, that means I will just have to wait here a little longer until he falls asleep. But what if he hangs his clothes in here before going to bed? I panicked a little. No, that wasn't likely to happen, men never hung their clothes up. They just left them lying over a chair—or, more likely, in a heap on the floor.

But if he *didn't* visit the wardrobe before bedtime, and I *was* lucky enough to have him fall asleep without finding me, how on earth would I get back to my room again? I couldn't go out of the door—even if I did get through it without him stirring, I didn't have my key with me to get back into my own room again.

I heard Sean moving about and then I heard him mumble something that sounded like "What's this?" and there was a rustle of paper.

Oh no—my note!

"Meet me at the Eiffel Tower…" His voice trailed off. "Oh, Scarlett," I heard him say softly.

I listened intently, my ear pressed up against the wardrobe door, but all I heard next was another door open and close.

What's he doing now? I wondered impatiently. Then it dawned on me…

Quickly I opened the wardrobe door and ran toward the

balcony. Through the open windows to my room I could hear Sean knocking hard on my door.

With any luck he'll assume I'm asleep when I don't answer and leave me alone, I silently prayed, as I grabbed hold of the drainpipe again.

The knocking subsided.

Phew...I carefully swung my leg over toward my own balcony, got it safely over, and was just about to swing the other one across when I heard Robbie Williams's "Let Me-ee... Entertain You..." booming from my back pocket.

Shit, Sean was only calling my mobile now.

Hastily I swung my other leg across the gap and reached into my back pocket just as Sean appeared on his balcony.

He looked at his phone and then he looked at me. "What are you doing out here?" he asked. "I was just at your door, knocking. When you didn't answer I assumed you were still out."

"I was out—well, out here taking a call...from David. I didn't hear the door. I must have just hung up as you called."

"Oh, I see. Are you OK, Scarlett? You look a bit...flustered."

"Yes, I'm fine."

"Did you have a good night?"

Here we go, I thought. Wait for it...

"It was...all right," I answered hesitantly.

"Only, I just found this." Sean held up my note.

"Ah...that."

"I'm so sorry. I've only just got back from...my meeting. I didn't see it before."

"No worries," I said with a shrug. "It was a bit of a joke really. Just another movie moment for me to add to my list."

"Oh." Sean looked thoughtfully at the piece of paper. "Look, do you want to come over here for a while, or shall I come to you? I feel a bit silly talking to you across our balconies."

"I'll come over to you." I was relieved, yet puzzled as to why Sean hadn't ribbed me about the Eiffel Tower. Maybe he was saving it until he'd found out for sure I'd spent all night up there alone.

I grabbed hold of the drainpipe and began to climb back over to Sean's balcony.

"Scarlett! What the hell are you doing?"

"Oh…yeah," I said, blushing as I quickly pulled my leg back. "Maybe it would be easier if I just came around to your door."

Twenty-Four

'd fled inside, leaving Sean still standing on his balcony. Now as I stood outside his room, thinking what a dope I'd just been, he opened the door to let me in.

"What on earth were you thinking of?" Sean asked, still looking at me strangely.

I shrugged as I walked past him into the room. "Don't know, really—just seemed the natural thing to do at the time."

"Right…" Sean said, closing the door behind me. He held up my note again. "I'm so sorry, Scarlett—if I'd known where you were tonight…"

"You'd have what?"

"I'd have cut short my dinner and come at once. I did try and phone you."

"I know, but I accidentally left my phone in my room when I went out." I walked over to the window and looked at the street below. They were just pulling the shutters down on the bistro opposite. I hoped they hadn't seen me earlier, doing my Spiderman impressions. "So how was business tonight?" I asked casually, turning back to face the room again.

"Fine, why?"

"Where did you go?"

"Nowhere interesting really. Listen, you didn't spend *all* night on top of the Eiffel Tower alone, did you?"

"I might have done." *Two can play at avoiding the questions, Sean.*

"I'm really sorry, Scarlett. Honestly I am."

Why was he being so nice to me? It must be guilt, because he certainly wasn't telling me the truth about Jen.

"Have you eaten tonight?" Sean asked, looking about him for the room service menu.

"Have you?"

"Scarlett, what is this? Why aren't you answering *any* of my questions?"

"Why aren't you answering any of mine…truthfully?"

"What do you mean?"

Without looking at him, I walked away from the window and sat down at the desk. I picked up one of the hotel pens and doodled on the headed notepaper that lay in front of me. "Does the name Jen ring any bells with you, Sean?"

Sean jumped. "How do you know about Jen?"

Oops, how did I know? Oh yes… "I saw the two of you earlier—in the restaurant over the road."

Sean's eyes flickered toward the window for a moment. "Oh, I see. Yes, I did have dinner with Jen. It was a thank-you for her helping us out with the information about your mother—she's the contact I was telling you about."

"Did you not think *I* might like to thank her too?" I asked, swinging round in the chair to face him.

God, I was good. I could almost have been Reese Witherspoon

at the end of *Legally Blonde* putting my client under pressure. But strangely, winding Sean up like this wasn't as much fun as it should have been—he looked extremely uncomfortable as he tried to justify his actions to me.

"Yes, perhaps I should have asked you along as well. But," he added brightly, as an excuse occurred to him, "I couldn't, could I? Because I couldn't get hold of you—the dinner was what I was trying to call you about earlier." Sean gave a satisfied nod of his head and visibly relaxed again.

Damn you, Sean—touché!

"Hmm, that's true, I guess. So this Jen, is she just a work colleague?" I asked, pushing on ever further.

"Actually she...wait a minute," Sean said, narrowing his eyes. "How do you know the person I was having dinner with was called Jen if you only saw us through a window?"

"I...er..." *Now he'd got me.*

"Did you hear us in here earlier, when you were out on the balcony? I didn't think we were that loud—our voices must have carried."

That would be the reason—yes!

"Yes, they did. I didn't hear everything, though—only her name really because I was on the phone to David for most of the time."

Sean looked relieved again. "Good. I mean I'm glad we weren't too loud."

"Why?" I inquired politely. "Were you shouting then? Was there a problem?"

"No, no problem. Look. I asked before if you'd eaten. Would you like me to order something up for you?" He reached across the desk for the room service menu.

"No, thanks, I had a snack at the top of the tower."

Damn, I didn't want to bring that up again.

"So you *were* up there a long time?"

"A while…maybe I am a little peckish after all." I pulled the menu away from Sean and began to examine it, eager to steer the subject quickly away from *that* embarrassing topic.

Sean snatched it back and knelt down in front of me.

"Hey, I was looking at that!" I cried, trying to take it back from him.

Sean held the menu away from me at arm's length. "Not until you answer my questions." He looked up at me in earnest. "Why did you ask me to meet you up there, Scarlett?"

"I told you, there's a movie where—"

"Forget the movies for once. Is that the only reason?"

I looked down at Sean—his eyes were fixed firmly on my face; they didn't waver. "I don't know," I said flippantly. "What other reason would there be?"

Sean closed his eyes, sighed, then sprang to his feet again. "*That* is just what I was rather hoping you might tell me, Scarlett." It was his turn to walk over to the window now. He stood with his back to me, supposedly gazing out of it.

"Maybe I'm not telling you for the same reason you didn't tell me about Jen being your ex-girlfriend?"

I saw Sean's back stiffen, then he turned around.

"You heard that?"

I nodded. "I heard all of it, Sean. I know she was the one you told me about in Glasgow—the one who broke your heart."

"I'm sure I didn't say that," Sean said lightly. "That sounds more like something Oscar would say."

"I never discussed you and Jen with Oscar."

"Oh."

"It doesn't matter anyway," I said, standing up and joining him at the window. "I don't mind if you want to see your ex while she's in town, why would I?"

Sean shrugged. "I didn't want to see her particularly. When I rang her for help, I thought she was in New York, not in Paris. I'd forgotten she'd be over here for fashion week. As far as I was concerned, if I'd never seen Jen again for as long as I lived, it would have been too soon. In fact, it was bad enough speaking to her over the phone."

"Then why do it?" We were facing each other now and it was my turn to look up into his eyes. "Why did you even call her?"

"For you, Scarlett, you know that. I swallowed my stupid pride and called my ex-girlfriend to help you."

We were moving closer to each other all the time. I should have moved away then, backed off before something happened I'd regret. But I couldn't—Sean's intense gaze paralyzed me. It buried itself deep within me, taking a hold in places I shouldn't have allowed it to go.

"Now I've told you the truth about Jen, it's your turn, Scarlett," Sean said in a low voice, still not taking his eyes away from mine. "Why did you leave me this note?" He pulled the folded piece of paper from his pocket and held it up in between our two faces.

"I wanted to see if you'd come."

"Why? You know I would have if I could. I wouldn't have just left you stranded up there all alone."

"No, I mean…oh, I don't know what I mean, Sean. I just needed to prove something to myself."

"Let me try proving it to you another way." Sean released the note from his fingers and we both watched it flutter down on to the carpet. Then in perfect unison, our faces lifted to look at each other once more. Sean reached up his hand and gently stroked my cheek with his fingers. I felt my eyes close at his touch—it was almost too much to bear. *Pull away, Scarlett. Pull away now!* a tiny voice inside me urged. *Before something happens you'll regret!* Now Sean was cupping my face in his hands…But I didn't want to pull away. I wanted Sean to kiss me. I wanted to know what it felt like to have his lips on mine, to taste him, to—

There was a knock at the door.

My eyes snapped open as our heads both spun toward the intruding noise—then back toward each other again.

Sean shook his head. "Don't look at me. I don't know. We didn't get around to ordering any room service in the end, did we?"

"Well, I have no idea," I said, staring wildly at him. "It's your room!"

Sean took a look through the peephole. His expression was puzzled as he pulled open the door.

"*Bonsoir, monsieur,*" a waiter said. He was carrying a tray laden with champagne, chocolates, cakes, and pastries.

"I didn't order this," Sean said, looking even more confused. "You must have the wrong room."

A smarter-looking man wearing a suit and carrying a huge arrangement of flowers followed the waiter into the room. "Excuse our intrusion so late in the evening, sir, madam," he said, nodding at me as he placed his flowers on the table. "Allow me to introduce myself—I am Francois, the duty manager." He gave a small bow. "These," he said, waving his hand over the tray of food and the vase of flowers, "are with the compliments of the hotel. We were unaware when you booked with us that you were on your honeymoon."

"But..."

"It was only when two of our elderly guests informed us earlier tonight of some strange goings-on in our honeymoon suite that we realized our mistake, as we have no one staying in the suite at present. When they mentioned this room number, and said you had just got married, we felt we had to do something special for you. There will, of course, also be a champagne breakfast for you both in the morning, again with our compliments."

Sean looked at me in astonishment.

I shrugged.

"Er...thank you, Francois," Sean began to say, "but I really think I should explain—"

"What my husband is trying to say, Francois," I quickly interrupted, "is that it is most kind of you to spoil us in this way, and we are very grateful, of course, to both yourself and the hotel."

"It is our greatest pleasure, madam. *Bon appétit.*" Francois gave another little bow. "Come along, Tomas." He beckoned to the waiter.

Tomas obediently followed Francois. They paused at the door and wished us a good evening before quietly closing it behind them.

"Well," Sean said, looking at the tray in front of him. "What on earth gave them the idea we were newlyweds?"

"Beats me," I said innocently. "But let's not look a gift horse in the mouth, eh? Come on, Sean, this looks lovely. Let's tuck in."

Sean hesitated.

I hoped he wasn't going to mention what had happened—or what was just about to happen before Tomas and Francois had arrived.

"Not hungry?" I asked, picking up a plate and placing one of the cakes on it. "Can't I persuade you into something a little bit naughty but nice?"

I blushed when I realized what I'd said.

Sean grinned. "You almost did, Scarlett," he said, coming over to the table and picking up the bottle of champagne. "And I'm sure it would have been an awful lot nicer than any of these cream cakes are ever going to be."

Twenty-Five

After we had eaten all of the chocolates, most of the cakes, *and* had drunk all of the champagne, Sean and I sat propped up against the bed on the thick soft carpet feeling a little tipsy. Well, I was anyway; I wasn't too sure about Sean, but he was grinning more than he usually did, so I took that as a sign of possible inebriation.

Nothing more had been said about what had happened before Francois and Tomas had shown up, and I was glad. My life was complicated enough without adding Sean as anything more than just a friend into the mix.

"So," Sean said, tipping his empty champagne glass upside down. "What now?"

"I guess I'd better head back to my room," I said, although I didn't really want to. That was the thing about Sean, he was such good company I never wanted our time together to end, wherever we were. "We've got an early flight in the morning, remember?" I knelt forward to reach for my shoes which I'd kicked off earlier when we'd flopped down on to the carpet together.

"Did you know your foot is as big as your arm from your

elbow to your wrist?" Sean said, grabbing hold of my right foot. "Let's measure yours."

"Hey, stop it," I said, praying he wouldn't start tickling me.

"Why, you're not ticklish, are you, Red?"

"No," I said, managing to flip myself back over. In an attempt to deflect him I decided to counteract his Julia Roberts foot quote from *Pretty Woman*—although I was pretty sure Sean wouldn't realize it was used in the film—with my own from *Notting Hill*. I pretended to inspect Sean's sock-covered foot.

"Hmm, that's an awfully big foot you've got there, Mr. Bond. You do know what they say about men with big feet."

Sean raised his eyebrows at me.

"Big feet, big shoes," I teased as I wriggled my foot away from him.

Sean laughed and moved nearer to me. "Please don't go just yet, Scarlett. This weekend has been so much fun—well, most of it has—it seems a shame for it to end now."

I smiled as I thought about everything that had happened since we had arrived in France together.

"What are you grinning at?" Sean asked.

"I was just remembering you in that Goofy suit—now *that* was class."

Sean rolled his eyes. "Tell me about it. The things you make me do, Scarlett—no one else would have got me to do that."

"You didn't have much choice, if I remember rightly. It was that or walk back across the park soaking wet."

"No, I mean you seem to uncover things about me that even I don't know exist."

Sean was lying close to me on the carpet, propped up on one elbow with his head resting in the palm of his hand. He pulled himself up, so his face was level with mine.

"I'm sure that's not always a good thing," I said jokily, while at the same time trying to persuade my stomach that it was supposed to be resting not performing today, as it began one of the complicated routines it did when Sean was this close. I attempted to stand up and move away from the dangerous feelings beginning to engulf me once more. But Sean caught hold of my hand and pulled me back down. We were even closer now.

"It *is* a good thing, Scarlett," he said, toying with a strand of my hair that had come loose from my ponytail. "Believe me—it is."

Our faces were just millimeters apart now—but this time I didn't try to get away. As Sean's lips gently brushed mine with the lightest of kisses, I closed my eyes, allowing all the feelings I'd wanted to experience earlier but hadn't allowed myself to surge through my body. Then there was a tiny pause as I felt Sean pull away. I was about to open my eyes to see what was wrong, but then I felt his lips on mine once more. This time, though, all his initial politeness had gone; his kisses were now more passionate, more urgent.

I felt his fingers firmly caress the nape of my neck as he tried to pull me closer. And I let him—I wanted this to happen—I'd wanted it since...

When *had* I started to feel this way about Sean? A couple of weeks ago I'd thought the only reason I half liked him was because he happened to resemble a couple of my favorite movie stars, and now here we were virtually rolling about in a hotel room together. No, forget the virtual; we now *were* actually rolling about, as Sean moved onto his back and pulled me down on top of him.

Our lips parted for a moment.

"Scarlett," Sean said breathlessly as he pushed my hair, which was fast becoming extremely tousled, back off my face. "I've been wanting this to happen for so long."

"Have you?" I asked in a matter-of-fact way that was not in keeping with the passion of the moment at all.

Sean didn't appear to notice. "Of course, even before we came to Paris, before the wedding, before David, before…"

I froze when he said David's name.

What was I doing lying here on top of Sean? Hadn't I just said earlier that I'd been stupid to take a chance on someone else when I'd already got a man who loved me waiting at home? And now look what I was doing. This had to stop—immediately.

I jumped up, hurriedly backing away from him across the room. "I'm sorry, that shouldn't have happened. I…I shouldn't have let it happen."

Desperately I tried to smooth my wayward hair back into its band. At least I could control that if nothing else.

Sean propped himself up on his elbows. "But why…" he said, looking completely bewildered. "I thought you felt the same way about me as I feel about you. Isn't that what the whole Eiffel Tower thing was about? I don't understand—what's wrong?"

I paced about the room in a dramatic fashion.

"Nothing's wrong—for you, but it is for me. I'm engaged, Sean—I'm supposed to be getting married at the beginning of April, for goodness' sake."

Sean pulled himself up so he sat cross-legged on the carpet in front of me. He looked composed again now. "You must know what I think about that."

"I can probably guess, but you don't know the whole story."

"Perhaps not, Scarlett, because there's always something more going on than meets the eye where you're concerned. But maybe you could listen to me for one moment, let me state the facts as I see them."

I nodded. I had little choice.

"OK then." Sean took a deep breath. "One—even before you met me, you were more than happy to leave your fiancé behind for a month and charge off to London to house-sit a stranger's home. Just to prove some silly notion you've got about movies and real life. This, I would suggest, would seem unusual to most people."

I listened silently, trying to look anywhere except at Sean.

"Two—all the women I've ever met that are getting married never stop talking about it, especially in the run-up to the big day. You hardly ever mention your wedding or have anything to organize for it. How does that work?"

I opened my mouth to point out that was the whole point of having a wedding planner, but Sean continued with his interrogation.

"And three—for some reason I can't understand, you appear to be marrying someone who you have absolutely nothing in common with, who doesn't seem to excite you that much, and most importantly, doesn't even make you that happy." Sean folded his arms. "There, how does that all sound to you? It hardly adds up to the romance of the century."

"Do *I* get to respond now?" I asked indignantly.

Sean nodded and leaned back against the end of the bed to await my defense.

I sat down on the chair by the desk. It didn't feel right to go on standing while Sean remained on the floor. But I still didn't trust myself to get down to his level again.

"First, Sean, I thought you understood why I came to London for a month and why the cinema is so important to me."

"No, Scarlett, I don't really understand," Sean said with a shrug of his shoulders. "You've never really explained why you *want* to prove this to your family, only that you're trying to do it."

He was right, of course—as always. I'd hidden my real thoughts and feelings from the start. "If you want the full version, Sean, it's a long story."

"Well, I'm not going anywhere—are you?"

I still felt too high up on the chair, so I knelt down opposite Sean on the carpet. But this time, I kept a safe distance between us.

I told him all about how my life was usually. My boring days in the office with Dad, David's and my DIY disaster zone of a home, and how the only way I could find any romance and excitement in my life was through other people's fictional lives at the movies. I then explained that David's parents were not only paying for our wedding but, with the assistance of the wedding planner, doing most of the organizing too. Which at the time of our engagement I'd happily agreed to, so long as I got to choose my own dress for the big day. Then I told him my feeling that there had always been something missing from my life, and how this, and the chance to do something different for a month, had made me jump at the opportunity of getting away from everything and everybody for a while.

"So?" I asked when I'd finished recounting my tale of despair. "Now do you understand why?"

Sean thought for a moment. "It ties up a few loose ends, yes."

Loose ends? I'd just about told him my entire life story!

"But what it doesn't explain, Scarlett, is just why you're marrying David."

"Because I love him, of course."

Sean tipped his head quizzically to one side. "Oh really?"

"Yes, really," I said defensively.

"I don't believe you."

"Well, it's true," I said, folding my arms and turning my head away like a sulky teenager. "I do love him."

"I'll accept you *think* you love him." Sean narrowed his eyes. "But there's something else, isn't there?"

"No."

"Hmm…now what could it be?" Sean said, pulling himself up on to his feet. It was his turn to pace the floor like a detective in an old black and white movie trying to solve the mystery at the end of the film, while I sat tight-lipped on the carpet watching him.

"Stop this, Sean," I said eventually, breaking the silence that had enveloped the room while he thought. "Why does there need to be something else? Why can't I just love David, and that's that?"

Sean turned and raised his eyebrows at me. "You forget—I have actually *met* David."

"That's not fair; David is a good man."

"I don't deny it. But that's not what's in doubt here, Scarlett."

Sean rubbed at his forehead. "Oh, what is it…what *is* the missing link to all this?"

Sean was right—again. There was something else, but there was no way I was going to tell him what it was.

"Got it!" Suddenly he clicked his fingers and spun round. "Scarlett," he said, looking accusingly at me. "Surely it can't be true—can it?"

"What?" I asked suspiciously, as Sean began to pace around the room again.

"You told me David's family owns a chain of cinemas, right?"

I nodded reluctantly.

"And you and your father's business is popcorn…am I getting warm?"

"Popcorn machines," I corrected.

"OK, popcorn machines, so am I seeing a little business opportunity coming your way if you marry into this vast family of movie theaters?"

I tried to appear unfazed.

"Am I right, Scarlett?"

I got up and walked over to the window. I couldn't let him know how close he was.

"Well?" Sean asked again. "Am I?"

I spun round. "Yes," I snapped, "you're right. Happy now?" I swung back toward the window again.

I felt Sean's hand on my shoulder. "Scarlett," he said, his voice now soft and calm. It was as though he had been playing both parts of a good cop, bad cop routine in the last few minutes. "You can't marry someone just because you think he might give your father's business a bit of help."

"It's not just a *bit* of help," I said, turning to face him. "If I marry David, our popcorn machines will be in every cinema foyer in David's group. Do you have any idea just what that would mean, Sean? Their chain is not only one of the biggest in this country, but in Europe too. Dad would be made for life."

"But what about you, Scarlett?" Sean said, his eyes not leaving mine for a second. "Will you be made for life if you marry David?"

I couldn't bear to look at Sean as I answered him. My eyes dropped away from his down to the floor. But I had to make him see that it was what I really wanted.

"I'll be settled and in a happy, stable relationship," I said, raising my head and lifting my chin. "With a man who loves me and won't let me down."

"That *definitely* isn't you talking now."

"It is me talking, Sean—this is what I want." I could feel myself beginning to build momentum now. "Anyway, you wouldn't understand. Dad built up this business from nothing. He had to work so hard just to keep it going *and* look after me when I was small." I stopped to think about Dad for a moment. Something I hadn't done enough of lately. "He's given up so much for me over the years, and now it's time I gave up something for him."

"What, your freedom?" Sean asked, raising his eyebrows.

I stared at him as coldly as I could.

"So I take it your father doesn't know about this...this business merger of your souls then?"

"No, he doesn't, and don't call it that. Dad likes David, and he's happy I'm marrying him. Anything else will just be a bonus once we're wed as far as he's concerned. And David's not callous if that's what you're thinking either. It just happens his present supplier's contract runs out after the wedding, and he mentioned it would be a good opportunity to unite our families."

Sean looked skeptical.

"Anyway, you're supposed to be the hot-shot businessman—I thought you of all people would approve." I half turned away and folded my arms defiantly.

Sean shook his head. "I deal with property and companies that are in trouble. I buy and sell commodities, Scarlett—I don't deal in people."

I turned my head back and this time when I stared coldly at Sean I meant it. I could feel tears beginning to well up inside my eyes. But I wasn't going to give him the satisfaction of seeing them fall.

"That fact, Sean, has been all too apparent since I met you, I'm afraid."

Sean's whole body tightened as his face drained of color.

But he'd asked for that—suggesting I was selling my soul and all his other clever analogies. "And now, I'm going to go to bed—before one of us says something we may regret, even more than what's already been said and done in this room tonight. Good night, Sean," I said, walking to the door. I turned back briefly to look at him.

Sean was facing the window again, so I couldn't see his expression.

"Good night, Scarlett," he said coolly. "Sleep well, won't you? If your conscience will allow you to, that is."

Twenty-Six

The atmosphere on our journey back to London the next day was muted. When we did speak to each other we were polite and civil, but we only conversed briefly on subjects that were necessary to our journey home—like flight times, taxis, and luggage allowances.

When we finally reached Notting Hill, Sean paid the taxi driver and then, without asking, carried my suitcase to the top of my steps.

"Will you be all right from here?" he asked, choosing not to make eye contact with me.

"Yes," I said, suddenly feeling very self-conscious in his presence. "Thank you, Sean, not just for the case—I mean for coming with me this weekend, helping me with my mother and everything."

"Not a problem. If that's all?" He walked back down the steps, pausing at the bottom to look up at me.

I couldn't think of anything more to say, so I smiled at him half-heartedly.

"See you later, Scarlett," he responded with a tight smile. But it was the "see you later" that meant "see you around some time" rather than "I'll see you very soon," and immediately the thought that I wouldn't be seeing Sean later on today, or even at any time in the near future—other than perhaps on these very steps, as we happened to enter or exit our houses at the same time—filled me with sadness.

Sean sprang up the steps to his own house and quickly disappeared through the front door with his suitcase. Despondently I unlocked the door to my temporary home. It felt cold and empty as I walked inside.

Even Buster's wailing seemed subdued as I swiftly silenced him, picked up the post, and made myself a cup of tea. I spent most of the afternoon and evening sobbing, as I sat and watched every film that I could think of containing a touching or tear-jerking scene that Belinda and Harry had in their vast collection.

I didn't know whether I was crying because I wasn't going to see Sean anymore, because Sean had made me face up to a few home truths about my life, or just because I was a complete sucker for a soppy scene in a movie.

The only thing I knew was that every time I watched one of those big romantic finales, I was more certain than I'd ever been that I never would experience one for myself. And that thought made me cry all the more.

The next morning I waited in front of the big bay window that looked out on to Lansdowne Road. I hoped I'd see Sean heading off to work, so then I could just "happen" to be going out at the same time as him and we would "accidentally" bump into each other again.

But he must have left pretty early that morning, because at 11 a.m. there was still no sign of him.

I sighed as I sat in the window. I didn't like this feeling—up until now everything had been fun and new since I'd arrived in Notting Hill. I'd always had somewhere to go and someone to go with. But now I had no one. I felt very, very alone.

This routine continued for the next couple of days. I'd rise early and wait fully dressed and made up for Sean to leave his house—but every day I seemed to miss him. I'd then watch movies or, if I was desperate, the occasional bit of daytime TV for the rest of the day, until I thought it might be time for him to return in the evening. I would then begin the same vigil by the window, just watching and waiting. During this time I played Belinda and Harry's copy of *Bridget Jones's Diary* over and over again. Not always the whole movie, quite often just the part where Bridget mimes to "All by Myself," as it seemed particularly appropriate.

I had to pop out occasionally for food and supplies, and it must have been on these brief occasions that I missed Sean returning to his house.

I didn't know why I was going through this ridiculous charade every day—after all it was me that had cooled it between us in Paris, not him. But I couldn't bear the thought of us not being friends, not after everything we'd been through together recently. I just needed to see him again and hear his voice reassuring me everything was all right between us.

But after nearly three days of waiting, I still hadn't seen him.

I knew I should really try to start going out a bit more, there was no point in spending my remaining time in London shut up in the house. But I just couldn't summon up the enthusiasm if Sean wasn't there alongside me.

But this afternoon I had no choice about whether I left the house or not. I was forced into going out for longer today, because I had an appointment I had to keep—for a fitting for my wedding dress.

I was just about to input Buster's code into his box on the wall when the doorbell rang.

I looked though the peephole and saw Oscar and Ursula standing on my doorstep, chatting and laughing together.

"Scarlett!" Oscar said, hugging me as I opened the door to them. "Where have you been hiding yourself? We haven't seen you for days." He popped Delilah down on the floor. "Away you go and be a good girl for Daddy."

Delilah, wearing a pale lilac knitted dog coat, trotted off into the lounge.

"Sean said you got back on Monday," Ursula said, appearing next to Oscar. "What have you been up to since then?"

"You've spoken to Sean?" I asked.

"Yes, he phoned from New York the other day—he's buying some business or other over there at the moment. I think from the sounds of it, it's turned out more complicated than he first thought it would be. Anyway, he asked how you were and if we'd seen you at all. When I said no, he asked if we'd come and check on you."

"I feel awful now for not doing so before, darling," Oscar said. "But we thought you must have been out and about finding your movies and hadn't had time to call in on us for a bit of gossip."

"I've just been under the weather since Paris," I said. It was partly true—I had been feeling pretty rough.

"But you look lovely today, darling. Are you off out somewhere? You're all dressed up."

"Er, yes I am, actually."

"Ooh, somewhere nice?"

"I'm going for a fitting for my wedding dress."

"Oh, how lovely," Ursula said. "Somewhere local?"

"Not too far away from here. It's at a shop that my friend Maddie's sister owns."

"Is Maddie meeting you there?" Oscar asked, looking around him.

"Er, no. She's still on her own honeymoon unfortunately."

"Oh, that's a shame," Ursula said. "She's going to be your bridesmaid like you were for her, isn't she?"

"Yes, that's right." I could see where this was heading. I looked at my watch. "I'm sorry, but I'm really going to have to go in a minute."

"So who's going with you?" Oscar blurted out. "To give an opinion on your dress, I mean?"

I looked between the two of them. How sad was I going to sound now? I had thought originally I might ask Sean along to this. It would have been a good excuse to re-create another movie moment—there were so many films where the bride went for a fitting for her wedding dress, but I was specifically thinking of *Four Weddings and a Funeral*. All I had to do was to get Sean to say something about a meringue and I was home and dry. But after everything that had happened between us, it wouldn't have seemed appropriate, even if I had seen him to ask.

"It's just going to be me and my wedding planner at the fitting," I said, trying to sound positive at the thought of an afternoon spent with Cruella.

Oscar and Ursula looked at each other. Then they turned and looked at me.

"Mind if we tag along, darling?" Oscar asked. "I'm a sucker for a shop full of bridal gowns."

I smiled gratefully at them. "Are you sure you want to come?"

They stood either side of me and slipped their arms through mine.

"It would be our pleasure, Scarlett," Ursula said. "There's nothing like a bit of romance and some pretty dresses to brighten up a Thursday afternoon."

I stood in front of the three of them now.

Oscar in his emerald-green geometric-print shirt and purple designer jeans and Ursula in her sixties-style white minidress, black tights, and black pumps sat on a velvet half-moon settee in the center of the changing room.

They were a stark contrast to Cruella (or Priscilla, as her business cards told us she was really called) who was wearing a gray jacket and skirt suit, and white high-necked blouse. Her silver hair was tied up tightly at the back of her head in a very efficient looking bun.

She stood away from them at the side of the room making notes in her folder. Or my wedding "objective," as I was supposed to call it.

"What do you think?" I asked, spinning around in front of them. "Is it too much?"

I'd always thought when it finally came to the time for me to choose my own wedding dress the task would be easy. I'd go for something slim and sleek, simple and not too fussy. But when I'd got into the shop for the first time a few months ago and seen all the dresses and the books of samples, my common sense had gone right out of the window.

It was *my* day, after all, and this was the *only* thing I was having my say on. Why shouldn't I choose something a bit more...memorable?

"It's...big," Oscar said, tilting his head to one side.

"Is it?" I asked, hurrying over to one of the many mirrors lining the walls and turning to and fro in front of it. "Where, around the bodice?"

"No, I mean the skirt is big. I just imagined you in something a little more...fitted."

"So did I originally," I said, coming back over to them. "But when I saw this I knew I had to have it. It just makes such a statement."

"It sure does that," Oscar said, pursing his lips.

Ursula nudged him.

"I think it looks lovely, Scarlett. It's so romantic to have a dress like that these days." She stood up and came over to me. "It's like the sort of wedding dress you imagine you're going to have as a little girl." She looked wistful. "Big tulle net skirts, a beautiful bodice encrusted with pearls, maybe even a long train carried by six pretty bridesmaids…"

I could tell Ursula had thought a lot about this.

"I've got the white tulle skirts, Ursula," I said, swishing them about a little. "And the bodice is embroidered—with tiny white beads though, not pearls. But I'm afraid I have to draw the line at the six bridesmaids and the long train. I'm just having Maddie."

Ursula shook her head. "I'm sorry, I got a little carried away there for a moment. Sean always said I was too romantic for my own good."

"What do you think?" Oscar asked, looking over his shoulder at Cruella.

She slowly lifted her head from her notes and her electronic organizer.

"It's quite suitable," she said, looking at me over the top of her rimless spectacles.

"Glad you approve!" Oscar turned back to us, sticking out his tongue and pretending to slit his throat with his finger.

"She doesn't have a choice," I whispered, as we all leaned in toward each other in a conspiratorial huddle. "This is the *only* thing I'm allowed; she can't quibble about. It was part of the deal in me allowing David's parents to hire her."

"However," we heard her say, "I *do* have an issue with your choice of bridesmaid's gown. Perhaps we could take a look at it when you've finished here. It's hanging in the next room."

I rolled my eyes. We all stood up straight again from our huddle.

"Maybe I can help?" Oscar said, winking at me. He leaped up and bounded over to Cruella. "I run my own very successful fashion chain based in Kensington. I have more experience in gown dilemmas than you've had..." He paused as he looked at Cruella's bony frame. "Than you've had carb-free meals, darling!"

I watched as he guided Cruella in the direction of the exit.

Ursula smiled. "It really is a princess of a dress, Scarlett," she said, gently stroking some of the fabric. "You'll have a happy ending when you wear this dress, that's for sure."

I looked at myself in the mirror again.

"You said before that Sean said you were *too* romantic, Ursula. Isn't he ever, then?"

Ursula turned and faced the mirror too.

"Why do you ask?"

"It's just when I was at his house once I saw all these books on his shelf."

"Sean's always been a big reader."

"Yes, I know, but among them were authors such as Jane Austen and Charlotte Bronte; there was even a book called *Love Letters of Great Men*. Those aren't the sort of books read by someone who's *un*romantic, are they?"

"Oh, that's where it went," Ursula said, rolling her eyes. "That book is mine. I bought it because it was in the *Sex and the City* movie—but of course you probably knew that."

I nodded.

"I must have left it at Sean's when I was waiting in for a delivery for him once. I wondered where it had gone." She laughed. "I can't imagine Sean reading that, can you? It's not really his scene."

I tried not to let the disappointment show on my face.

So that explained it. Sean wasn't romantic at all, and he never would be.

Ursula must have sensed something. "It's not entirely Sean's fault he's the way he is," she said, turning toward me. She glanced toward the door where Oscar and Cruella had just exited, and she lowered her voice. "A few years ago there were some...problems between Sean and Oscar's sister, Jennifer."

"Yes, I know, Sean told me."

"He did?" Ursula said, sounding surprised.

"Yes, when we were in Glasgow. Oh, and he mentioned it when we were in Paris too."

"I see." Ursula looked thoughtful. "Anyway. That experience knocked Sean pretty badly at the time. He's never been quite the same since."

I was about to ask how when Oscar and Cruella returned.

I stared at Cruella. She looked different.

What was it about her, had she changed her clothes?

No, she was actually smiling for once.

"All sorted," Oscar sang as he twirled around in the center of the room. "Just ask Uncle Oscar to wave his magical wand and all shall come good!"

I wondered if Oscar might like to wave that wand over some other areas of my life that were needing a sprinkle of magic right now.

When the wedding dress fitting was over Oscar and Ursula suggested we go on somewhere else.

"That's why we originally dropped by earlier, to invite you out for the evening, isn't it, Ursula?" Oscar said as he skipped down the street carrying Delilah (did she ever walk? I wondered), admiring his reflection in the shop windows he passed.

Ursula nodded. "We thought we'd take a trip to the cinema tonight—you'd be up for that, Scarlett, wouldn't you?"

It was a rare occasion I wasn't, and they knew it. "There is a new Hugh Grant movie out I haven't seen yet."

"Oh, I love Hugh," Ursula cried. "What do you say, Oscar? Do you fancy a bit of Hugh Grant tonight?"

"Darling," Oscar said with a flourish. "I fancy a bit of Hugh *every* night."

The Coronet in Notting Hill Gate had to be the most wonderful cinema I'd ever been in. The opulent red plush interiors edged with gilt took me back to the height of Hollywood glamour.

"Ah, I do love it here," Oscar sighed, as we relaxed in our velvet-covered seats. "It's so glam."

The Coronet cinema, I discovered once we were inside, was originally a nineteenth-century theater, converted in modern times to a picture house. So, unusually, when we bought our tickets we had the choice of whether to sit in the stalls or the upper circle to watch the film.

We plumped for the upper circle, and now, while we sat there waiting for the adverts and trailers to begin, I felt as if I was going to watch a theater production rather than a movie.

"It's lovely, isn't it?" I said. "So different from our local multiplex back home."

"I should have searched out some diving goggles to wear

when I dropped Delilah back at the house and then you'd have felt even more at home," Oscar said, holding his fingers over his eyes in two circles.

"Diving goggles? I don't get…wait, is this the cinema from *Notting Hill*?"

Ursula nodded. "Yep, I thought you'd have recognized it straight away!"

"I thought it looked familiar," I said, taking a good look around me. "Well, we may not have any diving goggles to re-create that scene, but Hugh Grant is going to be joining us in a few minutes, so I guess that will have to do!"

The lights in the auditorium dimmed, and the curtains were pulled back to reveal the huge cinema screen. Immediately I was plunged back into my comfort zone again. A zone where someone else's life was all I had to concern myself with for the next two hours, and my own, ever more complicated one, could temporarily be forgotten.

It was a good movie, as nearly all Hugh's were. The only thing that could have made it better was if Sean had been sitting there next to me rather than Oscar.

You have to stop this, Scarlett, I told myself as the final credits rolled up the screen. *You've made your choice, now you have to live with it.*

"Shall we go for something to eat?" Ursula asked as we left the cinema. "There's a lovely Indian restaurant just up the road from here. Oscar and I often go there when we've been to see a movie."

"Yes, why not?" I said, thinking of the empty house waiting for me. "That would be great. Hold on, let me just check how much money I've got left, I may have to stop at an ATM along the way." I felt for where my bag would usually hang but instead felt only my hip. "My bag! Oh, I must have left it in the cinema—just wait here a minute. I'll be right back."

I hurried back to where we'd been seated a few minutes ago—but there was no bag waiting for me when I got there.

I felt under the seat, then looked all around where we'd been sitting in case it had been kicked along the floor when everybody had been leaving, but there was still no sign of it.

"Excuse me?" I heard a voice calling from down below. I looked over the top of the balcony, and saw one of the usherettes holding up a bag—my bag. "Is this yours?" she asked.

"Yes," I called out. "Yes it is! One minute, I'll be right down."

I rushed to the exit and then down the stairs.

"Thank you," I called, as I hurried toward the woman. "I thought I'd lost it."

"You're lucky," she said. "It's a good bag too. Gucci, right?"

"It's a fake, actually," I admitted. As I approached her, I realized she was older than I'd thought.

"I did know, I can tell."

"Can you really? How?" I'd thought it had been a pretty good copy when I'd bought it off eBay a couple of months ago.

"It's all in the logo," she said, pointing at the clasp on the front. She looked up at me as I arrived in front of her. "You see just here, it's..." Her voice trailed off.

"What?" I asked. "What's the difference?"

But she continued to stare at me. It was unnerving; she didn't speak—she just stared. I knew I shouldn't have bought a fake handbag off eBay. Knowing my luck she'd turn out to be some sort of part-time counterfeits officer, on the lookout for fake designer goods.

Her eyes dropped away from mine, and she swallowed. "Here—just take your bag," she said in a low voice. A strand of black hair fell across her face.

I reached out and took my bag. As I did so my hand brushed against hers. What felt like a bolt of lightning shot up through my arm—and spread right through me like an enormous wave of emotion.

I looked closely at her again and in the dim light noticed that her eyes were an intense shade of green, just like mine. She stared helplessly back at me.

I glanced down at her badge; it stated that *Rose* would be pleased to help me today.

I opened my mouth to speak—but nothing would come out. It was like being in one of those awful nightmares where your body won't do what you want it to. There were so many questions I suddenly wanted to ask this woman—but I couldn't.

So instead, she asked me one.

"Scarlett, is that you?"

"Mum?"

Twenty-Seven

We stood in the empty cinema staring at each other.

"Scarlett?" she said again. "Is it really you?"

I nodded helplessly.

"I…I can't believe it. My little baby."

Suddenly it was all too much and I burst into tears.

"Scarlett, are you still in here?" I heard Ursula call. "Oh, there you are." She came rushing toward me. "We wondered where you'd…what on earth is wrong?"

Ursula looked between Rose and me.

"Ursula, this…" I hesitated, it sounded all wrong. "This is…my…my mother."

"Your…but Sean told us you couldn't find…oh my! You mean you two have just…like just now in the cinema?"

I nodded.

"But that's incredible."

"Isn't it," my mother answered for both of us. Actually, I couldn't even think of her in that way just yet. So I decided to think of her as Rose for now—like her name badge stated. Rose looked as bewildered and disorientated as I was feeling.

"You two must have so much to talk about. Perhaps I should—"

"No, no don't do that, Ursula," I said, panicking. Now I was face to face with my mother, I didn't have a clue what I wanted to say to her.

"But…" Ursula said in embarrassment.

"Scarlett, my shift finishes in about half an hour," Rose said gently. "Maybe we could go somewhere…just for a coffee or something?"

I nodded again. I still couldn't bring myself to speak to her properly.

"There's a little café just up the road from here, called Kelly's. Do you know it?"

I shook my head.

"I do," Ursula said. "I'll make sure she gets there OK."

"I guess I'll see you in a bit?" Rose said, trying to force a smile.

Again I just nodded. Ursula had to forcibly turn me around and walk me out of the cinema, as my legs, and in fact my whole body, had become incapable of functioning on their own.

"Don't ask!" she instructed an astonished Oscar as we emerged on to the street. "I'll tell you in a minute. Come on, we're going this way."

She grabbed my hand, pulled me along the street, and into the first pub we came to.

"But this isn't a café," I said weakly, looking around me.

"No, I know, but you need a stiff drink before you go and meet your mother properly."

"Her what?" Oscar asked in astonishment. "But I thought…"

"So did Scarlett until about ten minutes ago. Come on, let's get a drink first—I'll go up to the bar, you find us some seats, Oscar."

Oscar looked around him, then wandered over to the other side of the pub where he spied a small table in the corner with three empty seats. "Over here," he said, beckoning me across. When I didn't move, he returned to my side and gently guided me in the right direction.

We sat down at the table and waited for Ursula.

"Do you want to talk about it?" Oscar asked after a minute or two of us sitting in silence.

I looked at him sitting there in his bright green shirt and purple jeans. No one but Oscar or a Wimbledon umpire could get away with that color combination, I thought in admiration. A man at the next table cast an appreciative glance in Oscar's direction—so he was obviously doing something right. "I would, Oscar—but I don't really know what to say."

Ursula arrived with the drinks. "Usual for you, Oscar," she said, plonking an energetic-looking cocktail down in front of him. The drink, with its lurid umbrellas and swizzle sticks, even seemed to match Oscar's outfit.

"And a brandy for you, Scarlett."

"But I don't drink brandy," I protested.

"You do tonight—you've had a shock. Go on, get it down you; it'll do you good."

I began to sip gently at the brandy, still in a daydream, while Ursula briefed Oscar on what had happened at the cinema.

"It's unbelievable," I heard Oscar saying. "What if Sean hadn't phoned today and asked us to call on Scarlett? She might never have bumped into her!"

"I know, and if he hadn't suggested we take her to the cinema too—it doesn't bear thinking about, does it?"

I was fed up sipping at the rich, sweet liquid, so I picked up my glass, threw my head back, and downed the contents in two big gulps.

Oscar and Ursula stopped talking and watched me open-mouthed.

"Blimey, girl," Oscar said. "Steady on."

"It's got to be done," I said in a raspy voice after the brandy had burned the back of my throat.

"Better?" Ursula asked after a few seconds. "Are you with us again now?"

I nodded.

"So what do you think you'll say to your mother when you see her?"

"I have no idea," I replied truthfully. "I don't know her, and she doesn't know me. What the hell are we going to talk about?" I hesitated. "Perhaps I just shouldn't go after all."

"I'm sure you'll find some common ground," Ursula said, gently putting her hand over mine. "Oh, what I'd give to have five more minutes with my own mother again."

I was so wrapped up in myself, I'd forgotten about Ursula and Sean's mother.

"Yes, you're absolutely right. I should be grateful for this opportunity. But the difference is, Ursula, your mother didn't choose to abandon you. When she passed away, she had no choice in the matter."

"But she's still your mother, Scarlett." It was Oscar's turn now. "I moan about mine enough, with her constant badgering and interfering in my life. But I wouldn't be without her for the world."

I nodded. "Thanks for your advice, guys. Of course, you're

right, I must go. I'll just have to see what happens when I get there. After all, what do I have to lose?"

Ursula and Oscar quickly finished up their drinks, and we all left the pub together. We walked along the street until we came to a little cafe called Kelly's. It wasn't quite a greasy spoon, but it was getting on that way with its bright plastic chairs and easy-wipe tablecloths.

"Will you be OK?" Ursula asked as we hovered by the door. "Or do you want us to come in and wait with you until she gets here?"

"No, I'll be fine. It'll give me a bit of time to think about what I'm going to say to her."

Ursula gave me a big hug. "Good luck, Scarlett. I do hope it goes well."

Oscar did the same. "If you're not sure about her, check out her shoes," he instructed me in all seriousness. "You can tell a lot about a person by the shoes they wear."

"Sure, Oscar, I'll remember that. Thanks."

I opened the door to the café, and a bell rang above my head, announcing my arrival. "I'll call you later and let you know how it all goes," I promised.

"Yes, please do, we'll be crossing everything for you," Ursula said with an encouraging smile. "Including our eyes!"

I gave them one last nervous smile, then I took a deep breath and walked into the café. I found myself a table in the corner by the window and sat down.

A middle-aged waitress wearing a brown uniform and a white frilly apron tied around her middle duly appeared. "Evening, what can I get you?"

"Erm, just a cup of tea, please, milk no sugar. Actually no, I will have sugar, please." I still felt I was in shock: maybe a sweet cup of tea would help me more than that brandy had.

"OK..." the waitress said slowly, eyeing me up and down. "Anything else?"

"No, not at the moment, thanks...Oh, if you have *skim* milk that would be good in the tea too, thanks."

"Skim." The waitress wrote on her pad. "Sure, I'll check for you. I won't be long." She wandered back to the counter and spoke briefly to a man who I assumed must be the chef because he was wearing a large white apron. Well, it would originally have been white underneath all the food stains.

I sat back and surreptitiously looked around at the other diners in the cafe.

They were an odd mix of people. The youngsters that lolled about at one of the tables were obviously there to partake of their five daily food groups—chips, caffeine, ketchup, salt, and sugar. Most of the other diners were that bit older, but still obviously felt that their day was not complete without some sort of fry-up. And there were a few odd people like me just sitting on their own, sipping a cup of tea. The lone people looked quite desperate and sad, and I hoped I didn't look like that.

The dingy white walls were covered in old black and white photos. I glanced at the one closest to me and immediately recognized the handsome face of Gary Grant smiling back.

Then I realized that all the photos were of movie stars. Marilyn Monroe and Charlie Chaplin were hanging next to Clark Gable, Rita Hayworth, and who was that? I squinted to see across the room. Ah yes, Ginger Rogers, Fred Astaire, and Gene Kelly. Maybe the café was named in his honor?

I picked up the laminated menu that stood on the checked plastic tablecloth and flicked casually through the pages. Helpfully, there was a photo of every dish that Kelly's had to offer. This was presumably so you didn't have to tax yourself by wading through the one-line description of each meal. And intriguingly, all the dishes had Hollywood-inspired names, I assumed to try and inspire you into wanting to eat them.

Was this why my mother knew this place—because of all its movie connections?

I put the menu down as the waitress reappeared at the table with my tea. I was impressed that it was in a pot, and not just in a chipped cup and saucer as I'd half expected it to be.

"Would you like anything else?" the waitress asked hopefully. "I see you were just looking at our menu."

"No, not just at the moment, thanks—maybe later though," I added when she looked disappointed. "I'm meeting someone here."

"Righty-ho," she said, walking away. "I'll pop back in a while."

I turned my head and looked out of the window. I felt like I should have a red rose or something similar poking out of a book, so the person meeting me would know who I was. But Rose already knew what I looked like, didn't she? Just like a younger version of her, really.

I thought about what had happened only half an hour ago in the cinema. What were the odds of that? I wondered. All that time I had been chasing across London and Paris with Sean looking for her, my mother had been right here all along—in Notting Hill.

Sean! Oh my God, I had to tell him; he'd be so excited for me, and it would be an excuse to talk to him again. I'd ring him now, even if he was in New York. Hmm, what time would it be there?

"Hello, Scarlett."

I looked up and saw Rose standing at the other side of the table. "May I sit down?" she asked.

"Yes—of course."

I watched her remove her raincoat, hang it neatly on the back of the chair, then smooth her skirt carefully beneath her before she sat down. She arranged herself so that her knees were together and her lower legs, angled slightly to the side, were crossed at the ankles.

It was very elegant to watch. I noticed she had changed out of her cinema uniform too. She now wore a slim green skirt, white shirt, and matching pale green cardigan. Her hair, that had been pulled tightly up in a bun before, had now been brushed and lay gracefully over her slim shoulders.

The waitress appeared. "Hello, Rose," she said. "Usual?"

Rose nodded. "Yes, please, Greta. Would you like anything, Scarlett?"

I shook my head. "No, no, I'm fine just now, thanks."

The truth was I was far from fine. I had the strangest combination of sickness, apprehension, and curiosity all burning a hole inside me, and it was starting to make me feel a bit lightheaded.

"So," Rose said, when Greta had disappeared. "I guess you're still in as much shock as I am."

I nodded.

"When you came running toward me to get your bag I just knew—I don't know how, but..."

I nodded again. It was stupid, but I didn't know what to say to her.

"Have you worked there a long time?" I asked, then immediately felt dumb. Of all the things I needed to know, that was definitely not one of them.

"Not too long, no—it's just temporary really, until I find something better."

"Oh."

"So how about you, Scarlett, what do you do?"

"I work with my father," I blurted out without thinking. "We have our own company."

Rose stared at me for a few seconds. "That's good," she said, her cheeks flushing slightly. "How is your father?"

"He's well." God, I was going to have to think before speaking. One minute I don't know what to say, and the next I'm blabbing about Dad.

"I'm glad to hear it. The company you mentioned, is it anything to do with popcorn, by any chance?"

"Yes it is, why?"

"Your father was always talking about setting up on his own, even when I knew him. I'm glad he finally got to do it. And you work with him?"

"Yes, we're partners. Dad has the bigger share, but we both have the say-so about what goes on within the company."

"Good. So you should do."

Greta arrived at the table again. "Would either of you like something to eat?" she asked after she'd placed a mug of coffee on the table in front of Rose.

"Actually, I am rather hungry," Rose said. "What about you, Scarlett?"

"Yes, OK." I picked up the menu again. I fancied something

sweet—the brandy, and then the sugary tea, still hadn't been enough to stop my shakes. "I'll have the hot apple pie, please."

"Cream or ice cream?" Greta asked.

"I'd like ice cream, but only if it's vanilla, please. And can I have it on the side, not on the pie itself? Otherwise, it just melts straight away," I explained to Rose, who was looking at me with interest. "But if it's not vanilla ice cream," I said, turning to Greta again, "I'd rather just have cream, but only if it's fresh cream, not that squirty sort from the can."

"O…K…" Greta said, raising one eyebrow. "Apple pie with vanilla ice cream, but if we don't have vanilla, you want cream, right?"

"Yes, but only if it's *fresh* cream."

"And it's to be on the side, not on top?"

"The ice cream, yes."

"What about the cream?"

"That's OK on the pie, but only if it's fresh."

"What, the pie?"

"No, the cream."

"Right…" Greta said slowly, rubbing her forehead. "What if we don't have either vanilla ice cream or fresh cream?"

"Then I'll just have a jam donut."

Greta looked at Rose, who appeared highly amused at my ordering technique.

"I'll have whatever she's having," she grinned.

Greta rolled her eyes and headed back to the kitchen.

"*When Harry Met Sally*, right?" Rose asked. "The way you ordered your pie?"

I nodded. "Sally knows exactly what she wants—and she

wants to get it just right. So do I when I order food—it's just the way I am. By the way, I liked your line, the 'I'll have whatever she's having' one. It comes from the movie too."

Rose smiled. "Yes, I know. That's why I said it."

"Oh, sorry." I blushed. "I didn't realize you'd done it on purpose."

"You like films, then?" Rose asked, her green eyes sparkling with interest.

"Yes, love them."

"Me too."

"I know, Dad said." I closed my eyes. *Duh!*

Rose looked surprised. "Tom told you about me? I didn't know if he would."

"Only recently—he never said anything before."

"So what happened recently to make him start?" Rose pursed her lips. "I'm sorry, that's none of my business, perhaps you'd rather not say."

I shrugged. "It's fine. Don't worry." I wondered if I should tell her the real reason I'd come to London. But I decided against it for now. "Why did you leave?" I asked abruptly. I had no idea where the question came from—it certainly didn't run itself past my brain for permission to exit before it blurted out.

Rose sighed deeply. "I knew you would ask me that question one day, Scarlett. And I've always known I wouldn't be able to give you a worthy answer to it when you did."

I turned my face to the window and watched the passing traffic crawling by. I might have guessed she wouldn't tell me anything.

"You've turned into a fine young woman," Rose continued.

"Your father has obviously brought you up well on his own." She thought for a moment. "I'm assuming he was on his own… or did he…remarry?"

I shook my head as I stared out of the window. "No, he didn't get married again. Dad did it all on his own—he was the one who looked after me." I thought about Dad for a second. I tried not to think about how he'd feel if he knew where I was right now. Then I turned back to face Rose. "He fed me, played with me, and changed my nappies. He listened to me read and helped me study for my exams. He even made my outfits when I was in the school play, even though he had to handsew everything because he couldn't get the sewing machine to work. Dad let me cry on his shoulder when my first boyfriend dumped me, and he even came with me to buy my first bra. Yep, Dad was there for it all—when *you* weren't."

I took a deep breath to steady myself. Getting all that out of my system had left my heart pounding so hard I thought it might explode through my chest at any moment and land on the table in front of me.

"I'm sorry, Scarlett," Rose said, looking startled by my outburst. "If it's any consolation at all, I never stopped thinking about you."

"Do you know something? It's not!"

Rose looked down at the tablecloth while I stared hard out of the window again. This time I didn't even see the cars as they pulled up at the traffic lights. It had started raining, and the wet glass was a blur of colored lights merging like the inside of a kaleidoscope.

"So?" I demanded, turning back to face her again after a few seconds. "Where were you when all this was going on?" I was on a roll now—a floodgate had been opened on thoughts, feelings and questions that I'd had bottled up inside me for over twenty years. And it was going to take a lot to stem the fast-flowing river that contained them. "Living it up in London? Or was it New York then—or Paris?"

Rose looked confused. "How do you know I've lived in those places?"

"I...I don't. Lucky guess, I suppose."

"Scarlett, it's a very, very long story."

"So, we've got all night—unless you've got something better to do?" I challenged her, our eyes meeting across the table.

"No, nothing better."

"Plus, we have a bonus," I said, glancing behind her.

"We do?" Rose asked, looking confused again.

"Yes, it looks like we now have apple pie to sustain us through your long story," I said, as Greta placed two large helpings of apple pie covered in fresh cream on the table in front of us. There was a scoop of vanilla ice cream on the side of each plate.

"Now, if Greta can get that right, I'm sure you're going to be able to tell me just exactly why you ran out on us all those years ago, aren't you, Rose?"

Twenty-Eight

By the time Rose had told me what she'd been doing over the last twenty years, her ice cream had all but melted, without the need of a hot apple pie to help it along.

Rather than the wonderful, exciting life I'd thought my mother had had working in fashion and living in London, New York, and Paris, it appeared she'd spent most of her time rolling from one disastrous relationship to the next. It had been the men in my mother's life that had taken her around the world, not her career.

"So, Scarlett, my life has been quite a rollercoaster ride. One minute I'd be up in the air, living the dream with a rich man on my arm and a glamorous job to wake up to every morning. And the next, when it all went wrong, I'd plunge into the depths of despair, and sometimes even poverty, while I got myself back on my feet again. Now is one of those down times, I'm afraid, that's why I took the job at the cinema."

"But at least you've had an exciting life. It hasn't been boring, has it?"

Rose laughed bitterly. "No, it certainly hasn't been that. But if I could just go back in time…would I choose to do it all that way again? I'm really not sure I would."

"What do you mean, if you could go back in time? Are you saying you wouldn't have left us if you'd known then what you do now?"

Rose shook her head. "I really don't know, Scarlett. Things were different back then. Your father is probably a completely changed man now from the Tom I knew."

"How do you mean?"

Rose looked across the empty table at me. Greta had long since cleared our plates away—there were only two empty cups left now, and the rest of the café was deserted too. I think Greta and Charlie—the man in the white apron— were hoping to close up for the night. "Scarlett, do you really want to sit here and listen to me criticize your father? I don't think you do—because it's obvious that you won't agree with me, and then we'll just end up fighting, and I don't want that to happen."

"I won't say anything in Dad's defense, I promise. I'll just sit here and listen to your side of the story. All I really want to understand is why you left."

Rose looked around at the empty cafe. "Perhaps we should continue this elsewhere, then? I think they're waiting for us to leave."

"All right," I agreed. "But you will tell me the whole story, won't you? You at least owe me that."

Rose nodded. "Yes, I'll tell you."

We stood up and paid the bill. I insisted we go halves, even though Rose tried to pay for everything.

I still couldn't think of calling her anything other than Rose. Thinking of her as Mum was still too painful to contemplate.

"Where should we go?" Rose asked, once we were standing on the pavement. "My flat is only a few tube stops from here."

"Let's go to mine," I said. "It's just around the corner and the rain seems to be easing up now, so we won't get wet."

Our walk to Lansdowne Road was quiet. Occasionally one of us would make a comment about the weather or something in one of the antique shop windows we passed. When I turned off the Portobello Road in the direction of my house, Rose spoke again.

"You live along here? Either the popcorn business pays a lot more than I thought these days, or you've a very rich man in tow!"

"Neither, I'm afraid." Actually that wasn't altogether true. David was quite wealthy—but he wasn't the reason I was living here. "I'm house-sitting for friends," I explained, taking the easy option.

As we reached the house, I noticed that Sean's light was on in his hall, and my hopes were raised for a moment. But then I remembered that light had been on every evening since we'd returned from Paris. He must have one of those night light things set up on a timer.

I opened my own door and rushed through to deal with Buster.

"Gosh, this is very nice," Rose said, spinning around in the hall. "You've fallen on your feet here. How long are you staying for?"

"About a couple of weeks," I said, trying to remember how long I'd been here. Gosh, over halfway through my time already. "Coffee?" I asked, going into the kitchen. "Or perhaps something stronger?"

"Coffee is just fine. But don't let me stop you if—"

"No, I'll just take a coffee too." I still couldn't quite shift the aftertaste of the brandy.

"So?" I asked when the coffee was made and we were sitting down in the lounge together on one of the brown leather settees. "Let's hear it."

Rose took a sip of her drink, then put it down carefully on a glass coaster on the coffee table.

She sat back in the seat and looked at me before speaking.

"Scarlett, your father and I, we were always just a bit *too* different, I suppose. He was the calm, sensible one in the relationship—whereas I was livelier and much more...impulsive, I guess you'd call it." She thought for a moment. "It was fine while we were courting; our differences were what kept our relationship fresh and exciting. And your father—he was a bit of a looker in those days, Scarlett. I always thought he had a touch of Harrison Ford about him."

Try as I might, I couldn't help but smile at that image.

"In the early eighties Harrison Ford was considered to be a bit of a catch," Rose explained. "It was the height of the *Star Wars* craze."

I nodded. "Yes, I know." But I still couldn't see my father as anything but Dad, let alone Indiana Jones.

"Anyway, eventually we got married. Everything was fine at first. Things weren't a lot different than they were before. Except we now had the added worry of bills and mortgage payments every month—something your dad took a lot more seriously than me. And to be fair to him, it's a good job someone did. Tom always wanted us to save our money, put it away for a rainy day, that kind of thing. And I wanted us to go out and continue living our lives as we had done before we'd got married. I wanted to enjoy life while I was still young. So as you can imagine, that caused many an argument."

I nodded; this all matched up to what little Dad had told me.

"But whatever arguments we had over money, the bottom line was we still loved each other deeply, Scarlett, you have to remember that."

She paused and thought again.

"About a year after we got married I fell pregnant with you. This put Tom into super-saver overdrive, I'm afraid. We had to save money for the baby, for when I had to give up work, for when we needed to buy nappies, cots, and prams. I wasn't allowed to buy anything without your father wanting to know why I'd bought this or spent money on that—every penny had to be accounted for. And it drove me mad, Scarlett."

I couldn't blame her for that—it would have driven me mad too. David was bad enough, but at least I still had my own source of income.

"But then you came along, and for a while everything changed. I was besotted with you—I think that's the only way to describe it—really I was. You were the most important thing in my life—you have to believe that."

"So, what changed?" I had to ask. I'd been silent up until now.

Rose shook her head. "I really don't know for certain. I think now I may have had a form of postnatal depression. You have to remember back then it wasn't as widely recognized in all its various forms as it is today. Yes, we knew about the 'baby blues' and no doubt if I'd sat at home all day sobbing I might have been diagnosed. I've done quite a lot of reading on the subject since the Internet came along. I can't excuse what I did, Scarlett, but I can't take all the blame either."

"Why? What happened to you? What made you so different from all the other mums who chose to stay with their babies?" My questions were all asked in the same detached voice. It was as if I was a journalist interviewing Rose for a story that had nothing to do with me. It was the only way I could deal with all of this—by keeping myself as far removed from the subject matter as I possibly could.

Rose stared down at her hands which she had clasped together on her lap. "My emotions went in the opposite direction. There was no crying or endless sobbing; quite the opposite, in fact. I was so happy at becoming a mum that I wanted to go out and celebrate. The problem was I *kept* wanting to go out all the time. I think part of me wanted to cling to the fact I was still *me*—and not just someone's mother." She looked up at me. "You wait until it happens to you, Scarlett. You'll know what I mean then. First you're always Mrs. O'Brien when you go to the clinic, then Baby O'Brien's mum, then suddenly everyone only knows you as Scarlett's mother. You start to lose your own identity; no one calls you by your own name anymore."

"And this is the reason you left us?" I hadn't been very impressed so far by her weak excuses. I was sure that everything she was telling me was the truth, but it just didn't add up. Something was missing.

"Partly, but I'm afraid there's more to tell you yet."

Rose looked at me as if she was considering something.

"You said you'd tell me everything," I urged.

"Yes, I did, you're right." She took a deep breath. "Well, these feelings grew worse, until I felt completely trapped within my own life. I can't explain to you how awful that feels unless you've been there yourself, Scarlett. I almost felt I couldn't breathe sometimes, as if my life was being suffocated out of me. I was just desperate to get away from it all for a while."

I could appreciate that feeling.

"My only escape back then was going to the cinema. The funny thing is your dad and I actually met in a cinema; we used to love going to the pictures together. But when all this happened your dad changed—he wouldn't go with me anymore, even when we *could* get a babysitter. He said it was filling my head with all sorts of nonsense, and it was the films that were making me unhappy, not anything else. He said they were giving me unrealistic expectations of how life should be."

This sounded a familiar tale too.

"One day it all came to a head. I'd snuck off to the cinema to see an afternoon matinee while your father was at work. Unfortunately, he came home early that day and found you with one of our neighbors. He went mad when I came in. He said I was neglecting you and I wasn't fit to be your mother."

Rose paused as she took another deep breath. This obviously wasn't an easy story for her to tell. "He told me that if I thought life was so much better in the films I wanted to go and watch so badly, then perhaps I should go out and try to live my life in some of them."

I sucked in my own breath now. No...Dad would never say that, would he?

"Then he seemed to calm down a bit. He suggested I go

away for a while to clear my head and think about what I really wanted from my life. I think he thought some time away would get all the—well, he called it nonsense—out of my system once and for all."

"And did it?" I asked, already knowing the answer to my question.

"I think you already know the answer to that, Scarlett."

"But how could you just abandon me like that? I was a baby, for goodness' sake!" I knew I was being slightly hypocritical about this, considering my own current situation. But it was different. I'd only left David behind in Stratford—she'd left Dad and a six-month-old baby.

"I didn't want to at first. I thought your father meant for me to take you as well, but he insisted that you remain with him. He loved you so much I knew he couldn't bear the thought of losing you. Plus, I think he saw you as a sort of security that I'd return home again."

"But you never did?"

"No, I never did. But you have to believe me, Scarlett, at the time I didn't think it would be forever. I just saw it as a break from you both—time to get my head around everything. Like I said before, I wasn't thinking straight. I honestly thought I would return a better person *and* a better mother."

"So what happened, then?" I asked, unmoved by her excuses. "What was so wonderful that made you forget all about us?"

"I never forgot you, Scarlett. Never."

I just stared at her, waiting for an answer.

"I met someone else," she said quietly.

"Is that it?" I exploded, leaping to my feet. "You met

someone else! You left your family behind forever because you got chatted up by some guy in a bar!"

"No, it wasn't like that, Scarlett. Please sit down, will you?" Rose held her hand out and gestured to the settee. "I am trying to explain."

Sullenly I sat back down.

"You did say you wanted to know everything," Rose prompted gently.

"Go on then," I said, folding my arms in front of my chest and leaning back against the cushions. "Explain away."

Rose took a sip of her coffee before continuing, as if a small delay in proceedings might allow me to calm down. "I met this man," she began again, "not in a bar, but at the cinema, strangely enough. He was there on his own, and so was I. He was so different from your father—the complete opposite, in fact." Rose became lost in her memories as she spoke. "Nothing happened at first; we were just friends. But then it became obvious we both wanted more from the relationship, and the inevitable happened."

I didn't like this. It was all far too close to home.

"He lived abroad—France, to be exact, on the south coast. He asked me to go back there and live with him, and I agreed. He just seemed like my perfect soulmate…" Rose re-emerged from her reverie. "Scarlett, you must know that feeling when you meet someone special? You feel wonderful when you're in their company. Then when the two of you are apart, you both feel miserable and alone. After a while these feelings become so intense you simply can't imagine your life without the other person being a part of it."

I knew just how that felt.

"So I took the coward's way out. I left the country without anyone knowing I'd gone."

"And me and Dad? What of us?" I demanded, feeling myself tense up again.

"I wrote your father a letter a few weeks later, telling him where I was and what I was doing. I also told him that I'd be coming back to get you once I was settled in France with Jacques."

"But..."

"I know—I never came back. Not immediately, anyway. It was six months later when I returned to England again. Jacques had ditched me for another woman—that was my first experience of being dumped for a younger model. I tried to make ends meet in France, but I could hardly speak the language and so my job prospects were limited. I had to come home again. I took bar work for a while, a trade that's seen me through many lean times since, I can tell you. But the hours weren't suitable for looking after a young baby, so I promised myself that once I'd got my life sorted, I'd call around and see you and Tom again. I didn't expect him to take me back or anything, but I was desperate to see you. And I knew if I had a good job and a nice place to live, there might be a chance I could regain custody of you again, or at least see you on a regular basis."

"So, what happened?"

"I never got myself sorted. Well, I did, but that was only through a man again. Another rich one—this time he lived in London. Scarlett, I was living in a horrible little bedsit at the time. I saw a way out, and I took it."

"But at the expense of your family," I said without feeling.

Rose nodded sadly. "None of these men were interested in having children around—let alone one that wasn't their own. So by the time that relationship had gone down the pan—like all the others did eventually—you would have been about two years old."

"We moved when I was two, to Stratford."

"Oh, is that where he took you? I did try to find out where you'd gone, but no one would tell me. Tom's family just clammed up when I tried to get in touch. I can't say I blame them, really."

I didn't comment on this.

"So that was it, end of the line—I had no choice but to get on with my own life then. But you have to believe me: I never wanted any of it to happen that way. I never wanted to abandon you. I always thought I'd be able to come back for you. And you have to know, Scarlett, I've always thought about you and wondered how you were doing—especially on your birthday."

"Which is?" I asked, testing her.

"The 19th of March, of course."

She was right. I stood up and aimlessly wandered about the room. I couldn't get my head around all this.

This evening I'd not only met my estranged mother in the orchestra pit of a cinema, but I'd found out exactly why she had abandoned me almost twenty-three and a half years ago. And the even crazier thing was it had happened for almost the same reason my father had encouraged my fiancé to allow me to go and do for a month.

Why would he risk the same thing happening again?

"I know all this must be a bit of a shock to you, Scarlett," Rose said, standing up. She walked over to me. "Believe me, it's been quite a shocker for me tonight, meeting you again."

I thought for one awful moment she was going to try and hug me, so I rapidly backed away from her.

"I...I just need to think about everything for a bit, Rose...I mean Mu...I mean..."

"It's OK, Scarlett. I understand, of course you do. Perhaps you'd like me to go now."

I nodded.

Rose picked up a pad that was lying on the table. "Do you have a pen? I'll jot my number down for you. Perhaps you'd like to call me sometime, when you've had a chance to think about everything."

"Erm, there's one in the hall, I think."

Rose found the pen and returned to the room to write her telephone number down. Then she laid the pad and pen on the coffee table in front of me. "That's both my home and mobile numbers. Call me any time if you want to talk some more."

I nodded again.

Rose picked up her bag and coat. "Well, good-bye, Scarlett. I do hope I'll hear from you soon."

"Yes...bye then...er..."

"It's OK—I don't mind you calling me Rose. I used to be Rosie, of course, but I think Rose suits me better now. Rosie was the person I used to be, not the person I am now."

"Yes, good-bye...Rose," I said, still not able to face her properly. My head was spinning. I just couldn't deal with all this right now.

Rose gave me one last look and then smiled again before walking out of the lounge and into the hall. I heard her heels clipping across the tiled floor and the click of the front door as it shut behind her.

The strange thing was that that was exactly the same noise my shoes had made earlier when they walked across the floor of the hall.

And the reason it was the same noise?

I just realized Rose was wearing exactly the same pair of shoes as me.

Twenty-Nine

I hardly slept that night. It was not surprising really after what had happened to me earlier on.

I'd rung Ursula almost as soon as Rose had left and briefly told her what had gone on. I didn't feel like speaking to anyone, but I knew if I didn't they would phone me anyway. So I quickly got that call out of the way and settled down to do some serious thinking.

There was so much that was still unclear.

So I now knew the reasons why my mother had left. Perhaps I didn't fully understand them, but I knew more than I'd ever known before. But it was my father's behavior that was puzzling me more than anything. If *he'd* lost my mother all those years ago, why would he encourage David to do the same thing to me? Did he really think that lightning wouldn't strike twice?

I tossed and turned in my bed, going over and over all the possible scenarios that my next move might bring forth.

First, I had to decide whether I wanted to see Rose again—and my answer to that dilemma was an immediate yes. There were still so many questions I wanted answers to that I couldn't wave good-bye to her just yet. Though I couldn't imagine us ever being best friends like some mothers and daughters were. But she seemed likeable enough, for all her faults, and I wanted to spend more time getting to know her better.

I was going to have to speak to my father about all this at some point. But I didn't know how he would react when I told him about Rose. What if he tried to stop me from seeing her?

My father couldn't actually stop me from doing anything I wanted to—I knew that. I was, after all, a fully functioning adult. Although right at this moment I felt far from that as I huddled beneath my bedclothes like a frightened child, hugging my knees tightly into my chest and hiding away from the scary world outside.

But I couldn't risk upsetting Dad over this—the emotional stakes were too high. No, I'd have to wait until after my time in Notting Hill was over and I'd returned home. Then I'd be able to tell him everything that had happened and ask him all the questions I wanted.

The next morning I called Rose. I lifted and lowered the phone from my ear at least five times before finally I was able to summon up the courage to dial the number and let the call go through.

Surprisingly she answered straight away. "Scarlett, how wonderful, I didn't think I'd hear from you so soon."

"I was wondering if you were busy today. I mean, if you're working it doesn't mat—"

"No, not busy at all. I don't have a shift at the cinema until this evening. Would you like to meet up again?"

Part of me was hoping she *was* busy. "Yes, I would, if it's OK with you...I thought maybe we could meet in Kensington Gardens...or somewhere else if that's not suitable?"

"The Gardens would be lovely. What time?"

"Is eleven too early?"

"Eleven is just fine. Do you know the Peter Pan statue?" she asked. "I could meet you there."

I didn't. "Peter Pan, sure, no problem. I'll see you later then."

"I'll look forward to it, Scarlett."

She hung up.

I sighed heavily as I collapsed back against the scatter cushions on the settee. "Oh, Dad," I said out loud to the empty room. "If only you knew just what you'd started..."

Thirty

I sat on a bench opposite Peter Pan while I waited for Rose.

I'd got to Kensington Gardens early so I'd be able to find the statue in plenty of time. But it hadn't been that difficult, as the first person I asked pointed me in the right direction.

I ran my eyes over the statue while I waited. The Peter in this sculpture appeared to be standing on a tall tree stump playing a set of pipes. A crowd of fairies, rabbits, and other woodland creatures swarmed around the base of the tree—and I guessed it was probably Tinker Bell who was at the top of the stump looking up at Peter. It seemed quite apt, in my current situation, to be sitting in front of "the boy who never grew up." The reason I was waiting here now was because of something that had happened when I was just a baby—something that had never allowed me to completely leave my childhood behind.

While I waited, I watched walkers and joggers pass by, mothers and nannies push prams along the path in front of me, and dog owners allow their mutts to urinate on the gates that surrounded Peter.

Two women wearing baseball hats and tracksuits came

running along the path toward me. I expected they'd pass by like all the others, but they paused and leaned on the railings.

"OK, let's have twenty," one of the women said to the other as they began to do push-ups while leaning on the wrought iron.

They'd completed twelve when I heard a mobile phone ring. "Oops—really sorry, I'll just switch that off." The woman instructing, who I assumed must be a personal trainer, reached into her pocket.

"No need. Take the call…" the other woman panted. "It'll give me the chance for a break…I'll still do the last few push-ups, don't you worry."

The trainer answered her phone, then wandered a little way away to speak to the caller. Her client finished her push-ups and came and sat down next to me on the bench. Resting her elbows on her knees, she dropped her head down so she could catch her breath.

"She's working you hard, I see," I said, partly out of politeness and partly to take my mind off my mother's imminent arrival.

"Just a bit," she said, sitting up. "She always does. But that's what I pay her for; she's very good."

We sat in silence for a moment staring at the statue in front of us.

"It's amazing to think, isn't it, that that whole story was thought of by a man sitting here on a bench just like we are now," my companion said, still gazing up at Peter Pan.

I was surprised; people didn't usually converse with you much in London. Let alone a stranger you'd just met. "Yes, although I have to say I only really know that story because of the movie that was made about it—*Finding Neverland*."

"Yes…I believe I know it." She paused for a moment. "What did you think of it?"

"It's a lovely film," I said, thinking about the movie. "It also stars two of my favorite actors, which helps. And I've actually met one of its stars too."

"Oh, really?"

"Yes, Johnny Depp."

"And what was he like in real life?"

"Erm…he was cool."

"Yes, Johnny's definitely very cool."

"Oh, have *you* met him as well?" I was slightly put out my bench buddy wasn't more impressed at me hobnobbing with a Hollywood A-lister.

"Yes, just a few times."

"Kate!" The trainer was back on the scene now. "Come on, or your pulse rate will drop out of your ideal training zone."

My bench buddy turned to me now.

"Glad you enjoyed the movie," she said, standing up. Then she lifted her hat for a second and winked at me. "And all my other movies too."

And I sat and watched, aghast, as Kate Winslet and her personal trainer jogged away from me down the path and into Kensington Gardens.

Rose appeared seconds later from the same direction, hurrying along the path toward me. Out of her cinema uniform she was elegantly dressed again, this time in black trousers, leather boots, and a red wool coat. She didn't appear to recognize the Hollywood A-lister who jogged by in her tracksuit and baseball hat any more than I had.

"I'm so sorry. I'm not late, am I?" she asked as she arrived by my side.

"No, you're fine," I said, standing up to greet her. "I wasn't quite sure where Peter was, so I thought I'd better get here early. Though there's been lots going on to keep me busy."

"That's good." Rose looked up at the bronze sculpture. "You know I used to read *Peter Pan* to you when you were a baby. I know you were too young to understand, but it was always one of my own favorite stories when I was a child." She glanced at me.

I didn't know quite how to respond, so I said nothing.

"Would you like to go for a walk, Scarlett? Or perhaps we could just have a coffee?"

"A walk sounds good."

We set off together along the path. At first we kept to the safe subjects of the weather, the news, and the people we passed in the park. Then we moved into the semi-safe territory of my life, and I told her about David and Maddie and a bit more about the business.

That led us on to Dad again.

"Have you told him yet?" Rose asked, looking straight ahead. "About me?"

"No, not yet."

"Will you?"

We had reached the Diana memorial fountain. I stopped walking and watched the tourists taking photos and the people just stopping for a moment's reflection in the clear flowing water.

"I don't know. Probably."

"What do you think he'll say?"

I turned to Rose. "I have no idea. I'm not expecting a good reaction, though."

"Will it cause trouble? Between the two of you, I mean?"

I shrugged. "Possibly—for a while. But Dad's usually OK about most things in the end. Once he gets used to the idea, that is."

"The idea?"

"Of me seeing you…" I paused. "I mean if we continue to see each other…in the future."

"Would you like that, Scarlett?" Rose looked as if she might burst if she had to contain the smile any longer that was so desperate to break free and spread across her expectant face.

"I think so…yes, yes, I would."

Don't hug me. Don't hug me, I silently prayed.

To my great relief she didn't. Instead, she just allowed her smile to escape at last.

"Oh, Scarlett, I was hoping you'd say that."

"It doesn't mean I've forgiven you or anything like that. For leaving us," I added, as if she needed reminding.

"No, that goes without saying, of course. Oh, I'm just so happy you feel this way, Scarlett. I'm glad I brought this with me now." She held up a large shopping bag. I'd noticed she'd been carrying it earlier but I hadn't liked to ask what was inside. "Here," she said, handing it to me. "Don't open it now, have a look when you get home."

The bag was quite heavy. "What is it?" I asked, taking a quick peek. Inside was one of those large decorated boxes with a brass-cornered lid and handles, the type you put wedding mementoes in or old photos.

"It's something I've kept for you over the years. No," she insisted when I tried to lift the lid up inside the bag. "Please look at it later, when you're back home again."

"OK, but you've got me intrigued now."

"It's not much, honestly. Shall we get a drink?" she said, changing the subject. "There's a little café over there that looks as if it might be open."

We spent a further hour together in the café, chatting and drinking coffee. And I actually quite enjoyed it. Rose was good company. I think I'd have liked her even if she hadn't been my mother. In fact, it would have been so much easier if she wasn't.

I watched her as she sipped her cappuccino.

"What is it?" she asked, noticing my stare.

"It's nothing, really." I averted my eyes.

"Scarlett, if this is going to work, I think we've got to agree from now on to be honest about everything with each other, yes?"

I nodded reluctantly. "Yes, you're right, of course."

"Well then?"

I took a deep breath. "I was thinking that if you were a person I'd just met casually then this would be a lot easier, that's all."

"What, you mean easier to like me?"

"I guess so."

"Then why don't you pretend that's what I am for now— just a friend and nothing else."

"Are you sure?"

She nodded. "And keep calling me Rose if it makes you feel more comfortable."

"I think it would, yes."

Rose sat back in her seat and lifted her coffee cup. "I think that deserves a toast, don't you? Here's to friendship with a total stranger you met in a cinema, and nothing else!"

I lifted my teacup in agreement. "Yes, here's to that—nothing more, nothing less…"

I went straight back to the house after Rose and I had parted in Kensington Gardens, Rose promising to call me the next day to arrange another meeting.

I didn't even glance in the direction of Sean's house as I climbed up the steps and let myself inside. I swiftly dealt with Buster, threw my coat on to the chair in the hall, and then hurried into the lounge to open up Rose's box.

I don't know what I expected to find in there—some old diaries maybe, a pair of baby booties, that kind of thing. But what I found as I lifted the lid on the colorful box momentarily took my breath away.

Inside were lots of tiny presents—all gift-wrapped in brightly patterned paper. There was one with pink rabbits hopping about on it, and another with numbers, one that was covered in lipsticks, and the next flowers. All the boxes were small, but all were beautifully wrapped with bows and ribbons.

There was a note lying on top, so I opened it—

My darling Scarlett,

Although I was not able to be with you for any of your birthdays in the past I want you to know that

I always thought about you on your special day, and never forgot you.

Every year after I left, I bought you a small gift on your birthday, wrapped it up, and placed it here in this box.

As every year passed and it became fuller, I lost a little more hope that one day you would be able to open the gifts for yourself.

But now I have been given a chance to pass this on to you. I hope you will understand that although I may not have been with you in person on these very special days, I never forgot my little girl.

Mum x

I read the letter through one more time before placing it to one side, and as I carefully picked up the box covered in the pink rabbit paper, I noticed my hands were shaking. The tag attached to the present read—

On your 1st birthday.

I hesitated. I knew that by opening up this box I was going to be opening up so much more than just a gift.

Cautiously I peeled the paper off the box. Inside there was a tiny red teddy bear. I looked at the label around its neck. *My name is Scarlett bear*, it proudly announced, *Please look after me.*

I held the teddy close to my face for a moment and closed my eyes. Then I sat it down carefully next to me, so we could do the rest of the present-opening together.

You are 2! the next gift declared. Inside this one was a soft cloth book, *Amelia's Alphabet.* The front cover had a picture of

Amelia—a cheerful-looking rag doll, with ringlets and a red checked dress.

There followed a succession of toys just perfect for a toddler. Then there were more books, a wooden game, and a real rag doll, who looked very much like Amelia. Then we moved into my teens—where I opened cassettes, and then CDs, of music that strangely I had actually liked when I'd been that age. Some jewelry followed, and a tiny jewelry box, a small evening bag, a couple more books, some earrings, and a bracelet. Then the final few—a beaded makeup bag, an ornate photo frame, and a beautiful silk scarf. When finally I came to the last present, I held it carefully in my hands. The last few minutes had been like traveling through time at supersonic speed, watching my life unfold in front of me.

The truth was, every single present my mother had bought for me was something I knew I would have loved at that age; she'd got it spot on every time. I peeled the paper off the last gift as carefully as I'd opened all the others, trying to rip it as little as possible.

Inside this one was a small red velvet box. I gently lifted the lid and found inside a heart-shaped locket. I could tell the locket wasn't brand new, because it had that slight tarnish all antique silver has. I lifted it up in my fingers to examine it; it was surprisingly heavy, and the floral engraving on it was exquisite. There was a tiny note caught inside the box lid. Carefully I pried it out.

Dear Scarlett,
I wore this necklace on my wedding day, as did your grandmother many years before me. I don't know why

this of all years it seems the right time to give it to you.
But something tells me in my heart that perhaps it is.
    So happy 23rd birthday, my darling, I hope this year is
the year that true love will cast its spell upon you.
    Mum x

I cradled the locket in my hand for a few more seconds before folding up the note, placing it inside the box, and firmly closing the lid.

Then I placed it down alongside all the other twenty-two gifts, which now sat in a huge semicircle around me on the floor. Each gift sat upon the carefully folded wrapping paper it had been encased in for so many years.

I looked slowly along the line from start to finish before I returned to my first birthday once more. I picked up the little red teddy and held it up against my face again.

And it was then that I began to cry.

I must have sat there on the floor sobbing for at least twenty minutes before I was finally able to compose myself. I then packed all the gifts away as carefully as I could back into the box, quickly went to the bathroom to clean up my mascara-streaked face, then grabbed my coat and bag and headed out of the front door.

As I hurried along the pavement I rummaged in my bag for a piece of paper. Once found, I glanced at it briefly before shoving it in my coat pocket.

I walked down into the depths of Notting Hill Gate station. I found the correct line on the map up on the wall and then had to sit patiently on the tube train for a few stops, before I could alight and go back up into the fresh air once more.

I pulled the piece of paper from my pocket, glanced at it again, and then had to ask for further directions before winding my way along a few more streets, eventually arriving at a block of flats.

I looked up momentarily at the towering gray building in front of me before I hurried into its core. I had to wait while I rose up excruciatingly slowly in the lift until the light above my head lit with the number 5, and the doors jolted open.

It was after I had made my way along a dark and dingy corridor that I finally found what I was searching for.

I took a deep breath before knocking purposefully on the door of flat no. 504.

After a few seconds the door swung open and Rose stood staring at me in astonishment.

"Scarlett, what are you doing here so soon?" she said, her expression one of concern.

My voice quivered as I tried to speak.

"What on earth is wrong?" Rose asked in alarm. "What's happened?"

Tears began to fall from my eyes. "M…Mum," I just managed to utter before the tears cascaded down my cheeks in a tidal wave of emotion.

"Oh, Scarlett," Rose said, clasping her hand to her mouth, as tears began to spring from her own eyes now. "What's changed?"

"I have," I sobbed, running toward her.

And it was then, for the first time in my life, that I hugged my mother.

Thirty-One

Mum and I spent lots of time together over the next couple of days. We visited galleries, took walks in the park, had lunch, and even managed to watch a few movies together—both at the cinema and at home on Belinda and Harry's huge plasma screen TV.

"My shifts change next week," Mum announced on Sunday when we were on our way back from seeing a double bill of Cary Grant films. We'd had to travel quite a way on the tube to find this particular cinema, which only showed classic movies. But it had been worth it for an afternoon of *An Affair to Remember* and *The Philadelphia Story* the way they were originally intended to be viewed, on the big screen. "So I won't be able to spend so much time with you, I'm afraid. Besides, I expect you're starting to get fed up seeing me every day."

"Of course I'm not," I protested, genuinely meaning it.

Mum smiled. "That's lovely to hear, Scarlett. But unfortunately I'll be working days next week, so I'll only have my evenings free. Anyway, I expect you'd like to catch up with David. I bet he's been missing you."

"Actually, I think I have been neglecting David a bit

recently, and I wanted a chance to introduce him to my new friends, and to you, of course. So you having your evenings free is good, because I was hoping to have a dinner party next week. David has some business in London so he's going to stay over one night."

"Oh, I'd love to meet your fiancé," Mum said, looking pleased.

"I thought I'd invite Oscar and Ursula too—they're the two people who were with me the night we met at the cinema. They're dying to meet you properly; they know about everything that's happened."

So did my mother now. Over the last few days I had explained not only how Sean and I had searched all over London and then Paris for her, but also the other reason I was here. And, as I thought she might, my mother had heartily approved of my plan to prove everyone wrong about the movies.

"I shall certainly look forward to your dinner party, Scarlett," Mum said now. "But you must promise me you'll try to get out and find some more films next week—you've not got long in London now, and one of us has to prove your father wrong. I certainly never managed it."

"Stop worrying, Mum," I assured her. "Everything will be just fine—I'm sure of it."

As I stood in front of Belinda's cookbooks trying to decipher how long you marinated and how often you should stir, I highly doubted it *would* all be fine...well, the dinner party I was holding tonight anyway.

I was sure that people like Oscar and Ursula who frequented trendy London restaurants all the time wouldn't expect to come to a dinner party and be served up my trademark dish of spaghetti bolognese. But knowing those two, I highly doubted they would complain—they were far too lovely and polite for that. And David…well, David would be surprised to find I was even cooking at all; it wasn't usually high on my list of successful pastimes.

But I wanted to impress my mother. She might not be living in the lap of luxury at the moment, but I got the feeling from some of the stories she had told me about her life that she had sampled some of the finest cuisines in the world at one time or another.

"Oh God, what do you mean, you stupid man?" I said, staring at the pages of the cookbook, where the celebrity chef grinned smugly back at me from a tiny photo at the top of each page. "What the hell is *braise-deglaze*?"

The doorbell rang.

"Oh no—who the hell is that at"—I glanced at the clock on the cooker—"at four bloody o'clock in the afternoon!"

I stomped impatiently to the door in my apron, with my cookbook still gripped tightly in one hand.

"Hello, stranger," the person standing grinning on my doorstep said. "Long time no see."

"Sean!" I nearly dropped the book in surprise. "What are you doing here?"

"I just heard the good news from Ursula—about your mother—so I thought I'd pop round." He looked at my apron-clad body suspiciously. "Can I come in?"

"That depends."

"On?"

"On whether you know what *braise-deglaze* means."

Sean wrinkled his forehead. "It's a way of cooking food in liquid, until the liquid evaporates—I think."

"You're in then," I said, pulling him into the house with my book-free hand.

"What *are* you doing?" Sean asked when I'd shut the door behind him and he was following me back into the kitchen.

"Cooking—well, trying to anyway. I'm having a dinner party."

"Oh, I see."

"I would have invited you, of course," I said hurriedly. "But I thought you were still in New York."

"I got back last night—been sleeping off the jet lag since. Then Ursula phoned and told me about your mother. I can hardly believe it, Scarlett, she was right here all along."

"I know—mad, isn't it?"

"So how have things been between you?" Sean said, picking up an onion from the counter and casually tossing it up and down in his hand. "Are the two of you getting on all right?"

"We are now. Look, it's a really long story, Sean. Which I really want to tell you," I added truthfully. I *did* genuinely want to tell him. In fact, now he was here in the house with me again, I didn't want him to go at all. "But I'm in way over my head here with this dinner party and I really don't have the time at the moment. Maybe we could meet up tomorrow?" I suggested hopefully.

"Or maybe we could just kill two birds with one stone and I could stay here and help you cook while you tell me all about your mother."

I smiled gratefully at him. "You can cook?"

"I'll give it a try," Sean said, throwing the onion on a chopping board and starting to roll up the sleeves of his shirt. "Now, how bad can it be?"

"I've just about managed to light the oven successfully," I said in a pathetic voice. "But not much more, I'm afraid."

Sean quickly took charge and the kitchen was soon filled with countless delicious aromas—suggesting to me that he might have played down his culinary talents somewhat. I ran about the kitchen like his commis chef and, in between chopping, slicing, and stuffing, I told him all about what had happened with Mum.

When I got to the part about the gifts I watched carefully for Sean's reaction. He had his back to me stirring something in a saucepan, but I saw him pause for a moment before he continued to move the wooden spoon around again in a slow, circular motion.

"Pass me that knife, will you, please?" I asked, gesturing to a sharp knife that lay next to him on the counter. "I think this one is a little blunt."

Sean picked up the knife and turned toward me. As I looked up at him I noticed his eyes glisten under the bright kitchen spotlights. "I do wish you'd chop those onions under water like I said, Scarlett," he said brusquely, hastily turning his face away. "They play havoc with my eyes."

I didn't like to point out I'd actually finished chopping the onions ten minutes ago and I was now well into the mushrooms and carrots.

"So everything's going well, then?" Sean asked, when I'd finished my story and he was fully up to date.

"Yes. That's partly what tonight is all about, so Mum can meet some of my friends—well, most of them. Maddie and Felix are still away on their honeymoon."

Sean was silent. He pretended to concentrate hard on something in the recipe book.

"Look, why don't you stay for dinner tonight too, Sean?" I suggested, putting down the casserole dish I was carrying. "After all, you've practically cooked the meal yourself."

"But won't it throw your numbers out?" he asked, turning his gaze from the book toward me.

I shook my head. "No, there were only five of us anyway; six will make it look much neater."

"Who's the five?"

"Me, obviously, and Mum. Then there's Oscar, Ursula, and David."

I saw Sean's shoulders tighten when I mentioned David's name.

"David's coming?"

"Yes, Mum wanted to meet him."

"I see."

"But I'm sure she'd love to meet you too, Sean," I said hurriedly. "She's heard all about you from me."

"Has she?" Sean asked keenly, his eyes bright with anticipation.

"Yeah, I told her all about how you helped me search for her."

"Oh, right." Sean turned back to the book again.

"Please stay, Sean," I said, walking across the kitchen toward him. "This is an important night for me. I'd like you to be here." I touched him gently on the shoulder.

"Of course I'll stay, Scarlett," he said, turning to face me again. "If that's what you'd like?"

"I would, Sean—yes."

As we stood silently staring at each other, I had to fight the urge to reach out and wipe away the small beads of sweat that had formed on Sean's brow. Because if I did so, I knew my fingers would want to continue to trace a line along his nose to his mouth, where they would pause, and I would slowly replace my fingers with my lips…

There was a sizzling sound. It took me a few seconds to realize it wasn't coming from me.

"Sean, the sauce!"

Sean spun round to see red wine sauce bubbling over the side of the saucepan on to the hob. "Damn, it's not supposed to boil," he cursed, hoisting the saucepan aloft. "I'll have to start again now."

Hurriedly we returned to our kitchen duties, and all sizzling—of any kind—was momentarily forgotten.

Thirty-Two

Y ou know what's just occurred to me, Sean," I said a little
later when things were back under control again. "You
could be Mark Darcy standing there cooking in my kitchen."

"I don't think Mr. Darcy cooked, did he?" Sean said, looking
puzzled. "Not in the Jane Austen I've read anyway—he would
have had staff to do that for him."

"No—not Mr. Darcy from *Pride and Prejudice*. Mark Darcy
from *Bridget Jones*!"

"Oh right, one of your movies again."

"Yeah, I haven't notched one up for a while. But you've given
me another scene this afternoon with all your cooking efforts."

Sean thought for a moment. "Wait, haven't I been him
before? This Darcy fellow?"

I considered this. "Yeah, I said you and David's water
fight at Maddie's wedding was like the one out of the second
Bridget Jones film."

"What about when I was in the boat, on the Small World
ride at Disneyland? I'm sure you mentioned it then?"

"No, that was Hugh Grant's character—Daniel Cleaver—I
compared you to."

"Ah, I see—I think. Which one's better? To be compared to, I mean?"

I thought again. "Mark Darcy. Yes, definitely Mark." After all we were talking Colin Firth here—and no woman who ever saw him emerge from that lake ever quite got over it.

"You had to think about it though. Why?"

"I…I'm not sure. Colin Firth is this quite staid, reserved character in the film, a bit like the real Mr. Darcy—the Jane Austen version. But you just know that deep inside he'd be really passionate and sexy once you got his guard down. And Hugh Grant—that's Daniel—his personality is out there from the start—there are no hidden depths with him. He's a bit of a cad…a smooth talker…a ladies' man, I guess you'd call him. They both have their attractions from a female perspective, just in different ways."

"But you liked Colin better?"

Sean had stopped what he was doing at the stove and was giving me his full attention during this questioning.

"Yeah, I think so. What is all this anyway? I thought you hated the cinema—why the sudden interest?"

"No reason," Sean said mysteriously, turning back to his saucepan. "I just wondered, that's all."

I opened my mouth to question him further, but the doorbell rang again. I never had visitors—mainly because I only knew Sean, Ursula, and Oscar in London. Who could this be?

I excused myself from the kitchen, walked through the hall, and pulled open the front door without my now customary glance through the peephole.

"Surprise!" my father called from the top of the steps with his arms outstretched.

"Dad! What on earth are you doing here?"

"What sort of welcome is that for your old dad?"

"He came with me, Scarlett," David said, appearing from behind Dad on the steps. "I hope you don't mind?"

"No...no, of course I don't. I'm just surprised to see you, that's all."

"Good surprise or bad?" Dad asked.

"Good, obviously."

"You're a good liar, Scarlett—I know you hate surprises."

"Not always," I said vaguely. I was trying to think which film the lines we had just inadvertently spoken had been from. Oh, it was on the tip of my tongue...Oh yes, *Notting Hill*, of course! The part where Alec Baldwin turns up to surprise Julia Roberts at the Ritz hotel.

"Aren't you going to invite us in?" David asked.

"Yes...yes, come in." I stood back, and they piled in, David with an overnight bag but my father, rather more worryingly, with a suitcase.

"How long are you here for, Dad?" I asked, suddenly remembering who was coming to dinner tonight.

"Just for a few days, Scarlett. It's been ages since I've been down to London, and David had some sort of rail voucher that if you bought one rail fare you got one half price. So we split the cost, and I thought I'd come and see how you were getting on."

Now David and the railcard made sense, but my father rarely took time away from the business, and for both of us to be away at the same time was unheard of.

Dad and David gave each other a conspiratorial look, and suddenly I got why my father was here. He didn't want to risk anything going wrong like it had with my mother—not now the end of my time away was so near, and neither did David. They'd cooked this little scheme up between them to keep an eye on me. Is that what David had meant in Paris when he said he'd given my father his word? Were they in this together all along?

I was about to tell them in no uncertain terms that I didn't need keeping an eye on when Sean appeared unexpectedly from the kitchen still wearing an apron.

"Scarlett, have you any—"

I spun round toward him.

"You!" I heard David say behind me.

Sean looked calmly between David and my father. "And it's a pleasure to see you again too, David." Then he ignored him and walked toward Dad. "I don't believe we've had the pleasure?" he said with his hand outstretched.

"Sean, this is my father."

"Mr. O'Brien, pleased to meet you at last, Scarlett has told me so much about you."

I didn't know whether Sean was doing all this just to annoy David—but if he was, it was working, because David's face was now quite an alarming shade of red.

My father, looking surprised, shook Sean's hand.

"Dad, this is Sean, my neighbor."

David made a snorting sound.

"Pleased to meet you, Sean," Dad said. Then he glanced at David. "Are you all right, David? You've turned a funny color."

"I think it's time I went," Sean said, untying his apron. "I hope I've been of some help to you, Scarlett." He pulled the apron over his head and walked toward the door.

David—his color returning to normal again—stepped aside to make room for him. "I hope you're not going on our account, old boy," he sneered as Sean passed.

"Yes, Sean, you really don't have to go." I glared at David.

"Yes, I think I do," Sean said, focusing on me and choosing to ignore David. "I hope all goes well tonight, Scarlett. I'm sure your guests will enjoy the food you've so carefully prepared." He winked at me as he reached for the door.

"Wait a moment, Sean, and I'll see you out properly. Dad, David, the lounge is just through there," I said, pointing to the door. "If you'd like to go through, I'll be there in a minute to help you find somewhere to put all your things."

My father looked in the direction I was gesturing. "Righty-ho then. Nice to meet you, Sean." He nodded at him.

"And you, Mr. O'Brien."

David made what sounded like a growling noise at Sean.

"You really want to get that cough seen to, David," Dad said, as David followed him obediently into the lounge. "It can get much worse if you leave it untreated too long."

I waited until they were out of sight before stepping outside with Sean.

"Please don't go," I pleaded with him again. "I still have room for seven around the table, it's huge. And I'm sure David will behave himself if I have a word."

Sean smiled at me. "Oh, Scarlett, I would have thought me being there would be the last thing on your mind right now."

"What do you mean? Oh, Dad. I had no idea he was going to turn up today—apparently it's a surprise."

"Yes, I couldn't help overhearing your conversation from the kitchen. But no, I don't mean your father turning up unexpectedly. I mean, what are you going to tell your mother?"

"How do you mean?"

"About the dinner party—how will you put her off? You can't have her turning up tonight with your father here, can you?"

I stuck my hands in the pocket of my apron and idly watched a man trimming a hedge over the road.

"Scarlett?" Sean prompted.

"They're going to have to meet each other again some time now Mum's back in my life," I said, turning to face him. "It's not my fault Dad's turned up out of the blue like this."

Sean's eyes widened. "But they haven't seen each other for over twenty years; there could be bloodshed if they just turn up at the same dinner party!"

"But there might not be...it could all work out just fine."

Sean rubbed his forehead in a way that suggested he didn't agree.

"Just how much of that red wine we were marinating with did you drink? Scarlett, just ring your mother and tell her the dinner's off."

"No, she's been looking forward to meeting everyone."

"Including your father?"

I pulled my apron over my head and folded it up. "Look, Sean, I didn't orchestrate this, fate did. And now I'm going to let fate take its course."

"You're asking for trouble."

"Maybe...maybe not." I shrugged. "Look, are you going to come to dinner tonight or not?"

"And miss this? You've got to be kidding. It'll be like Christmas in the Queen Vic—just without the cockney accents."

I had to smile. "I know you think what I'm going to let happen is the wrong thing to do. But maybe that's what all this has been about—me coming to London, so I can have two parents in my life. Everything happens—"

"For a reason. Yes, I know, you've said so before. But maybe this isn't the only reason for you coming here?"

"And maybe it is. Look, I have to get back inside. I'll see you later, yes, about 7:30? I'll tell Mum it's eight, and then everyone will have a chance to chat to Dad a bit before she arrives."

"I don't think that's a good—"

I held up my hand. "No more, Sean. I'll see you later?"

Sean nodded. "But you could end up regretting this decision, Scarlett. Maybe not today, maybe not tomorrow, but soon, and possibly for the rest of your life."

I stared suspiciously at Sean. "Are you absolutely sure you never watch movies?" I asked him.

"Not often, why?"

"Hmm, it just seems you have an awful knack recently of making me feel like I'm in one."

Thirty-Three

I looked around Belinda and Harry's lounge at my guests all enjoying themselves and I felt a sense of great achievement.

Everyone had arrived within ten minutes of the requested time of 7:30, and they were now all standing around with glasses in their hands, chatting amiably to one another.

Ursula arrived looking quirky yet elegant as always, in a lilac and pink 1960s vintage dress from Oscar's boutique. And Oscar, who was currently looking very bored talking to David, tonight sported a mustard-yellow suit with a black shirt and red tartan tie.

My father had put on his best trousers and a shirt that I bought him last Christmas, and at this moment was surprisingly deep in conversation with Sean.

After Sean had left earlier this afternoon, I had quickly returned to the kitchen to make sure that nothing was burning or boiling over on the stove—but everything appeared to be under control. Luckily Sean had prepared a series of sticky notes to remind me just when I had to start cooking each dish and what gas mark to put them on at.

I watched him now as he chatted with my father. Tonight he

was wearing a deep-purple shirt—unbuttoned just far enough for me to make out the beginnings of the fine hair that I knew covered his broad chest. And a pair of black trousers that sat on him so perfectly and fitted him so snugly in all the places they should that they must have been tailor-made.

"When is your mother arriving?" Ursula inquired, appearing by my side and making me jump.

"Hmm? Oh, I...I told her eight o'clock," I said, looking at my watch. "So she should be here soon." I had briefed everyone—except Dad, of course—on what was happening tonight, and so far the response hadn't been exactly enthusiastic.

"Are you nervous about her coming?"

"I wasn't. But now the moment's getting closer I am starting to get a bit worried."

"Finally," Oscar gasped, breaking free from David and rushing to our side. He took a large gulp of his wine. "Oh sorry, darling, I know he's with you, but if I have to hear one more word about his wood laminate flooring issues, I think I'll scream!" Oscar looked from Ursula to me. "So who did I hear you say is arriving at eight?"

"Scarlett's mother?" Ursula prompted.

"Oh, of course, your mother. Scarlett, I'm so sorry, I almost forgot. My brain's been quite numbed." Oscar put his hand to his forehead and took another gulp of his wine. "You know best, darling, but it sounds like a recipe for firework pie if you ask me."

Ursula shot Oscar a warning glance.

"So," she said brightly, turning to me. "How have you and your mother been getting on? We've hardly seen you since that night at the cinema."

"Really well, actually," I said, keen as I always was these days to talk about Mum. "We've spent loads of time together and had such fun. Meeting her again has made me face up to quite a few things too."

"What sorts of things?" Oscar asked, intrigued.

"Just things like how important certain people are to me. To be grateful for what I have in life and not to keep chasing after the unattainable." I glanced across at Sean.

"We should always be grateful for our nearest and dearest," Ursula said softly. "But never give up on your dreams, Scarlett."

I looked at her.

"But what if your dreams never come true, Ursula?"

"If you stop believing in them, how will you ever know if they would have?"

I was about to question her further when the shrill tone of the doorbell interrupted me. Everyone in the room froze except my father. He carried on his conversation with Sean until he realized that everyone else had stopped talking and the room was silent.

"Carry on, everyone," I said brightly, trying to force a smile. "It's only the doorbell, for goodness' sake."

As I walked out of the lounge a sudden dread about what was going to happen next began to wash over me. And as I reached the front door and slowly swung it open a huge sense of foreboding flooded through my body.

Perhaps everyone *had* been right. I had to try to stop this now, before it went any further.

"Good evening," my mother said cheerfully, standing on the step in front of me clutching a bottle of wine and some flowers.

"How is everything going? I'm not late, am I?" As I stood staring at her, desperately trying to think of a reason for her not to come in, she walked past me into the hall.

"The thing is...it's..." I stuttered as I closed the door behind her.

"What's up, Scarlett?" she teased. "Surely cooking for us all hasn't taken it out of you that badly? Actually you do look a bit pale. Are you all right?"

"Mum, there's something I have to tell you."

"Yes?" my mother asked, looking concerned. "What is it?"

"Scarlett, where's your corkscrew?" my father said, appearing from the lounge. "We need to open..." His voice trailed off as he saw the newest guest to join the dinner party. The bottle he was carrying slipped from his hand and crashed onto the tiled floor. The green glass smashed into what looked like a thousand tiny pieces, and the red wine inside flowed out around his feet, making him look as if he was standing in a huge pool of blood.

The crash brought everyone running from the lounge to see what had happened. But my father didn't appear to notice; he just stood staring at my mother. His face had drained of color, just as the bottle had been of its wine.

"Hello, Tom," Mum said, recovering from the shock much quicker than Dad. I quickly grabbed the bottle of wine from her hands—just in case. "It's been a long time."

My father opened and closed his mouth a few times, like a goldfish gasping for air.

"Dad, let's get this cleaned up," I said, moving toward him to pick up the pieces of broken glass. "Then maybe we—"

"What is *she* doing here?" my father boomed, finding his voice at last.

I stopped dead in my tracks. Dad had rarely shouted at me, even when I was little.

"I can assure you I had no idea *you* were going to be here either, Tom," my mother replied calmly. "Or I definitely wouldn't have come and upset everyone's evening like this."

"*You* wouldn't have come?" my father bellowed again. "When did *you* ever care about anyone else but yourself? You certainly didn't care twenty years ago when you walked out on us, did you, Rose?"

My mother looked around at everyone staring in shock at the situation unfolding in front of them.

"If you'll just let me get this wine cleaned up," I said, trying to move toward Dad again, "then I can explain—"

"Stay right there, Scarlett," he said, holding up his hand. "I think *you've* done enough already."

I turned back toward my mother.

"Mum?"

"Perhaps I'd better just go, Scarlett. I don't want to ruin your evening further." She glanced back at my father. "It's quite obvious I'm not welcome here." She made a move toward the door.

"But..." I didn't know what to do. What to say. I'd messed up big time and I was scuppered whatever I did next. Whichever parent I tried to appease it would look as if I was taking sides.

"Mum, please don't go."

She turned around, her hand still on the doorknob. "Scarlett, I must. It really won't be pleasant for anyone if I stay. I'll call you tomorrow and we can talk about this then."

I just nodded at her.

She gave a quick glance back into the hall. "I'm so sorry. I do hope I haven't ruined your evening too much. Good night, everyone."

And then she was gone.

I felt my heart wrench as the door closed behind her. Slowly I turned back to the waiting guests.

Among the emotions on the row of faces that greeted me, the strongest by far was anger on that of my father. He still stood in the pool of spilt wine, his face even paler than it had been before.

"Dad?" I said in a small voice. "I'm really sorry. I didn't mean for it to be like this."

Dad still didn't speak. He just stood there. So I moved toward him.

"No!" he said, finding not only his own voice now but those often others at the same time. "No, don't *you* come anywhere near me."

"But, Dad..."

"How could you, Scarlett? How could you after everything we've been through together? Everything I've told you about her? How could you do this to me?"

I stood in the middle of the hallway feeling the weight of everyone's eyes upon me. My father's were full of anger, Oscar's shock, Ursula's sorrow, and David's pity. When my eyes made contact with Sean's, I felt myself begin to shake.

"That's enough," Sean said immediately, stepping in between my father and me. "This stops now. You two need to sort this out later, quietly and in private when you've calmed down." He looked about the room. "Ursula, can you get something to clean this red wine up with, please. And Oscar, could you take Mr. O'Brien into the lounge again and pour him a large whiskey?"

Oscar opened his eyes wide at the thought of trying to take my angered father anywhere.

"Scarlett," Sean said, coming over to me and putting his arm around my shoulders. "You're shaking. Are you OK?"

"And *this* stops now!" I heard yet another angry voice say, as David marched over to Sean. "She's my fiancée, and I'll be the one to comfort her if she's shaking."

"Why didn't you do something just now, then?" Sean asked, his arm dropping away from my shoulders as he turned on David. "If you care so much about her, why was I the one who had to step in to rescue her in her hour of need yet again?"

I stood silently watching them all: Ursula trying to mop up a bottle of red wine from the floor around my father's feet; Oscar trying to persuade my father to move away from the wine and go through to the lounge for a drink; and Sean and David arguing over me once again.

And very slowly I felt myself backing away from them. I lifted my jacket that was hanging on the coat stand and gently pulled open the front door. As I did an icy wind blew through my body and back into the house.

Everyone stopped what they were doing and turned toward the opened door.

I must have looked quite dramatic silhouetted in the doorway with the wind billowing my hair all around my face, so I took up a theatrical stance.

"You all warned me that tonight would be a disaster. And it was, of epic proportions. And I didn't listen to any of you, did I? I never do. I just carry on blindly, assuming everything will work out and hoping everyone will have a happy ending. Well, congratulations—you were all right, and I got it all spectacularly wrong. Just like I always do."

The wind blew another icy cold blast around my back. I didn't really want to go out into the cold February evening at all—but I couldn't go back now, could I? Not when I'd just made that dramatic speech. Oh, why did this sort of thing always work in the movies and not in real life?

"Now before I cause any of you any more trouble, I'm going out. To somewhere I can't cause any problems."

Then I turned and, without looking back, ran down the steps outside, slamming the door behind me.

Now where can I disappear to for a while in Notting Hill? I asked myself as I ran quickly down the street, pulling on my coat as I went.

I knew the answer straight away.

Thirty-Four

I hurried down the road until I came to the black railings that surrounded the gardens, and after checking quickly around me, I hoisted myself up and over the bars in exactly the same place I had the night I'd met Sean.

I was grateful I hadn't worn the dress I'd been thinking about wearing earlier tonight, and had plumped instead for a pair of smart black trousers and a sparkly top, otherwise the maneuver could have been a lot trickier.

I landed on the other side with a thud and toppled sideways into a bush—luckily for me one of the non-thorny varieties; my stiletto heels were not an ideal platform for landing on soft ground. "Damn," I mumbled, as I scrambled to my feet again and brushed my trousers down. "If only I'd had my keys with me I could have saved myself all this mountaineering lark." I had found out after my first visit here with Sean that Belinda and Harry too had a key to this little park. But of course my diva-like exit from the house tonight hadn't allowed me the luxury of collecting keys. I was lucky to have a coat on.

So now I was in here, what was I going to do?

I found the wooden bench that Sean and I had rested on

a few weeks earlier and sat down. I was starting to feel very guilty at just storming out and leaving everyone to sort out the trouble I'd caused. But it was too late to go back now; I'd acted on the spur of the moment, and now I would have to suffer the consequences.

I wondered what was happening back at the house.

I hope Sean remembers to take the meat out of the oven, I thought, suddenly panicking about the carefully prepared dinner. But it was hardly likely that anyone would be tasting it tonight after what had just gone on, so I suppose it didn't really matter...as long as it didn't set light to the house...

"Stop it, Scarlett," I admonished myself. "You've got more than a burned dinner to worry about now."

I was right for once. What I'd done tonight was unforgivable. I'd put everyone at the dinner party in an awkward position, and I wouldn't blame any of them if they never wanted to speak to me again—particularly my parents.

"Oh, poor Mum." I buried my face in my hands as I recalled the expression on her face as she'd looked around at everyone in the hallway staring at her.

And Dad. How was I ever going to explain all this to him?

I rested my head on the back of the bench and looked up at the sky. It was a clear night and I could see the stars twinkling above me. It was just like the evening I'd sat out here with Sean—the only difference was, that night I'd felt excited and optimistic about the days that lay ahead of me. Now I only felt sadness that my time here was so rapidly coming to an end and I seemed to have caused so much pain and achieved so little.

I sat on the bench for quite a while just thinking, until my feet began to feel like they were encased in ice, and my hands, even though they were shoved in my pockets, would have sat well on the end of Jack Frost's arms.

When I'd left the house earlier I'd secretly hoped that someone might come after me. Or that by now I might at least have heard the faraway call of my name floating down the street. But instead I saw no one and heard nothing.

If this had been a movie, the hero would have known right away where to come looking for me. He'd have found me sitting here all alone on my little bench and come along and comforted me in his big strong arms. While everyone else had no idea where I'd gone, my hero would have known straight away.

Perhaps everyone was right? Maybe life never did happen the same way it did in the cinema. I thought about all of the movie scenes I'd added to my list so far. Every time I'd tried to orchestrate one of those scenes myself something had gone wrong. I'd been lucky enough to pick up some coincidental ones along the way, but even those weren't quite the same as the originals. Had I just been imagining the similarities for my own benefit? And now, I'd just made a wonderfully dramatic exit from my house in the dead of the night—in a scene that would have made any director proud—and yet not one person had come looking for me. I'd have thought at least Sean might have guessed where I was and come to my rescue.

I looked toward the gate hopefully, in case he might be there desperately searching through the railings for me. But sadly he wasn't. Instead, a bright white light shone through the bars, almost blinding me.

I held my arm up over my eyes.

"Are you OK, miss?" I heard a voice call.

The spotlight was aimed at the ground now, so at least I could see again. I blinked at the railings and saw a young police officer peering through them.

"Yes, I'm fine. Thanks, officer."

"What are you doing sitting all alone there in the dark?" he asked, shining his flashlight around the surrounding area.

"Nothing really, officer," I said, racking my brains for a reason to be here.

The policeman rattled on the gate. "This gate appears to be locked, miss. You do have a key for this park, don't you?"

"Yes, of course," I said, telling the truth. OK, I might not have it on me just now...

"Would you mind coming over here and showing me?" the officer asked. "Only we get quite a few reports of vandals trying to get in these gardens, so I have to check, you see. It's all because of that film they made here a few years ago. I don't know if you know it at all—*Notting Hill*, it was called."

"Er yes, I do know it." I got up from the bench and made my way slowly across to the railings. I tried to make small talk while I felt around in my pockets, praying I'd find a key. "It's a good film, have you seen it?"

"Yeah, several times, my girlfriend loves it. Loves old Hughie boy, more like. We have to go and see every bloody film he's in."

"But you must have enjoyed watching Julia Roberts," I said, stalling for time.

"Yeah, she's OK. Prefer blondes myself. Cameron Diaz—now she's much more my cup of tea."

My hand struck on something hard—hoorah!

"Here's my key," I said, confidently holding up the key to Belinda's jewelry box. I'd been having a nose about the house on one of my "down" days a while ago, and had bent the tiny key while trying to get it into the lock on the box. I'd put it in my pocket to remind me to get a new one cut while I was out. But then everything had kicked off with my mother, and I'd never got around to it.

The police officer looked doubtfully at the key. "It looks a bit small, miss."

"No, this is the key. How else would I have got in here otherwise?"

"Perhaps you'd like to open the gate for me then, miss. Then I can leave you be and carry on my way."

"Er…right then." Hopefully I tried the tiny key in the lock, praying that it might just "pick" the mechanism and open it. Well, stranger things had happened.

But unfortunately they weren't going to happen to me tonight.

"Ah, it appears to be stuck," I said, rattling the key about in the oversized lock.

The police officer raised his eyebrows at me. "I think both of us know that key has never opened up this gate, don't we, miss?"

I looked down at the ground and made patterns in the dust with my toe.

"I'll ask you my earlier question again, miss. Just what are you doing in that garden?"

"I do have a key, honestly, Officer. It's just I came out in a rush—and forgot it."

"In that case, Miss, just how *did* you get into the garden tonight?"

"I climbed over the top," I mumbled.

"I beg your pardon, miss?"

"I said I climbed over the railings."

"I think you'd better wait right there, miss." The officer bent down to his lapel and spoke into his radio. "Bravo One to Charlie Four—I require some assistance at the gardens just off Rosmead."

"Roger, Bravo One, right with you," came back the crackly reply.

"Look, I'm not a hooligan or anything like that," I protested, imagining myself being handcuffed and carted away in the back of a police van. "I really do have a key—I live in Lansdowne Road."

"Could I see some ID then, please, miss?"

"Yes, of cour—" I reached for my missing bag. "No, I don't actually have any on me right now."

"I thought not. If you could just wait there, please, miss."

I leaned my head against the railings. Could tonight get any worse?

Charlie Four quickly showed up. He was a fair bit older than Bravo One, and although he didn't quite say, 'ello, 'ello, 'ello, what 'ave we 'ere then?" he might as well have, as he inspected me standing miserably behind the bars. Oh my God, it was like being in prison already!

"What's all this then, Constable?" he asked Bravo One.

"Well, Sarge, this lady claims she has a key for this park, but she admits to entering it earlier by climbing over the top of the railings."

"I see. Is this right, miss?"

"Yes, but—"

"One moment, Miss," he said, holding up his hand. "Your turn will come. What else, Constable?"

"She also claims to live in Lansdowne Road but doesn't have any ID on her to prove it."

"I see. Anything else, Constable?"

"No, Sarge. That is the situation as it appears to me."

"'Right, miss. Do you wish to add anything to the constable's statement?"

Didn't I need a lawyer present before making a statement to the police?

"I guess that's kind of what happened. But you don't understand. The reason I don't have a key or any ID is because I had an argument tonight at home, and I had to come out in a hurry. I'm not a criminal."

"Is that everything, miss?" the sergeant asked, eyeing me up and down through the railings.

I nodded my head sadly. Wasn't it enough?

"Right then, you leave us no alternative. Constable, go to work."

Bravo One looked blankly at his sergeant.

"The equipment, Constable?" Charlie Four demanded. "You do have it?"

Bravo One's cheeks flushed and then he shrugged and shook his head.

Charlie Four rolled his eyes and sighed. "Then I shall have to improvise." He reached for his handcuffs.

Oh no, were they going to cuff me to the gates until backup was called?

But instead of removing the handcuffs from his belt, he lifted them up and groped about in his pocket. "Nope, I don't seem to have anything suitable," he announced. "Constable, empty your pockets, please."

"Sarge?"

"Your pockets—empty them. I'm looking for something to pick the lock with."

The constable slowly emptied his pockets. One by one a tissue, a piece of string, a stick of gum, and a condom were placed into the sergeant's outstretched palm.

The sergeant raised his eyebrows at the condom.

"I was a Boy Scout," the constable explained. "Be prepared?"

"Indeed, Constable, we'll discuss that fact later. But none of this is any good for getting the lock undone, now, is it?" He looked at me through the bars again. "I don't suppose you have a hairpin on you, do you, miss?"

"Er, no," I said, absentmindedly feeling about in my hair. I had worn it down tonight, so there were no accessories of any kind hidden in there.

"Then I shall have to ask you to remove your hat, Constable," the sergeant instructed.

"But why, Sarge?"

"Come along now, Constable. I think you know why? Let's not mess about in front of the lady."

The constable slowly removed his hat and the sergeant swiftly plucked a hairpin from his head.

"There now, that's better," he said, inserting the pin into the lock.

"It was my girlfriend's idea," the constable quickly explained to me while the sergeant expertly picked at the lock. "I have an unusually small head for a man, and they didn't do a hat small enough to fit me properly. The pins help me keep it up above my eyes, see."

I nodded, thinking how bizarre this was—one policeman picking a lock in front of me while the other explained the benefits of hair accessories.

"There. All done," Charlie Four announced at last, swinging open the gate. "Now, if you'd like to come this way, miss."

"Are you taking me down the station?" I asked worriedly.

"You've been watching too many episodes of *The Bill*, miss," he said, holding out his arm in an "after you" gesture. "We're just going to walk you safely home, that's all."

"But I thought—"

"*Notting Hill*, right?" the sergeant asked, giving me the onceover again now I wasn't "behind bars."

I nodded. "How did you guess?"

"You look the type. All full of romance and nostalgia. We've seen it a hundred times since that film came out. They're not usually on their own though, like you—are they, Constable? We usually find them in pairs."

The constable nodded.

"Well, I…" My voice trailed off. It was much too long a story to explain why I was there on my own.

"Never mind, miss. We don't need to know why. Let's get you home."

Charlie Four and Bravo One escorted me back to the house.

They may not have been arresting me, but I felt like a criminal being walked home by two policemen. Thank goodness it would probably only be Dad and David there when I got home; everyone else would be long gone by now.

There was still a light on in the hall as I approached the house. I climbed the steps while the sergeant and his constable watched me from the pavement below. I held my hand up to knock gingerly on the door, but it swung open before I had the chance to.

"Scarlett!" Sean exclaimed. He hurriedly crept out on to the step next to me and pulled the door to behind him. "Where the hell have you been?" he asked, lowering his voice. "We've all been worried sick." He looked down at the two policemen standing on the pavement. "Are you all right? Has something happened?"

"I'm assuming you know this lady then, sir?" Charlie Four called to Sean. "And you can confirm she does actually live here?"

"Yes, yes she does, why?"

"That's all we need to know, sir. We'll leave her with you now, if we may? But perhaps you can do one thing for us in the future?"

"Yes?" Sean asked, looking mystified.

"Next time she goes out, sir, just make sure she takes a key with her, OK?"

As the two policemen ambled away together down the road, Sean held his finger to his lips and pulled me silently inside the house. Then he gently closed the door behind us. "What's he talking about, Scarlett?" he whispered. "What's been going on?"

"It's a long story, Sean." I looked around the house. It seemed very quiet. "Has everyone gone home?" I asked, keeping my own voice low. "Why are *you* still here?"

"Oscar and Ursula have left, yes. But I didn't want to go home until I knew you were back safely. Your father is in the lounge. But David and I have been trying to keep him calm."

"Thanks," I said gratefully. "You didn't have to stay."

"I wanted to." Sean smiled. "You don't need to worry about your mother either. Ursula and Oscar found her in a café down the road. And she's fine."

"How did they…oh, it must have been Kelly's they went to. And she's really OK?" I asked him. "You're not just saying that? What did they say?"

"She's fine, Scarlett. A bit shaken up, but once you've spoken to her and explained I'm sure all will be well again."

How did Sean always know how to make everything right?

"You look frozen, Scarlett," he said, putting his hand on my shoulder. "Why don't you go upstairs and put something a little warmer on? I'll make you a cup of tea and then you can deal with your father. Five more minutes won't hurt, will it?"

I nodded at him gratefully. "You're too good to me, Sean, do you know that?"

"Yes," he said, smiling, "I do."

I began to climb the stairs and then I turned back. "Wait, you said before you and David had been working *together* to keep Dad calm? How did that happen?"

Sean shrugged. "I guess we both had something in common for once."

"What's that?"

"We both love you, Scarlett," he said, looking up at me for a moment before he disappeared into the kitchen. I heard my father's voice from the lounge, and David replying, so I quickly ran up the stairs to my bedroom, dissecting Sean's last comment as I went.

What did he mean—love? Did he mean love as in "care about"? Or love as in "fall in love"?

I rubbed at my forehead. Now was not the time to be throwing even more complex questions into my pounding brain. I knew there were going to be plenty of those later.

Thirty-Five

When I'd got changed and tidied up I ventured downstairs again. I stood in the hall, taking deep breaths to calm myself. David emerged from the bathroom while I was standing there. He jumped when he saw me. "So you decided to come back?"

"Yes, and I'm really sorry for storming out the way I did earlier…So, how's Dad?"

"He's a bit shaken after seeing your mother, which is understandable. But I've been keeping him calm with the inside of your friends' liquor cabinet—so you may have to replace a few items before they return home."

"Sure, I will. Thanks, David…for everything. I know it can't have been easy for you being here tonight with Sean."

"Hmm, that…I think we have a lot to talk about, Scarlett—and soon. But right now you have a more important issue to deal with waiting for you in the lounge."

I hugged David. "What was that for?" he asked, holding me in his arms and looking at me with a puzzled expression.

"For putting up with me and understanding. You're too good to me, David, do you know that?"

"Yes," he said. "I do."

I froze, realizing that I'd just said the same thing to Sean a few minutes ago.

"But that's all right," David continued. "Because I love you—and I know once this is all over everything's going to return to normal again. These hitches are only temporary ones."

I was about to ask him what he meant by temporary hitches, when Sean appeared from the kitchen carrying two mugs.

Quickly I wriggled from David's embrace.

"Scarlett," Sean said, not looking me in the eye. "I've told your dad you're back, and he'd like a word when you're ready."

"Ah, right," I said, looking with trepidation toward the lounge door.

"You'd best take these," he said, passing me the mugs, one of which was my tea and the other a mug of black coffee. "He might be needing it."

I took the mugs from Sean as David dived for the lounge door to open it for me.

"Good luck, sweetheart," he said as I passed him.

When did David ever call me that?

"Thanks," I said as I saw Dad sitting on the sofa flicking through the channels on the TV. I glanced back at Sean standing in the hall.

"Go for it, Red," he mouthed silently as David closed the door behind me.

My father looked up as I entered the room.

"I brought you some coffee," I said, holding the mug out as a peace offering.

Dad looked at the coffee mug and then he looked at me.

And for one awful moment as we stood staring at each other I thought he wasn't going to take it.

"Thanks," he said, eventually reaching out and taking the mug. With his other hand he switched the TV off with the remote control.

I sat down next to him on the sofa, strangely in the exact place I'd sat with Mum only a few days previously.

"I'm really sorry, Dad," I began, taking a deep breath. "I should have told you about finding Mum here in London and that I'd been spending time with her. It was wrong of me to keep it from you."

Dad just looked at me over the top of his coffee mug while he sipped steadily at its contents.

"But I just wanted to get to know her a little better first before things kicked off—as I was sure they would do when you found out. And for once it seems I was right."

I gave a little smile, hoping to lighten the moment. I didn't like it when my father was silent like this. It wasn't his usual style at all.

Relieved I'd made the first move, I relaxed a little and tried to lean back against the cushions behind me. But they were further back than I thought, so I kind of toppled backward and had to balance my tea high in the air like some sort of circus acrobat to prevent myself getting scalded.

My father leaned across, lifted my mug away from me, and placed it safely on a glass coaster on the table in front of us.

"Do I still have to look after you even after all these years?" he asked, speaking for the first time.

"Looks like it."

Dad placed his own mug down now too.

"Why, Scarlett?" he said, looking at me with sadness in his eyes. "Why didn't you tell me you were going to come and find her?"

"I didn't know I was. It's all just happened by accident."

"You mean this wasn't the reason you wanted some time away—so you could come and find your mother?"

"No. I hadn't even thought about it. I mean, yes, I had thought about her, obviously, but I didn't come to London so I could find Mum. I came to prove something else."

"What?"

Oh. Now I was cleverly digging myself out of one hole by burying myself deep in another.

But it couldn't get any worse, could it?

"I came here to try and prove to you and to Maddie and to David that movies do exist in real life. And that I'm not wasting my life by loving them so much."

My father rolled his head back and closed his eyes.

"Oh, Scarlett, not this again."

"Yes, this again," I said, standing up. "And do you know something? I was right, because since I've been here I've managed to live my life in..." I tried to do some quick calculations in my head. "I don't know how many movies, Dad, because there have been so many I've lost count. So movies do exist in real life, because I've proved it!"

"With your mother's help, no doubt," my father muttered. "I bet she was there goading you along. I can just see her loving all this. I bet it took her right back."

I stood and looked at my father sitting on the sofa. He was

scowling down at the carpet, caught up in his own thoughts and recriminations. And suddenly I felt I was fighting Mum's battle as well as my own.

"Actually, Mum had nothing to do with any of my movie scenes. I only met her for the first time a few days ago. But she has told me the *whole* story as to why she came to leave you in the first place."

My father's eyes darted up at me.

"She's what?" he said in a low voice.

"I asked her to. I wanted to know everything that happened back then. But why, Dad? Why would you risk it all happening again? Did you want me to run away, like Mum?"

"Oh, my darling Scarlett, no, of course I didn't." Dad stood up now too and reached his hand out toward me. "It... it's complicated."

"Tell me, Dad, please. I need to know your side of the story too. So I can fully understand."

He nodded and gestured for us to sit again. Then he took a deep breath.

"As much as it hurts me to say this, Scarlett, you've always been like your mother—not only in looks. So however hard I tried I could never get rid of the memory of her altogether. And unfortunately, I could see you beginning to make the same mistakes she did."

"So you thought you'd send me away, just like you did her?" I asked. "How was that going to help?"

My father shook his head. "No, let me finish, Scarlett. You have a good life and a good job—no, business; it belongs to us both equally. And more importantly, you have a good man who wants to marry you and spend the rest of his life with you. David *is* a good man; you do know that, don't you?"

I nodded. "Yes, of course I do."

"But you still weren't happy, Scarlett. I could tell that. You were growing increasingly dissatisfied with everything—just like your mother was all those years ago. It frightened me seeing you beginning to turn into her. So when David came to see me and told me how worried he was about you, I knew I had to do something to help.

"So that's when I suggested we give you the same chance I had your mother. I knew it was a risk—but it was a risk worth taking for your sake."

"But why—what would it achieve if it didn't work out the first time?"

"That's true—it didn't work out well for *me* back then. But I'm guessing it worked out well for your mother. I bet if you ask her now she's glad she took the opportunity to get away from me and didn't continue living what she would now consider the boring life I have."

I decided now was not the time to be telling Dad about Mum's very colorful, yet quite unstable past.

"But what I still don't get is why do it all again? Why persuade David to do something that worked out so badly for you?"

"Because I love you, Scarlett—and there's nothing that means more to me in my life than your happiness. But I knew if you married David, and continued the same way as you were, you wouldn't ever be truly happy and neither would David. You'd always be wondering 'What if?' I know what it's like living with someone like that, Scarlett. I did it for long enough, and let me tell you it's far from easy. And what if it had gone on longer and you'd ended up like your mother? I wouldn't want that for you or for David. Even though I wouldn't change our time together for the world, Scarlett, the aftermath of one parent leaving and trying to bring up a child alone is so hard I wouldn't wish it on anyone."

I was feeling really guilty now. I was putting my dad through all this unnecessary hurt. He'd done so much for me, and this is how I was repaying him.

"Plus, Scarlett, I *knew* if you went away on your own for a while you'd almost certainly try to live out this wonderful life you think everyone has in the movies, and I hoped you'd quickly realize that no one really lives like that—and it's all made up. Then if my plan went well, you'd return home and be content with what you'd got. You'd be happy with David and happy with me—just like your mother wasn't able to be."

"Oh, Dad," I said, leaning forward across the settee and putting my hands over his. "I've always been happy with you—that was never in question. You were right though; I *was* unhappy with the way things were back in Stratford. But what if it had gone wrong, what if I *had* found something better—then what?"

"Scarlett, only you can answer that question. *Have* you found something better?"

I thought hard. Had I found something better here in London than I'd known back home? I'd met new friends, had new experiences, yes. But was it better than my life before? I tried not to think about Sean.

I took a deep breath. "Yes, I have, Dad. I have found something better since I've been here. It may not be something life-changing in the way either of us hoped it might be when I left, but it's certainly changed mine for the better. And that something is Mum."

I waited for the explosion to come from my father. But strangely it didn't.

He sat back on the sofa looking thoughtful.

"Is that the *only* thing you've found since coming here, Scarlett? Your mother?"

"How do you mean?"

"I mean, you said yourself you only met up with her in the past few days. What about the rest of the time you've been here? You must have met some other people and had some other experiences you've learned from?"

Just what was my father getting at?

I picked up my tea from the table and casually took a sip of it. Yuck, it was barely warm now.

"I've made a few new friends since I've been here, yes."

"And?"

"And what? What are you trying to say, Dad?"

My father stood up and walked around Belinda and Harry's lounge for a few moments, supposedly inspecting the few ornaments that they allowed in their minimalist interior.

"I spent quite a bit of time with both Sean and David this evening," he said, suddenly spinning round to face me again.

"Yes, they said you had."

"And do you know what they both spent most of their evening talking about while they were with me?"

I shrugged. "Football?"

"Scarlett!" My father came over to the sofa and placed his hands purposefully on the back. "You silly girl. They both spent nearly all their time talking about you tonight. I don't know what exactly you've been up to while you've been here in London—nor do I want to know," he added, holding up his hand as I opened my mouth to protest. "But what is obvious to me, and anyone else with half a brain, is that these two men both care about you very much."

I thought about David and Sean waiting for us in Belinda and Harry's house right now. They hated each other, and yet tonight, just like Sean had said, they'd put aside their differences to help me.

Dad sat down next to me again. "You need to be careful, Scarlett. Or someone's going to get hurt."

"But I don't want to hurt anyone, Dad. I never do. I didn't want to hurt you or Mum either. I just want everyone to be happy for once in my life."

"But sometimes your actions, intentional or otherwise, can have a ripple effect. You have to think carefully before you make your choices in life, Scarlett. Use your head for a change."

I sighed. If only Dad knew the truth. I had been using my head for far too long to make my choices—especially those involving David.

"Sean uses his head," my father said out of the blue.

I stared at him. "What do you mean?"

"He uses his head. In his business *and* in his personal life as far as I can see."

"And how do you know this?"

"I spent some time with him earlier tonight. We talked business—"

"Yes, I know," I said, cutting Dad short. "I saw the two of you together earlier, but what's that got to do with Sean's personal life?"

"If you'll let me finish, Scarlett. As I said we talked earlier, and while you were out, Sean was also gone for some time too: 'A little business to attend to,' he said."

"But I thought Sean was here all night with you and David?"

Dad shook his head. "No, David was here with me for most of that time. Sean got back just before you did."

Sean was out tonight doing business deals? So much for me thinking he'd been worrying about me all evening.

"That doesn't surprise me," I said, trying to sound like I didn't care. "Sean's business is pretty important to him."

Maybe he and David weren't that different after all.

"It surprised me, Scarlett. Until then I'd thought Sean was completely focused on you this evening, and I'd been impressed by that. But when I found out what he was up to while he was away from the house, my opinion of him began to sway even more."

"What on earth do you mean, Dad?" I asked, as a feeling of unease began to flutter around at the base of my stomach.

"Apparently, Sean went to find your mother tonight. I understand from David your other guests found her in a café not far from here. So while he was out Sean went to check on her as well."

"What's wrong with that?" I asked defiantly. "I'm glad someone went to make sure she was all right."

My father raised his eyebrows at me and shook his head slowly.

"Oh, Scarlett, you've so much to learn."

"What, what is it?" I screwed my eyes closed and shook my head. "Just what are you going on about, Dad?" I said, opening them again. "What are you trying to say?"

"That Sean is playing a very clever game with us all. I don't doubt he cares about you very much, Scarlett. But to win you over he tried to manipulate the situation we all found ourselves in tonight for his own ends. He had a chance to look good in front of me, your mother, and, most importantly, you, all in one evening. And he took that chance and ran with it tonight."

I sat there for a few moments trying to take all this in. No, Dad was wrong, surely. Sean wasn't like that.

But then why hadn't he said he'd been to Kelly's to check on my mother? And why did he suggest he'd been in the house all night with Dad and David if he hadn't? It just didn't add up.

"I'm not saying Sean's a bad person—far from it," Dad continued when I didn't respond. "I actually quite like him. But perhaps he's not quite the person *you* think he is?"

I nodded slowly.

"Scarlett, you may think that all that's happened to you since you came to London is finding your mother again. But I think we both know a lot more has taken place than that. You've got some serious thinking to do and some big decisions to make about your life, and for once, you can't hide out in a movie theater to make them."

"But how do I choose, Dad?" I asked in desperation. "How do I know what the right thing to do is?"

"You'll just know, Scarlett," Dad said, taking my hand and holding it firmly in between the two of his. "Something will come along and, believe me, then you'll know."

Dad slid along the sofa, put his arms around me, and immediately I was returned to that safe and secure little girl once more.

Thirty-Six

Dad and I sat together for quite a while on the sofa, just snuggled up together like we used to, both of us lost in our own thoughts and memories. Eventually Dad unwrapped himself from around me, stretched out his arms, and yawned.

"It's been a long day, Scarlett. I think I might head off up to bed now. Plus David and Sean must be wondering what we're getting up to in here now it's gone so quiet."

I uncurled myself from the sofa and saw him to the lounge door.

"Night, Dad," I said, kissing him on the cheek. "And thanks."

"Good night, Scarlett," he said, glancing across at Sean as he appeared from the kitchen. "Sleep well, darling." He tilted his head in Sean's direction. "Good night, Sean."

Sean nodded and watched until Dad had disappeared at the top of the stairs. Then he turned to me.

"You look exhausted, Scarlett. Would you like another cup of tea—or maybe something stronger? I think your father may have left *some* alcohol in the bar tonight."

Considering the vast quantity of alcohol Sean and David

had suggested Dad had put away tonight, he had seemed quite sober to me, and his thought processes surprisingly clear.

"Something stronger would be good. It has been quite a night."

Sean followed me back into the lounge. "Where's David?" I asked, suddenly realizing he hadn't reappeared.

"He went to bed. Just a few minutes ago, though," Sean added, as if that made it better. "He said he had an early start in the morning."

"Oh, that's right, he does. He has a breakfast meeting, I believe, over in Surrey." *But he might have waited up to see how everything went*, I thought as I sat down again on the sofa.

"Ah, I see," Sean said as he poured us both a whiskey. I knew he was probably thinking the same thing. He added some ice from a bucket and passed me the glass. "Is that OK for you, or do you want it watered down a bit?"

"No, this is just fine," I said, taking the cut-glass tumbler. I was glad it wasn't brandy this time. I didn't think I'd ever drunk so much alcohol for "purely medicinal" purposes in my life.

Sean sat down next to me. "I hear you've got a meeting with your future parents-in-law tomorrow, to discuss the wedding?"

"Yes, that's right. David's parents have a house in London; we're holding the wedding reception there in a tent."

"I'd have thought you'd have got married in your home-town. Isn't that the tradition?"

"I suppose it is. But it's going to be a big wedding with people flying in from all over the world. Lots of David's business contacts are coming, so it just seemed easier to hold it all in London."

"Ah, I see," Sean said again.

We both took a gulp of our drinks. The whiskey burned at my throat—but at least it wasn't as sickly sweet as the brandy.

I sighed heavily.

"What's up, Red?" Sean asked, winking at me. "Tough night?"

I tried to raise a smile but couldn't. "I'm sorry. It's just I've got a lot to think about."

"You mean about what your father said?"

"Partly."

I looked at Sean. I was trying hard not to think too much about what my father had said. After all, Dad had only just met Sean tonight; he didn't know what he was really like. But there were too many things that kept bugging me about it all. Was work so important to Sean that it meant more to him tonight than me? And even if the business thing was just a bluff so he could go out and see Mum, was Dad correct, was Sean using my parents to get to me? No, that couldn't be right; Sean wasn't like that. But why then hadn't he told me he'd seen Mum? It just didn't add up.

"Do I get any more than just a partly?" Sean asked, tipping his head to one side. "How about a two-thirdsly, or even, if I ask nicely, a three-quartersly?"

I half smiled at him. "Sorry. I was thinking about how I messed up again tonight. I was lucky it didn't turn out a lot worse. I seem to have very understanding parents *and* very understanding friends."

"That you do," Sean said, nodding. He took a drink from his glass. "So what *did* your father say?"

"About?" *Was Sean fishing to see if Dad had mentioned him?*

"About everything. About your mum, about your movie chasing, about everything else you seem to do that annoys him."

"I'm not doing the movie thing anymore."

"Why ever not?"

"Because there's just no point in trying to prove my theory any longer—I told Dad earlier that I'd had loads of experience of life being like a movie since I've been here, and I still don't think he believed me. So what's the point? Maybe I was never right in the first place anyway. Maybe they *were* just all coincidences."

Sean stared at me in amazement. "I cannot believe I am hearing you say this."

"Why? I'm entitled to change my mind, aren't I?"

Sean raised his eyebrows.

I sighed. "It's just after everything that's happened over the last few weeks—and especially tonight—I'm beginning to think that Dad and David and whoever else has said it to me in the past was right, Sean—life really isn't like a movie. You can try as hard as you want to make it that way, but there never is that perfect fairytale ending you get at the cinema, and there never will be."

I drank some more of my whiskey while Sean continued to stare at me in disbelief.

"Scarlett, stop it," he said eventually. "This is not you talking. What's happened to you? You were so full of hope and optimism when I first met you, and now you're so...so..."

"Realistic," I said flatly. "That's the word you're searching for. If this experience has taught me anything, it's taught me realism, Sean. I thought the reason I came to London was to prove my family wrong about the movies. But I've discovered the true reason was so I could find something that's been missing from my life all these years—my mother. I'm telling you, Sean, everything happens—"

"Yes, I know, for a reason. You've said so before—many a time. But finding your mother could just have been an added bonus while you're here. Why does it have to be the *only* reason for what's gone on?"

"It's not the *only* one—it's the main one. These last few weeks have also taught me that I'm luckier than I ever realized with the life I have back in Stratford. Meeting my mother and hearing about the life she's had, and the men she's met since leaving my father, has made me realize that the grass *isn't* always greener on the other side. It may seem it for a while, but then when the grass withers and dies, and there's nothing left, you have to start all over again from the beginning—sowing the seeds and watching it grow again."

"So what are you saying, Scarlett?" Sean said, putting his whiskey down on the table. "You'd rather your life was full of plain gray concrete—solid and virtually indestructible—so that nothing could ever come along and damage it?"

I nodded.

"Bullshit," Sean said. "I don't believe you. Before you came here, you'd have wanted more than just a neat green lawn. You'd have wanted a whole meadow full of long grass and wild flowers for you to run through."

"Yes, you're probably right. But I've changed."

"No, you haven't. You've had a few experiences that have made you see life a bit differently—and that might not be a bad thing. But the romantic, idealistic Scarlett still lurks in there somewhere—I know it. It's who you are, Scarlett, it's what makes you tick."

Oh why did Sean have this ability to read me so well? It was so annoying. I'd just made all these decisions about how my life was going to be in the future—and now here he was turning them all upside down again.

"How would you know what makes me tick?" I said haughtily. "You don't have a romantic bone in your body, Sean Bond—let alone an idealistic one. You don't even like Robbie Williams or Ronan Keating, for heaven's sake! Everything's got to be black and white with you—there's no room for daydreaming."

Sean was strangely silent.

I thought I'd hurt him with my words—which wouldn't be the first time—and I was just about to apologize when he leaned toward me and spoke.

"You could be right there, Scarlett," he said, looking deep into my eyes. "On the other hand, you might be wrong. You'll just have to wait and see, won't you? Maybe you're not the only one changing your view of life right now."

Now what did he mean? But before I had time to question him further, the phone rang in the hall. I rushed through to answer it so it didn't disturb David or Dad.

Sean followed me.

"Mum!" I said as I recognized the voice at the other end of the line. "Just hold on a moment, will you?"

I put my hand over the receiver.

"It's about time I got some sleep too," Sean said, heading toward the door. "So I'll leave you with your phone call. I'm flying over to Dublin tomorrow on business, so I won't see you for a few days. Will you still be here when I return?"

I was surprised he was off again so soon. But then it was *business* so perhaps I shouldn't have been..."Yes, I think so. I have to house-sit until Belinda and Harry get back from Dubai at the end of next week, so I should still be around."

"Because I wouldn't want to miss you to say good-bye," Sean said, pausing at the open door.

"No...that wouldn't be good." I couldn't imagine ever saying good-bye to Sean. But I guess it was going to have to happen sooner or later.

Sean gave me one last smile and then closed the front door behind him.

"Mum," I said as I carried the phone into the lounge and shut the door, "I'm so glad you rang. I'm so sorry about earlier. I didn't mean for it to happen like that, honestly, I had no idea that Dad was going to turn up here today or I would never have invited you to the dinner party and—"

"Scarlett, Scarlett, just slow down, please," Mum's calm voice came floating back down the line. "I haven't rung for explanations at this time of night, simply to check if you'd got back safely. When Oscar and Ursula told me you'd run off I was worried about you. And I know all the circumstances surrounding what happened this evening, because Sean explained them to me earlier, so please don't fret."

"I know, but I'm really sorry, Mum."

"And like I told you, Scarlett, we can talk about it properly when I see you again. But now I know you're home safe and sound I can relax, and we can both go and get some sleep; it's late."

I hesitated for a moment. "Can I just ask you something before you go, Mum?"

"Yes, of course."

"You met Sean tonight."

"Yes. I met Sean."

"And…what did you think of him?"

It was Mum's turn to hesitate now.

"Why?"

"I just wondered, that's all. Since it was the first time the two of you had met properly."

"We promised to be honest with each other, didn't we, Scarlett?"

"Uh-huh."

"I liked him."

"Is that it?"

I heard her sigh. "All right—he seems like an amusing and intelligent young man. Quite good looking too, I suppose, if you like that type."

I had a feeling I was going to regret asking this, but I had to. "What type do you mean, Mum?"

"Look, Scarlett, I can't fault the way he dealt with the situation tonight. He came to see if I was OK and was polite and attentive while he was in the café with me. He was extremely concerned over your welfare too."

"But…"

"But he's good looking, Scarlett, and has a smooth line in chat when he wants it. So I'm guessing he's probably extremely fun to be with when you first know him. But then he's likely to turn out to be completely unreliable after you've known him for a while."

"How can you tell all this?" I asked in a small voice.

"Because I've been there before, Scarlett, I'm afraid. If you're asking my advice—which I think indirectly you are—the last thing you want is to get mixed up with Sean when you've got David already waiting for you in the wings."

I stared into the phone. This was the last thing I'd expected my mother to say.

"You're making Sean sound like some sort of modern day cad."

"I never said he was that. I just don't think he's as reliable as your David's likely to be. In the long term, I mean. You did ask for my opinion, Scarlett."

"Yes, I know. And thank you, it's helped me...clarify a few thoughts."

"I'm sorry if it's not what you wanted to hear, Scarlett."

"No, it's fine. It's given me some things to think about."

As if I didn't have enough of those already...

Thirty-Seven

Even though my head was still spinning with thoughts and conversations when finally I climbed the stairs to bed that night, I felt as if a great weight had been lifted from my shoulders now that Dad knew about me finding Mum. But when I arrived at the bedroom door and saw David sleeping in my bed, I felt the same weight descending upon me again.

The purpose of taking some time away on my own hadn't originally been to find out whether I wanted to marry David or not; purely to put my mind at rest that I was doing the right thing. But now after everything that had happened, I found myself standing at the bedroom door wondering just that.

To anyone who didn't know David well, he did appear to be quite staid and reserved, and he didn't give too much away. But I knew that deep down he could be very passionate and loving once you got to know him. And that was the David I loved—the one he didn't show to anyone but me.

But since Sean had come into my life it had made me question whether what I felt for David was enough. Sean was the complete opposite to David, his personality was…well, how would you describe him? My mother had portrayed him just now as a bit of a cad...a smooth talker...a ladies' man, even. He wasn't really that. She'd also said he was an amusing and intelligent young man—fun to be with at first, but likely to let you down in the long run. Even Dad had said he used his head to get what he wanted, not only in business, but in his personal life too.

I screwed my forehead up; those descriptions sounded familiar, particularly Mum's...where had I heard them before?

Then I realized. That's just how I'd described the characters of Mark Darcy and Daniel Cleaver from the *Bridget Jones* movies to Sean earlier today—almost word for word!

I'd told Sean then that I'd preferred Colin Firth's character of Mark Darcy to Hugh Grant's Daniel Cleaver. Is that the way I really felt about David and Sean?

Oh God, this is just getting ridiculous. Didn't I just say this evening how I wasn't going to try living my life like a movie anymore? And now here I am only an hour or so later doing it again already.

I entered the bedroom and tiptoed in the dark across to the bathroom. *Too much has happened tonight for me to even be thinking about all this right now, let alone to be making any decisions.*

When I had finished in the bathroom, I returned to the darkened bedroom again. I tried crossing the room as silently as I could; the last thing I needed was for David to wake up and want to start yet another discussion with me—especially about our relationship. I think I'd done enough soul-searching for one night.

I stubbed my toe against the chair in front of the dressing table and swore under my breath, so I reached out and fumbled for the lamp that sat on top of the table. A soft glow filled the room. David stirred in the bed and I watched him for a moment, praying he wouldn't wake up. But he didn't—he just turned over and carried on snoring.

Normally if I'd heard David snoring I'd have been immediately thinking of ways of getting him to stop before I tried to get some sleep myself. But not tonight; in fact, I hardly heard him—I just stared at the offending chair that had attacked my innocent toe.

On the seat of the chair lay David's clothes for the next morning. Not his suit and shirt; they hung on wooden hangers against the outside of the wardrobe. The items that were causing me so much interest were his socks neatly laid out in a pair, and more importantly, his underpants. They sat folded just as neatly on top of the seat too—just like Mark Darcy's underwear had done when he'd been in Bridget Jones's flat...

I looked at the boxer shorts and then I looked at David.

And suddenly everything that had been a jumbled mess in my head up until now became crystal clear.

What Dad had said to me in the lounge.

What Mum had said on the phone.

It all made sense now.

Dad had been through so much to raise me on his own. He'd made so many sacrifices for me, and now it was my turn to repay him.

Mum had spent too many miserable years all alone, just because she chased some wild, romantic dream that didn't exist with the wrong type of man. I didn't want to end up like that.

Now it was my turn to do the right thing. Dad said I'd know

what to do when the time came, and now this must be the time. He was wrong about one thing, though; it *was* something to do with the movies that was helping me make my choice.

"Well, if Mark was good enough for Bridget," I whispered quietly into the darkness.

Thirty-Eight

Vivaldi could be heard filtering from the church as Maddie made the final adjustments to my train and Dad held out his arm to me.

That's funny, I thought, as we entered the church and began to walk down the aisle. I don't remember my dress having a train when I was fitted for it.

In fact, I'm sure this wasn't the dress I'd chosen with Oscar and Ursula for my big day at all. This dress was a *very* fitted gown in raw ivory silk. I could hardly breathe as I tried to waddle down the aisle with a smile fixed rigidly to my face.

But I couldn't stop to complain because my father was whisking me toward the altar at such a speed that I could hardly feel my feet on the ground below—was he that desperate to get rid of me?

We arrived in front of the vicar, who looked suspiciously like Rowan Atkinson, and Dad passed my hand quickly to David. At least that part was right.

The vicar rushed through the preliminaries swiftly, and it was soon time for the first hymn. I looked about me for a hymn sheet, but there didn't seem to be one.

"What are you looking for?" David hissed at me. "Surely you of all people should know the words to this one?"

A band appeared out of nowhere among the congregation and part of me wanted to shout, "Hey, that's just like in *Love Actually*!" But then I remembered I wasn't counting movie scenes anymore—so I just stood and silently listened as they began to play the first few bars of...no, it couldn't be, could it?

But it was—and then suddenly up in the pulpit there he was, wearing the biggest pair of feathery white wings I'd ever seen: Robbie Williams, and he was singing "Angels."

I wanted to rub my eyes—but I daren't in case my mascara smudged. Robbie Williams—at my wedding—singing "Angels"? This couldn't be happening. I looked around at everyone, but they all seemed completely unmoved by the whole thing, as if Robbie Williams singing at a wedding was just an everyday occurrence. I decided to ignore them and enjoy it; after all, this *was* Robbie. But when "Angels" quickly turned into "Let Me Entertain You," and then "Rock DJ," the romantic ambience was soon lost.

Robbie finished singing and disappeared back down into the pulpit as quickly as he'd appeared. I began to applaud loudly but was the only one who did. Embarrassed, I quickly hid my hands behind my bouquet.

What was wrong with these people?

The vicar resumed the service and soon came to the part about anyone having any reasons why David and I shouldn't get married. I secretly hoped I might hear Sean's voice floating across the church pews toward me. But sadly I heard nothing, only a deathly silence.

Then there was a polite cough at the back of the church, and all heads swiveled round to look at the offender.

"Does somebody have something to say?" the vicar asked, seeming worried. I looked at him closely—he looked even more like Rowan Atkinson now than he had done at the start of the service.

"Yes, I have a reason," I heard a familiar voice call from the back of the church.

"Please, stand up," the vicar requested, squinting into the distance.

I nearly dropped my bouquet when Hugh Grant stood up. What the hell was he doing here?

"You have an objection, sir?" the vicar inquired.

"Yes," Hugh said in his clipped English voice. "I do."

Wasn't I supposed to say that?

"Perhaps you'd like to share it with us?" the vicar asked.

I looked at Hugh in amazement—what on earth was he going to say?

"I suspect the bride is having doubts," he said. "I suspect that the bride does, in fact, love someone else."

The congregation's heads swiveled in unison away from Hugh and back toward me again.

I looked at Father Rowan. "Do you?" he asked me sternly. "Do you love someone else, Scarlett?"

My breathing was quick and shallow, and I could feel my chest rising up and down as I tried desperately to get enough air into my lungs to speak. I turned frantically to David. But David had vanished and in his place, and his morning suit, was Colin Firth.

"Well, do you, Scarlett?" Colin now demanded of me. "Do you love someone more than you love me?"

I opened my mouth to speak, but nothing would come out. I looked desperately into the congregation for help, but all my family and friends had disappeared now too. Replacing them on the groom's side of church were Darth Vader and the cast of *Star Wars*, and on my side the pews were now filled with Mickey Mouse and his Disneyland friends.

I searched frantically for my father. He would help me; Dad was always there for me when I needed him. But in the place where my father had been standing until a few minutes ago was Harrison Ford dressed as Indiana Jones complete with fedora and whip.

I turned to Colin again. He just stared at me; like everyone else in the church, he was awaiting my answer.

"Yes!" I shouted at the top of my voice. "Yes, I do love someone else! I do...I do...I do!"

I awoke with a start and sat up in bed. Still breathing heavily, I wiped away the sweat that was pouring down my face.

"Scarlett," my mother said, rushing into the room in her nightdress. "Are you all right?"

My breathing was beginning to calm down now. "Yes...I had a bad dream, that's all."

My mother sat down on the side of my bed. "Was it about the wedding? Only you were shouting out 'I do' at the top of your voice."

"Yes, it was about the wedding. Things were...well, they weren't going too well at the service." Apart from Robbie being there, of course—of all the dreams I'd had about Robbie Williams, I couldn't say I ever recalled being in a church with him before.

"That's quite understandable the night before your wedding. I'm sure most brides have the odd strange dream about their big day."

Strange? Nightmarish, more like.

"Well," my mother said, looking at her watch. "There's not much point in going back to sleep now, is there? Not now your big day is here at last." She jumped up to the window and flung back the curtains. Sunlight streamed through the glass and down onto my bed. "And it looks like it's going to be a beautiful day!"

I yawned and rubbed my eyes now mascara wasn't an issue. "After that dream, as long as no more instances of movies where the wedding goes disastrously wrong crop up during the service, I'll be quite happy, whatever the weather does."

Mum came over to the bed again. "Weddings don't always go wrong in the movies, Scarlett."

"Oh, come on, Mum," I said, holding up my hand ready to count on my fingers, "there's loads. Apart from *Four Weddings*, there's *The Runaway Bride*, *The Wedding Planner*, *Bride Wars*, er…" I tried to think of one from my mother's era. "What about *The Graduate* when Dustin Hoffman runs off with Anne Bancroft's daughter at the end? It's hardly a recipe for success, is it?"

"Scarlett," Mum said, taking my hand. "Like you said, they *are* just movies. This is *real* life and everything is going to turn out just fine at your wedding. Trust me."

I sighed and gave her a half-smile. "I suppose just as long as I don't look like the Bride of Frankenstein when I walk down the aisle later this morning, there is half a chance it could just be a perfect day for love—actually."

Thirty-Nine

Yes, it was finally my wedding day—the day every girl dreams of.

As I began the long process of trying to transform myself into the perfect-looking, radiant bride I had plenty of time, in between manicures and hairdressing appointments, to ponder what had happened over the last few weeks to lead me to this most important of days.

After the disastrous dinner party that never was, things had been decidedly calm in Lansdowne Road.

Belinda and Harry had decided to return a few days earlier than expected from Dubai, so I'd had to vacate their home sooner than I'd originally planned. They'd been extremely grateful to me for looking after their house so well, and as Belinda said, "putting up with our neighbors." And they had brought me several expensive gifts back from their travels, as a thank-you.

The day I left Notting Hill, Oscar and Ursula had been the only two people there to see me off. Sean was still in Dublin on business, so I hadn't actually seen him to say good-bye to properly.

"Sean will be so upset he's missed you," Ursula said, almost in tears as I loaded my final bits and pieces into the waiting black cab.

The taxi was a luxury, but today was stressful enough as it was without having to battle to the train station on the hot and crowded underground system.

"Darling, you must send me photos of you in your wedding dress," Oscar said, hugging me. He kissed me on each cheek. "You're going to look absolutely divine—I just know it."

"I can do better than that," I said, reaching into my bag and pulling out two envelopes. "Here—invites to the wedding." I'd had to fight tooth and nail with Cruella to get these invites for Oscar and Ursula because, apparently, "There isn't any more room to squeeze in two miniature chihuahuas, let alone two more guests," I'd been told when I'd asked for two of my friends to be included on the guest list. But fight is what I'd done, and for once I'd come out victorious.

"Ooh we'd love to come, wouldn't we, Oscar?" Ursula said, eagerly opening her envelope. "What about Sean—have you put one through his letterbox?"

"Er…no. I think he's had enough of weddings just lately. He probably wouldn't want to go to another one."

Oscar glanced at me. "And especially not *your* wedding," he said, exchanging a knowing look with Ursula.

"No," she replied. "Perhaps not."

I pretended not to have noticed and gave them both one last hug. Then I bent down and gave Delilah a quick stroke before climbing into the back of my taxi and driving away from Lansdowne Road and Notting Hill forever.

And now, as I held on tightly to my father's arm—who, thankfully, looked nothing like Harrison Ford today in his steel-gray morning suit and burgundy cravat—and we walked together down the seemingly never-ending aisle of the vast church my wedding was being held in, I saw Oscar and Ursula again for the first time since that day.

You couldn't really miss them, because Oscar was wearing a startling lime-green shirt teamed with an electric-blue suit. And Ursula, a red and white polka dot 1950s dress with a huge, red, wide-brimmed floppy hat.

They waved at me as I passed by, and Ursula mouthed "good luck."

Unlike last night when I'd "walked down the aisle," today I was actually wearing the same dress I'd picked out in the wedding shop with the two of them that day. The white silk embroidered bodice, although fitted, wasn't so tight that I couldn't breathe, and the yards upon yards of white tulle that made up my skirts floated airily around my legs, allowing me to move freely.

I wouldn't have wanted to run a marathon in this dress, or these four-inch stiletto heels for that matter. Or even the diamante headdress that was balancing precariously on top of my curled and tonged hair. But for moving around at the sedate speed I was going to be required to move at today, they'd do just fine.

When we finally arrived in front of the minister and the service began, I watched carefully while my father "gave my hand away" to David. He then went and sat down next to my mother, and for a split second a look passed between them that proved to me they had once genuinely cared about each other very much, and I was pleased that my wedding had formed, even for just that brief moment, a small link between them again as they shared their pride.

The vicar, who I was relieved to see looked nothing like Rowan Atkinson, continued with the service in a clear and confident manner, and everything seemed to be going just fine.

I can't say I felt blissfully euphoric that this was my wedding day and I was finally standing here opposite David about to take my vows. After all the dramas of a few weeks ago, I just felt glad to get it over with at last and to be able to get on with living a normal life once more.

Yes, this feeling of stillness inside me must be how normal people felt. It wasn't an emptiness at all like I'd worried it was before I came to London. No, today this was simply a feeling of calm. There was no need for the exhilaration and excitement I'd felt in my month living in London...no need at all.

"Therefore, if any man can show any just cause why they may not lawfully be joined together," I heard the vicar saying, "let him now speak, or else hereafter for ever hold his peace."

As there always is at weddings, there was a deathly silence in the church as the congregation waited (hopefully?) to see if anyone did have any objections to our marriage.

When it appeared that no one was going to burst through the doors, declare their undying love for me, and whisk me off on a galloping white charger, the vicar opened his mouth to continue.

"Wait," a voice said, breaking the silence. Embarrassingly, I quickly realized it was mine. I was sure I could hear something outside, and if he started prattling on again I wouldn't be able to hear it properly. "Wait, please. Just a moment—listen."

Everyone fell silent for a second time. And there it was again, I hadn't imagined it—the definite sound of someone singing in the church grounds. And it was a song and a singer I recognized immediately.

I knew then that I had to go and find out.

I knew that I couldn't just carry on with the ceremony without checking first.

What if it wasn't just a coincidence? What if that song meant what I thought it meant?

I turned and looked at David.

My head was saying, "This is your wedding day, Scarlett..."

But my heart was saying...

"David, I'll be right back."

"Scarlett, you can't just run off in the middle of our wedding ceremony!"

But I was already halfway down the aisle.

"Get out of my way," I instructed Cruella, as she tried to bar my exit through the doors.

"Miss O'Brien, I really don't think you should go out there. I've managed to stop them from coming in. But it's nothing, really. Please just continue with the service."

"Get out of my way now—or I *will* move you myself!"

She hastily stepped aside.

"And if you want to retain your reputation as London's top wedding planner, then I suggest you try and stop them from coming outside for a few minutes," I said, as I saw David, Maddie, and my parents all hurrying down the aisle behind me.

I ran the last few steps down the aisle and tugged open the heavy wooden doors at the end, and as I did so the music immediately got louder, because sitting alone on the steps of the church was a CD player. And it was playing a song that was instantly familiar: "When You Say Nothing At All" by Ronan Keating.

It was the theme tune to *Notting Hill*, the song that had been playing while Hugh and Julia sat on the bench in the movie.

The song Sean and I had discussed while we sat in the park together the first night we met…

While the song was playing I became aware of two pairs of eyes watching me. The eyes were trying to disguise themselves behind two pairs of dark glasses, and they in turn appeared to belong to two bodies that thought they were hiding themselves behind two gravestones.

"Do you know something about this, by any chance?" I called, pointing to the CD player as I carried it to the bottom of the church steps.

The two pairs of eyes turned to each other, then one of the heads nodded, and slowly two bodies emerged from behind the graves. Then walking across the churchyard toward me came two men who wore black suits and black hats to match their dark glasses.

"Allow me to introduce myself," the shorter of the two men said, removing his hat from his head in greeting. "My name is Dermot, and this is my brother Finlay."

Finlay gave a small bow of his head.

"And can I assume that you are the lady in question?"

I stared blankly at them.

"Scarlett?" he prompted.

"Yes, that's me—but who are you, and what's going on?"

"All in good time, miss," Dermot said. "First we must apologize to you that we've turned up here today in this manner." He smiled ruefully and straightened his tie. "And please also send my apologies to the lady inside who tried to bar our entrance for the slight, shall we say, altercation that took place a few minutes ago."

"Who? You mean Cruella? Tall woman, silver hair in a bun?"

Dermot nodded. "That's her."

"Ah, don't worry about it—I'm sure she can handle herself."

"She certainly can. Finlay was unconscious for over a minute."

I looked at Finlay, who nodded his agreement.

"Oh, er…I'm really sorry about that, Finlay."

Just then the church doors burst open and, unable to be contained any longer, David, Maddie, and my parents burst forth from the church and poured down the steps behind me.

"What on earth is going on, Scarlett?" David demanded, looking with disdain at Dermot and Finlay.

"*That*, David, is just what I'm trying to find out," I said impatiently. "Dermot, please continue. I'm sure everyone will be quiet and listen—*won't you?*"

Everyone nodded silently. I don't think I looked like I was in a mood to be messed with.

Dermot glanced nervously at his new audience.

"Anyway, as I was saying before, I must apologize not only for turning up here today, but also for being so late."

"Late—by how long?"

"About sixteen hours, give or take a couple."

"Sixteen hours! I don't understand."

Dermot cleared his throat and looked a bit embarrassed.

"We should have been at your house yesterday evening. I say we…Finlay and his missus should have. You see, it was them that was booked to do the drop."

"The drop?" I asked, mystified.

"Yeah, that's what we in the trade call the booking—see?" He lifted his dark glasses momentarily to wink at me, then saw David scowling at him and he hurriedly continued. "Finlay and his missus, well, they was booked to turn up dressed as Scarlett O'Hara and Rhett Butler from *Gone with the Wind*. Finlay does a stunning Rhett Butler, don't you, Fin?"

Finlay blushed under his black hat.

"But due to unforeseen circumstances—namely the lovely Scarlett having to be rushed into hospital yesterday with suspected appendicitis—Rhett and Scarlett were not able to make an appearance at the appropriate time or place yesterday."

"Oh dear," I said, addressing my remark to Finlay, although I didn't for one moment expect him to reply, as Dermot seemed to do all the talking in this relationship. "I do hope your wife is all right."

Finlay simply nodded while Dermot answered for him. "She's fine—we just got her to the hospital in time, apparently. But it means we're a Scarlett O'Hara down for a few weeks now, which is going to mean a lot of canceled bookings…and a lot of lost revenue…"

He looked me up and down for a moment. "I don't suppose *you'd* be interested in joining our books for a while, would you?

You've quite a look of the Miss Scarlett about you and you do suit a fuller dress."

I smoothed my tulle skirts down. "That's very kind of you. But no, I don't think so. And what books would they be anyway? What is all this?"

"We," Dermot said proudly, producing a business card from his pocket, "provide the highest quality, top notch, can't-be-matched message delivery service in London. We currently have over thirty different options of message delivery service available to our very discerning and dignified clientele. We never fail to deliver; our messages *always* get through."

"Oh," I said, looking at the business card Dermot had thrust into my hand. "I get it. You're like a singing telegram service."

Dermot and Finlay recoiled in horror.

"Madam," Dermot said, lifting his hat again and placing it over his heart. "We pride ourselves on being much more than just..."

Finlay patted him encouragingly on the back as he struggled to repeat my damaging words.

"More than just a...a...telegram service!" he almost spat out. "And I can assure you we definitely *never* sing!"

"Oh my God, you don't strip, do you?" I asked in dismay, looking from one to the other of them. Finlay was tall and gangly with black, slightly greasy-looking curly hair, and Dermot was short and fat without enough hair left on his head to tell what it had once been. Neither of them were exactly oil paintings.

"No, miss, we certainly do not! We," Dermot said, squaring his shoulders, "are London's only Moviegrams—we deliver messages dressed as characters from the silver screen. And as I said before, we have 100 percent success record at getting our messages delivered. Which is why," he said, glancing at Cruella, who had now appeared outside the church, "we would not be thwarted by a minor setback such as a Chanel-wearing Rottweiler when it came to delivering this message to you before its deadline expired at midday."

"Oh, right," I said, relieved Dermot and Finlay weren't going to strip down to their boxers, or even further, in front of me in the churchyard. "Now I get it. Oh," I said again as something else just occurred to me. "You're dressed as the Blues Brothers today—right?"

"Yes," Dermot said, looking pleased I'd guessed. "We had to substitute costumes at the last minute because of the circumstances I mentioned before—and since we couldn't get hold of Mr. Bond, we had to choose something ourselves. The Blues Brothers are one of our favorites, see—"

I cut him off before he went any further. "Wait a moment; you said Mr. Bond—is that Sean Bond you're talking about? Is he the one who booked you to do this?"

"Er, yes, he is—and actually we'd best continue with the task in hand; we're starting to drift a bit off course." He squared his shoulders and adjusted his tie in preparation. Then he gave me a nervous smile.

I simply stared at him. I just wanted them to get on with this, now I knew Sean was at the bottom of it. What did it all mean? I glanced at David; his face was thunderously dark.

I noticed that Oscar, Ursula, and some of the other guests had joined us outside to see what all the fuss was about.

Dermot rummaged in his pocket for a piece of paper, then took a quick look at it before stuffing it back in his pocket again.

"So, now we need to ask you how you feel?"

"What?"

"How...do...you...feel?" Dermot repeated slowly as if I was hard of hearing.

"At...this...very...moment?" I repeated in the same tone of voice. "Extremely confused."

"Not angry?"

"No."

"Not cross."

"No."

"Irritated?"

"No—but I'm going to be in a moment if you don't get on with it!"

"Good, then we can give you this. Finlay?" Dermot held out his hand and Finlay pulled a red envelope from his jacket and passed it to him. With a flourish Dermot passed it to me. "Mr. Bond said if you reacted in the right way to the song then we were to give you this."

"What is it?" I asked, turning the envelope over in my hands.

"We're not privy to that sort of information, miss. We were simply instructed to give you this if you seemed at all moved by the music we played. Just as well you like Ronan Keating, eh? Lucky you're not a full-on thrash metal fan, or we might have had a different result on our hands!" Dermot and Finlay both laughed at his joke.

"Er...yes." I looked down at the envelope. "Should I open it now?"

"I guess so. Well, *we're* interested to know what's in it anyway, aren't we, Finlay?" Dermot turned to his silent partner. "We've never had a booking like this before."

Finlay nodded.

"I guess I'd better open this." I turned and looked back at the others. "I'm assuming that's OK with everyone?"

Everyone nodded with enthusiasm except David, who stood motionless next to the group now crowding around me.

Slowly I opened the envelope.

Inside there was a postcard and, underneath that, a ticket. I didn't look at the picture on the postcard because handwritten on the other side in black ink were the words—

> *If you feel the same…*
> *Meet me on top of the London Eye tomorrow.*
> *I'll wait until midday.*
> *S x*

I read the card aloud.

"What does he mean—the top of the London Eye, Scarlett?" my father asked, speaking for the first time. "Why would Sean want to meet you there? And how can he meet you at the top? Isn't it constantly revolving?"

"It's like the movie, isn't it?" my mother said, smiling. "*An Affair to Remember.*'"

"I thought that was *Sleepless in Seattle*?" Maddie asked, joining in. "Meg Ryan tries to meet Tom Hanks on top of the Empire State Building."

"It's both of them, actually," Dermot piped up. "*Sleepless in Seattle* was based on *An Affair to Remember.*"

Everyone turned and stared at him.

"It's my girlfriend," he said, blushing under his hat. "She

watches all those kinds of films." His voice deepened. "I'm more of an Arnie guy myself, obviously."

We all turned back to the card still held in my hands.

I shook my head. "This is all just madness. I can't believe I'm standing out here now even looking at this—let's all go back inside and continue with the service. I...I shouldn't have dragged you all out here, I'm sorry."

I looked to where David had been standing a few minutes ago but he'd gone.

"Where's David?" I asked, looking wildly around me.

I felt a hand on my shoulder. "He's gone back inside the church, Scarlett," my father said gently. "I think he'd heard enough."

I looked up at the church and felt a wrench in my stomach. *Poor David—what was I putting him through on our wedding day?*

"Are you absolutely sure about this, Scarlett?" Dad asked in the same gentle voice. "Are you sure it's what you want—to go back in there and marry David? This invite, and the way it was *supposed* to be delivered," he said, looking at Dermot and Finlay, "seems just the kind of romantic ending you'd get in one of your movies. Except this time it's happening for real. Are you sure you don't want it to end a different way?"

"I...I don't know."

"How *do* you feel about Sean?" my mother asked, appearing on my other side. "Do you love him?"

I hung my head. "Yes, I think I do. But it's complicated."

I could feel everyone willing me to tell them why.

"It just is, OK?"

"He obviously loves you, Scarlett," my mother said, "to go to all this trouble."

"I thought *you* were against him?" I said, turning to her. "I thought you said he was a Daniel Cleaver."

My mother looked confused.

"I believe he's a character in *Bridget Jones's Diary*," Dermot suggested helpfully.

We all stared at him again.

"Yes, I'm aware of that—thank you," my mother said, slowly turning away from Dermot. "But what's that got to do with anything, Scarlett?"

Oh, this was just getting far too complicated to explain now. "Look, forget I said that. It just makes more *sense* to marry Mark...I mean David."

"Why does it, Scarlett?" Maddie asked now. "If you love Sean more? Yes, I know you're here at the church about to get married, and it would be easier to just go through with it all now. But this is just one day—we're talking about the rest of your life."

"Because..." I stuttered.

"See?" Maddie continued. "I knew this would happen after I saw you two together at my wedding."

"Sean is the chap you took to Maddie's wedding?" Dad asked in surprise.

"Yes—why?" I asked, wondering what that had to do with anything.

"Because David told me about this absolute cretin that went with you to Paris, said he was a right slimeball and was all over you that night. He described him as a complete loser."

"David would say that, though—he hates Sean."

"And with good reason, it would seem now. But Sean's not a loser," Dad said, defending him. "Nor is he a cretin, come to think of it. He's a very smart, astute businessman. And a nice genuine young fellow too."

"How do you know all this, Tom?" Mum asked. "How are you able to form such a rounded opinion of someone you've only met the once, like me?"

My father sighed. "Look, Scarlett, Sean asked me not to tell you this—but I feel now with so much hanging in the balance, I must. Sean has offered to invest in our business. He's recently bought a chain of cinemas over in the States, and he wants us to provide not only the popcorn makers for every single outlet, but all the food concessions too."

"He's done what?" I asked, slowly absorbing this information. "But that means..."

"Our business will be made for life, Scarlett—yes."

"But..." I couldn't take all this in. *If we exported to America with Sean, that meant we wouldn't need David's cinema chain...*

"Sounds like he cares more about your welfare than you realize, Scarlett," Maddie said knowingly. "If he's gone to all the trouble of buying a chain of cinemas for you."

I shook my head. "They're not for me—they're just a business venture. There must be money in it, or Sean wouldn't be involved."

"May I just say something?" a polite voice asked, and someone stepped forward to join our debate. It was Ursula. "I haven't said anything up until now, because being Sean's sister you'd all just think I was biased. But it was actually Sean who helped reunite you with your mother, Scarlett."

I looked at Ursula.

"No, it wasn't. We just bumped into each other accidentally in the cinema one evening—you should know, you were there."

"That's what I thought at the time too. But it was Sean who encouraged us to go around to your house that day. Sean who suggested we take you out for the evening, and Sean who absolutely insisted we take you to that exact cinema."

I turned to Oscar, who nodded in agreement.

"Scarlett, you know Sean and I don't exactly see eye to eye," he admitted. "But Ursula's right. He was the one who insisted it had to be the Coronet. He told us it was because of the *Notting Hill* connection and we'd be helping you out with your movie thing by taking you there. But the truth of the matter is we found out later he'd actually tracked your mother down, found out she worked there, and even knew what shifts she was on so he could guarantee you'd bump into each other."

I stared in astonishment between Oscar and Ursula for a few seconds before turning first to my mother, and then my father, and then Maddie, who all stared back at me with similar expressions.

"I…I don't know what to say…I don't know what to do." I returned my gaze to my mother. "Mum, what do you think?"

She thought for a moment. "Forget what I said to you on the telephone, Scarlett. I think Sean has put an awful lot of expense, but more importantly thought, into trying to win your heart. And you won't find many men who can do both—believe me, I've spent long enough looking for one. And, if it hadn't been for him, it seems I wouldn't be standing here now. But only *you* can decide what to do for the best."

"Dad?" I asked, looking at my father again.

"Scarlett, you have my blessing whatever you decide to do—both now and in the future. But whatever you decide, all I ask is, you forget about the movies for once. This is real life you're dealing with now, not a film script. You *must* take it seriously."

"But I do take it seriously. That's what I've been trying to tell you all along. In the month I was away I had so many experiences that completely back up my theory, but you wouldn't listen when I tried to tell you. Life *can* be like a movie—perhaps not always in the same saccharine sweet way they portray it to be in the cinema, but maybe living with that sort of hope and those types of dreams is the only way you'll ever find a happy ending in life."

"Then why stop now?" I heard a voice behind us call. I turned around and saw David standing high up on the steps of the church. "Why stop, Scarlett, when you're on a roll? Let's live out a real movie scene right here, right now."

"David, I…"

"Perhaps we'd better go inside," my father said, attempting to herd everyone together. "David, you and Scarlett should discuss this in private."

"No, why bother?" David said in a tight voice. "You've all heard everything else. You might as well hear this too. Plus," he said, looking directly at me, "it will be so much more dramatic this way, and that's what Scarlett likes, a bit of drama and excitement in her life—don't you, Scarlett?"

Even though it was a warm April morning, I felt a shiver run through me as I stood and watched David speaking at the top of the steps. I never wanted to hurt him. I hadn't meant for any of this to happen.

Everyone around us stood in silence as I gazed up at him. Out of the corner of my eye I noticed Dermot and Finlay removing their hats.

"I'm going to make this really easy for you, Scarlett," David said, looking down at me. "You know when we hired a wedding planner to help us plan for this wonderful day in our lives, you thought she would be just like Jennifer Lopez in the film?"

He waited for my answer, so I just nodded.

"And she wasn't—she turned out to be more like…now what did you call her? Cruella De Vil?"

I nodded furiously as Cruella scowled at me from where she was perching on a nearby gravestone.

"Well, this part of our wedding is going to be just the same as in that movie. Do you remember it, Scarlett? The bit just before the couple are due to get married."

I looked up at David glowering at me from the steps above, and I nodded sadly.

"You do? Good. Well, just like the groom in that movie, Scarlett, I'm going to make this really easy for you and take the choice between me and Sean out of your hands. Because guess what? *I* don't want to marry *you* anymore."

There was a sharp intake of breath around the churchyard.

"I don't want to marry someone I can't rely on and trust to be there for me 100 percent. I don't want to marry someone who thinks I'm only second best. And"—his voice that had been so strong and devoid of emotion when he'd first stood on the steps was beginning to break now—"most importantly, I don't want to marry someone who is, without question, so completely and utterly in love with someone else."

I made a move toward him but he held out his hand to stop me.

"No, Scarlett. You wanted it this way—you wanted to live like you were in a movie and now you are. I've given you your dramatic last scene, just like in *The Wedding Planner*. But I bet you never expected to be the bride jilted at her own wedding."

"David, please," I pleaded with him as he descended the steps of the church, obviously intending to leave this hellish situation I'd put him in as quickly as possible.

I caught up with him at the bottom and grabbed hold of his arm.

"David, wait…"

"Go to him, Scarlett," he whispered to me. "He doesn't deserve you, but go to him if that's what you want. Maybe you *can* have that fairytale ending you've always wanted—even if it's not with me."

Then I watched as he marched out of the churchyard, quickly hailed a passing taxi, and was soon swallowed up into the swarming London traffic.

I turned back to the others, who were watching everything that was unfolding in front of them. Then I glanced down at the invitation I still held tightly in my hand; this time I saw the picture on the other side of the postcard.

"But it can't be," I whispered to myself. "How did he know?"

The postcard was one of those art cards, the sort you get in galleries as a souvenir of one of their paintings. And the painting on the card was of a bride on her wedding day—it was *La Mariée*.

It was the painting that had hung in the art gallery I went to visit with Maddie. The one Julia Roberts had given to Hugh

Grant in the movie *Notting Hill*...The song that had been playing earlier had been from the same film. Ronan had sung it in the movie when they'd sat on the bench together in the moonlight—just like Sean and I had.

Notting Hill was also where Sean and I had first met, in a bookshop—just like Hugh and Julia had.

Now Sean was giving me this painting too...if I didn't know better, I would have sworn that Sean knew these films as well as I did! But that was a mad thought, because he hated movies, didn't he?

I turned the postcard over and read it once more.

"Oh my God!" I exclaimed as the realization of something awful hit me. "Where are Dermot and Finlay?"

Replacing their hats on their heads they emerged from the crowd again. "You were supposed to deliver this yesterday, weren't you?" I demanded of Dermot.

"Yes, that's right, but I did explain—"

"But it says for me to meet Sean tomorrow...that means he's there now...today, at the top of the London Eye—waiting for me!"

I looked for the church clock. "What's the time?" I asked impatiently when I couldn't see it.

Everyone looked at their watches.

"It's half past eleven," Maddie answered first. "He's still there if you're going to go to him. Is that what you want, Scarlett? Do you want to go and find Sean?"

"I do," I said, almost as though I needed to reinforce the decision for myself now it was finally made. "I do, Maddie. I'm going to go and find Sean, and I'm going to have the happy ending

I've always wanted." I hugged her. "Now then," I asked, looking around at everyone else. "Just how do you get to the London Eye from here?"

"We'll take you," Dermot offered. "We've got our car parked around the corner."

"No, I couldn't possibly ask you to do that."

"It's OK. I used to be a London cabbie once upon a time. I have the *knowledge*," Dermot said proudly. "Plus it would be our pleasure to help—wouldn't it, Finlay? After all it's our fault the invitation was late getting to you, it's the least we can do."

"If you're sure?" I looked at Finlay, who nodded his agreement silently as always.

"Come on, let's go!" Dermot called, already heading down the path. "You've no time to lose!"

I ran after the Blues Brothers, clutching the card and ticket to my chest. "I love you all," I called back to my parents, Maddie, Ursula, and Oscar as they followed us along the path to the waiting car.

"And I love you too, Sean," I whispered, looking down at the card in my hand once more. "Wait for me, won't you—please."

Forty

I think Dermot fancied himself as a bit of an action hero, because we took off at breakneck speed in the very authentic-looking American police car that he and Finlay had arrived in.

I'd assumed they'd meant they had a normal car parked around the corner—not a replica from the original *Blues Brothers* movie. But it seemed that Dermot and Finlay took their business very seriously indeed. I was grateful now they hadn't been able to turn up as Scarlett and Rhett today—because a horse-drawn carriage from the American Civil War wouldn't have been traveling at anywhere near the speeds the "Bluesmobile" was doing right now.

But it wouldn't have mattered what form of transport we'd taken once we began to hit the central London gridlock. As I sat anxiously in the back of the police car, waiting for us to shunt forward another few meters, I suddenly realized what I was wearing.

"Oh my God, I'm still in my wedding dress!" I panicked from the backseat. Finlay turned the stereo down that had been constantly playing the *Blues Brothers* soundtrack since we left, and Dermot glanced at me in his rearview mirror.

"But you do look lovely in it," he said, smiling.

"I know, but I can't just roll up and meet Sean in a wedding dress I was going to marry another man in, now can I?"

"Hmm," he said. "That is a bit tricky when you put it like that."

"What choice do I have? I can't very well change now. I don't have the time or anything to change into." I leaned forward between the two front seats and looked through the windshield. "Damn it, is this traffic ever going to move?"

It was just like Glasgow all over again—the day when Sean and I had ridden to the wedding on the back of mopeds. Except this time, I was the bride—running away from my own wedding.

And yes, I know I was in yet another movie. And yet again it was a Julia Roberts one. But I didn't have time to reflect on that now, as we slowed right down and virtually came to a standstill a few yards away from the entrance to a church.

As we sat there waiting to move forward, I realized there must be another wedding taking place today, as the sound of church bells ringing filled the air. *I hope yours is more successful than mine was*, I thought as I sat well back in the car. I saw a man in full morning dress walk out of the church gates, and I wondered, as he walked toward us, if he was the nervous groom.

It was when he got right up to the outside of our car that an uneasy feeling started to spread over me.

He grabbed the door handle just as I went to push the lock down and thrust the car door wide open.

"You're early," he said, peering into the car. "The bridesmaids aren't even here yet. I'm Max by the way, one of Graham's ushers, we've not met before." He held out his hand for me to shake.

"I…I'm not the bride," I hurriedly said, trying to grab the door again and pull it shut.

"Don't be daft, of course you are, Teresa—that's just nerves. I didn't know you were having a Blues Brothers theme?" he said, staring at Dermot and Finlay in the front seats. "But that's cool—I like it. Now which one of you is Dad?"

"I'm telling you I'm *not* the bride," I said, managing to wrangle the door from his grasp. "I'm *not* Teresa. And this is definitely not my wedding!" and I slammed the door shut again.

"Get us out of here, Dermot…please," I implored him, as I recoiled from Max's flattened face pressed up against the car's rear window.

"Our Lady of Blessed Acceleration, don't fail me now!" Dermot called out as he thrust the car into gear.

"It's from the movie," Finlay explained, breaking his silence for the first time. "He's been waiting his whole life for an opportunity to say that line."

Luckily, just then a significant gap opened up in the traffic and Dermot was able to accelerate away from the church, leaving Max standing on the side of the road looking dazed.

"Oh God," I said, my head in my hands. "I should have known this would be a disaster. Everything I do always is."

"I think it's only going to get worse, I'm afraid," Dermot said, looking at the traffic backing up in front of us. "There's no way we're going to make it across London by midday."

Finlay turned and looked at me. "Can't you phone him?" he asked sympathetically. "And let him know you're on your way?"

I looked up at him, surprised he had spoken again—I

guessed he was usually a man of few words. Then I looked down at my dress, and held out my hands. "All I came away with was these," I said, holding up the card and ticket. "I don't have my phone with me, and I don't remember his number to use someone else's."

"Finlay, I think you're missing the point," Dermot said. "It wouldn't be very romantic if Scarlett just called him up and said, 'I'm on my way, but I'm stuck in traffic,' now would it?"

"It would save a lot of hassle though," Finlay said matter-of-factly.

"No," Dermot continued. "She needs to race along the Embankment with only seconds to spare—hoping against hope she'll make it on time—before her true love, in despair, gives up on her and disappears from her life forever."

Finlay and I both stared at Dermot.

"You not only watch too many films, but you've been dressing up like characters from them for far too long," Finlay said. "Let's be realistic—Scarlett's not going to make it there on time. This isn't a movie script; this is *real* life, in *real* London traffic. I'm sorry, there's just not going to be a happy ending this time."

"Right," I said, my hand already on the door. "That's it. I'm getting out. I'll run there if I have to, even in this stupid dress. There is no way I'm not making it to the London Eye by midday. There *will* be a happy ending for me this time, just you wait and see."

I climbed out of the car. "Thank you both so much for getting me this far," I said, smiling gratefully at them as Finlay rolled down his window. "Can I just ask you one more favor though?"

"Sure, what's that?" Dermot asked.

"Could you lend me my tube fare?"

I ran along the pavement as fast as I could in my awkward and now very uncomfortable wedding shoes until I found the nearest underground station, then descended into its depths and quickly bought myself a ticket.

I tried to ignore the stares I got from commuters as I ran down escalators and along corridors to shouts of, "Late for the church, are we?" or, "Been jilted at the altar darlin'?" and a rousing chorus of "I'm Getting Married in the Morning" from a gang of Arsenal supporters on their way to a home game.

It seemed an eternity as we trundled along on the Bakerloo line—every time the train stopped in the tunnel or at a station, I'd try and glance surreptitiously at someone's watch to see the time. But eventually we arrived at Embankment and I emerged into the fresh air once more. I could see the London Eye, dwarfing everything around it as it stood elegantly by the side of the Thames. So, running as fast as I could manage, I crossed the Golden Jubilee Bridge, holding my white tulle skirts aloft like a lady of the bygone age in her crinolines. I glanced at Big Ben in the distance—it was two minutes to twelve.

As I descended to the footpath that ran alongside the South Bank of the Thames, I managed to overtake tourists taking photos, children rollerblading, and even a couple of slow joggers. It was only as I ran past a coffee shop, with a few tables waiting hopefully outside in the early April sunshine, that I suddenly pulled myself to a halt.

Slowly I reversed to the shop. Was that who I thought it was sitting at one of the tables toward the back of the outdoor seating area? I stopped and stared.

And then slowly, as if he sensed me looking at him, although I wasn't actually that inconspicuous, standing there in a full-length wedding dress with a tiara balanced precariously in my hair and my skirt pulled up around my knees, Hugh Grant turned around and stared back at me.

He spoke quickly to the man sitting opposite him, and then they both turned to look at me. Hugh's dining partner looked familiar too—he had whitish gray hair and spectacles. And then, as I stood there still staring, I realized that not only was I looking at Hugh Grant sitting having a cup of coffee in the middle of London on a sunny April day, but Richard Curtis too.

I hovered there for a moment—these were two of my biggest movie heroes, sitting right there in front of me—I had to go over, I had to...then I heard the chimes of Big Ben signaling it was about to become midday and I snapped back to the real reason I was here.

No, Scarlett, not this time, I told myself. *Sean is more important than the cinema.* "Put this in one of your movies!" I shouted to them both, as I hoisted up my dress once more and began to run the final few hundred meters along the footpath. Each chime of Big Ben brought me that little bit closer to the Eye, until I arrived by its side just as the last chime declared it was now officially midday.

Breathlessly I stood at the bottom of the huge wheel and watched the glass capsules rotate slowly around. I looked up desperately to see if I could catch a glimpse of Sean in one of them, but most of the insides were not visible to me down on the ground.

Then I saw the queue.

It snaked around the turnstiles several times before ending a few feet in front of me. But people were joining it all the time—if I got in that queue I'd never spot Sean, and there was no way I'd ever make it to the wheel before he got off.

"Excuse me," I said, beginning to push my way up through the queue. "It's an emergency—thank you," I'd say, as I got a bit further. "Thank you—emergency—sorry; have to get through—emergency, see."

"Looks it, darlin'," a man said as I passed by him. "Lost your groom, have you?"

Finally I reached the front. "I'm so sorry to push in like this," I said to the attendant on the gate. "It's really important I get to the wheel—I'm supposed to be meeting someone there."

I expected there'd be an argument, or at least a look of "We get them all here, trying to push in—and look at this one, she's even come in fancy dress!" But instead, the lady just smiled at me.

"Are you Scarlett?" she asked.

"Yes, yes, that's me."

"We've been waiting for you to turn up all morning. He's been going round on this thing since 9 a.m."

I looked up to where she was pointing and saw Sean coming into view at last. He was wearing a smart black suit and a crisp white shirt unbuttoned at the neck. He looked despondent as he rested his head dejectedly against the glass window of the capsule.

But then he glanced down in our direction, and his expression immediately changed. A huge smile broke out over his face and then an even bigger grin as his capsule finally came down to ground level.

"Quickly, miss," the attendant said. "Be ready to board when the pod comes past. Otherwise you'll miss it and have to wait another half an hour."

There was no way I was going to let that happen. I leaped up onto the area where people were boarding the capsules as they passed slowly by. There were about fifteen to twenty boarding each capsule at a time. But when Sean's finally came into view, there was only him inside.

"Hop on, miss," another attendant said, helping me on board. "Safe ride." He winked at Sean, who was standing up against the glass on the far side of the pod.

Inside the capsule, there seemed to be flowers everywhere.

Roses and lilies were arranged elegantly in a long glass vase. How did Sean know they were my two favorite flowers? Had I mentioned it to him in passing one day and he'd remembered?

They stood on a small table next to an ice bucket, which held a bottle of champagne patiently waiting to be poured into two empty glasses. I looked down and saw more flowers—a sea of pink and red rose petals covered every inch of the floor. It was one of the most romantic settings I'd ever seen.

"Oh, Sean, it's just beautiful," I said, walking toward him. "I'm so sorry it took me so long to get here. But it was the

Blues Brothers, they didn't arrive until today, and when they did finally arrive, as you can see"—I gestured at my dress—"I was already at the church. But oh, Sean, when they played that song to me, and said it was from you, I knew I just had to come here and find you. And then there was the painting, Sean, it's just all so romantic, and so unexpected. How did you even know about that?"

Sean didn't speak—he just held up his hand to stop me coming any closer.

"What? What's wrong?" I asked.

Sean reached down and picked up some large white pieces of card. He held the first one up in front of him, like a flash card. Then he proceeded to communicate silently with me in lines from the movies I knew and loved so well. Except they weren't the exact lines spoken by the actors on the screen; Sean had cleverly changed them to fit in with our own story. It was just like the scene from *Love Actually* I'd told him about—only better.

I say it best, when I say nothing at all.

I grinned at him as he turned over the next card.

In the spirit of Love Actually (The Bee Gees, and latterly Boyzone) I should like to tell you how I feel in Words, if I may?

I nodded eagerly. Oh my God, I couldn't believe he'd done all this for me.

Firstly, don't apologize for being late, because when you're in love with someone, apparently you never have to say you're sorry.

First, how did he know I'd be late? And second, he was of course referring to the classic line from *Love Story*.

Sean turned another card while I silently watched him.

When I met you, frankly, Scarlett, I didn't give a damn. And

I wondered, of all the bookshops in all the towns in all the world, why you had to walk into mine.

I laughed at the classic lines from *Gone with the Wind* and *Casablanca* as he turned over the next card.

But then I thought, well, nobody's perfect, & I should give you a chance because this could be the beginning of a beautiful friendship.

The second part was obviously Casablanca again. I thought hard for a moment about the first before I realized it was from the Marilyn Monroe film *Some Like It Hot*. Wow, Sean really had done his homework.

But I knew we were supposed to be together. I knew it from the very first time I held your hand, Scarlett. It felt just like…magic.

"Oh, Sean," I mouthed, silently knowing he was referring to the "magic" moment from *Sleepless in Seattle*.

Sean dropped another card and it fell among the rose petals on the floor—while I tried to stop the tears that were springing to the corners of my eyes from escaping, pouring down my face and joining them. This was fast becoming more emotional than any "weepie" I'd ever sat through in the cinema.

And even though I knew we'd always have Paris, I knew you wanted more; I knew you wanted the whole fairytale.

I smiled again at another classic quote from *Casablanca* and his *Pretty Woman* fairytale reference.

So I asked you to meet me here today like this on the London Eye, because when I realized I wanted to spend the rest of my life with you, I not only wanted the rest of my life to start as soon as possible, but in a way we would remember forever.

I nodded in agreement, loving his twist on the classic quote from *When Harry Met Sally*.

So Scarlett, I ask you to excuse the fact that I am just a bloke you met in a bookshop, standing in front of the most beautiful girl he's ever laid eyes on, asking her to love him.

A parody of the final bookshop scene in *Notting Hill*, of course…

Because I love you, Scarlett, just the way you are. You complete me…and I hope I complete you too…

Sean put down the final card—the classic *Bridget Jones* and *Jerry Maguire* quotes mismashed together to give yet another Sean-esque-style twist. And slowly he raised his head to look at me.

I ran toward him. "Can I speak now?" I asked breathlessly.

He nodded.

"That was just *the* most romantic thing anyone has ever done for me, Sean. And I love you too—very much. I think I always have."

Sean had looked ever so slightly worried since I'd arrived in the capsule with him. Now relief, mixed with joy, replaced that look of concern as I spoke the words he so desperately wanted to hear.

As I stood in front of him, I gently stroked his cheek with my hand. And he, in turn, equally gently took hold of my hand and tenderly kissed the palm.

Then he pulled me closer to him and silently wrapped his arms around me until there was nothing between us but our love.

Sean gazed into my eyes forever before he finally kissed me. But when he did, my heart only reinforced what it had told me earlier—by beating so fast that I think the entire Russian gymnast team must have been performing on it this time.

When we could finally bear to be parted again I looked up at Sean while he held me in his arms.

"There's something I still don't understand, Sean. You were the most unromantic person I'd ever met up until today. How on earth did you know all those lines from all those movies if you never watch them?"

"I watched them for you," Sean said, speaking for the first time since I'd arrived in the capsule. "I started when I went over to New York, and I've been watching them ever since."

I shook my head in disbelief as I continued to gaze up at him in amazement.

"I wanted to prove to you just how much you meant to me, Scarlett. By doing this with the wheel and the cards, I knew it would mean so much to you if I was romantic. But I also knew I had to do something a bit more than just send you a few flowers. I would have got you the real painting if I could. But even my budget doesn't quite extend that far."

I stood up on tiptoes and kissed him again. "I know you would. But you really didn't have to, Sean; the cards and the flowers and everything. I love it, of course, but it wasn't necessary."

"I think it was," Sean insisted. "I had to make sure I was your Mr. Darcy and not just your Daniel Cleaver."

I smiled at him. "Oh, Sean, you're better than either of those two. But you really didn't have to go this far. And do you know why?"

Sean shook his head.

"Because after everything we've been through together over the last few weeks—and to part-borrow another quote from *Jerry Maguire*…" I smiled at him. "You had me at…Ronan Keating."

A smile twitched at the corners of Sean's lips and then it broke free into one of the infectious grins that I knew and loved so well now.

I grinned back at him and leaned forward to kiss him once more, but he stopped me, as the serious expression returned to his face again.

"There's something else, Scarlett. Something very important I need to tell you."

"OK," I said, wondering what it could be.

Sean cleared his throat and then, to my surprise, a voice sounding incredibly like Sean Connery's came floating from his lips.

"My name is Bond—Sean Bond," he said with a completely straight face. "Scarlett, you've left me feeling shaken and stirred. I'll be licensed to love you for the rest of your life, if you'll have me."

I tried to keep a straight face as I answered him.

"Sean, I'd go to Russia with love for you."

Sean thought about this for a moment. "How about from Notting Hill with love...actually?" he suggested, grinning.

Then we could keep up the pretense no longer, and we fell into each other's arms, laughing uncontrollably with happiness and love.

So while the rest of the world went about its daily business below, Sean and I held each other tightly while we gazed down at the London skyline together. Knowing this time, as the credits rolled, we were the ones with the happy ending.

MORE ABOUT NOTTING HILL...ACTUALLY!

A visitor's guide to Notting Hill

You've seen the movie. You've read the book. Now visit the place itself!

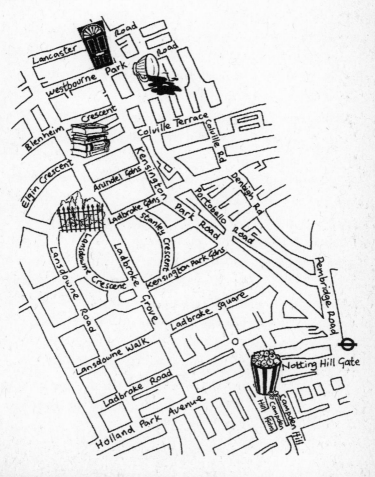

Alighting from Notting Hill Gate Tube station for the first time, just as Scarlett did in the novel, take a right turn onto Penbridge Road. Cross the street and follow the signs for Portobello Road. On your way, the eagle-eyed among you will spot to your right a plaque on the wall which marks the house where George Orwell once lived.

The day on which you visit will definitely affect how much of Portobello Road you can actually see! If you have chosen to come on a Saturday when the famous antique market is in full flow, you will quickly be enveloped and swept along through the brightly colored stalls by the huge crowds which flood this area every weekend, out to hunt down a bargain, or their own Beavis & Butthead stained-glass window as featured at the beginning of the *Notting Hill* movie.

If, however, crowds aren't your thing, and you're visiting on a quiet day, carry on down Portobello Road at your own pace (hopefully you won't be dragging a heavy suitcase behind you like Scarlett was!). Browse at the various antique and craft shops along the way, until you come to the junction with Westbourne Park Road. Look to your right; on the corner is now a Coffee Republic. This is the spot where Hugh Grant spilled orange juice down Julia Roberts's shirt in the movie. But if you turn left, you'll see a very plain looking, black painted door directly opposite you at number 280. That door was originally the site of the famous blue door in the movie—the one Hugh Grant came in and out of, and the one Rhys Ifans's character famously posed in front of in his underpants for the worlds' press!

Continuing down Westbourne Park Road, turn left at Ladbroke Grove, then left into Blenheim Crescent where you will find the Travel Bookshop. This isn't where they filmed the bookshop scenes for the movie, but this is the bookshop Will's was inspired by. And when you've finished having your photo taken outside, take a moment to go in for a browse (just as Scarlett did when she met Sean for the first time) because you'll find the interior of the shop is exactly like the movie version!

When you leave the bookshop, turn left (but be careful not to bump into any dog-carrying boutique owners like Scarlett did!) and continue down Blenheim Crescent, turning left when you get to the junction with Ladbroke Grove again. Continue a little way along the street, passing one of Notting Hill's many locked gardens along the way. Stop and peer through the bars for a moment and imagine Hugh and Julia sitting on a bench there or, now you've read this book, Scarlett and Sean too. I don't advise you try to climb over the top of the railings, though!

Follow the road a little further until you come to Lansdowne Road. This is where Scarlett's and Sean's houses would have been in the story. The houses on the left-hand side as you enter the road have steps leading up to their front doors—exactly the sort of steps that Scarlett and Sean had many encounters on during the novel.

Find your way back to Portobello Road. Why not finish off the day with a visit to the Coronet Cinema on Notting Hill Gate? I can't guarantee you'll find Hugh Grant sitting in the stalls wearing snorkeling goggles or that one of the usherettes will surprise you in the same way they surprised Scarlett. But you might just catch a good movie.

(Perhaps not quite as good as *Notting Hill*, though.)

—Ali McNamara

SCARLETT'S MINI MOVIE QUIZ

Are you a true movie buff like Scarlett? Do you really know your stuff? Take this quiz on Scarlett's favorite movies and find out!

1. In *Notting Hill*, Anna checks into the Ritz with a cartoon character's name. Which two names did she use in the movie?

    A. Flintstone & Pocahontas
    B. Pocahontas & Bambi
    C. Flintstone & Rubble
    D. Simpson & Flanders

2. Also in *Notting Hill*, what does Hugh Grant's character, Will, exclaim when he tries to climb over the garden fence, but slips?

    A. Golly gosh!
    B. Whoopsy daisies!
    C. Oh bother!
    D. Crikey!

3. What type of car is Edward driving when he picks up Vivian in *Pretty Woman*?

A. Porsche
B. Ferrari
C. Lotus
D. Lambourghini

4. Sticking with *Pretty Woman*, what street are Kit and Vivian working on?

A. Beverly Hills Boulevard
B. Los Angeles Boulevard
C. Hollywood Boulevard
D. Rodeo Drive

5. Which two authors made an appearance in *Bridget Jones's Diary*?

A. Jeffrey Archer & Salman Rushdie
B. Agatha Christie & Jeffrey Archer
C. Salman Rushdie & Dan Brown
D. JK Rowling & Dick Francis

6. What did Bridget put in the soup to make it turn blue for her birthday meal?

    A.   Blueberries
    B.   Gin
    C.   String
    D.   Food coloring

7. In *Sleepless in Seattle*, where is Sam when he first sees Annie?

    A.   On a highway
    B.   At a train station
    C.   At a restaurant
    D.   At an airport

8. Which newspaper does Annie work for?

    A.   Baltimore Sun
    B.   New York Times
    C.   Washington Post
    D.   Chicago Tribune

9. Which of these people are not mentioned when Hugh Grant's character lists the great things that have come out of Britain in *Love, Actually*?

A. Jeremy Clarkson
B. David Beckham
C. Harry Potter
D. Sean Connery

10. What is on the last card that Mark shows to Keira Knightley's character Juliet?

A. Merry Christmas
B. To Me You Are Perfect
C. My Wasted Heart Will Love You
D. Enough Now

Answers:

1. Flinstone & Pocahontas; 2. Whoopsy daisies; 3. Lotus; 4. Hollywood Boulevard; 5. Jeffery Archer & Salman Rushdie; 6. String; 7. At an airport; 8. Baltimore Sun; 9. Jeremy Clarkson; 10. Merry Christmas

SCARLETT'S FAVORITE MOVIES

If you're head-over-heels for movies, just like Scarlett O'Brien, why not clear the whole day and sit down to watch a marathon of your favorites? You could start with Scarlett's top five—just make sure you have enough popcorn at hand to last you through all five films! You'll find some top trivia here to really get you in the mood…

Notting Hill

Directed by Roger Michell, 1999
Starring Hugh Grant and Julia Roberts
Notting Hill is a classic British romantic comedy. It was written by Richard Curtis who had previously penned the just-as-classic *Four Weddings and a Funeral*.

Hugh Grant plays bookshop owner Will, who literally bumps into international movie star Anna, played by Julia Roberts. Their will-they-won't-they love story plays out in Notting Hill, with the most iconic scene taking place in a private garden.

The movie won several awards, including a BAFTA, a

Golden Globe, a British Comedy Award, and a Brit Award for its soundtrack.

Three facts you might not know…

1. Will's house—at 280 Westbourne Park Road—was once owned by Richard Curtis, and behind the famous blue door featured in the movie (now painted black), there is actually a very impressive house, not at all like the grubby dwelling in the film (the flat we see is actually a movie set).

2. During the dinner party scene, Julia's character Anna Scott is asked how much she was paid for her last movie. She replies, "15 million dollars." This is the amount Julia Roberts was paid for her role in *Notting Hill*.

3. The film features the painting *La Mariée* by Marc Chagall. Richard Curtis is a big fan of Chagall's work. The producers had a reproduction made for use in the film, but first had to get permission from the British Design and Artists Copyright Society and the painting's real owner. The producers also had to agree to destroy it at the end of the movie in case the fake was too convincing!

Pretty Woman

Directed by Garry Marshall, 1990
Starring Richard Gere and Julia Roberts
Pretty Woman is a well-loved American romantic comedy from the nineties, written by J. F. Lawton. Richard Gere plays

Edward, a workaholic businessman in L.A. on business. He meets Julia Roberts' character, Vivian, when he stops to ask for directions. The movie features some truly iconic moments—who hasn't laughed at the snapping jewelry case or sighed when Edward braves his fear of heights and climbs the fire escape?

Three facts you might not know …

1. The iconic moment when Edward snaps the jewelry box shut on Vivian's fingers was entirely improvised by Richard Gere. Julia Roberts's reaction was so natural and charming that it was kept in the final version of the movie.
2. Lots of leading actresses turned down the part of Vivian before it was offered to Julia Roberts—including Meg Ryan, Michelle Pfeiffer, Molly Ringwald, and Winona Ryder.
3. When filming the scene where Vivian sings along to the Prince song "Kiss" in the bath, the cast and crew played a prank on Julia Roberts. Emerging from the bubbly water, Julia found the whole set deserted—everyone had left the studio, even the cameraman!

Bridget Jones's Diary

Directed by Sharon Maguire, 2001
Starring Hugh Grant, Renée Zellweger, and Colin Firth
This movie is based on the novel of the same name written by Helen Fielding, who also wrote the screenplay for the

movie along with Richard Curtis and Andrew Davies. Renée Zellweger plays Bridget, the ever-single Londoner who keeps track of all her romantic ups and downs in her trusty diary. And she certainly has a lot of ups and downs with Mark Darcy (played by Colin Firth) and Daniel Cleaver (played by Hugh Grant) rivaling for her affections. The sequel, *Bridget Jones: The Edge of Reason*, was released in 2004.

Three things you might not know...

1. When writing her novel, Helen Fielding ironically based the character of Mark Darcy on Colin Firth's portrayal of Mr. Darcy in the TV adaptation of *Pride & Prejudice*, which aired in 1995. There are also several other links to this Jane Austen novel in the film. Bridget and Daniel work at Pemberley Press; Pemberley is the name of Mr. Darcy's ancestral home in the Austen novel.

2. To prepare for the role, Renée Zellweger gained nearly twenty-eight pounds and worked undercover at a British publishing company for a month. She practiced her British accent while she was there and kept a framed picture of Jim Carrey, her boyfriend at the time, on her desk.

3. The director, Sharon Maguire, is a close friend of Helen Fielding. The author actually based the character of "Shazza," one of Bridget's best friends, on her, so it seems fitting that she directed the movie of the novel!

Sleepless in Seattle

Directed by Nora Ephron, 1993
Starring Meg Ryan and Tom Hanks

Sleepless in Seattle was inspired by the classic romantic movie from 1957, *An Affair to Remember*. The final scene at the top of the Empire State Building (where Meg Ryan's character Annie Reed and Tom Hanks's character Sam Baldwin meet for the first time) is a direct reference to the scene in *An Affair to Remember* where Cary Grant and Deborah Kerr fail to meet at the same spot. Meg Ryan plays the sensible and reliable Annie, engaged to equally sensible Walter, but when she hears Sam talking on a radio phone-in one night, she begins to fall in love with him before they even meet.

Three things you might not know …

1. The scene when Sam and his brother-in-law discuss the movie *The Dirty Dozen* and pretend to cry was made up on the spot by the two actors.
2. Meg Ryan was not the first choice for the role of Annie. Kim Basinger, Michelle Pfeiffer, Jennifer Jason Leigh, and Jodie Foster all turned down the part. Julia Roberts was actually the first actress to be offered the part.
3. In the whole film, Meg Ryan and Tom Hanks have roughly just two minutes of on-screen time together. That's a lot of chemistry in just two minutes!

And one last interesting fact about Richard Curtis: in each screenplay that Richard Curtis writes, he puts in an annoying or silly character called Bernard. This dates back to Curtis's twenties, when a past girlfriend married a man called Bernard. In *Love, Actually*, the character is Emma Thompson and Alan Rickman's annoying son.

Keep your eyes peeled for a "Bernard" or a "Bernie" in all of Richard Curtis's other movies.

Acknowledgments

Thank you to my wonderful agent, Hannah, for taking a chance on me, and to my editor, Caroline, and everyone at Sphere for all your help and support.

To all the original RKMB girls who read, laughed, and demanded more! Without you lot, I definitely wouldn't be writing this now. Especially Karen, Carol, and all those who remember "the hotel, the BMW, and the cliff…"

And to my family: Mum and Dad, thank you for fueling my overactive imagination by making me an only child! And finally to Jim, Rosie, and Tom: thank you for everything, you are my world, I love you, x.

About the Author

Ali McNamara lives in Cambridge in the UK with her husband and two children. This is her first novel. Get in touch with Ali at www.alimcnamara.co.uk or @AliMcNamara on Twitter.